KU-022-765

The Promised Land

David Hewson

W F HOWES LTD

This large print edition published in 2007 by
W F Howes Ltd
Unit 4, Rearsby Business Park, Gaddesby Lane,
Rearsby, Leicester LE7 4YH

1 3 5 7 9 10 8 6 4 2

First published in the United Kingdom in 2007
by Macmillan

Copyright © David Hewson, 2007

The right of David Hewson to be identified as
the author of this work has been asserted by him
in accordance with the Copyright, Designs and
Patents Act, 1988.

All rights reserved

A CIP catalogue record for this book is available
from the British Library

ISBN 978 1 40740 998 6

Typeset by Palimpsest Book Production Limited,
Grangemouth, Stirlingshire
Printed and bound in Great Britain
by Antony Rowe Ltd, Chippenham, Wilts.

The Promised Land

DATE DUE FOR RETURN ꟼ√

11 JAN 2012

15 AUG 2013

13 JAN 2014

1 - FEB 2014

17 FEB 2014

15/11/14

15 SEP 2016

-9 DEC 2017

21 DEC 2017

a/18

Renewals
www.liverpool.gov.uk/libraries
0151 233 3000

R.267

LV 21462917
Liverpool Libraries

ALSO BY DAVID HEWSON
FROM CLIPPER LARGE PRINT

The Lizard's Bite
The Sacred Cut
A Season for the Dead
The Seventh Sacrament
The Villa of Mysteries

The gurney wheels stop squealing. I dare to look. There's someone new there. He's got the face of an Andy Warhol doll: bright eyes gleaming like glass, a shock of white, spiky hair and yellow tombstone teeth locked into a smile that has all the sincerity of a cosmetics salesman peddling cheap aftershave.

'Hi!' he says brightly. 'Good day to you, sir. It's a fine day. A sunny day. Outside the birds are singing.'

His speech is too old for his looks. I remember voices like that, back from before, from outside. It's the jaundiced, bored intonation of the wage slave trundling through his daily routine.

'Very loudly I might say.'

He pauses theatrically, as if waiting for a sound. I can't hear a thing except the hum of air conditioning and electrical equipment, the stupid tinnitus that's lived alongside me for twenty-three years, three months and four days.

All the same, I try to speak. The words come out incomplete, a mumbled half-sentence mashed by the sedative shot I got before they strapped me to the gurney.

'Yeah, yeah, yeah . . .'

He's cross. He doesn't appreciate being interrupted.

'I like birds too. Don't we all? Please don't talk. Some of us are working here. Or trying to.'

The fierce rays of the surgical lighting dazzle me. For a moment the bright white hair looks like a halo, like a shining mantle rising from a slender, almost girlish neck.

'My . . . name . . . is . . . Martin . . .' The man in the green gown says this very slowly, very precisely, as if speaking to an idiot. 'Call me Martin the Medic. Call me God. Call me anything you like. I am merely your willing attendant on this short but meaningful journey. It's a job, chum. Someone's got to do it.'

I just manage to see as he retrieves something from a place beneath my range of vision: a silver kidney-shaped bowl sitting on a trolley alongside a line of implements and containers inside, neatly arrayed, ready for use.

Martin the Medic raises his right hand. In it sits a syringe, long, gleaming and, as yet, empty.

'This is just beer money, a part-time thing, you understand,' he says, then reaches down and plunges a needle deep into my right arm, piercing the flesh, hunting for the vein, finding it, then holding the metal spike there as he reaches round with his other hand and firms it down with tape.

'Killing people, I mean,' Martin adds, working the needle into my flesh till it hurts. Then, brightly, 'Oh!'

4

The yellow teeth gleam.

'We do have something in common.'

I mumble again and I can't even hear the words. Martin has replaced the syringe and picked up some ampoules. He's talking to himself. I'm just some eavesdropper here.

'Sodium thiopental. *Check!* Saline. *Check!*'

He touches two slender, feminine fingers to the line in my arm again and dabs the area with a piece of cotton wool.

'Old nursing habits. Crazy, I know. Here I am swabbing and flushing with all this clean-up routine. As if it matters.'

He picks up two more ampoules and flicks a fingernail against the labels.

'Fifty ccs of pancuronium bromide. Fifty ccs of potassium chloride.'

He seems satisfied. The glassy blue eyes are back on my face.

'Listen to me, friend. This is important. It's probably the last important thing you'll hear. First, I pump in the thiopental. Which sends you to sleep, straight off pretty much, just like a baby. Not that they sleep easy all the time, but you were a father once. *Before* . . . So I imagine you know that.'

The vial comes up close to his face. He stares at it myopically.

'Then I flush the line clean. After that it's the pancuronium.'

He holds up another glass bulb for me to see,

then, for show, turns round to some people I can just make out behind a glass screen to the left. They're not clear but somehow I know what they're wearing: dark suits and grim faces because there's a dress rule for such occasions, even though a good half of them think this is a day to throw hats in the air, scream a little joy from the rooftops.

Martin lets them see the vial because it's why they're here. In a way, the thing belongs to them.

After this he returns to face me and speaks, in a rapid, businesslike voice, 'You may know this already, but pancuronium is very neat stuff. It paralyses the diaphragm, the lungs. All quick, all clean. Given the choices, you picked the right place to be, let me tell you. This is *so* much better than electrocution. More hygienic. Let me tell you a secret. Want to know what happens when they fry a man? Everyone shits themselves. *Everyone.*'

He sighs.

'Where's the dignity? I ask you. If we *have* to do this work – and when I look at you, I know we do – let's manage it with a little decorum. You agree?'

It feels as if a ball of cotton wool is stuck in my throat. I couldn't scream if I tried.

'Behold.'

A syringe is in his hand again, with a different vial. I can just read the details on the bottle: a pharmaceutical company, one that's vaguely familiar. Once, a long time ago, in a different lifetime, we bought cough medicine for Ricky that bore this same logo. It tasted sweet. The boy loved it so much he'd pretend-cough sometimes just to get some.

'Progress . . .' the medic goes on. 'So the thiopental here is in. The pancuronium's chasing it. You don't breathe too well but – and this is important, follow me here – you're still not dead. OK?'

One more vial. One more familiar brand on the paper covering the glass.

'I flush with the saline again. And finally we come to the potassium chloride. This – *listen to me when I'm talking*!'

Something had popped into my head at that moment. Some memory: an image from the last time Ricky suffered a cold. I remember the small room he commandeered the moment he was old enough to talk. The wallpaper had cartoon characters running up and down it. There was a full-size bed, too big for the boy, but that was what Ricky wanted. So we gave in, and on his fifth birthday I lugged the thing up the old wooden stairs of the house in Owl Creek, then stood by my son, holding his hand, as Miriam made the bed: white cotton sheets, tight and perfect, by the window where the apple tree had recently come into bloom.

The bed. Another memory enters my head. The two of us between creased white sheets, hovering on the edge, me wondering whether she wants this or not. Then Miriam smiling, saying, 'Sometimes it's good slow. Sometimes fast. Today . . .'

Ricky would be twenty-eight now. Maybe we'd have had grandchildren. Then one more memory starts to rise from the dust.

'Listen to me!' Martin orders once more, and he's winding the needle of the line round and round in my arm, stirring some deep, hard pain to get my attention.

The recollection – a five-year-old boy in bed, while I read him Dr Seuss, still in my police uniform – fades into darkness and I wish, more than anything, I had the strength to claw it back from the lost, damaged part of my mind where it's now cowering.

The vial is in front of my eyes. Closer up, I see the logo has changed. When it was on a bottle of kid's cough medicine it had more colour.

'This,' Martin the Medic insists, 'kills you. After a little while, thirty seconds maybe, you get hit by cardiac arrest. You're long unconscious by then. You don't feel a thing. Sadly. In total I guess we're looking at . . .'

He examines his watch. It's a fake Rolex, too fat and shiny for the real thing, with a metal band, big and bulky. I can see the second hand ticking away, faster than it ought.

'Oh . . . two minutes from now. Three max. Then I'm away for breakfast, and you're getting cleaned up for the box. Nothing fancy. No one wants to pay. I guess you know that. You're incinerator fuel, Bierce. Nothing more, nothing less.'

The man in the green gown puts a finger to the dimple in his chin and thinks about something.

'Orange juice. And fruit. Mango and citrus. Got to stay healthy. Any questions?'

I struggle again, trying to speak, but the sedative's really kicking in. My head's thick with dope and formless, swirling thoughts.

The medic laughs.

'No, no, no. That was rhetorical. I've heard it all a million times. You know. Is there life after death? My opinion? People who ask that should really be thinking: is there life *before* death? Honestly . . .'

He picks up a second syringe, inserts the long needle into a vial and checks the level.

'Here's another I get all the time. You want to know how much I'm getting paid for this modest little professional appointment?'

Martin shakes his head, as if he can't quite believe it himself.

'A hundred and fifty an hour, less tax. It's the operating theatre plus twenty or something. Not a lot, my friend.'

He pauses. The bright eyes are no longer gleaming.

'Still, let me tell you something,' he adds.

The needle's coming closer, a glittering silver spear in front of my face, with not a tremor, not the slightest sign of hesitation.

'I would do this for free. I would *pay*, for God's sake. This . . .'

He has flawless skin. Pale and lightly tanned.

I can feel him grip the line in my arm once more, harder than ever this time, twisting it, lifting the needle until it runs tight against the inner wall of the vein.

I fight to pull in enough breath to shout, to say anything. The heavy weight of the sedative keeps me still, a straitjacket in the blood doing everything to paralyse me except remove the pain.

'. . . is for your wife and kid.'

Somewhere – in my imagination or the frantic flickering of my eyes as I struggle to shake my head – I see a man move, rise from the seats beyond the glass.

Not a harbinger of hope. After all this time they're gone, every last avenue of appeal extinguished, every channel of possible life closed. Except one, a simple act of mercy. The last thing anyone in this city would grant for a man called Bierce.

From the corner of my eye I see the needle enter the line.

Martin the Medic leans over, peers into my eyes and says, 'It's been a pleasure working with you, sir.'

A cold, hard sensation begins to creep along my arm. It makes a ringing noise at the back of my head, like the distant chimes of the old Chinese church, half a mile from home.

The Warhol face closes in for a last good look. His breath is stale and fetid. His smile has returned. It's different: eager and hungry.

'For in that sleep of death,' he whispers, yellow teeth shining, lips damp, blue eyes feasting on his work, 'what dreams may come?'

He pauses. A smile. I wish I had the time and the strength to tell him what I think of quoting Shakespeare out of context. The trouble is, a part of me doesn't care. About anything much at all.

There's a new pain now, a fierce chemical dagger rising from my spine, chasing upwards.

I shriek. I can hear myself. I flex my muscles against the tight surgical bonds, steel my body for the coming embrace.

We're in the kitchen, looking out on the garden that final summer. Wild briar roses bloom in the strong wire fence that runs on all three sides. A string of honeysuckle rises yellow and fragrant among the thorns. These are the barriers, one sweet and perfumed, one hard and painful, between ourselves and the bleak, dark tenements beyond.

A letter sits on the table.

It's the force annual medical. *Again.*

I want to avoid it. *Again.*

Her fingers touch the back of my hand, her soft warm mouth falls lovingly against my cheek for one bitterly brief moment.

'You think you're immune from all this, don't you?' she asks in a teasing, gentle voice, the one I first heard that day when I went, in a fresh new uniform, to her school. 'You think that all the

11

physical things that happen to other people are beyond you somehow. That it's all different inside. Nothing to go bad. Nothing to go wrong. Bierce?'

I'm not really listening. There's a shadow in the garden. I see it now and wonder: *is this real or not?*

I squint. I cough into my fist. I do all the things I do when I'm trying to make up my mind. Then I open my eyes, and it's hard this time, harder than ever before.

This is not the garden, the piece of paradise belonging to a house we once owned, a place that stood for family and warmth and contentment. This is the death room in the grim, antiseptic prison that is Gwinett, and Martin the Medic is there leering at me, triumphant. He grins then winks then turns, pirouetting by the flat table, twisting, twirling, singing a little song I can't quite hear for the roaring rushing sound in my ears, blowing kisses towards the figures behind the glass, writhing like a dancer racked with glee, the star of some small, private show, a performer taking his bow.

I can see them all now. Four ranks of men and women, sober suits, sober faces. Watching me, waiting for my death to release them.

No one moves. Not even the one figure I thought I recognized earlier: the thin black man in a tight black suit, with the familiar long face and heavy jaw, the gloomy eyes and a head of wavy hair. He looks so much older, and as miserable as sin.

'Stapleton,' I try to scream.

I can't hear the sound of my own voice. I can't believe that among the last words I shall utter on this earth will be the name of a once-crooked police officer I turned into a straight man, in a different world, another time.

'I saw . . .'

I saw what?

Nothing I could remember. That was the problem. That was always the problem. But not now.

A shadow moves through the garden.

Something is shooting into my brain, some wild, stark compound, chasing down my consciousness, extinguishing everything it meets with the subtlety of a chemical jackhammer stomping on living cells.

The seated man in black doesn't move, not a muscle, not a finger. Then my vision is gone altogether, ripped away by some black falling sea of nothingness. It grows from inside the crude searing presence of the drug, roaring up from my veins, fighting to extinguish the last living part of my being, a place where some faint, fading memories of Miriam still lurk.

I'm afraid.

I'm relieved.

This was always coming. Always.

'Bierce?' her dead voice says.

My heart races. The rhythm of my lungs locks into a single, solid beat. This sound is now the warmest thing in the universe and I know full well that behind it lies an empty space, a void that goes on forever.

It's Owl Creek again and I know what day it is without looking at the newspaper that lies, unopened, on the table.

Thursday, 25 July 1985, part of a memorable month, one that has stayed frozen in my memory, its events trapped like a scorpion suspended in amber.

A lot happened in the world that month. Coca-Cola gave up on new Coke. The French bombed the *Rainbow Warrior* in New Zealand. George Bush Senior stood next to a bright-looking teacher called Christa McAuliffe and announced she'd be the first woman ever to ride aboard the Space Shuttle, a particular one too, called *Challenger*. Six months later, in the Gwinett TV room, I'd watch that burn up in the sky like a fiery spear, after which I pretty much gave up on the news for good. They were asking for the death penalty by then. Seven months later they had it, and the long stay in the execution wing, twenty-two years in all, began.

Not that any of this matters. What does is this. That very afternoon my real five-year-old was supposed to be taken by his mother to see his – *their* – last movie: *Pee-wee's Big Adventure*. And it hadn't happened, for some reason I don't know, can't work out in the sullen silence between them.

14

Stupid thoughts dog you when people you love die. This one had eaten away at me for years: I just wish the movie they hadn't seen could have been something better.

We sit in the kitchen, Miriam and me. At this moment there is high pressure out over the distant water that lurks just a little under two miles away, beyond the line of apartment blocks straggling the horizon like bad teeth. Desiccated, stifling weather has been hanging in a bright pall over the city for days. There was a riot two days ago in the tenements of St Kilda. An entire building burned down during a turf scuffle between the gangs. One teenager was dead; thirteen more were licking their wounds. It was another short-staffed week in the station. I'd seen none of this. For reasons I never did understand, they'd had me out of uniform for seven weeks, on surveillance watching an empty warehouse on the edge of the docks, twenty-seven hours with scarcely a break on this last shift while other men and women tried to push the lid back down on something that stemmed from the simplest of causes. The heat. The poverty. The boredom.

Exhausted, I close my eyes, and at that moment I understand this same dank lethargy is everywhere. This is my city, a part of my character. Every inch of it is known to me, its small beauties and large blemishes, its people, good and bad and indifferent. I see them now in Greenpoint,

15

out by the clean sea just a few miles south, beyond the industrial outflows, where four beaches, two marinas, and the estates of white apartments and luxurious villas allow the rich to live unmolested. I see them in Yonge, down by the docks, where stevedores and truck drivers, drunks and street women all hide beneath the shadows of the idle cranes, too exhausted to work or play or do much except drink beer and grow more surly, more resentful with each passing hour.

They populate my mind as they have for years, since I started to ride these streets on a police department motorcycle, a badge and a gun visible on my person if I can make it that way, because the uniform is a part of my personality, one I refuse to hide. I never wanted to sneak inside a suit. I never wanted to be invisible, peering in to try to see what was going wrong inside their lives. The law needs to make its presence known, and when I am there that presence is me.

Along the broad business streets of Westmont men in black suits, white shirts, ties tight into a button-down collar, scuttle between their offices like beetles fleeing the sun, snatching glances at the pretty girls in their skimpy dresses, both too weary to make or take a pass. On the deserted hills of Eden, the old, original quarter, now a declining residential area of decaying houses and shuttered stores, with the polyglot mess of Chinatown at its heart, the trams travel half empty, squeaking iron wheels on ancient tracks, shuttling between stops with names that have lost their meaning, Fair Meadow and Leather Yard, God's Acre and Silent Street, carrying a meagre load of the poor and the elderly, passengers tracking the old metal road for want of anything else to do.

This is summer, mirror image to the hard freezing days of December and January. For these few brief months the marina yachts should have been out on the blue, blue water. The single remaining piece of green in Eden, Wicker Park, ought to have filled with families watching the ducks and geese on the pond, eating ice creams from the Italian *gelati* stands, imagining they could smell the sea over the stink of smog from the traffic and the factories by the Yonge docks. But the city is in stasis, for rich and poor, black and white, young and old. This scorching, heartless weather recognizes neither colour nor class, poised as it is, airless, without a breath of wind, over everyone.

It's always like this in July and only some interior sense of self-deception manages to keep a perpetual truth at bay: *no one escapes the city easily*. Going north, there's the long, viewless drive the length of the peninsula, then three hours through endless spruce forests before another metropolis rises into view. South, across the De Soto bridge, it takes almost as long to reach civilization, following the winding line of AIA, past abandoned coastal hamlets and dead fishing ports, just, in the end, to find another city much like the one left behind.

And turning away from the coast, going west, lies the dead wasteland of the plains, a sprawling, barren region where a few farmers eke out a living, their numbers winnowed each year as their children gravitate to the cities, looking for work in the factories and offices, the fast-food stores and the malls, dreaming, all the time, that something will snatch them from the daily tedium, give them what the young always want: celebrity, status, money.

We never had the cash to travel, but in truth it hadn't mattered. In the end you always wind up where you started: a place where rich and poor and the middling masses in between fight each other for the right to go home in the evening, having survived another day. If they're lucky, with a scrap of dignity and a little something to show.

We haven't been outside the city in the seven years since we married. There was never the time, never a bill that didn't need paying. Sometimes it irks her. But not a lot. She's been here most of her adult life. She knows it lives like a rogue gene in the blood.

'Bierce?' she asks that last morning, reading my thoughts easily, the way she can.

I hold a cup of coffee. It doesn't taste rich and comforting, the way her coffee normally does.

Then I look at Miriam, enjoying this small moment of intimacy, as I always do. She has on a long, loose scarlet cotton dress, low at the neck.

Her bare arms are suntanned from so much time in the garden with the boy. This is the kind of thing she wears at home. Her face, dark and beautiful, a little Spanish-looking I always think, doesn't seem to own a care in her world. She has eyes the colour of expensive chocolate, beautiful eyes, full of interest and consideration and, in the presence of her family, love. Miriam is an attractive, striking woman. We never go anywhere without some man taking a second look. She never believes me when I tell her it was the eyes I noticed first, that time I went round to the school to check up on some small case of theft, a childhood prank she'd found amusing when I pulled her out of class to talk about it.

No matter what she believes, it's true. I could stare into those eyes forever.

Mine are fixed on the garden. It looks more beautiful than ever. The place was a tip when we moved in, taking a mortgage we can still scarcely afford, most of it for renovation, on one of the last remaining original houses in Eden, the first city district, created back when the settlers came and took the land without asking who'd lived there first. Miriam found it on the agency lists, talked to the authorities to save it from demolition, negotiated the loan and a long pay-back period, one that seems endless, and still manages to bleed us dry. When we finally took possession she went through every last mid-nineteenth-century corner, restoring wood and plasterwork, removing vile modern paint, stripping the place back to the plain, pristine condition it once had when it was an upper-middle-class mansion, next to the small stream that gave the cul-de-sac in which it sat a name.

Owl Creek.

The last time I'd slept, in the big bedroom at the front, I thought I heard an owl, shuffling, screeching low from its sharp beak, hooting secretly to itself on the roof. The Pocapo natives said that birds – all birds – were harbingers of death, couriers that flitted between this world and the next. When it came to owls, I could almost believe it. Later that night I listened as the bird returned with some kind of prey, a small animal that squealed and screamed as it was torn apart and consumed alive just a few feet above our heads, as we lay in the big iron-framed bed, on the soft mattress, just a sheet to cover us during the long hot night.

Sometimes it's good slow. Sometimes fast. Today . . .

Miriam hasn't heard a thing. It's a dream. It has to be. There are no owls these days. Ours is the only residence in Owl Creek. Next door, just thirty feet away, is a deserted warehouse that has lain unoccupied for thirty years. On the other side sits a small two-storey factory occupied during the day by immigrants, mainly illegals. They make cheap clothing and handbags that get sold, for the most part, in the sprawling local market in St

Kilda. None of them ever looks me in the eye, though I do nothing about them. Still, they know. Everyone does. That's part of the job. You don't become a cop for anonymity.

In those first few months I lugged barrowloads of junk – scrap metal, an old bath, rotting furniture – out of the back yard. I watched the way she coaxed back to life the old plants and trees there, as if some magic lived in her fingers. While I was working, she built a swing for the boy, made this small patch of life in the grey, faded landscape of the city her own.

One August morning, three years after she began, when the long, patient time she'd spent pruning and repairing the old tree began to bring rewards, Miriam put fresh fruit on the table in a new olive-wood bowl she'd bought from the immigrants next door. Ricky was too young to try them raw, so she cooked some and mashed them up into a pulp he devoured, sitting giggling in his high chair, next to the kitchen table. The apples tasted a little of the city smoke, even after several dowsings under the tap. Neither of us mentioned it. The house and the garden were our private places, though a century and a half of constant development had transformed, completely, the area around them.

The stream now runs in a hidden culvert, its water polluted by industrial filth. The fields and orchards beyond Owl Creek, of which our fruit tree is a solitary survivor, have been consumed by

21

the uncontrolled, haphazard growth of St Kilda, transformed into housing blocks and clumps of low, grimy lockups, workshops and shanty huts where, from shadowy doorways, the dope dealers hang out, looking for trade.

Something moves in the garden, beyond the apple tree, hidden by its heavy, leafy branches, which contain green gems of bright round fruit growing, but still bitter, dangling from thick stems, like ornaments attached to an out-of-season, out-of-shape Christmas tree.

'Where's Ricky?' I ask.

Silence. The kind we get before an argument. I don't understand.

'You never listen.'

'Please,' I say, exasperated. 'Where's Ricky?'

I look at her when there's no reply. Miriam seems different. The room seems different.

Out in the garden the shape moves. I see more of it this time. It looks like a man, someone who must have got across the high wire fence, through the wild briar and the thick tangle of honeysuckle, finding a way into our small, private haven.

'Stay here,' I say, and get up from the table.

A stray finger catches the coffee cup. Liquid falls on my hand. It contains no heat whatsoever – nor cold. It merely exists.

I open the solid timbered door, a modern one – I'd insisted on that. Security is important. Then I go outside and look around.

The place seems more lush, more luxuriant than

I recall. The apple tree is covered in flowers and tiny fruit the size of elongated cherries. Ferns and fennel and green, spiky artichokes rise from a vegetable bed down near the end fence, close to the old well and the covered creek culvert, now a hard concrete vein rising from the earth.

I walk forward and stand on the drain for a moment. The water inside is beating, pulsing, roaring. For reasons I can't understand, this disturbs me. I blink, I fight to stop myself keeling over, then step off, stumbling, trying to scan the garden, the house, anywhere, everywhere.

Someone could have walked inside during that brief period in which I wasn't watching. Lapses like these cost you everything in the end.

Feeling a sudden foreboding, I look behind me. The kitchen door is wide open, thrown back on the hinges.

I never leave it this way.

My eyes shift upwards to the first-floor room, Ricky's, with its white cotton sheets and the over-sized bed. We let him use the one at the back because there was less noise. The cul-de-sac gives on to the busy main thoroughfare of De Vere. Our own bedroom shakes sometimes when a heavy vehicle roars down the road in the middle of the night, rattling the iron manhole covers, slipping a gear for the hill ahead, rising towards north St Kilda.

The double windows are open. Ricky's favourite mobile – plastic dolphins dancing over ripples of blue cardboard waves – moves gently in an invisible breeze there, then, as I watch, almost on cue, begins to go round and round, faster and faster.

I close my eyes again and try to breathe. There's no wind. There's scarcely any air. Just the dusty city smog, so meagre it's hard to believe anyone can find oxygen inside it.

Then I look at the house again, just starting to think, cursing my slowness. The kitchen is empty. This is wrong. She was there. Ricky was in bed. She wouldn't disturb him. Not without good reason.

For the first time I feel some real sensation, some genuine emotion, chilling the blood in my veins, making my teeth chatter with fear.

Suddenly, it's cold, bitterly cold, even in the harsh late-afternoon sun, and none of this matters: Miriam is upstairs now and this is wrong. I can hear it. Not a scream. Not a cry for help. It's Miriam's voice and she is furious with someone, filled with an anger I've never heard, not in the entire time we've been married.

She's yelling with all the force her lungs can muster, with a fear and a rage I barely believe can exist.

Though if she yelled at anyone like this, it would surely be at me.

I begin to run for the kitchen. When I'm partway through the door something falls, a weight so heavy I expect and believe its mass will run straight through the top of my skull, keep on going, down and down, until it enters the throat and the neck or works its way clean out through my body.

I fall to my knees, starting to sob silently with the pain, an agony so harsh, so cruel, so intensely internal that, for a moment, I think only of myself, not of them.

For a moment.

My arm reaches out. There is blood on the hand, thick and red, from wrist to fingertip.

'Miriam . . .' I say.

Then no more, because from above come other sounds, other noises.

Screaming and the slow, blunt rattle of blows, something hard and heavy on flesh and bone. Ricky's voice, her voice, both among the damaged, these I hear, and they make me want to rise from the ground, full of hate and vengeance, if only my limbs could move, if only I possessed the strength to save them.

Miriam's voice grows higher, louder, reaches a crescendo and then is silent.

A thick line of blood begins to move down my vision like some red stain descending from an unseen sky.

I fall backwards, can't help it, find myself flat on the floor in the old kitchen, hard on the ochre tiles she recovered from the dump one day, cursing someone else's lazy ways before laying them herself, patiently fitting each one.

I stare at the ceiling. It stares back, perfect white,

the way she painted it, now tinted with the blood flooding into my vision.

A foot obscures everything, stamps on my face, stamps again near one eye.

I feel nothing. I can think of nothing but the agonizing sound coming from above . . .

Daddy, Daddy, Daddy, Daddy.

I want to die now. Or I would if the same damn thought didn't keep running through my head.

There are three.

This is new. Before, in all the long years waiting in a cell, trying to recover some memories from the black, pained past, there had been just an empty well of not-knowing, a void that, before long, filled itself with my own self-doubt.

That infuriated them – judge and jury, even one-time friends – more than anything.

I never revealed the single truth of which I was certain: it infuriated me too, made it impossible to sleep most nights, to close my eyes without seeing their faces, the way I found them, when I discovered the strength and the courage to crawl up-stairs, then wait there, too weak to reach the phone, for how long I never knew, until the screaming squad cars arrived, threw themselves across the dead-end road, between the deserted warehouse and the little factory, outside what had once been a simple wooden porch in a country field on the outskirts of a nascent, new-born city made alive by ingenuous hope.

I couldn't tell them what happened because I

simply didn't know. Even, in the blackest moments, whether I was victim or the perpetrator they believed.

'There are three of you,' I murmur through lips that can barely speak, lips that feel swollen and useless, like those of a man with the plague. 'Three . . .'

'"There are three of you." What in God's name is that supposed to mean?' I was still on the hard, flat, surgical bed, in the same white medical gown I wore into the death room. This place was different. There was a window, a hard summer sun streaming through it, past a high fence topped by a watchtower with three crows on the roof, then, in the distance, what looked like sky-scrapers and gleaming towers in the direction of Westmont. Not that they seemed how I remembered them. Thanks to the time I'd spent in the Gwinett jail, the last twenty-two years in the third of the jail reserved for condemned men, I had no idea what the city looked like now.

The ragged line of corporate monoliths, like upright gleaming tombstones, disappeared just as I was beginning to recall the low, smoke-stained office blocks I thought should have been there. A black man in a tight-fitting dark blue suit walked into my line of vision, reached down, then unfastened the fabric restraining straps that still held me tight to the table.

His voice was familiar.

'Stapleton? Is that really you?'

My throat felt raw and painful. My head was still spinning. I wasn't sure whether this was part of the dream or not. Or how I found out which.

'What? Of course it's me. Who else gets dumped with this kind of shit job? You're babbling to yourself, man. Get it together.'

The straps fell free. I pushed myself up and slid round to sit on the edge of the bed. There was a throbbing pain in my arms. I looked. The line was no longer there. All I could see was a red mark over the vein and a livid yellow bruise stain spreading out from under it. Martin the Medic, with his shock of white hair and bright blue eyes, must have undone his work while I was unconscious. There was just Stapleton, the individual who once used to ride the squad bike next to mine, the lean black man who'd come out from St Kilda, put some dark, messy past behind him and clawed his way to some respect on the force before getting promoted out of the mundane place the rest of us worked.

'How long have I been out?'

Stapleton glanced at his watch.

'Three hours. They kept you under just to make sure there was no permanent damage.'

'If there was I guess I would never have woken up.'

'You were always too quick for your own good. They just wanted to do things right. These people are trained to finish lives, not revive them. They needed a little specialist help.'

Thinking, I reached over quickly and pinched his arm, finding flesh between thumb and forefinger, squeezing hard.

'Hey!' Stapleton yelled. 'What the hell do you think you're doing?'

'Just checking. I might be dreaming this.'

'Yeah. You might be. You're just the kind of screwed-up jerk who'd invite the likes of me into your dreams.'

'You didn't say welcome back, Stape.'

'You noticed?'

He looked unhappy. He often used to. Just not this way. About me.

'What am I doing here. What . . . ?'

Stapleton silenced me with a fierce stare.

'I talk. You listen. This is one short and very rare opportunity for a second chance. I don't care one way or another if you think this is real or not. I say my piece. Then I'm gone. You've got a decision to make. Be smart or be stupid. Either way it means nothing to anyone except you.'

He retrieved a sheaf of printed documents out of a leather briefcase. This interested me. The Stapleton I knew before he left the force never owned a briefcase. He moved papers around in a supermarket bag. Then he took out some pages, flicked through them, handed them over and sat down on a metal chair by the window.

'Sign these and you get to walk out of here today. Free. It's a great deal. The best you'll ever get. *All* you'll ever get.'

He'd aged. A lot. We all had, I guessed, though on those rare moments when I looked into the plastic mirror in the communal shower rooms in jail I didn't detect much change. Prison stopped my clock running in many ways. I was twenty-nine when I went inside, fifty-two now. The rest of the world got on with its business, not knowing, not caring, just getting older while I ran through all the rounds of predictable emotions: bewilderment, anger, fear, then finally a dull acceptance. Maybe that last preserved me somewhat. Stapleton was one year younger than me yet his once-black hair was grey with white streaks. His long, miserable face fell down in two jowls from his cheeks. There were bags beneath his sad, staring eyes. He used to be about my size, just under six foot tall, muscular, fit. Sometimes, when we were in uniform on the road together, we'd mixed up each other's jackets. Either fitted. Once we had a few issues out of the way, I'd liked this man, mostly, during the couple of years we worked together, before he got promoted to detective work, then left the force al-together. I believed he felt the same way about me.

That was then. *Before.* We wouldn't swap clothes any more. He'd got a gut on him, a pouch of belly that jutted out over his belt. His chest had sunk in somewhat, in an old man's way. There was a hint of envy in his eyes when he looked in my direction. I don't think he meant to hide it. This new Stapleton had found one more reason to hate me and that seemed to give him a buzz.

'I thought I was supposed to be guilty,' I protested.

'This is about the law, Bierce. Not justice. Two different things. You taught me that. Remember?'

Stapleton used to be on the take from some of the drug runners we were supposed to look out for. One day I found him getting paid off in a parking lot on the edge of the Yonge docks. After I watched the scurvy brother who'd been financing him flee the scene in some shiny new Toyota sports car, I delivered a brief lecture, part spoken, part physical, about honesty and what it meant to be a cop, even when most of those around you still hadn't quite received the message. I got through to him back then. It wasn't hard. There'd always been something to get through to, and I'd recognized that in the man all along.

I took the papers from his hand and looked at them. Page after page of legal bullshit, that mix of English, arcane and real, we always had to wade through before going to court.

There were three places for me to sign.

'What are these?'

'Waivers. Statements that say you're willing to forgo your right to sue anyone – the mayor, the chief of police, judges, lawyers, the prison people, me if you feel cranky, *everyone* – in return for getting out of here.'

I stared at the print and tried to take in the details. 'Why?'

Stapleton swallowed, got up. The gut apart, he looked thinner all round, and more than a little unwell. This question had been inevitable, and he hadn't been looking forward to it.

'What does "why" matter? Can't you just put your arrogance to one side for a change, take a gift and walk away with it?'

'No. That was your speciality if I remember correctly. Until I taught you otherwise.'

'Oh, Christ! Are you going to play the insufferable pain-in-the-ass all over again? After what you've been through? After what's on your record? Give me a break.' He was standing next to me now.

I put a hand on Stapleton's jacket and gripped the lapel. The material was a lot better than anything he wore when we worked the streets.

'I want to know,' I said very carefully.

What I got in return was a look I'd learned to recognize over the last two decades, one that said: *but you know already, you bastard, just stop pretending.*

'So it's still that game, is it?' Stapleton grumbled miserably. 'Let's get this straight. I am not here to plead with you. I am not here to convince you one way or the other. I am merely a messenger from people who, for reasons beyond me, are feeling a touch generous in your direction right now. Are we clear on that?'

'Sure,' I agreed. 'After this I hope never to see your ugly sick face again too.'

His mouth curled up in a timid little snarl. I remembered what was wrong. Stapleton used to have a pencil moustache above his thin upper lip.

There was just rough stubble there now, flecked with white and grey.

'I am assuming,' he went on, 'that your supposedly damaged memory does not extend to forgetting Frankie Solera?'

Names. Faces. Sometimes they came back quickly. Sometimes it was as if I'd never heard them before in my life. This was a familiar one.

'Dopehead,' I said. 'We put him inside in the summer of '83. "We" being you and me. Armed robbery in the company of one Tony Molloy. We chased them over the De Soto bridge until they ran out of gas on the highway. They came without protest if I recall correctly. Twelve months with parole.'

Solera and Tony Molloy were a team, both violent street hoods who belonged to one of the gangs smuggling goods – dope, contraband, anything worthwhile – through the docks. Not that they didn't take on freelance work when it came along.

'So?'

'Two nights ago Solera died in hospital. Cancer of the colon, in case you're interested. It was a long and painful time coming, so perhaps there is a god. We'd been talking to him for a while. About what happened at Owl Creek. About other things. We thought maybe you and him . . .'

I just looked into his sick face. Stapleton got the message.

'You said there were three,' he pressed.

33

'You said I was babbling. How many times do I have to tell you this? I don't remember a thing.'

Barely, I added, but to myself.

'So you say. Anyway, he confessed. Said it was just him.'

'What about Molloy? Was he around or in jail?'

'I don't know! Do you think we've got nothing better to do than chase old ghosts?'

'I didn't realize you'd developed the giving-up habit.'

'Don't get smart with me, Bierce. Or I may just walk straight out of here and let you stew for the rest of your pathetic little life. Solera said there was no one else. Then he died. Personally, I don't believe him, not for a second. It doesn't matter. The legal department thinks your conviction could go before a judge if someone pushed it. There's some procedural shit involved no one but a lawyer would understand. So maybe it's best we come to some quite private arrangement. *If* you're willing.'

Stapleton's eyes flashed at me and there was some hesitation, maybe even some hate, there.

'Why you?' I asked. 'Why not some lawyer?'

He twisted his mouth into a kind of a smile.

'In case you don't know, I saw that house afterwards. I just wanted to see what you looked like when you walked out of here thinking you'd got off scot-free.'

This was interesting. This made me think.

'You weren't police then, were you?'

'Your memory's still working there too! My,

34

is it one selective organ. This is none of your business. Whatever I was, I saw that house. One man
couldn't do all that damage. Forensic said so.
Common sense said so. But I'm not paid to make
those kinds of judgements.'

'You're not paid to make private arrangements
either. What happened to the law?'

He hesitated, wondering whether to say what
was on his mind.

'There's something you have to understand,
Bierce. I'm saying this just once, so that I can
tell myself you've been warned. Not that I
imagine it will make a difference. You're an obsti-
nate son of a bitch and always will be. But hear
this anyway. Life is different now. A lot different.
All the rules you thought existed, such as they
were . . . Don't assume anything. That would be
stupid, and stupidity is one thing I never thought
you guilty of.'

I rubbed my arms. Some life was coming back
into them. Maybe.

'Is there any evidence linking Solera to the
house?' I asked.

'What does it matter? What do you care?'

'That was my wife and son. I care.'

Stapleton pushed the papers at me again.

'If it means anything, he said he still had the
knife in his apartment. The moron kept it as a
trophy all these years. The blood was hers. And
Ricky's.'

I thought about what he said. Thought about

the dream too. It seemed oddly ironic that it took a shot of dope designed to soften me up for execution to start to loosen all those locked memories from years ago.

'You found my blood on it?'

'No!' Stapleton spat back at me. 'You know damn well where we found your blood. Underneath Miriam's fingernails. You used to be a police officer once, how do *you* think it got there?'

'I have no idea,' I answered. 'And that's the truth.'

'The truth . . .' he muttered. 'I don't really care about that. These are strange times, and forgiveness is a part of that strangeness, I guess. So are you signing those papers or not?'

I'd been glancing through them in the few minutes while we talked. Even wrapped in legalese, the release came with heavy conditions.

'This doesn't make me innocent,' I pointed out. 'It just puts the conviction on ice. It's like parole without the conditions.'

'Listen to me,' Stapleton replied. 'Guilty or not, you get to walk out of here. Also you pick up four hundred and sixty thousand in cash as recompense for the time you spent in jail. Twenty thousand a year for twenty-three years.'

'I'd have earned more than that on the force.'

He smiled.

'Only if you'd lived. To get this you need to sign on the line, go your way quietly, keep your mouth shut, stay away from stirring the shit with lawyers or anyone else. Plus the usual condition we'd impose on any ex-con. Do not touch any kind of firearm whatsoever, on pain of immediate re-imprisonment. This is all, by the way, non-negotiable and comes with the shelf life of a mayfly. Take it now or lose it forever. Everything's off the table if I walk out of this door without your name on those documents.'

He pulled a gold pen out of his jacket and placed it on the table.

'Maybe I ought to talk this over with someone,' I stalled.

'Do that and it's gone. Here's the deal and it's the only deal there'll ever be. Sign and you get a little of your life back. All that money and a little upfront. Twiddle your thumbs for one second beyond my limits and you're back in Gwinett, staring at the wall forever and ever amen. Well?'

He reached into his jacket, took out a fat wad of used notes and threw the money on the table. It looked like a lot.

'Here's twenty thousand cash to be going along with. The rest we'll pay into one account you get to specify. This could buy you a few nights of heaven out there. Alternatively, you can be some stuck-up, stupid prig and you stay in solitary for life. Without parole. It's your choice. And if you're thinking you can call in a lawyer later and try to revive this deal, let me enlighten you now. These papers . . .'

Stapleton waved them in my face.

'. . . they don't exist. They came out of some private safe on the way here. They go back in if you sign. Or hit the shredder if you don't. This is all happening outside the judge's rooms, Bierce. Bear that in mind. If you want to get prissy we're talking years and years of argument and in the end you'll lose. We'll make sure of that. Think on this. There's enough circumstantial evidence to let us treat Solera's confession as that of your accomplice if we want. Remember Miriam's fingernails. I do.'

I shook my head.

'Didn't I teach you anything? This is the law you're dealing with. You can't cut deals like that, Stape. It doesn't work this way.'

He sighed.

'I keep telling you. These are different times. Don't argue with them. It's not productive. Also . . .' He pointed a finger straight in my face. 'Don't get familiar with me again. Should we meet in the street after this, ignore me, 'cos I will surely ignore you. Should we meet professionally – and I pray for your sake that does not occur – it's Agent Stapleton these days. I get some respect.'

I smiled.

'Agent? Congratulations. I guess you're glad I punched your lights out when I caught you taking money that time. You might have stayed in the police. And prospered.'

He laughed. Briefly there was a little sparkle in his tired eyes.

'Jesus, Bierce.' His voice went down to a whisper. His eyes flickered nervously round the room. 'I could have been up for commissioner right now. Different times. Bear it in mind.'

This man was once my friend. It was hard to believe everything was gone.

'You don't honestly believe I killed them, do you?'

The smile dropped like a stone.

'Can you honestly say you didn't?'

That was the problem, and had been all along. I told them the truth. What else was there to say? They found me unconscious, my wife and son battered to death upstairs. All the physical evidence pointed to a struggle with Miriam before she died. My blood and prints were on the sledgehammer used in their murders. And I didn't remember a thing, not a single moment of the events leading up to the killings. I didn't deny the facts of the murder because I couldn't. All I could rely on was my own emotional instinct, which told me, without a possibility of error, that I couldn' have committed the acts of which I stood accused. That was the only honest answer and, as a stratagem in court, it was disastrous.

There was no remaking the past. Only a possibility of its recovery. Of comprehension.

So I took the pen and signed three times, promising to be quiet from now on, not to talk to the media, break the law or be anything but the good citizen that, in my mind, I always was. Four hundred and sixty thousand dollars, more money than I'd ever owned in my entire life, ought to be enough to work out what to do next.

My name looked odd on the paper. It had been a long time since I'd written anything.

'I will organize transport,' Stapleton said, watching. 'Where do you want to go?'

'Home.'

There was a brief silence.

'You mean Owl Creek?'

'I mean Owl Creek. It's the only home I have.'

I didn't let them sell it, not even when my lovely lawyer, Susanna Aurelio, was moaning, very sweetly, for money. Nor could they make me. Through some odd irony, the insurance money had paid off the mortgage automatically, before the court case. Susanna expected the insurance people to come hunting me for the money once I was convicted. For some reason they never did. It was just one more question that bugged me for a while. But not long. The endless days in Gwinett saw to that. Owl Creek was 100 per cent mine two months before I was sentenced to death for the murder of Miriam and Ricky, and stayed that way throughout my time as a condemned man, not that I ever expected to see it again.

'That house has been empty for twenty-three years, Bierce. With all the money I'm handing you, why not go to a decent hotel for a few days?'

'Because I want to go home.'

'Fine,' he snapped. 'I rather thought you'd say

that. It can pass for now, though I seriously suggest you find yourself somewhere more healthy soon. That neighbourhood is not coming up in the world. Particularly for a friendless individual like you. I'll make some calls. It's in both our interests that the media stay off your back. They've been warned already. Doesn't do any harm to be a little more emphatic.'

I tried to think straight. This didn't ring true. So much of what he said didn't.

'Warned? How the hell can you warn people like that?'

'There are only so many times I can say this. Things have changed. Do yourself a favour. Remember that. Do yourself a bigger favour.'

The man in the suit stood up and took my arm. For a few seconds I thought I saw a flicker of sympathy, some concern, in his eyes.

'Take a plane out of here. Go to the other side of the country. The world. The universe. Somewhere no one has a clue who you are. As long as you stay here you're just a man in limbo, Bierce, and limbo's not a nice place to be.'

I nodded. I knew how to be co-operative when it felt right.

'I'll think about that. So what took you?'

'Excuse me?'

'Solera died two nights ago. You had the confession then. This morning you had me on the slab, thinking I was about to get dead. Events like that kind of mark you.'

I pointed to the documents on the table.

'If you'd been a little later with those . . . Even with your lousy timing that was cutting it fine, Agent Stapleton, don't you think?'

He picked up the papers, examined the signatures, then placed them in a plastic folder which he inserted into the briefcase.

'Oh! You mean these?' he asked, wide-eyed, sarcastic. 'No. I had these last night. I was just asked to put them aside for a while. Where were you going anyway?'

I felt my fists clench. It was a long time since I'd hit anyone.

Stapleton took my right hand in his lean black fingers, pushed it down, smiled, just briefly.

'Hey. You taught me something once. Now it's my turn. This is educational, friend. Think about it. There are people out there who want to see you sweat a little. To make sure you understand how the land lies in the hope you will adjust your future behaviour accordingly.'

He nodded at the money on the table.

'I wonder if it worked. I'll send out for some clothes before the car arrives. After that, you're back where you always were. On your own.'

It was dark by the time the car pulled into the narrow dead-end turning that was Owl Creek. Stape was right. From what little I could see, the area hadn't come up the way Miriam had expected. I'd slept most of the way, still doped. No dreams.

Nothing. I still felt wiped out when the car's movement jolted me awake as it negotiated the ragged cobblestones of the short dead end that led towards my front door. The warehouse on the left looked even more decrepit than I recalled. There wasn't a window or a door intact in the place any more. From the back seat of the vehicle I could see straight into the interior: broken walls, missing floorboards. We told Ricky never to play in the place. He'd done as we said. He always did. The factory opposite looked unchanged. There was a light in one room on the first floor, a single bare, yellow bulb, and the silhouette of someone working at a desk. Apart from that, the building seemed empty.

I got out of the car and gazed at the single street lamp in front of the house. It was flickering into life, looking as if it might never quite get there. I thought I heard an owl hoot somewhere nearby, but perhaps I was dreaming.

'Thanks,' I said to the driver, some plain-clothes guy Stapleton had called.

'Don't walk around here at night,' the man said, still gunning the engine.

I hardly heard him. I was staring at the house, feeling its presence come back into my life, the good and the bad. But mainly the good. People are made that way. Sane people anyway, and in spite of the years in jail, and the dope Martin the Medic had pumped inside me that morning, I still felt sane.

It would be just a few steps up the broken paving stones to the front door. I could see a heavy, rusting police padlock and chain there, now hanging loose and broken, a clear, perhaps deliberate, indication that someone had been inside of late. Stapleton had given me my old set of house keys from the belongings bag they'd stored for twenty-three years. There were no clothes, of course. They, and their attendant bloodstains, had gone into the evidence file. Just a set of keys and a wallet with nothing but an expired driver's licence and police ID card inside. I'd left the latter for him as a souvenir, but now I couldn't help but think about what he'd said. I could have gone somewhere else, some anonymous hotel, placed my head on a comfortable pillow for the first time in a third or so of the average lifetime, and forgotten about the past. The trouble was, I didn't feel I had a choice. This old house, with its rotting weather-boarded timbers and cobwebbed windows, looked grey and old and dead, but I still saw it in another way too, as somewhere my family once lived, in a semblance of brief happiness. One night of horror doesn't obliterate seven years of normality. Not quite.

'I'll bear that in mind,' I said, then walked up to the wooden porch, removed the shattered chain, found my old key, amazed how it still felt familiar in my fingers, unlocked the door after a struggle with the rusty, stiff lock, took a deep breath – smog and ocean, drains and, from somewhere out back, the slightest hint of apple blossom – and walked inside.

It didn't smell old or dead. The house still had the odour I'd noticed the first day we moved in: drying, antique wood, on the floors, the stairs, around the long, generous windows. Cedar maybe, or something else aromatic. I never did find out.

Instinctively, I reached for the light switch. To my surprise, it worked. Quite why, in a house that had been empty all this time, all bills, except the city taxes, unpaid, was beyond me. But this was a new century, a new world. A lot would be beyond me, I guessed, and standing there, in the place that had once been the focus of the only family I'd ever have, I realized I couldn't care less. What mattered was then, not now, and maybe it would always be that way.

What I saw in front of me was both foreign and familiar. The house had been in legal limbo since my conviction, incapable of being sold or rented, visited only by lawyers and the police over the years. Cobwebs ran everywhere, geometric grey skeins with a covering of dust like the first frost of winter stored somewhere dusty, somewhere it could grow old. A line of yellow police tape still ran across the foot of the stairs. I strode up and brushed it to one side with my hand. As I did so, something rose in my memory. It came from my working days. The touch of the plastic tape, so distant yet so familiar, brought back a mental picture of a case I'd handled once, many years before. The rape and murder of a young girl found in the rocky, seaweed-strewn dead land beneath the Greenpoint side of the De Soto bridge. Stapleton and I had been the first to the scene. I could recall the sight of her ruined, broken body, the smell of the place, the sound of the waves lapping over the algaed rocks where she was found. I could recall, too, Stape gagging into the bushes, choking as he threw up, moaning about how unjust it was that this job had fallen on his shift.

We never did catch that girl's killer, not while I was out on the streets. Still, that was a memory in itself. They did keep coming back, which gave me pause for thought.

I glanced up the wooden staircase and thought: not yet.

Then I turned round and walked through the ground-floor rooms, slowly, methodically, trying to recover the mental map stored somewhere deep in my head.

The parlour faced on to the street. I went in. Nothing had changed. I walked to the upright piano that sat against the end wall, lifted the lid and played a chord: G minor seventh, the one I always remembered from a couple of months of lessons at school because it was my favourite, sad, resigned yet not entirely devoid of hope. The instrument was hideously out of tune. The chord didn't sound right. I crossed the hall, went past the foot of the stairs and entered the dining room.

Only one light bulb worked here. It cast a hard shadow across the large, eight-place mahogany table, still with the set of high-backed chairs tucked in between its legs as if awaiting guests.

It had been a standing joke between us: the Bierces only ever had eight guests at Christmas, when Miriam's small and argumentative family descended. We found it hard to fill this house with family at other times, until Ricky came along, and after that it didn't much matter.

I ran a finger through the dust and spiders' webs on the table. Beneath it lay the hard, polished shine she'd put there through days of dedicated labour after we found it languishing, half wrecked, in a St Kilda junk yard.

It made me try to remember the last meal we ate here. It was impossible. All of a sudden I felt giddy, aware that I was deeply exhausted, maybe a little unbalanced and prone to hallucinations from the stuff still circulating in my veins. I was desperate to lie down and sleep. Just not ready. And not upstairs either. Not yet.

There was a sofa in the parlour, beneath the window out on to the street. When I needed it, that would do.

These two rooms were untouched by the savagery. I knew in my heart that was why I came here first. But self-deception was never one of my talents. So I turned round and walked to the back of the house, into the big kitchen, with its French windows out on to the garden, a pool of semi-blackness now, just illuminated by the washed-out lighting from the nearby tenement blocks.

The bright fluorescent tubes came on, flickering, as if nothing had ever happened here. I saw what I knew I'd see, and still it made me catch my breath, fight to stem the nausea rising with the memory of the pain, that all-consuming agony that came when the blows, from an unremembered hand, rained down.

There were blue chalk marks on the floor and scribbled annotations from the investigating officers. I moved my foot across them quickly. The ochre tiles had lost their warmth under a dusty azure film. These stains wouldn't go easily.

Through the windows, in the garden, I could just make out the shape of the apple tree. It seemed huge, a sprawling, low mass of branches. Miriam pruned this thing carefully each spring, brought it back to shape. It needed that. So many things did. Perhaps I could do the same again, and in five or six years it would look like it used to. Or – this thought wouldn't go away – perhaps I could do what Stapleton wanted, turn my back on everything here and run, for good. I had the money. I could walk out to De Vere, pick up a cab, book into a clean, bright, antiseptic place with no memories, nothing to keep me awake at night. Then, in the morning, go to the airport. Take the first flight out, to anywhere.

All this was possible, I thought, and then my

mind seized on itself, like an engine abruptly starved of oil.

There was a sound upstairs. It was someone moving, softly, as light as a cat.

I thought for a moment, then walked back into the hall, placed my hand on the warm wood of the banister and started taking the steps, two at a time.

When I reached the top I heard the sound again: the bare wooden floorboards, once polished, creaked under a step that was light. Like a woman, not like a child.

There were more chalk marks on the landing. I tried to move my foot to obliterate them but there was too much blue dust, too many scrawls on the floor. I fought to remember what this level was like in detail. A design still lived in my head, but it wasn't specific. The house had become a part of us, almost a member of the family too, a jumbled-up, rambling collection of rooms, running from the cellar, where Miriam had made some small den for herself, up to this bedroom floor in a crooked, illogical tangle of half-staircases and dead-end corridors. I was never a man to work on a home; Miriam did that or found someone. So it became something close, accepted for what it was, not broken down into some kind of precise, visual inventory. And this section of it always puzzled me more than anywhere else. It should have been bigger, not just three bedrooms – ours, Ricky's and a third for rare guests – along with a bathroom, a closet and, on the blind side of the building, looking out on to a small scrappy field of scrub kept in permanent shadow by high walls on both sides, so it was invisible from the house, a tiny boxroom for storage.

I flicked the landing light switch. One more burnt-out bulb. The entire garden end of the house – Ricky's room, the guest bedroom, the boxroom – was still in darkness.

I walked forward and said, in what I took to be a calm, flat voice, 'Who's there?'

Feet scampered ahead in the gloom, making swift, light movements across the boards. A shape flitted through the shadows, got lost in the gloom so thoroughly I couldn't see where she came from or where she went.

My heart skipped a couple of beats. My mouth went dry. Noticeable physical symptoms, proof I was alive. That hadn't happened in a while.

I'd seen enough to know she was wearing a dress, scarlet probably, loose and flowing, open at the neck. Like all those dresses Miriam kept on buying because they were so comfortable in the scorching summer heat.

Like the dress she died in. I'd never forget the pictures. Bendinck, the sour-faced detective who led the investigation, seemed to take a particular pleasure in thrusting them into my face, even in hospital, when I could scarcely open my eyes. Those shots, taken from every angle, unforgiving in their brutal honesty, had stayed with me, would stay with me, always. The colour of the blood and the fabric seemed so closely matched.

I walked forward, turned left into the boy's room and hit the light. The sight made me want to weep. The bed was still there, stripped of sheets. The cartoon characters remained stuck to the walls, each in mid-flight, hitting, running, chasing, doing what cartoon people did: things we weren't supposed to in real life. Many were now marked by the work of the forensic men, whose pens and crayons had disfigured every-thing, everywhere. In places there was a fine spray on the paper. It jogged a phrase at the back of my memory: blood spatter.

Blue chalk lines ran across the floor, the walls, on to the cupboards and the low table where Ricky used to work, crouched over a book, head lolling on the desktop, pencil in hand.

Like slender, writhing snakes, they all ran outwards from the chalk silhouette of a small body curled on the floor, a single arm raised defensively to his head, a curving, organic shape that looked as if it was scrawled there in one single, sweeping movement.

Ricky died here. This stark blue impression on the bare floorboards was the only physical evidence our son existed, a moment snatched from a single human life and pinned to the ground as if to say: *here*.

My foot reached out to touch the shape. Then

I stopped. There was so much blue chalk. I couldn't obliterate it all, not with a simple gesture.

From somewhere behind came a sound again. I went back to the landing, trying to locate it in the darkness that squatted like a black, dead pool in the corner, out of reach of the bulb in the stairwell.

I knew where it came from. The bedroom. Nowhere else. And as I watched, something skipped through the door: in and out, teasing. I saw the briefest of glimpses of a scarlet cotton dress, a lithe naked leg, an outstretched bare arm, shifting tentatively into the light, then disappearing.

She had so many of those dresses. She couldn't stop buying them. They were like a uniform, like a second skin.

I went forward, past the guest room, past the boxroom, over the lines of blue chalk on the floor, like tattoos on the face of some primitive being, and entered, holding my breath, determined to see this through.

Something tried to burst into life by the Victorian metal bed where we'd slept. A smell reached me: it was dry and vile and burning. I looked and saw a gigantic moth trapped inside the bowl of the upright tungsten lamp she kept on the cabinet, stuck to the burning glass by its own dissolution, struggling, flapping, to get free.

In the corner, she was dancing.

Round and round the scarlet dress turned,

revealing the long, loose limbs, bare and brown, tanned from the summer sun.

Her hair flew about her head, a brown, shining mantle over her face and the dark, slender stalk of her neck.

There was another blue outline on the floor. A larger shape, contorted in agony. I stepped over it, towards the figure, trying not to shake.

She skipped round me, round the bed, past the mirror, hair flying, long, slender hands curving, curling in theatrical gestures.

The cassette in the clock radio was playing a song from a tape I'd owned in jail for a while, until they took it away when I did something wrong, like breathing in six/eight instead of four/four.

It was Bruce Hornsby's rolling piano and soft, sad voice.

This is no fond farewell.
You can be sure I could wish it was
no farewell at all.

I tried to remember the title, cursed my own failed memory. Then the music told me anyway.

This is my swan song. I'm gone, gone.

I walked up to the head of the bed, hit the stop key and punched the eject button. The tape sat in its little hole, pale plastic. Scrawled on the top, with the cheap black felt tips they gave us in

Gwinett, my writing said: *Property of Bierce. Steal me and die.*

The scarlet figure moved towards the door. My hand swept the air in front of me, touching nothing except cobwebs falling long and loose from the old fan in the ceiling down to the iron bedstead. It fell hard on the burnished bronze frame at the foot. The springs squeaked, a sound I hadn't heard in more than two decades, one that filled me with despair and a sad longing.

Sometimes it's good slow. Sometimes fast.

In a low voice, one filled with some fear and fury I hadn't expected, I murmured, 'Who are you?'

Then I sprang forward, caught hold of the scarlet cotton, pulled, feeling a body, a real body, exert momentum in return.

I was grateful for that.

The mantle of brown hair subsided. She had her back to me. I placed my hands on her naked shoulders and turned her round.

Two green, unfamiliar eyes stared into mine.

'Hi.'

The girl was about twenty-five, slim, beautiful in a marked, damaged way. There was a hint of something Oriental in the oval shape of her face. A small horizontal scar ran above once eye. She smiled: even white teeth and a silver stud in the tip of her tongue.

She stood there, her body twisted into the inviting curve of some dancer in a cheap St Kilda sex dive.

'Who the hell are you?'

The girl's face fell. It was still pretty.

'You don't look pleased to see me.'

Her voice didn't quite match her slightly foreign appearance. It had the hard city inflection to it, the mark of a local.

'Get out of my dead wife's clothes,' I said. 'Then get out of my house.'

She touched the scarlet fabric.

'So many things to wear here. They don't do her any good now. Do they?'

'Get out,' I said, and didn't feel mad for some reason. Someone had sent her, and if she was the kind of woman who could be bossed around that way, it wasn't hard to guess the rest.

'Hey, Bierce. Don't be so prissy. Why shouldn't someone live here? No one else does. Who do you think put back the electricity and the water and the gas? Who washed a few things so they don't smell musty and bad? Me. That's who. A big house like this needs a woman around.'

She reached out. Her fingers touched my hand, stroking the skin gently. Almost with tenderness.

'My name's Alice. If you let me stay you won't regret it.'

'Out,' I said, and I could hear how weak it sounded. I felt exhausted, screwed up by Martin the Medic's dope and the events of the day. I was alive but I didn't feel it.

Also, I was aware I couldn't take my eyes off her. The girl's body was so like Miriam's, slim, lithe, like an athlete's but a little worn down and damaged by use. If I didn't look into her face, if I couldn't remember or imagine . . .

'You want the dress,' she said. 'You take the dress.'

With that easy two-handed movement a woman has, she reached down and pulled the scarlet cotton past her head, dragging it over her hair. Then she stood in front of me, slouching a little, her mouth midway between anger and a pout.

She pressed the dress into my hands. I felt the soft seersucker fabric, smelled its freshness, so familiar, once a part of the ritual that began here, ended here, sometimes made me believe this room was where we'd live forever, locked into each other, not moving, scarcely daring to breathe, in rapture that two people could become one like this, could find so much in each other that nothing else in the world beyond the shutters mattered at all.

I let it go. The thing fell through my fingers and drifted to the floor. She watched it land gently on the old carpet, then picked it up, carefully I thought, and threw it on the bed, looking at me, leaning her slim, bronzed body the way she did before.

She had small upright breasts with dark nipples, almost black. The triangle of hair at the apex of her long, slender legs had been fashioned into an artificial geometric shape, like some twisted astrological symbol. A small green and red dragon tattoo nestled above the final curls in the soft curve of her lower stomach.

She reached out and stroked me through the cheap pants the prison had provided.

'I think you're going to need some work there,' the girl whispered tentatively, with no confidence at all. Almost shy, I thought. And reluctant.

It didn't seem to be an offer, even if she thought that was what was expected of her.

'I've got work aplenty,' I said, then turned round and walked down the stairs.

Just the touch of her fingers had broken some spell. With that came a memory.

It was in the garden and it mattered.

Two of the four security floods came on like small silver suns. Shaded by high walls on all three sides, the garden was unrecognizable.

The lawn was thigh deep in long grass and weeds. The roses had defeated the honeysuckle in the wire fences, which were now thickets of thorns and white, simple flowers, rambling down to the ground.

The broad crooked path of broken paving that led to the end wall, and the old wooden door to the scrub land beyond, was barely visible beneath the weeds and wild flowers that covered it. Then there was the tree. Uncared for, uncut for more than twenty years, it had grown into a behemoth of heavy branches, stooping low on one side under a surfeit of fat green fruit, a rough, misshapen giant, bent in on itself, malformed by the shade.

Things thrived, after a fashion, in spite of neglect. It didn't always work out for the worse.

I heard a sound behind me and looked back. It was the girl, Alice, skipping across the kitchen. She was wearing jeans and a cheap white T-shirt now. She looked more natural.

'I never went in here,' she said quietly, coming to a stop by my side. 'I never lived anywhere with a garden before. What's it for?'

I walked up to the good side of the tree and pulled off a couple of apples. They were just like the first ones Miriam had picked for me. Half green, half rosy red. I gave her one. She watched me, cautious. I rubbed the shiny skin with the arm of my shirt and took a bite. She did the same, not taking her eyes off my face for a moment.

They still tasted a little of smog, not quite sour, not quite sweet. I didn't mind. It was better than anything I'd eaten in Gwinett.

'Gardens exist to remind you there's something else in the world apart from buildings and cars and money.'

She laughed.

'There is?'

The memory was firm now. It could wait.

'I'd like the key,' I said.

The green eyes glittered, a little resentful. She didn't like being found out.

'Take 'em.'

She kept the bunch in her pocket. They were new and still had a label on them from the shop where they were cut.

'Was it a black guy who put you up to this?

Stapleton? Old. Grey-white hair. Stubble where he used to have a moustache.'

She nodded.

'I didn't know his name but it sounds like him. You don't ask when it comes to this kind of work. I just heard they were putting it round they needed someone who'd be happy to make up a welcoming party. They let me in last night. Said to clean up the worst places. Get things going.'

She folded her arms. The next thing didn't come easily.

'Part of the deal was that, when you got here, I'd do whatever you liked. I think he wanted you to be happy. Sorry. I didn't mean to upset you.'

'You didn't,' I answered honestly.

'They gave me five hundred, Bierce. That's a lot of money.'

No, it wasn't. Not even twenty-three years ago.

'You could make that with two tricks in Westmont,' I guessed.

'What?' Her face lit up with anger. It looked keen and intelligent when that happened. 'I'm no hooker.'

'So what are you?'

She thought before answering.

'Someone who scrapes along. Or tries to. This is a profession followed by the masses these days. Maybe a man in jail forgets that. Besides, I've got reasons.'

I reached forward and took her by the wrists,

turned them over and looked, slowly. There were no marks.

'What particular reason happens to be yours?'

'Huh?'

They always kept it about them. I patted the pockets of her tight jeans, ignoring her struggles. The bottle was in the lefthand one. I took it out and waved it in front of her face. Brown-coloured glass. A pharmaceutical label. Something about this didn't make me feel smart.

'It's for hay fever, you jerk,' she squealed, wriggling out of my hold. 'Talk about once a cop, always a cop. Can I have my medicine back now? Jesus, getting accused of being a hooker and a junkie in two consecutive sentences is a little tough to take. Even for me. How'd you get married in the first place? Was your wife allergic to charm or something?'

The funny thing was, Miriam used to say something very like that at times. When we lay back in bed, after. I was feeling sleepy. She was feeling talkative.

Is that what got you here, Bierce? Charm?

No. I never did unlock that secret.

I looked at the label, then opened the bottle. It was half full of white, innocuous-looking pills. There had to be something, I thought. A real reason. A good one.

'Thanks for the apple,' she said, then pulled back her arm and threw the spent core straight ahead as hard as she could. It flew through the bright beam of the security lights and went over the high wall, into the dead land behind the abandoned warehouse. A good shot. A powerful shot.

'You're right. I should go now.'

'Stapleton gave you the Hornsby tape? The one you put on in the bedroom.'

'Is that who it was? Some of this old guy stuff is really cool.'

I blinked.

'It's not old. Eighties. Early nineties at the most. I was in solitary all the time after that. I never got anything.'

Alice licked her lips, wondering whether she ought to say it.

'Bierce, that's old. *You're* old.'

I looked at my hands, my arms. Looked at the parts of me I could see.

'I don't look any different. I don't feel any different.'

'OK,' she agreed. 'You haven't changed. It's just the rest of the world. Same thing.'

'Did he ask you to keep tabs on me?'

'No.'

'What did he ask for?'

'Nothing. I told you. He wanted you to be happy. That was all.'

'So for five hundred you'd just go and spend the night with a man convicted of killing his own wife and child? In the house where he was supposed to have murdered them?'

She blushed.

'All the dress stuff was my idea. I said I'm sorry. Sometimes . . .' She winced. 'Look. Being physical is the easiest way to converse with most men. It gets round the awkward questions. It's a way of saying hello.'

I laughed. I really did, though it took me a moment to recognize the sound that came out of my own throat.

'That's a hell of a way of saying hello.'

She was peering at me. She looked worried.

'Twenty-three years?' she asked.

'Plus forty-seven days,' I added. 'And just for the record, I do not, and never have, fallen into the category "most men".'

'God, you have a lot to learn. You said you didn't kill them anyway.'

I nodded towards the high wall at the end of the garden.

'Tell the people out there that.'

'I don't need to. It wouldn't mean a thing anyway. They don't know who you are, Bierce. They don't care.'

She didn't like the way I was looking at her.

'Besides,' she added, 'you got let out. They don't do that to guilty people. Remember?'

'No, I don't,' I said honestly. 'That's the problem.'

I strode over to the small lean-to by the south wall where we kept all the garden stuff. There was a rusting shovel next to a tangle of rakes and sieves. I dragged it out of the trumpet vine tangle that held it down, then walked through the mess of weeds and high grass to the end of the garden, close by the cement culvert, where the creek would have run back when it was something real, not an imaginary line on a map.

Most cops in the city had a private store. It was a dangerous profession. Occasionally it took a ride home with you. What I remembered in the bedroom, when Alice's fingers brushed against me, was where I'd kept mine. In the foot of the concrete stump I'd put in place to keep the bird table Miriam had always wanted.

It made a kind of sense. If there was trouble, I said, just run to the garden, find the table, look for the little handle in the cement block at the foot.

It was overgrown now: thick, heavy weeds and rye grass covered the metal hook I'd buried into the cement slab I made for the lid. I turned away the earth with the shovel, found what I was looking for, pulled hard until it moved, then peered into the small rectangular hole I'd dug into the hard clay earth all those years ago.

It wasn't quite as I remembered. A little deeper, and the metal box sitting in the bottom, rusting slowly, seemed rather more visible than I recalled. But there were leaves and dead beetles and all manner of stuff stuck above it. No one had been around here in more than two decades. So I got my shoulder to the ground, reached down with my right arm and pulled out the box. After several attempts on my own, Alice groaned and loaned me a coin. With that I managed to open the water-proof seal and put my hand inside. It was still there, a service revolver, already loaded, and three boxes of ammunition. Stock-keeping had never been good on the force range. Most officers managed to smuggle a gun out of there when they needed one.

'Wow,' Alice gasped. 'Are you sure you've got memory problems?'

'Some,' I replied, and let the weapon hang in my hand. It felt strange. Wrong somehow.

'There's a law in the city these days,' she said. 'If they find you with a gun and no licence you go straight to jail. No arguments. Unless you've got friends. If you've got friends you can do any damn thing you like. I thought you ought to know.'

In that case I'd go back to jail twice over if they found me carrying a piece. I'd bear it in mind.

'Do you have a vehicle?' I asked her.

'I got a bike. A 1993 Kawasaki 500 twin. Looks like a wreck.'

She smiled. A real smile. It changed her.

'It isn't,' Alice added. 'I did a hundred and forty on it on the big road south from the bridge last summer.'

She hesitated.

'Is this a job or something?'

'Fifty a day. Cash. A hundred when it gets into overtime.'

'For what exactly?'

'Let's call it personal assistance. I want transportation. And a little advice when I need it.'

She was smirking.

'What's so funny?'

'You wanting advice. What's that they say about alcoholics? Acknowledging the need is the first step on the road to recovery.'

'You really don't know me,' I said ruefully.

At that moment I wasn't sure I knew me either.

'You didn't kill them, Bierce,' she said again forcefully.

She looked convinced. It was ridiculous.

'I am grateful for your trust.'

'It's not that.'

She nodded behind her.

'My mom used to work in that little sweatshop next door. With all the other illegals turning out cheap crap for some crooked jerk in Chinatown.'

'So . . . ?'

'So she saw you. Every day, when she was slaving over her stupid sewing machine, praying it wouldn't bite half her arm off like it did some of the others. You wonder why I do what I do?'

I shook my head.

'You never said what you did.'

'Don't play the smartass. She saw you come home on that big shiny police motorcycle you had. She thought that was really brave back then, given the neighbourhood. Now . . .'

She stepped forward and looked into my eyes.

'She saw you with them too. Your wife. Some

lovely little white kid. My grandma, Lao Lao, told me all about this. More than once. My mom watched you and your wife and your boy and she thought . . . one day. I will have something like that. I will make it for myself. I will have that kind of family, that kind of house. All this *will* be mine.'

'Oh,' I said.

The reason was here somewhere.

'What made your grandma so talkative about me?'

'She brought me up. She was OK, even if she did think I was something slightly less than human as a result of my mom getting knocked up by some white guy who took the next train the moment the test tube came back blue.'

'Well, Alice. What's your last name?'

'Loong. Don't bother asking one of your police friends to look me up. I don't have a record. Nothing interesting anyway.'

'Good. I don't have any police friends either.'

I held out my hand for her to shake. She took it and laughed.

'Do I get a little cleaning for that money too?' I asked.

'For that money you get any . . .'

'No.'

I didn't want her to say it. I didn't want to hear it, even as a joke.

'Get rid of the chalk, will you? All of it. Every last piece of police crap in there. This is a home, not a carnival show.'

Miriam never lived in the past. She thought it

was a sin. It always seemed a crazy idea to me back then. Experience makes you, breaks you sometimes. But I knew now what she was getting at.

'No blue lines,' I said again.

My eyelids felt like lead. My head was aching. I was already dreaming of a quiet, uneventful night on that big, fat sofa downstairs.

'No dust. No cobwebs. I woke up dead today, Alice. This gives a man pause.'

'Huh?' she asked, green eyes wide with puzzlement.

'It's a private joke. I'll let you in on the secret some time. Where are you going?'

I watched her amble into the kitchen and thought for a moment: this could have been Miriam. But it wasn't. She was just some desperate young woman who'd been press-ganged by Stapleton into doing something that maybe half interested her in the first place.

For a reason I still didn't understand.

She stopped and looked back at me over her shoulder. Miriam never did that. She always turned to face you. These two were different. Every last person on this planet was.

'You'll need a pillow, Bierce. Even on a sofa like that.'

A small shadow of uncertainty crossed her face.

'Does it bother you if I sleep upstairs?' she asked. 'In the big room? If it freaks you out . . .'

'No. I don't mind if you don't.'

'Never had much time for ghosts,' she said, then

walked on until she was out of sight, leaving me to the smell of apple blossom and the buzzing cloud of mosquitoes swirling in the bright hard beam of the security lights.

The pillow was there when I made it to the sofa. I was so tired I thought nothing in the world could keep me from sleep.

I was wrong.

After tossing and turning for the best part of an hour I went up those old familiar creaking stairs. Something had happened. I walked around, through each part of the floor, before going into the back bedroom. The chalk marks were gone already, along with the tape. Alice Loong had been working before going to bed, which I hadn't, in truth, expected. Also, it meant she hadn't got out of her jeans and T-shirt by the time I walked into our old room. Not quite.

She stood by my old double bed, staring back at me, hands on her undone belt, puzzled, not wanting anything, probably not refusing anything either.

'It could have waited until tomorrow,' I said. 'But thanks.'

'I should have done it before. It was thoughtless of me.'

'No . . .'

'I wanted you to wake up to a new day or something,' she interrupted.

'Thanks. Why did your grandma bring you up?' I asked.

'That took a while,' she observed.

'I've had other things on my mind. Why?'

Alice Loong sat down on the bed and looked up at me. She could have been a teenager at that moment.

'Do we have to do this now, Bierce?'

'Yes.'

'Why?'

'Because you're in my house and it matters.'

I must have let a little cop attitude drift into my voice then. She didn't like it.

'Please,' I added.

She folded her arms, which seemed skinny but strong too.

'The same day someone killed your family, my mom got murdered. Grandma was out working. My mom had called in sick for work because I was down with a cold or a headache or whatever.'

'I'm sorry,' I replied. 'And?'

'Someone beat her to death with a sledge-hammer. Just like happened here. She knew they were on the way somehow. I was three. She pushed me into a cupboard, told me not to say a word, not to breathe even, not till she said it was OK.'

Alice took a deep breath.

'I listened for a while until I managed to stuff my fists into my ears so hard it kind of stopped. Not everything. I was there three hours, Grandma said. I didn't start screaming until she came and found me. I don't remember much and what I do remember . . . I don't know if it's real or not.'

'I'm sorry.'

She came up and stood in front of me. She looked really small and young, not the twenty-six or so she had to be.

'You're fired,' I said.

'What?'

'You heard. I hired you to clean up around here and lend me your bike. I don't want someone sticking their nose into my affairs, thinking some personal reasons give them that right.'

'Bierce!'

'You can stay the night. In the morning I want you gone.'

'Look . . .' She was shaking her head, fighting for the words. There were tears of rage in her eyes. 'You stuck-up dinosaur. You haven't been in the outside world for more than twenty years. You don't know what it's like here. You don't even belong.'

'Hey,' I replied, opening my hands. 'This is my city. I was born here. I know this place.'

'Really?'

She walked out to the landing, marched over to the little boxroom we used for junk, stepped through the cases and stuff on the floor, then, with me following, watching, threw open the curtains and waited in silence while I caught my breath. It took a while before I could stop shaking, and in that while, that long while, I thought of only one thing: how easy it would be, how comfortable, to be back in Gwinett, even in the same old twelve by ten cell that stood just stumbling distance from Martin the Medic's death room.

I still remembered the view we used to have when Miriam and Ricky were alive. That gave on to one piece of open green scrub, the last remnant of pasture from the old days of Eden, not that long ago, when cows must have grazed within the city limits. True, it was in shadow from the high walls of the warehouse in Owl Creek to one side and something similar on the other. But it was grass, real grass, and beyond that was nothing but scrappy single-storey homes and lock-ups.

I cursed myself for sleeping all the way here. The grass was gone. I was blinking at a sea of winking lights rising so high they went beyond the window: floor upon floor of apartments or offices, or both for all I knew, a massive wall of stone and glass where once there was nothing but scrub and kids playing ball.

She came back from the window and stuck a finger in my face.

'You need me, Bierce.'

'My mentoring days are over. The answer's no.'

'Whoever killed your family killed my mom,' she insisted.

'Tell the police.'

'The police *knew*! They didn't care then. Why are they going to care now? This was all in St Kilda. No one cares. No one gives a shit. That's how animals like us are supposed to live.'

There had to be a reason they let me out. A part of me – the thinking part – was screaming that I ought to focus on this. Finding someone to blame. A part of me also said I needed to be wary of Alice Loong too. Perhaps she was what she appeared now, nowhere near as tough as she thought, and naive enough to walk into a situation that might get dangerous. Perhaps that was part of the act too. Stapleton recruited her, and he was one sneaky beast.

I didn't much care what happened to me so long as someone paid for Miriam and Ricky, if that someone was still alive. I didn't need any other corpses on my conscience.

'So what the hell do you think I can do?' I asked.

'I want them. I want to know who they are. If they're still alive, I want to look them in the face and ask why. Don't you want that too?'

I closed my eyes for a moment and thought of this place in the happy times. And of that big black hole in my memory. Not knowing could drive you crazy, but it couldn't kill you.

'I know my wife and my son are dead. I know I wasn't responsible. That's more than I was sure of this morning.'

She was in the shadows. I couldn't see her eyes. She said, 'Are you really certain of that?'

'Yes.'

It didn't sound so convincing.

'You mean you know it? You *remember* it wasn't you?'

I didn't want these questions. They sounded too much like the ones people had been throwing at me for more than two decades in jail.

The lights in front of the window disturbed me. I moved forward and closed the tiny curtain. They were so bright they shone straight through the fabric.

'I mean I know. And that's enough.'

I was lying to her. And to myself, I think. Sometimes, when you're dog tired, it's hard to tell.

'I wonder,' she said quietly.

Alice Loong, who wasn't a hooker, I now knew, but would have given herself to me that night, if that was what it took, walked out to the landing.

I waited, listening to her footsteps travel the familiar path across the creaking floorboards to the bedroom. The door closed with a groan so distantly familiar it tore at my ragged memories.

Then I went downstairs, found the sofa and closed my eyes.

Twenty-three years. An entire generation had passed while I was stuck in a stinking cell in Gwinett beating my head against the wall. I was fifty-two. How many more chances did a man get?

WEDNESDAY

They didn't used to nail dead men to telegraph poles when we first moved into Owl Creek. They didn't even used to do that in the worst parts of St Kilda, the back streets where stray cats walked around on tiptoe, skeetering from trash can to trash can, trying to stay in the shade.

I inhabit a world in motion. Alice Loong had reminded me of this on several occasions. So had the man I still thought of as Stape. All the same, neither of them quite prepared me for what I saw that morning, my first day of freedom, after the caterwauling klaxon dragged me from sleep and sent me staggering out of the door.

It was bright, so bright my eyes hurt a little after all those years inside. There was a squad car there, dirtier and a little more beat up than I remember, and two slouching patrol monkeys in ill-fitting uniforms mooching around the first telegraph pole on the right, outside the abandoned warehouse, the one that Ricky liked to use in his counting games, touching the tips of his little fingers.

Pole, wire, rose bush, trash can, gate, fence . . .

He hit ten on our front door.

Things still kept coming back slowly, when they felt like it.

This was my first day outside a prison cell in more than twenty-three years. I dimly acknowledged the fact that it was a beautiful morning: a fiery sun sat in a sky the colour good summer skies were supposed to be. There was a keen, cool breeze coming in from the ocean, full of enough fresh salt and ozone to disguise most of the industrial pollution. This was the taste of freedom. A part of me liked it.

And there was a dead man nailed to telegraph pole number one, stuck there like flesh in a sack. I walked over. The nondescripts took an interest but clearly lacked the energy to move or say anything. A spike of metal, red and rusty, joined their stationary charge together at the ankles and through the palms, stapling him to the black wood of the pole so he hung there, limp in a blood-stained T-shirt and shapeless jeans, head drooping down so that his fleshy chin sat on his grey, scrawny, whiskered neck. He wore a black hood, like a velvet bag over the head, the kind they used to put on people before they hanged them, at least in the movies. Not that we got that kind of touch today. What we got, in this modern, civilized world, was Martin the Medic.

Even so, this was something new. Just like the voice I kept hearing at the back of my head. It was Ricky's and he was singing . . .

Pole, wire, rose bush, trash can, gate, fence, dead guy, cops, dead guy, cops, dead guy, cops . . .

Be quiet now, Ricky, I thought. Daddy's got things on his mind.

Pole, wire, rose bush, trash can, gate, fence, dead guys, cops, dead guy . . .

Things like this. You're dead too. And so is your mother. Maybe I killed you. Maybe I didn't.

Pole, wire, rose bush . . .

And if I didn't, then who did? That was all a blank, even after a long night in my own house for the first time in twenty-three years. So much was just a big black hole in my imagination hunting for facts to fill it. In truth the only certainties I had at that moment were about what had happened since the strange performance that got me released from the death room at Gwinett, with Stape looking as if he was going through the motions of some deed he hated to the core, just as he hated me for some reason. Not that it was a good enough one to stop him handing over all that money and a ride home.

Here was the kicker. The only things I could remember with any clarity were nasty, malevolent, scary little recollections, each of them bleakly insignificant on its own, but, when I strung them together, they got me shaking the way I should have been when Martin the Medic was standing over me, looking for the right vein to match his needle.

Here was the bigger kicker. Martin's tombstone

teeth apart, there was, for some reason, little I had found scary about lying on a hard steel bed waiting to die. I'd had more than a couple of decades to get ready. It all seemed natural in a way. Someone might have felt cheated had the show been cancelled.

But now . . .

Now I was scared.

My kid was chanting in my ear, a high-pitched laughing voice rising from a grave I'd never seen.

Pole, wire, rose bush, dead guy, dead . . .

Inside my house was a pretty young half-Chinese woman called Alice Loong who turned up out of nowhere, offered me her body and some cheap, unlikely story about her mom that made no sense whatsoever, then just nodded like a rear-window dog when I said no, but it would be really useful if she could clean up the chalk marks that outlined where the battered, bloodied corpses of my wife and child once lay.

I felt naked and stupid, the most stupid man in the world, a dumb willing target with a bullseye on my chest, waving it at anyone who ventured near, be that Stape or Alice or some vicious, dread bastard I'd yet to meet in this strange new world that seemed so unlike the one I remembered.

Also – and this was the worst by far – this was the first time in twenty-three years that I'd seen a dead person. They tidied them away in jail, swept into bags in the morgue like unwanted dust in need of disposal. Back when I wore a uniform the sight of a body wasn't so rare. They weren't usually lying around the street, waiting for you to trip over them. But they were there, part of the landscape, still and stiff, looking up at the sky through blank eyes that always, to me anyway, seemed to ask: *why?*

But here, in the grubby little street outside the house that was the closest I'd ever got to home . . . here was wrong. Here was a place I felt I knew, had some duty to defend. The city was never kind or sensitive or compassionate. Still, it had its limits, and nailing bodies to poles in some ordinary suburban street was one of them.

I looked at the poor bastard, all that pain, all that blood and agony, and when I did I saw something back from *then* again, something that hurt. I listened . . .

Pole, wire, bush, cops, dead guy, dead guy, dead guy . . .

. . . and I thought, and then I saw myself nailed there, out in the hot dry day for all to see, in just the pose they wanted me, taking the blame, carrying the guilt for something I didn't do, maybe.

I closed my eyes and when I did I saw it all: me on the pole, Miriam there in front, staring, not laughing, not quite, saying nothing, just with that expression on her face, the one that said: *this time you really screwed up.*

That was the truth. I did. I had. I always would. They should have stuck the right ampoule on the

81

end of the needle in Gwinett, because what happened there really was that I died in some way I didn't quite understand yet. Everything after . . . the voices, the memories, Alice Loong, Stape and these ugly drone cops huffing and puffing at some stinking corpse hanging by nails stuck through old wood . . . was irrelevant. I cared about one thing only. *Knowing.* What happened. What I did or didn't do. How, maybe, I could make amends, then sit back and let the big black rush begin.

Nothing really mattered any more apart from that.

So I looked at the uniforms in front of me and said, 'Good day to you, sirs. It's a fine day. A sunny day. Could you kindly keep the noise down, please? A man's trying to sleep.'

The two cops were of identical size: fat. They had the same blank, angry faces and dead, tired eyes. At some point, probably on the operating table, someone had surgically excised what little charm, wit and intelligence birth had given them and left nothing in their place except a physical tic that jerked one side of their mouth up to the nearest eye in a permanent squint and seemed to say: *what?*

In the way of the modern world – I had learned this in jail, on the few occasions I spoke with my fellow guests – this was uttered, always, rhetorically. I recognized men like this from the old days. They didn't ask questions. They waited for answers to fall from the sky and slap them round the face, screeching, *Look at me! Look at me!*

Curiously, too, their shared tic was symmetrical: one mouth rising on the left side, one on the right.

They had thick black leather belts, the kind power-line repairmen used to wear, but these contained big guns, cans of what I took to be some kind of nasty substance, radios and other gear I couldn't recognize, all hanging on neat little clips where the hammers and screwdrivers used to be. Progress. It made me feel like scampering back into the house, finding the bedroom and hiding under the sheets. Except someone, Alice Loong to be precise, was there already.

'Huh?'

Right Tic didn't look mad at me. He looked mad at everything, his own stupefied bewilderment most of all.

'This is a residential neighbourhood,' I suggested. 'I seem to remember from somewhere that you only hit the sirens and the flashing-light stuff when you're going on a call to the living. This, on the other hand . . .'

I looked at the body nailed to the pole. The bloodstains were dry and black. Rigor was setting in. It was now just after eight a.m. Sunrise must have been well before seven. He hadn't just been there for most of the night. He'd been hanging like a lone human scarecrow out in broad daylight for a good hour and a half before someone – a small crowd of faces at the broken and dusty factory windows told me who – had called the cops.

'I claim no expertise in these matters, but some small trace of ancestral memory tells me this guy's dead.'

They'd hardly looked at the man pinned to the pole. It was as if this kind of thing happened all the time.

'OK,' I said. 'I was just passing the time of day and that's done. It wasn't me, I swear, scout's honour. Do you think I can go now?'

Left Tic slapped his stick in his slack fat hand. It occurred to me then that he just might really hit me with the thing. Here, out in the bright light of day, a day I recognized, but only dimly. I shivered. I was trembling. It wasn't cold. A lot had happened since I last hung out with a squad car.

'That would be a very good idea,' he muttered. 'We're just waiting till the detectives . . .'

He pronounced that 'dee-tectives', just like a little kid.

'. . . arrive. You don't have anything to hide now, do you?'

'Officers,' I said, opening my hands, 'if I was that kind of a person, would I be out here talking to you?'

They stared at each other, wondering.

'So why are you here?' Right Tic asked at last. 'Be truthful now. We will find out. We will.'

I smiled, trying to look both harmless and stupid. 'I've lived an uneventful life. I've never seen a dead

84

man. Not a murdered man anyway, and – I'm guessing here – that same ancestral memory suggests this guy didn't nail himself to the pole.'

The two of them nodded. I felt they'd got about that far for themselves.

'Honestly?' I added. 'This sounds sick, I know. But I simply wanted to get a closer look.'

'Understandable,' Left Tic said with a shrug.

I winced.

'Trouble is . . .'

They still didn't get it.

'It's that hood. It's like . . . if you go into an adult movie and find they keep their clothes on. It provokes and unprovokes. Simply awful.'

Right Tic moved his head from side to side and chanted in a childish monotone rhythm, 'He wants to see the dead man, he wants to see the dead man, he wants to see . . .'

His hand was making a gesture. Finger and thumb, rubbing together greedily.

The last police officer I saw doing that was Stapleton, a quarter of a century ago. He regretted it deeply shortly afterwards.

This time round, though, I reached into my pocket, took out the wad, which, like an idiot, I'd failed to separate into smaller bundles, and passed over a fifty.

'Please,' I said. 'Pretty please.'

Left Tic took out something from his belt. It looked like a Swiss Army knife that had mated with a pair of bolt cutters: blades and screws and gadgets protruded from every inch of its squat little body. He clicked his podgy fingers and a pair of tiny scissors materialized out of nowhere. Then, with more care than I would have expected, he snipped his way up the left half of the hood, stopped to stare briefly at the two hands pinned together by the long sharp nail above him, before working his way down the other side.

It took a little tug. There was some blood keeping the fabric glued to a face that had, it turned out, taken a big punch to the mouth at some stage.

We all of us stared at the dead man's features. I'd done enough murder scenes to know what always tended to come out at this time. So I said it.

'He looks like he's sleeping.'

'He looks like he's dead,' Left Tic muttered, which made his partner crease over and hold his fat gut, consumed by an overdose of glee.

What I was unable to tell them was this: Tony Molloy always did look dead, even when he was a living, breathing, slouching six-foot streak of semi-human slime working the Yonge waterfront. He still had the same grey acne-scarred skin, the same dyed black hair, bushy eyebrows and bulbous nose, a little more pockmarked than I recalled. The crooked mouth, frozen on one side, from a knife fight back in his teens, though now it looked like a middle-aged man's stroke, hadn't improved. The truth was, if you knew the man, he simply looked *more* dead than usual, and that annoyed me greatly, because of all the people I had on my list to talk to that day, Tony Molloy was close to the top.

Stape would have second-guessed my interest in Tony Molloy. Anyone who knew me and the case and possessed an IQ edging just a touch south of three digits would have guessed that.

This was interesting, if a little depressing too.

A man who'd been the partner of the creature that had confessed, supposedly, to slaughtering Miriam and Ricky was dead outside my home, killed the night I happened to get out of jail. The sequence of events facing me was beginning to contain far too many subtly prolix personal elements for it to enter the comprehension of either of the uniformed amoebae who were my present company.

There were too many coincidences here and coincidences could kill me for good. There was also a stolen police department handgun sitting by the side of my bed with three equally illicit boxes of shells.

'It's a pleasure to know we still have officers of your insight and respectability in the police,' I said quietly.

The Tics twitched at me in silence.

'Presumably, gentlemen, you'd rather I didn't go anywhere for a while. Not until the *dee*-tectives arrive.'

Right Tic sneered at me, 'This is a gang thing, man. Always killing each other for fun. You don't have the tattoos. Or the colour.'

'Gangs,' I said, raising a finger. 'Excuse me. We don't have them back home.'

'Where the hell is that?' Left Tic asked, bemused. 'The moon?'

'East,' I said immediately, as if that explained everything.

He and his partner shared the look called 'caustic'.

'I should be surprised,' Left Tic grunted. 'But you *will* have to talk to someone. Unless . . .'

The fingers made that gesture again.

'That money came out easy,' Right Tic observed.

'I guess it did. I await your pleasure, sirs,' I replied with a little bow, then turned and walked back to the house.

Alice wasn't sleeping. She was smart and observant. I imagine she hadn't been sleeping for a while. Now she was watching me carefully from behind a curtain in the sitting room. She had a duster in her hand.

Shame. The cleaning was going to have to wait.

Maybe it was the half-Chinese gene, but a part of me wondered whether Alice Loong could read minds. By the time I'd walked back into the house, she had a light bag packed and ready to go. The gun was on the top.

'What's the rest of the stuff?' I asked. 'The gun is all I have.'

Her hands were flying over the fabric. It occurred to me she took a very professional approach to fleeing the impending arrival of the law.

'If you're in trouble – and judging by the smug, "nothing's going on here" look you were showering over those idiots you *are* – I am out of here too. I gave that Stapleton guy a phoney name. That's what you do with people who pay cash. I don't want him in my face, asking where the hell you've got to.'

This was not a good idea. Or rather it was an excellent idea, and one I felt I couldn't go along with.

'No, no, no. Listen to me. There's a dead man nailed to a pole out there. He is not unknown to me. Some people might even say I'd be prime candidate for making him that way.'

The green eyes glared at me.

'Stupid people you mean? Why would you dump the corpse outside your own home? Are you putting out an ad campaign too? Got a website?'

I shook my head.

'A what?'

She was checking through the bag. From what I saw she didn't own much either.

'You've been in jail, Bierce. Not in suspended animation.'

There was an important point to be made here.

'Look,' I said, watching her pick up the bag, ready to go. 'This is important. I am the person I was when I went inside. I intend to remain that way. All that modern stuff leaves me cold. When I communicate with a fellow human being I wish to see into their eyes.'

Alice Loong gave me a withering look.

'In that case you might as well go out there again and sit in the police car. They will walk all over you, Bierce. They will kill you. And me if they like. This is the world now. The one we live in, not the one in your head. They've got . . . things.'

'Things like what?'

'Things that know where you are! Things that can track you down just 'cos you used an ATM machine.'

'A what?'

'Oh, for Christ's sake! This isn't 1985 or whenever. You can't live like you did then. You need money.'

I reached into my pocket and waved some of the remaining hundreds.

'Gone in two days,' she snapped back. 'And you with it. We need more information!'

I'd thought about that already. It was on my list.

'What about libraries? You're telling me they're gone already?'

'Jesus,' she said with a long, pained sigh. 'This is like having a child in tow. Or a caveman.'

I snapped my fingers.

'The keys. I won't damage the bike, I promise. Not if I can help it.'

She folded her arms.

'You're not fit, caveman.'

'I rode motorcycles for a living, Alice. In uniform. Also, you don't know where I want to go.'

'Tell me!'

'The keys . . .'

'*No!* And I'll scratch your eyes out if you try to take them. I came here for a reason. We have the same problem if only you saw it. If I'd known you were the selfish, arrogant, macho, antiquated pig you are, maybe I'd have stayed at home. But there you go. This Stapleton guy's seen me. If you think they're going to come for you, then you surely know they're going to come for me. I will *not* be abandoned. Understood?'

I held out my hand.

'Understood. But like I said. I know where we're going and it's a place you couldn't even find. The keys.'

She hesitated.

'Trust me,' I pleaded.

'In this century,' she said, 'men normally say that just before they disappear.'

'It's your century, not mine.'

I pulled back the curtain a little further. More vehicles were arriving outside. Two marked cars, two plain ones. The *dee*tectives were surely here.

She reached into her pocket, took out a single stub of battered old metal and held it in front of my face. I glanced at it. If this was the key I could probably have started the thing with a paper clip.

'This is my bike,' Alice Loong said. 'You ride on the back or not at all.'

I could see two men walking towards the house. Men in dark suits. They didn't look stupid.

91

'A word of advice,' she added, picking up the bag and throwing it into my arms. 'Hold on tight.'

The battered, grubby blue and rust Kawasaki was in the garage, leaning on its prop stand like a drunk struggling to stay upright. When I saw it I was almost glad she didn't want me up front.

The problem was obvious to both of us straight off. If we opened up the doors and roared out into the street, past the Tic Twins, we'd be facing a roadblock within minutes. Even in the eighties I wouldn't have expected to make it far. If they really had these new toys now . . .

We had five miles to travel and even then I'd no idea what we might meet at the other end. Miriam's kid brother, Sheldon, was the family failure. He ran a low-grade motor repair shop, principally for people too poor to run a vehicle legally, out beyond Yonge, where the docks melted into the grey polluted estuary mud of the Pocapo river, an area I'd known well since childhood. I was sure he was still there because once a year he wrote me a letter that said nothing much at all, except, after a page of rambling self-pity: *sorry*.

Sheldon never visited me once in jail. Still, for all I knew, during those years he was the only living person on the planet who believed I wasn't responsible for murdering his sister and nephew. Even my own lawyer, the lovely, cold and utterly ineffective Susanna Aurelio (she preferred her maiden name, possibly because she was now on her fifth husband in the two decades she'd owned me as a client), had some doubt in her eyes from time to time.

Susanna usually delivered Sheldon's annual letter. That thought came back to nag me when I was in the garage looking at the bike, wondering how fast the thing might go. I couldn't work out why, but now, with my mind freed from the dumbing effect of being locked in a cell pretty much twenty-four hours a day, and wandering illogical places it sought just because it could again, the Susanna–Sheldon link seemed odd. There was precious little in the way of a professional reason for a big-time lawyer to keep in touch with a man like him. Socially they were planets apart, she slowly working her way through the moneyed husbands in Greenpoint, picking and choosing as she pleased, while Sheldon, unmarried, with never a girlfriend that I ever saw, lived over his repair shop next to the stinking grey flow that the Pocapo became once it worked its way into the city.

'Bierce!' Alice hissed at me through clenched teeth, and I came back down to earth.

Someone was hammering on the front door. No. I was wrong. Someone was beating down the front door with a hammer. Which, in the circumstances, seemed both impolite and ominous. Even in this strange new world, cops surely rang the bell first.

Starting to shake again, a physical side effect, it seemed to me, of Martin the Medic's dope, I went to the rear of the garage, opened the rickety screen door there and took one last look at the garden.

'You can see the gate?' I asked.

It was rotten, almost off its hinges, with undergrowth behind. We didn't even have time to open it, but that didn't matter. The thing was barely usable when Miriam and Ricky were alive. Today it would just shatter the moment the bike edged through it.

'Where does it go?' she demanded.

It took a moment for me to remember, and when I did a low, nagging bell began to ring at the back of my head, singing . . . *but that was then.*

'Just scrub land,' I said, with some false authority. 'We can make our way out to the back roads. Trust me. I'll show you.'

If luck was on our side – and statistically I felt it was about time the old bitch stirred herself and put in a little work on my case – we'd be able to make our way out to Sanderton on the largely deserted minor road that mirrored the busy trawl of De Vere just half a mile south.

I walked over to the bench, blew dust off my old helmet and put it on. The fit was a little loose for some reason and the strap didn't close well. When I turned round she was straddling the bike, helmeted, arms crossed, with a look behind the visor I was beginning to recognize.

I retrieved the handgun from the bag, checked it was loaded, stuffed it into my belt, filled my pockets with shells and climbed on behind.

The bike started first push, though the battery sounded a little weak. Alice raised the engine a little and worked it slowly out of the garage into the bright morning. She blipped the throttle once out of habit. Mistake. Someone in the house started shouting. I heard a window getting opened. The back door was rattling.

It was locked.

It was strong.

They had a sledgehammer.

She turned and looked at me. She was scared.

'Now . . .' I said, and wished to God she'd let me ride.

Alice opened the engine wide and let loose the lever.

She was right. I did need to cling on tightly. The old Japanese bike came out of the shade of the garage like a crazed animal, so quickly my arms fought to keep a grip on the slim body in front of me. She held the Kawasaki down in first all the way, found the trellised gate, aimed straight at it and barrelled through. Brambles and vines and tall, flowery weeds consumed us.

Alice started screaming. So did I. The earth was falling away in front of us, and it wasn't supposed to be like this, this *wasn't* the scrub land I imagined. We'd roared through the old planked door and found ourselves on the summit of some new, steep hill, one that disappeared from beneath our wheels the moment the screaming bike came over the edge.

I leaned out and looked down, still thinking . . . So far so good. All she has to do now is land the thing amid the mess of abandoned refrigerators and other junk that must still litter this dead, deserted land, festering like an old scab right behind my home, thirty or forty feet lower than it should have been.

Someone else started screaming, and then there were more voices.

Young ones too.

As the bike flew forward through thin air, I pumped myself up on the foot stands, took hold of Alice's slim shoulders and looked down in front of us. There was a sea of faces there, none of them much older than five or six, hundreds of them maybe, or, on second glance, at least a dozen.

My mind did what it usually does on such occasions: wound itself into a congealed, swirly, sticky mass where fast and slow don't mean much but simply bump into one another, over and over again. It didn't help that I could see the neighbourhood now, and it might as well have been Mars for all I could recognize it. Streets and buildings, factories and low grey offices, spread in every direction where, in what I thought of as 'my day', there'd been nothing but endless green scrub and the odd illegal tin shack.

As we flew joyfully through the air, I saw a small swing, some other brightly coloured little rides, and toys everywhere: dolls and animals and board games and a line of blue buckets next to a sandpit.

96

But more than anything I saw children: boys and girls, in summer shorts and T-shirts, happily playing in that tiny world which only they can inhabit until two lunatics on an ancient motorcycle come roaring out of nowhere, like a monster falling from the sky.

Someone had turned my dead land into a kindergarten and never thought to drop me a line.

The sensible ones started to scatter.

Alice kept screaming, frozen on the handlebars. A chubby kid stood there like a human target, a blob of flesh in the path of the bike, oblivious to the fact that several hundred pounds of metal and adult flesh were, at this very moment, plummeting towards him at something like forty miles an hour.

Yelling 'Out of the way, fat kid' seemed somewhat pointless in the circumstances. I thought of the tricks I used to try out on the flats near the Pocapo river, all those years ago. In the scant microseconds that flashed by as we descended, it occurred to me that these were always performed as individual acts of derring-do. Passengers never really came into the equation.

But then neither did overweight infants who stood rooted to the spot a few feet from you, mouths wide open dripping kiddie-drool.

So I flicked my weight hard over to the right and angled the bike down with me. There was screaming at the front and some hard, desperate tugging. Alice didn't want me to tip the bike over. In truth, she didn't have much choice.

The Kawasaki hit the ground at a forty-five-degree angle. Dirt scuffed up in all directions. I put my left arm round her waist and held tight, then forced myself forward till I had hold of one bar, stomping down hard with my right leg, trying to do a decent impression of a speedway skid. Somehow, in the shock of the impact and all this strange, retro momentum, my helmet came flying off and whizzed straight into the sandpit.

We travelled maybe ten feet thereafter, at the same drunken angle, till the bike finally came to a stop, without touching a single child, which must have surprised them as much as it did me.

Alice marked this wondrous event by flying head first over the bars, hitting the ground, hands in the dirt, surrounded by plastic bricks and a couple of small ride-on animals, screeching in sudden pain, then aiming in my direction an expression full of an anger that was so deeply, unfailingly female I had to focus for a moment to work out what it truly was.

'Christ, Bierce,' she screamed, holding on to her left arm, tears of pain in her eyes. 'I broke my wrist. *You* broke my wrist.'

Through some miracle of gravity and fortune I was still on the bike. Its gutsy little engine continued to rattle beneath me. The fat kid walked up to the front, eyes wide open. He looked a little older than I thought. Perhaps seven.

Then he stuck out a hand and said, 'Cool. My name's Tim.'

'Tim!' I said, pointing a finger in his face. 'Don't you *ever* do this at home. You hear me?'

I looked at Alice. She was clutching her left arm and staring back at the wall. I did the same. Some guy in a suit was there, struggling through the brambles of the shattered gate. He looked mad. In his right hand a gun was waving erratically.

There was no time to discuss this. I shuffled forward, took the bars and blipped the throttle. It felt odd to hear the sound of a twin exhaust again, and at that moment I was far from confident I could fall back into riding one of these machines after almost a quarter of a century out of the saddle. Not that there was much choice.

'Are you coming?' I asked quickly. 'Or do you want to stay and play with the rest of the children?'

She said something I rather wished Tim hadn't heard, then leapt on the back, clutching me tightly with her good arm.

Nothing looked right. That is to say, nothing looked the same or felt the same.

Alice screeched and I couldn't work out whether it was my terrible handling of the machine or the instant shock of my reaction to this new world, transferred to her by our enforced closeness. I was in an alien world, a land that had once been mine and now belonged to other people, people I didn't know except to understand I wasn't much going to like many of them.

I glanced back and found some old, lost emotion rising up from a place it had slumbered for a couple of decades, one I only recognized when I thought about it, and remembered the name: anger.

The dark suit was standing in a crowd of kids, right arm raised, black pistol pointed straight in our direction. As I watched, his arm jerked and a loud, distantly familiar noise cut through the kiddie-screaming.

For the first time in years someone was shooting at me, and that at least provoked something I knew, the same old feeling of fear I got on the streets, sweating in a tight uniform, over two decades before.

It made me mad as hell.

'Bierce!' Alice yelled again, then ducked down hard into my back. 'Will you get us out of here?'

Sure, I thought. And just leave these kids to some maniac letting loose with a handgun in their midst. A maniac who, the small, rational part of my head reminded me, ought, by the looks of things, to be a plain-clothes cop.

I took my old handgun out of my belt. She grabbed hold of my arm. Her hand was covered in blood. She was in pain.

'You want to start shooting?' she yelled. 'With all these kids around? Would that make you feel better, huh?'

The man in the suit was running towards us in a way that looked very professional, his gun held upright all the way, as if it was attached to a child's gyroscope.

'No,' I answered, and stuffed the police revolver back where it came from.

I wound the bike wide open and we tore out of the side passage by the school, towards the road that had to be there, somewhere ahead, fighting to keep us upright, because riding a bike wasn't, I learned at that moment, a talent you never forget. I was relearning it all the time we were disappearing from the suit with the gun, racing into somewhere that was not now, and never had been, a part of any planet known to me.

Whatever street this was curved downhill, past line after line of low industrial blocks that looked like bricks from a child's toy box, heading roughly in what I assumed to be the direction of Sanderton, though nothing, not a single brick or yard of asphalt, sparked a moment of recognition in my fevered head. There was the sound of a gunshot behind me. Alice started screaming again, holding on ever more tightly. I jumped the bike down a gear and opened the throttle. Some four hundred yards later the road angled sufficiently to put us out of sight of anyone on foot emerging from the kindergarten. Once we'd rounded the bend, I eased the power down a little, aware that I had two visible accoutrements that were, perhaps, not good for someone seeking to remain anonymous.

I wasn't wearing a bike helmet in an alien city where this was now, in all probability, a capital offence. And that handgun in my belt looked all too visible out here in the penetrating light of day.

Not that there was anyone to notice at the moment. I couldn't see a single house or everyday human being anywhere. Just buildings and office windows, and one lone delivery van parked in the street. We were, I felt sure, near to Sanderton, though. Something that seemed half familiar was finally looming up ahead, a junction where a local farmer once sold fruit and vegetables from a stall by the side of the road. There was a video store there now, but I saw the name sign and, when we finally reached the crossroads, I turned left, as confident as I could be that this was the right direction. They could erect new buildings, create new roads, change names and places entirely. But rivers stayed around longer than a single life, and this route had to take us down to the Pocapo, where I could think of getting this thing off the road, then disappearing into some kind of territory I surely still knew.

That last, welcome thought, and the rattle of the bike over the road, just about quelled my internal shakes, for a few seconds anyway. Then I stopped thinking about the future altogether, because I looked around me and everything Alice Loong had said about me being some kind of a dinosaur was finally starting to make sense.

The Sanderton I recalled was a long, straight, dusty road of low, single-storey economy homes, plain, unpretentious boxes for plain, unpretentious working people, with picket fences around tiny patches of lawn, each with a single beat-up automobile on it.

This place was gone, long gone by the looks of things, though I couldn't believe so much could change in twenty years. There were parts of Eden, the peripheral parts with the adult stores and girlie bars, that seemed similar. But Sanderton wasn't that kind of neighbourhood. Quite. All I saw were long lines of identical single-storey shops and offices running down each side of the road, mirror images of each other complete with gaudy, over-sized signs: for pawn shops and bail-bond merchants, gun stores and tiny neighbourhood food outlets.

Most of the places had wire frames over their windows and metal doors that let through just a crack of light, though by this time it was ten in the morning or so. The places had to be open. Just scared open. Also, they were dirty, that special kind of grubbiness that's limited to cheap places that haven't been built long.

This ragged string of grubby development ran in a dismal strip of concrete in both directions, as far as my eyes, dashing front and back, checking out the best view of this nice new world, could see. Maybe the whole of the city looked this way these days. Or the world even. I was a foreigner in a place I once knew, a place that bred me, and for one brief moment I found myself pining once again for that plain twelve by ten cell in Gwinett. At least there I knew where I was.

I toed the Kawasaki into fourth and cut a steady speed, hovering around forty. Alice's arm relaxed, then I felt her move, get more comfortable behind me. We had to tough this out until we could find some place to hide. Still, I couldn't take my eyes off this different world that had supplanted all those innocent little homes of twenty years ago. There was nothing of that remaining now, just stores and auto lots, repair shops and places selling electronic gear I doubtless wouldn't understand. Someone had come down from on high, taken away the gardens and the little painted porches, deciding to colour this entire neighbourhood grey, sixteen shades of it maybe, not a lot more.

And then there were the people. I slowed down just to make sure of this.

Did we smile in the eighties?

I believe so. Not often, perhaps. Not without reason. But we did smile, and we walked along with our heads up straight, looking around us, talking to strangers from time to time, eye to eye. The latter was something I was very good at, and not only because it was part of the job. Talking to people always seemed to me to be an integral part of being awake, being alive. I lost the opportunity in Gwinett, but never the memory.

These people looked as if they didn't talk much at all, not even when they were meandering down the sidewalk in pairs. They just stared down at their feet, dreaming of nothing in particular, I guess, yammering from time to time into little black phones that they glued to the side of their head as if nothing mattered more to them than this call, this brief snatch of conversation, which would be so much more important, more vital, than a couple of simple words with someone, friend or stranger, a few feet away.

I rode idly through Sanderton, mouth open, collecting flies, trying to stop myself gawping at the men and women walking along the street, to force myself to rebuild a mental map of this part of the city in my head, and the way down to the Pocapo river, because the cops would surely come, and soon, with new toys I couldn't possibly hope to defeat.

I gunned the bike and went on, feeling ever more disconnected from the semblance of life I saw around me. A little further down the street there was another crossing and I just found myself drifting through the red light, wondering whether to abandon the bike and Alice Loong right here, take a cab back to Gwinett, hold out my hands at reception and plead for a cell.

A man of about thirty, in a well-cut khaki linen suit, one that made him look very elegant indeed, wandered out into the road. I pressed the horn. The Kawasaki made a sound like a baby seal crying feebly for its mother.

He had the regulation phone, but this time it was attached to his belt by some fancy leather holster. Over his ears were little white headphones, a fraction the size of anything I'd ever seen, joined by a thin white cable to some tiny white box pinned to his chest like a badge.

He was doing a bad boogie dance to some stupid rhythm only he could hear, which doubtless made it more precious, because if you looked at him you'd have thought the music coming into his ears, his music, no one else's please, was the finest ever made, so fine it didn't make him look twice to see if some idiot from another century had ridden the red light of his toy-town pedestrian crossing and was perilously close to mowing him clean down to the asphalt.

I braked hard, listening to the squeal, feeling Alice get squashed, hard and cursing, into my back. The bike came to a halt one foot in front of khaki suit.

He stared at me, affronted. So much so he actually pulled the little white things out of his head and started yelling in total outrage, using the kinds of words that, once upon a time, were not supposed to be available to people who had the wit to put together clothing that matched.

Then he leapt out of the way because another vehicle had arrived to join the party now, and it was just a touch bigger, a low, bright red sports car, not bad-looking either, like a Ferrari that had got shrunk in the wash. It screeched sideways on to the pedestrian crossing, tyres screaming, smoke coming up from the road, sending an acrid smell into my nostrils.

The smell was good. It woke me up.

The khaki suit took one look at the vehicle, ceased swearing, then dashed for the pavement on the far side, terrified, those little white ear cables dangling from his chest.

Strange.

I looked into the shrunken Ferrari. It was a two-seat coupé, both of them occupied. Men, judging by the way they seemed to fill up the meagre space behind the dashboard.

The driver had white hair and yellow tombstone teeth, grimacing not grinning this time. He had the window down and was hanging out, staring at me, looking as angry as a man might get at that time on a beautiful August morning.

Just seeing him brought back the medical smell and the pain in my arm.

'Martin,' I said pleasantly, and took a good grip on the throttle. 'To what do I owe the privilege? Are you here for a second attempt?'

He smiled, an ugly sight.

'If you don't pull over, I will be,' he said, and nosed the barrel of a black pistol out of the window, pointing it loosely in my direction. 'Off the bike. Wait for me over there,' he ordered.

Ordinarily I listen to people with guns. But there were four of us in this conversation now. Martin had just a two-seat coupé. Whatever was on his mind, it didn't involve an escorted tour of this new, changed city of mine.

'Sure,' I said, and twisted the plastic grip as hard as I could, let loose the left clutch lever and took Alice's Kawasaki veering in front of the coupé's red hood, which gave us a couple of seconds I reckoned, at least.

In my century, anyway.

By the time I reached the left intersection, praying it still went down towards the deserted mud flats by the Pocapo, we had a couple of hundred yards on Martin and his unseen companion. The trouble was, this was territory made for pursuit, not escape: level, open and visible in every direction. And I had an inkling that whatever breed of shrunken Ferrari Martin owned, it would, in the end, outrun a battered old bike.

I steered left towards the river, foot hard on the gravel, taking it as quickly as I dared, still jumpy from the power this little machine seemed to have, more than its size merited, more than a man of my age and rusty skills could handle. Then Alice began to chatter some scared refrain into my back. Somehow Martin had made up ground in the couple of seconds it took me to navigate that corner. His machine went faster than I could have guessed too. Everything did in this inexplicable new world in which I found myself. And what lay ahead looked bad: the same dead streets, everything so easy to see, not a sign of some sneaky little turn-off where two wheels might prove good and four bad.

Alice clung to me throughout. I regained a little distance coming out of the corner but I could sense it wasn't going to last. My legs hurt, my wrists were aching from the unaccustomed strain of throwing around a bike with two people on it. If I could have wound the clock back, found my old self, my old machine, then maybe . . .

Something moved behind me. I just managed to glance back. Alice had taken off her helmet and launched it out into the slipstream, towards the red coupé. It struck the windshield and bounced off harmlessly. The only visible effect was that it got Martin waving the gun out of the window again.

'Congratulations,' I yelled into the wind. 'Can't you just sit back and enjoy the ride while I try to figure this out?'

'Bierce!' she shrieked. 'Who the hell are these people in the Hyundai?'

Maybe it was all that time inside. Or maybe Martin the Medic's dope had done something to my head. Whatever the reason, words could have odd effects sometimes.

This road was a dead end. It had to be. The long, straight, quarter-mile-wide mud-stained stretch of the Pocapo had to lie somewhere at the end of it. A new century couldn't consume an entire river without leaving a trace. As I saw the line of high wire fencing come to greet us in the distance, I started to get a good idea of where it ought to be.

'That was a *Hyundai*?' I asked, not quite believing her.

She clung on more tightly and, when I looked back, had just managed to get a fraction of her face round my shoulder.

'*What?* We're talking automobiles now?'

No. Not really. We were talking about this strange century of hers. One where people walked down the street, eyes on the pavement, with white hearing aids in both ears, phones clamped to the belts of their khaki suits, thinking themselves immortal as a result. Where Sanderton, poor pathetic lost Sanderton, a quiet district old people lived in after they retired from the steel plant and working the railways, got turned into some bland, grubby and doubtless dangerous portion of homogeneous suburbia, a grey dusty nothingness that could, for all I knew, be anywhere on the planet.

We all have our limits and I felt I'd reached mine. The fast-approaching margin of the Pocapo river, which had a drop of around twenty feet from land to the bank around here, if I recalled correctly, only served to confirm my sentiments on this matter.

Martin and his new-fangled Hyundai didn't, couldn't, know this district. Otherwise the two of them wouldn't be shredding rubber on the asphalt behind me with such gleeful abandon at that moment.

I slammed on the brakes and wheeled the bike round in a badly handled curving skid, realizing my jail shoes had probably worn through judging by the growing pain that kept biting into the soles of my feet. When we circled to a halt I took both hands off the bars, turned towards the oncoming sports car, got out my gun and aimed carefully, the way the police range taught me, because it occurred to me that we were now a little like the fat kid in the kindergarten playground, a stationary target facing a mass of metal racing through space with a momentum that would take out anything dumb enough to stand in its way.

You can't flip a sports coupé round just by leaning over the side, even if this had been on Martin's mind at that moment.

I saw the bright white hair twitch as his hands began to work the wheel.

Then I let loose all six shells from the gun, the first into the hood, close to where the badge was supposed to be, the rest towards the tyres, since shooting people was not, at this point anyway, a part of my game.

A puff of smoke burst from the near front. The shiny red vehicle went down on that side, then began to slowly career sideways, sliding out of control. I could see Martin fighting desperately with the wheel. Whoever it was in the passenger seat had, wisely, slid down below the dashboard, out of view, and had every right to be wondering what it was like to be a crash-test dummy in Korea.

Enough, I thought, and popped the bike back into gear.

Badly. So badly the engine made a single loud metallic hiccup, then stalled, dead in an instant.

Alice swore, something about clumsy men.

I popped the starter button. It grumbled once, then nothing. I fumbled round for the kick-start, pumped wildly at it, banging my leg hard against the frame. The engine didn't even cough.

The Hyundai was starting to look big now, and I just knew from the way Alice's Kawasaki was sulking underneath me we weren't going anywhere.

There wasn't time to say a thing. I let loose of the bars, turned round, grabbed hold of her and half dragged, half pushed us out of the path of the oncoming metal beast as swiftly as I could. We fell into some low scrubby bushes by the edge of the wire fence. Martin the Medic's sports monster encountered some pothole in the dead end of the road, bounced once, bounced twice, then turned on its side, screaming sparks and smoke and debris as it flew towards the ragged cliff edge above the river.

'My bike!' was the first thing Alice got round to saying, once we'd picked ourselves out of the thorn bushes where we landed.

The coupé clipped the Kawasaki as it lay on the ground, sent it spinning out past the far side of the flimsy wire fence, bouncing off one lone, stripped eucalyptus tree, after which the bike somersaulted down into the river, falling with a loud, noisy splash and the sound of fractured metal.

I wasn't watching much. I was trying to see what was going on in the car. Something had exploded behind the dashboard. Two big white cushions that dimly brought back the memory of a fancy new contraption I'd read about in the prison library, back when they still let me in there. A concept I'd never quite understood: airbags.

Martin and his passenger would live, I guess. Which meant we didn't have much time to waste.

'We need to be going,' I said, leading Alice down the winding dust and rock path that several decades of kids had made from this cul-de-sac to the river bank.

It looked half familiar. There were cut-throughs like this along the length of the Pocapo. I'd probably used this one more than once back in that mythical era of my youth. We were some way from the estuary too. The water looked clean and lively, even with a dying Kawasaki steaming away in some low rock pool to one side.

Alice looked at the bike, tears in her eyes, and I felt, at that moment, worse than at any time since Martin the Medic had poked his little needle into my vein. My feet crumpled under me. I don't know whether it was exhaustion, Martin's dope or the air in this strange new world of theirs. But at that moment I felt as weak as a baby, and just as likely to burst into tears as Alice Loong. This was *not* my world.

It must have knocked the spirits out of her too. I never was good at hiding things.

'Shit,' she said softly, then hugged herself with her one good arm, staring down at the ground. I wasn't sure whether that was aimed at me or not.

She walked over and sat down next to me. I pulled myself together as best I could and took a look at her wound. Like a child, she let me examine it, gingerly. Tenderly, I might almost have said. She had a long, shallow scratch running from her wrist to her elbow. A big bruise was building. But as I gently squeezed around the unmarked skin it was clear nothing was broken, though it must have hurt like hell. I tore off one of the lower sleeves of my shirt and wrapped it round the cut, tying it carefully.

'Try to keep the dirt out,' I said. 'It feels worse than it is.'

She looked at what I'd done as if it was the work of a spaceman, with puzzlement bordering on gratitude. I don't think many men had behaved like that around Alice Loong, perhaps not in her entire life.

The riverside path was littered with stuff that could have been here forty years – candy wrappers and old newspapers, discarded fishing line, cigarette ends. And items I'd never associated with the banks of the Pocapo before. Just a quick visual sweep showed me two syringes and a couple of spent condoms. Then a heron flew lazily along the river like a slender grey spear, just a couple of feet above the surface, eyeing what lay beneath, looking for food.

'How beauteous mankind is,' I muttered to myself. 'O brave new world, that has such people in it.'

'What?' she asked, shaking her head.

'I got a little carried away with my reading for a couple of decades.'

The Hyundai had come to rest caught between two trees leaning drunkenly into the low cliff above us. I could hear people there. One voice, a familiar male one, sounded fit and healthy and deeply pissed off.

'We need to go,' I said, then waded into the water, recovered the bag from the bike, opened it and stuffed some shells into my pockets, planning on reloading the handgun as we moved.

'Where?' she asked.

'A good place,' I answered. 'For a little while anyway.'

When I was ten years old my parents went out for a drive and didn't come back. Some lumber truck shed its load running a narrow two-lane on the Peyton peninsula. They had the misfortune to be following meekly behind. In a Hyundai Pony as it happens. My dad never was one for expensive automobiles. Or overtaking. It just caused trouble, he said. Best wait patiently for everything to improve, as surely it would. Unless some trucker had failed to chain his load properly, in which case the wait would be very long indeed.

Had I not been in bed with flu, watched over from a distance by a friendly neighbour, I would have been in the back seat, dead too.

I wasn't a good foster kid. I wasn't a bad one. I just didn't give much back in the way of love and affection, for the very good reason, it seemed to me, that these were two things you couldn't invent at will, turning them on or off when you felt like it. The whole point about emotions was that they were beyond your control. Beyond your comprehension sometimes.

That was how it seemed to me anyway, at the age of ten, when two cops in uniform arrived to tell me my parents were 'gone', and did it with such quiet sympathy and skill I can still remember their faces now. And that was what made every foster home I went to move me on after a while, even though I behaved impeccably, being polite and helpful and always willing to clear away the dishes and wash whatever vehicle in the drive required my attention.

The river helped a lot in those years. Wherever I was fostered in the city I could reach this place on a pushbike and spend hours down by the slow, swirling waters, watching, waiting, thinking. My dad had taken me fishing here when I was so young I could barely walk. We'd sit for hours, never catching a lot to begin with. In time I got so much better than him that, by the age of eight, I was the one bringing home the trout, which both my parents found so amusing they could be reduced to tears just talking about it.

I can still recall the smell of fish frying in a pan in the kitchen as they sat around laughing at how hopeless he was at everything practical, while I became the one who fixed things, caught things, made a few modest repairs to the minor flaws in our small, small world.

The river wasn't about the fish, though. It was about us, about talking and looking at the water and the wild, green river bank that hadn't changed at all in hundreds of years, and would still have been recognizable to any of the natives who'd lived here back then, if the brute emergence of the city and the modern world hadn't wiped them out like back-yard pests needing eradication.

My dad liked music. Frank Sinatra, Mel Tormé, Perry Como, anyone from the era. He had a good voice too, and a feel for the occasion. One time we stayed so late the stars came out. I remember he began singing, word perfect, note perfect, 'The Night Has a Thousand Eyes', the whole song, including a little jazz riff in the middle, all while we packed away the gear and a couple of big fish suppers.

I never told him this at the time, but I didn't like that song. Not the words anyway. I was still just a little kid, whatever he thought, and the idea of all those eyes, in a deep black velvet sky, however beautiful, didn't make me feel good at all.

This was three weeks before he died. The first foster home I went to had that song on some compilation album. I played it over and over again until the man in the house went a little crazy and called the childcare people, asking for me to be moved on.

While we walked I told Alice Loong a little of this, for two reasons. First, she wouldn't stop asking questions. But second, and most important of all, I wanted to hear her talk about herself. I had heard a kind of reason for what she'd done the night before. She thought Miriam and Ricky's deaths were somehow connected with that of her mother. I still found that idea improbable, but I wasn't about to say it.

We walked that river bank, east, towards the ocean and the flat, industrial land that would surely engulf us soon, since no one could possibly build homes on these muddy grey flats, even in this dark century. After an hour or so we were both hungry.

'Do you eat fish?' I asked.

'When I can afford it.'

'Find me some dry wood, enough for a fire. Then wait for me here.'

She watched me take off my ragged shoes, roll up my suit pants, then wade into the river. It was a trick I'd learned to tease my dad. Most of the time he couldn't catch a thing even with line, a hook and bait. It used to drive him crazy that I knew how to stand in the slow, cool flow of the river, wait until the trout took me for granted, then scoop them out with my hands, straight on to the bank, where he'd club them quickly with the little toy he'd made at work, a lead weight on a short steel rod.

I waited in the river, not worrying about Martin the Medic or Stape or anyone, because they were city people, now of the twenty-first century, and nothing would suggest to them we'd be making our way along a narrow, little-used path through bulrushes and bramble thickets, down by the Pocapo river. The water swam around my toes and ankles. It reminded me I was young once. It also made me realize how much I needed some food.

The first dark shape wriggled my way after fifteen minutes or so. I scooped it straight out of the river with both hands, just as I used to, sent it flying to the bank, where Alice danced around it giggling, kicking the flapping thing with her feet, trying to stop it struggling back to the water. I watched, pleased. She didn't notice her hand much any more. I was right about that at least.

'What am I supposed to do now, Bierce?'

'Kill it,' I yelled back, not focused on her entirely, because another fat shape was stupidly wandering in my direction.

'I can't kill it! What with?'

'Bear with me . . .'

The second trout swam close enough for me to scoop that out of the water. It flew through the air and hit her clean on the chest, which provoked a little commotion. I climbed out of the river, picked up the wriggling fish and beat their heads a couple of times on the path.

The way women do, she looked at me as if I were some kind of animal, not the provider of much-needed nutrition. I smiled back all the while, aware of two things. I rather liked Alice Loong. And something told me not to trust her an inch, because there was a part of her story that didn't add up. Perhaps a very large part.

Once the disapproval had given way to hunger, it turned out she'd put a pocket knife in the bag, which was the kind of forward-looking act I'd never even have considered. After a little gutting, and the retrieval of her lighter – she was, she explained, 'in the process' of giving up smoking – we had two silver-head trout on twigs, cooking nicely over a small fire. The smell took me back to the kitchen in the only place I ever called home. This was disconcerting, but in a pleasant way, unlike most of that day.

'It's the caveman thing again,' she said after a while, as we squatted upwind of the smoke, me turning the fish to get them good and golden.

'Yes,' I agreed. 'It is. You have me named, labelled and pinned to a display board in some museum somewhere. So how about you?'

'Me what?'

'Who are you? What do you do?'

'You keep asking this, Bierce! There's nothing to say.'

'Come on.'

I moved the trout away from the flames a little and put on a listening face.

'I'm nothing. Just one more pair of hands in the minimum-wage economy, trying to get by. You want someone to work a few hours in your store? Alice will comply. You want a barmaid who'll dress nice and skimpy so the men in suits will get a little thrill on the way home from work? Done, provided they don't expect their hands to wander. How do you think I got to hear all the cop gossip?'

'I still don't know,' I said very seriously, 'how you came to hear all the cop gossip. Tell me.'

'Oh, right. You wreck my bike. You basically kidnap me. And now *I* have to provide the trust.'

'You came to me.'

The finger stabbed at me.

'I am twenty-six years old.'

'You don't look it. That is merely an observation, nothing more.'

'Well, I am. Also, I share – or perhaps this should be *shared* – an apartment with two other females of similar attributes. They worked the bars I wouldn't work. They got approached by this black cop and asked if someone would throw a welcome party for an ex-con who was secretly coming out of jail. Good money. He wasn't too specific about what was required. I was improvising there. How was I to know cavemen had scruples?'

'Scruples being something the human race has

acquired in greater quantity over time?' I asked, trying to puzzle this out for myself.

'Darwin,' she said. 'There. See. You're not the only one who's read books.'

'I never much believed in evolution. Sounds good in principle. But the more people you meet, the more you realize it doesn't add up. It's just . . .'

It felt strange having someone smart and contrary to talk with after a couple of decades in which the longest conversations I had were brief arguments with prison wardens about how the toilet was blocked. Again.

'Just what?'

'The idea of the human race getting gradually more intelligent, more *humane*, over time seems to defy analysis. When I was in jail I read people who've been dead two thousand years and still seemed brighter than most of the idiots penning editorials on big newspapers today. Also social things . . . Marriage. What is it? Half the time it ends in misery and hatred. If we're constantly evolving socially, how come we don't get better at it?'

'We are,' she insisted. 'By doing it less and kicking out the jerks when we don't need them any more.'

'Great for the kids,' I said.

She prodded the fish with a long twig. She was right. They were done. I was wandering, and I knew why. I took them off, wrapped each in some cleanish newspaper I'd found nearby and we ate two fresh Pocapo trout that ranked among the finest food

I've ever tasted. Some dimension of life returned to me at the moment, one that had been long absent. It was this: food can taste good, plain simple good most of all.

'Anyway,' she went on, wiping away some grease from her mouth, 'you were married. Happily. So what's the problem?'

'Maybe none,' I lied. 'Why do you think your mother's death and Miriam and Ricky's murders are linked?'

She hunched up her body and looked a little desperate.

'I don't know. They have to be, don't they? The timing. A sledgehammer . . .'

'The timing may just be coincidence. You can buy a sledgehammer in any hardware store. It doesn't take a genius to realize they can be used for pounding things that are not naturally inanimate.'

'She knew you!'

This puzzled me.

'You didn't say that. You said she saw me come home from work.'

'She felt she knew you. And she worked in that factory next to your place. That's a hell of a coincidence, isn't it? You're a cop. I thought things like that pushed your buttons.'

'I *was* a cop.' She had a point, though. 'What was her name?'

'Everyone called her May. It's fancier than that in Chinese, but May will do.'

May Loong. It didn't ring a bell. Not the tiniest of ones.

'You've no idea why she was killed? Still?'

She stared at the fish bones, picking through them, not eating any more.

'None.'

Alice Loong was very focused on the silver-head trout in her fingers when she said that.

'Was anything taken?'

'I don't think so. All I know is . . .'

She put down the fish. This conversation was ruining her appetite, and I blamed myself for that.

'. . . it didn't happen quickly. I was just three years old but I know that. It went on for a long time. They didn't kill her quickly.'

'They?'

She peered into my eyes. This woman possessed the kind of stubborn, steadfast determination that got people into trouble.

'Two voices. Two men.' Her voice went quiet. Her face became flat and emotionless. 'I suppose what I'm saying is I think they tortured her, judging by all the screaming.'

That ruined my appetite too.

'Do you remember what they were asking about?'

She shook her head.

'I'm not sure. Maybe I'm dreaming it. I don't know, Bierce.'

'Tell me.'

She hesitated, and that seemed strange.

'I thought they kept asking her about something called Sister Dragon. It doesn't mean a thing to me. Not a single thing. You?'

I was glad the fire was between us. It meant she couldn't see my hands shaking like dead leaves caught in the powerful, swirling current of the Pocapo, gripped by something that surrounded them, from which they couldn't shake free.

'No,' I said, and it was both true and a lie. I'd no idea who or what Sister Dragon might be. But I had heard that phrase before. It rang a bell from back in the black time, like Miriam's scarlet dress dancing around Alice's lithe body the night before and the taste of the red-green apple from the tree in the garden. These things were important, if only I could understand.

'It's probably my imagination,' she murmured, a sentiment to which I immediately agreed.

'Listen,' I added. 'This is crazy. My problems are nothing to do with yours. They're big problems. Maybe so big . . . You saw what happened back there. You don't look like the kind of girl who deserves to get shot at.'

'I am *not* a "girl".'

'Choose your own honorific. The point remains the same.'

'You're firing me again.'

'I don't ever remember unfiring you.'

'You stole my bike. You kidnapped me . . .'

I took out Stape's odd, tainted gift of the day before and laid the wad down by the fire.

'I want you to have this. You can use it. I can't. I never counted but there's supposed to be twenty thousand there. You could buy yourself several new bikes. Or, being a smart person, a ticket out of here. Go somewhere else. Find a new life.'

She stared at the money. I could see it looked like a lot to her.

'I've got a life already,' she answered.

This made me a little impatient.

'Well try and make sure you keep it. Let me put this less politely. There are people I may have to deal with, people who won't take kindly to having amateurs around. Nor will I if it comes to it. I thought you might have gathered that already.'

She didn't blink.

'No. I don't leave men, not even men I don't like or much care for. They leave me. That's the way it's supposed to be. Besides, you're just mad at me for mentioning marriage.'

'What?'

'I saw the way your face screwed up when that came into the conversation. What's the idea? You get rid of me and hope it'll just go away?'

'Hope what will go away?'

She picked up the trout again, ripped off a chunk of flesh from the side and stuffed it into her mouth, looking pleased with herself.

'That part always puzzled me,' she said, still eating. 'I went to the library a few times and read the court reports. Not that they were very detailed. I would have thought a city cop killing his wife

126

and kid would have made more than half a column on page thirty-three or whatever.'

This was interesting.

'That's all I got?'

'Six, eight paragraphs. Nothing more. Not in any of the rags. They only mentioned the motive thing once too, which I didn't get either.'

'"The motive thing"?'

'They said Miriam was having an affair and you found out.'

'Ah,' I replied, nodding, head suddenly spinning. '"The motive thing". That.'

I bundled up the fish and threw them in the river. Trout were cannibals. My dad had told me that.

Then I walked back into the water, washed my hands, and stayed there, staring upstream. There was nothing to see. Seeing wasn't the point.

'I'm sorry.' She looked it, a little. I'd made her wait ten minutes. We didn't really have that time. By now Martin the Medic and whoever else was chasing us would surely have started to narrow down the options on where we were. 'I shouldn't be bringing this up, but it's best I get it out of the way. I was always puzzled by the idea they could nail you on what seemed pretty flimsy evidence and amnesia alone. They needed a motive. A reason why you'd do such a terrible thing.'

She hesitated.

'Was it true, Bierce? Was she unfaithful?'

'I honestly don't know,' I answered without a second thought. 'I've no recollection that Miriam had a lover.'

'And on the day?'

'On the day, I remember nothing.'

'So if you'd found out. If what they said was true . . .'

'Then I'd still be in the dark. Did they use his name? In the papers?'

'No. Do you know it?'

I watched her closely.

'I remember the name they kept throwing at me in the interview room. Kyle McKendrick. Some cheap little crooked city councillor. I'd busted him once trying to pick up whores in St Kilda. He'd walked away scot-free for some reason, probably because he had friends. I don't know any more about him than that.'

Her tanned face went a little paler at the mention of that name.

It was my turn to be puzzled. Kyle McKendrick had never really entered my life except as a brief and unsuccessful customer of the city police department, and a name I kept hearing during interrogations where I couldn't really focus on much except what I'd lost. He seemed unimportant, irrelevant, whatever the angry faces across the table had said.

'You've heard of him?' I asked.

'Kyle McKendrick? Didn't you read *any* news-papers while you were in jail?'

'Not for a couple of decades. What was the point? I was never coming out.'

She still wasn't looking me in the eye.

'Bierce . . . Kyle McKendrick *is* this city now. He owns everything one way or another. The newspapers. The TV station. All the public services got privatized years back. Transportation. Health care. Some of the jails and the police system.'

'Jails?' I asked, bewildered.

'This is the enterprise era. Even the prisons. Why deprive convicts the privilege of getting a corporate logo on their dinner plates or whatever?'

'I didn't get a corporate logo on my dinner plate.'

'Are you sure?'

No, I wasn't. I'd stopped looking at everything for a while. They had moved me around for some reason, from solitary cell to solitary cell, which didn't help. A good decade and a half of my life was one big, fuzzy blur. I know I went into Gwinett. I assumed I came out of there, though that view from the window the previous day, when Stapleton offered me the deal, still puzzled me. It seemed *wrong*. The truth was they could have done anything they liked with me all that time inside. I wouldn't have known or cared.

'I see,' I said lamely.

'I doubt it. So they thought Kyle McKendrick was screwing your wife and that was why you killed her?'

'That's what they said. Is this guy really that important?'

'He's the new royalty. Big family man. If he doesn't own something himself, one of his kids owns it on his behalf. McKendrick could have got you out of prison just by clicking his fingers.'

'Why would he have done that?'

'I don't know. He could have got you killed too.'

'Oh,' I said. 'So he's that kind of royalty? The old-fashioned sort.'

'Word has it, not that polite or sensible people ask.'

I had to raise the question.

'Do you think . . . maybe . . . he knew your mother?'

'What, some cheap Chinese single parent working in an illegal flophouse sweatshop twelve hours a day?'

'She must have been pretty.'

'Oh, please . . .'

'That was simply another observation. I'm looking for strands here. That's all.'

She screwed up her face in disappointment.

'I thought you were supposed to be a good cop.'

'Is that good in the sense of "decent"? Or just highly competent?'

'Both.'

I shrugged.

'Oh, great,' she moaned. 'You don't even remember that either.'

'I have some intimations on the subject. You know if this is McKendrick, it can't be him alone now, can it?'

'Excuse me.'

'Someone set me free, maybe to line me up to take the rap for something. Me carrying twenty thousand in cash ought to be enough to raise a little suspicion in the first place. I don't know. But if that was McKendrick, why would he nail Tony Molloy to a post outside my house this morning? And who were the pair in the Hyundai? Not cops. They didn't feel like cops. They felt like . . .'

'Like what?'

She seemed interested.

'I don't know. I've been out of things for a while, remember? Someone wanted me out of jail, dripping in money, and knew I'd be in Owl Creek last night, hoping to get something out of it. On the other hand, maybe some other people want me . . .'

Dead, I thought, for no particular reason, and I wasn't sure whether I said the word or not.

'Ergo . . .' I went on.

'Please stop using words like that. You've read some books. I've got the message.'

'Ergo, I need a place to start. And that place has to be finding out whether McKendrick and Miriam really were an item, I guess.'

I hadn't told her about my brother-in-law Sheldon and his little motor shop, which probably lay less than a mile back up over the river bank, in the scrappy industrial landscape I hoped still existed there, unchanged by the years. It was always best to introduce Sheldon to people unawares.

'I concur,' she said. 'Now you'll have to excuse me.'

'Why?'

'The bathroom. Or the bushes, if you prefer. Do I have to spell it out?'

I tipped my hand to forehead in a little salute and watched her disappear behind a large clump of vegetation: wild rose and elder, fighting it out to see who could win. Four rowdy green-finches burst from the branches, screaming at her approach. They were very loud little birds.

Alice Loong seemed intelligent and selflessly dogged in her determination to get what she wanted, whatever that might be. These were both good reasons not to have her around.

When she was out of sight, I took out the wad of money again, retrieved a couple of hundred for possible future expenses and deposited the rest in her bag. Then, very quickly, I found a pen and scrap of paper and scrawled, 'He went that-away . . .' on it, with an arrow, which I pointed downstream, to the grey estuary and, eventually, the ocean at Blue Oyster Point.

Maybe she'd believe it. Maybe not. Either way she'd spend a couple of minutes puzzling over whether this was bluff or double bluff. Alice Loong was like that. She liked to understand things, or hoped to, before she made a decision. I have never felt shackled by such sensible constraints.

Though I hadn't mentioned it, I knew this

particular section of the river very well indeed, which was why I'd stopped here in the first place. This was where we'd fished many a time when I was young, the very place where my old dad had sung 'The Night Has a Thousand Eyes' to a young moon trapped among a celestial coverlet of twinkling stars. When he was gone, it remained one of my favourite places, alone or with the one good childhood friend I had, Mickey Carluccio, whose father owned the city fish market, where I worked for pocket money from time to time. Until that bond got broken up too. I hadn't thought about Mickey in years. There hadn't seemed any point. But the memories were starting to come back, in their own time. Some of them had to be useful.

It was easy to hoist myself up the bank using the low branches of the shrubs struggling to hold on to the red clay earth there. At the top there was another path leading to the low, ragged outlines of the industrial zone, all just as I remembered, only a lot bigger. Big enough for the nearest block to be just a short walk away, so I could get there and disappear behind it in less than a minute.

I didn't have a watch but I guessed it was now early afternoon. Sheldon would be dozing over the first beer of the day.

Ricky was just turned three when he got his Uncle Sheldon right. It was one day down at the beach, with Miriam secretly eyeing the fancy houses in

Greenpoint, wondering if we'd ever make it there. She thought I never noticed but I did. There seemed nothing wrong in dreams at that time. On this particular day Ricky looked up from his large and rather complex sand castle – more a fortress really, there was a touch of his dad there even then – pointed at Sheldon and declared, 'The Amazing Mumford. A la peanut butter sand-wiches!'

Miriam had to help me out with the reference. I didn't watch daytime TV much. Or the evening stuff either.

But the next day I sat down with my son and we watched an entire hour of *Sesame Street*, both screaming with joy when the Amazing Mumford did hop on screen to perform a very passable impersonation of Sheldon Jay Sedgwick.

The long, black, greasy hair was a little weirder, the baldness somewhat more apparent and the moustache more sleazily crooked. But I guess it was difficult to put all those real-life details on something as simple as a stuffed puppet made out of felt and cardboard. Still, the Amazing Mumford was damn close, most notably in the cack-handed way he approached even the simplest of tasks, starting out with one thing, ending up with some-thing else altogether. From that point on, Sheldon *was* Mumford as far as I was concerned, though it was a year before Miriam took me to one side and asked me to stop using the name, because Sheldon had finally plucked up the courage to complain.

He was that kind of human being. Timorous yet full of his own small self-importance. Utterly incapable of holding down a real job, yet convinced the low-grade, incompetent motor shop he'd run since getting kicked out of engineering school would one day make his fortune.

Sheldon – I've lost the habit of calling him Mumford, even if I still think of him that way – inhabited a world that existed inside his head alone, and as far as I could see he was reasonably happy there. He lived over the shop, which kept down costs. He had a steady stream of customers who couldn't afford to take their vehicles anywhere but a place where the primary fixing tool for any problem, large or small, was simple brute force. Nor did he have much in the way of friends – particularly female ones – who might introduce such awkward things into his life as relationships and human contact.

And he was the only person who wrote to me in jail. Now who would have predicted that?

The city may have been transformed while I was in jail but not Shangri-La Motor Repair. Six gutted automobiles stood on the forecourt, rusting away, either because the owners hadn't paid or come to collect, or because their problems were simply beyond Sheldon's rudimentary mechanical skills. Half the neon sign Sheldon had bought, at great expense, was now out.

At the time he acquired it I had queried this

135

purchase on the grounds that, since he opened only during the day, and then sporadically, a bright neon hoarding was, perhaps, something of a luxury. Miriam had thrown a large object in my direction. There was, you see, no way of offering Sheldon advice. He and Miriam were non-identical twins, the only offspring of a charming farmer from the Peyton peninsula whose wife had died when they were young. Their father doted on the pair, understandably in Miriam's case, expensively in Sheldon's. By the time old man Sedgwick died, Sheldon had run through the family's entire savings and mortgaged the farm too. I know because that was the one letter I got in jail in which he actually told me something. This said more about Sheldon than he realized, I suspect. He wasn't just indolent, untrustworthy and utterly friendless in life. He was also happy to let everyone know about it.

I worked my way past one half-burnt-out Volkswagen and a Volvo that looked as if rodents had taken up residence in the rear. There was, to my complete lack of surprise, not a sound coming out of the workshop, the doors of which were wide open to the sun, inviting any passing thief to enter and help themselves to whatever worthless junk lay inside. There was a clock just inside the door, though, and I was minded to think it half accurate, since the time there said just after three p.m., about what I'd reckoned.

If Alice Loong was sensible she'd be halfway

to the airport now, thinking of somewhere to go. A part of me hoped it would be a long way away, perhaps in another country altogether. A part of me thought this improbable, and was both pleased and sorry. Alice had told me only half the story, maybe not even that, and I wasn't sure I wanted to know the rest, or understand its implications.

A TV was playing somewhere: familiar sounds, grunts and sighs. I turned the corner into the office and there was Sheldon, feet up on a desk covered in sheets of paper, many of them with shouting red type on them, beer in hand, gawping at a porn video featuring two highly pneumatic women and a couple of plastic implements that would never make it on to *Sesame Street*.

'A la peanut butter sandwiches,' I said, then walked over and popped the off switch on the grubby little portable perched on top of a rickety filing cabinet.

Sheldon's grease- and oil-stained features creased in fear and disbelief.

'Oh, crap,' he muttered, and took a gulp of beer, most of which went down the front of his grimy blue overalls. 'Oh, shit and crap and . . .'

The beer can went up again.

He'd put on weight and, to my amazement, lost so much hair that all he had left were a couple of lank, black strands attached to the lower portion of his gleaming skull, like pigtails stuck on with drawing pins. The moustache had got bigger and uglier, but not so big it obscured much of Sheldon's flabby face, which was a shame.

He looked terrible. Old and fat and sick. And scared now too.

'What the hell are you doing here, Bierce?' he asked finally.

'Just looking up my last remaining relative. What do you expect a man newly released from jail to do?'

'Released?' he asked, seemingly amazed. 'When the hell did that happen? How?'

I brushed the remains of a long-expired pizza from the only other chair in the room, pulled it up and sat down next to him.

'Don't you keep up with the news?' I asked. 'I was under the impression that was my failing.'

'What news?'

There was a paper on the desk. I'll give him that. I picked it up and shuffled through the front pages and the local ones. The previous day's too. Nothing.

'They let me out of jail yesterday. Someone confessed. Frankie Solera. You heard of him?'

'Frankie Solera?'

He shook his head. The lank pigtails moved behind his shiny skull, one second out of sync.

'Never,' he insisted. 'Never!'

'Then this morning I found some guy called Tony Molloy nailed to a telegraph pole outside the house. Dead.'

He gulped on the beer and choked some.

'But,' I went on, 'since Tony Molloy was some kind of associate of Frankie Solera, someone you don't know, I guess he's a stranger to you too.'

'They let you *out*?'

'It's because I'm innocent, Sheldon. I thought you understood that. I thought that was why you wrote me that letter once a year.'

To his credit, he put down the can.

'I wrote you because I never thought you did it, Bierce. But I never worked out why you couldn't convince them of that either. You seemed to do everything else so easy.'

I said nothing.

'I wondered,' he added, 'whether that was because you hadn't quite convinced yourself.'

'That's an interesting observation.'

I looked around the office. One phone. Lots of bills. No obvious work. Cheap porn on the TV.

'So,' I asked, 'how are things in Shangri-La?'

'Lull before the storm,' he said, then leaned over, picked up a filthy computer keyboard, one which had no wires attached, and started punching it with his stubby fingers.

Something began to flash up on the tiny thin screen on the desk. It meant nothing to me, any of this.

'See, this business today is about knowledge. Being one step ahead of the pack. What those bums in the big auto shops out there don't know *will* kill them. You remember the second-series VW Sports Polo GTI hatchback, 97–2001?'

'We talked of little else on death row.'

He typed in something, then pointed to an unreadable page of text on the screen.

'Out of warranty now, natch. But there's a problem with the overhead valves on some of them. Not widely known yet. You have to understand where to look to get this info. The maker won't fix it, not without a lot of money. It needs a mod which you only get from Germany. Unless . . .'

More beer, and a broad grin which revealed that regular dental visits had not been part of Sheldon's medical regime in some time.

'. . . you know me. I have the parts. I have the knowledge. When those babies start coughing and wheezing and falling apart all over town, people are going to be beating a path to my door to fix them. *Big* money.'

I glanced at the empty workshop.

'When's this gold rush likely to start?'

He frowned.

'Six weeks. Eight at the most. The guy who sold me the mod parts says the problem only starts big time when the weather goes from hot to cold. Come the end of September, the streets out there will be littered with dead VWs and no one to fix them, short of paying a fortune to some dealer, except me.'

There were seven or eight cardboard boxes stacked in the corner of the office with Korean and Japanese writing on them, and a picture of a vehicle that looked as if it had been drawn by a three-year-old.

'You get these on sale or return?' I asked.

Sheldon's beetle brows curled in bafflement.

'What?'

'Nothing. Listen, Sheldon. I need . . .'

'I don't have any money.'

'I don't want money.' I looked up the little set of stairs that led to the loft that had been Sheldon's home since he left the farm. In desperate circumstances . . . 'The Airport Ramada is unexpectedly full. I need a place to stay, just for tonight. I need to talk to you about some things too.'

He shuffled and looked worried. Then he cracked open another beer and didn't think to offer me one.

'Things?' Sheldon asked, with that little nervous squeak in his voice I'd forgotten.

I came straight to the point.

'Were we happy, Sheldon?'

He wriggled in his seat.

'How the hell should I know? It was your marriage.'

'Did we *look* happy? Miriam, I mean.'

'Yeah,' he replied, nodding. 'I never saw her look as happy as she did the day you got married.'

'And after?'

'She looked pretty happy too. We didn't talk regular. I think she would have liked you to be home a little more. Maybe earning a decent wage. The Sedgwicks always had a thing about money, you know. Family failing.'

He cast a jaundiced glance around him.

'Miriam knew I was burning up the old man's inheritance big time ever since I started this business. That pissed her off. As she made clear to me on more than one occasion.'

Miriam and I had run through that conversation ourselves, several times.

'That was about you, Sheldon. Not the money.'

'No.' He said this carefully, as if he was scared of getting the words wrong. 'It was about both. Miriam had ideas, Bierce. Maybe you didn't notice that, but she did.'

I shook my head. This didn't fit the picture I'd stored in my mind, one that was, in many respects, very clear, since I'd taken it out and polished it so often while sweating in a cell in Gwinett.

'What kind of ideas?'

'Ordinary ones. A big house. A big garden. A pool maybe and a view of the beach.'

'She wasn't going to get to Greenpoint married to a cop. Not an honest one.'

'No.' He was speaking carefully again. 'I guess she wasn't.'

'Was she cheating on me?'

'Of course not! What the . . . ?'

He threw the half-empty beer can in my direction, which for Sheldon was tantamount to extreme violence.

'Hey. I don't have to listen to you insulting my dead sister's memory. OK?'

'I had to ask. You know what they hinted at in the trial. Not that they ever put a face to him.'

'I never came to the trial. I never read a word about it in the papers. I couldn't. Pop was getting sick by then, not that I expect you to be aware of that fact. I just . . .' He hung his head and sighed. 'I just wanted to be near him.'

'Inheritance time,' I said, and hated myself the moment the words floated out.

'There wasn't any left by then,' he said sourly.

'They said she was cheating. You must have heard that.'

'I heard it. I don't want to know any more.'

'With some jerk called Kyle McKendrick. That part never got into court somehow. But they ran the name past me all the same.'

He shivered and picked up the newspaper.

'Could that be true, Sheldon?'

He creased an inside page in half and thrust it in front of me. There was a long story, half the available space, about some charitable foundation and a gift it was making to one of the city hospitals. I scanned the details. Kyle McKendrick had come up in the world since I busted him for trying to talk cheap hookers into his Honda in one of the crappier parts of St Kilda.

The article described him as 'the city billionaire and philanthropist'. His foundation was giving the hospital twenty million for a new children's ward. There was a picture of him – a middle-aged man with well-kept grey hair and a face like that of some fallen angel, young and old at the same time – handing over the cheque to some pretty young nurse. I was surprised they used this particular photo. Mr McKendrick was leering straight down her neckline as he passed over the piece of paper. Maybe someone on the photo desk had a sense of humour.

'Seems a nice guy now,' I observed. 'A nice, generous guy.'

Sheldon grunted.

'He can afford to be. The only things in this city Kyle McKendrick doesn't own are the churches and the graveyards, and he's probably planning a takeover bid for them as we speak. You know who I pay the rent to on this place? When I pay it.'

'In person?'

'Nah! He's rich, Bierce. Rich people don't do things the straight way. It goes to his daughter's company, out on some Caribbean island, then straight back to him. I'll tell you one thing, though.'

He hesitated, as if he wished he hadn't thought of this.

'I'm listening,' I said by way of encouragement.

'It all comes back to Kyle in the end. Everything. He's a hands-on man. Doesn't delegate anything easy. Even the crooked stuff. Why should he bother? He's got everyone in his pocket anyway.'

'I understand. So was it true what they said? About Miriam?'

'How the hell would I know? Tell me that.'

There was a phone book on the desk. I just about recognized it. They'd changed the way things looked, the way things got organized. Also, judging by how thick the thing was – I noticed, after a couple of flicks through, that this was merely volume one – it appeared every last person on the planet now owned at least one phone number, if not several.

'Where can I call him? We need to talk.'

Sheldon was over in an instant, grabbing the book out of my hands.

'Are you insane?'

'Possibly. I'd still like to sit down with this guy all the same. We've things that need clearing up. Surely you can see that?'

'No, no, no, no, no. You do not call Kyle McKendrick. You don't go anywhere near someone like that. I don't know how the hell you got out of jail, but he could sure put you straight back in there, no questions asked.'

People kept saying stuff like this and it was starting to bother me.

'Did someone change the nature of the legal system while I was in prison? I still have this phrase "independent judiciary" running round my head. Is it an anachronism?'

'*You're* an anachronism. In this world money is everything. If you have it, you do what you like. If you don't, you stay alive by keeping your head down, getting on with the day and feeling glad when it's over. We're all just little fleas feeding off one another, then passing on a few of the spoils to bigger fleas because they *are* bigger. And Kyle McKendrick is the biggest of them all.'

'How did this happen?' I asked, genuinely bewildered.

Sheldon shook his head.

'I don't know. I really don't.'

'Then why the hell do you take it?'

'Because that's how things are! Listen. I don't want you getting any stupid ideas. I know what a stubborn bastard you are and on this point, brother-in-law, you are wrong. You may think the pinnacle of human civilization happened some time in the spring of 1985, and ever since then we've just been going down-hill . . .'

'You put that with a remarkable eloquence . . .'

'Well, it's bullshit! What we are is what we were all along. It just took us a while to realize it.'

'Cynicism does not become a man. Are you ever going to offer me a beer?'

It was the last one. That was why he kept shuffling his tubby body in front of it.

Sheldon Sedgwick sighed and threw the can across to me. I tried to open it and failed. A little swearing started.

'Gimme!' Sheldon yelled, then got up and snatched the thing from my fingers. He was furious all of a sudden. Over a can of beer. Or rather, over me. 'If you can't even open a beer, what the hell hope is there?'

146

I watched. It was different. In my day tabs got ripped off completely and came with razor-sharp edges that could stripe your fingers if you weren't careful. The opening on this thing just sort of turned in on itself, then hung there, meek and mild.

'Progress,' Sheldon said, and sat down. 'See.'

'Yeah,' I agreed. 'Now you can get shit-faced without fear of cutting yourself to ribbons.'

Nevertheless, I took a swig. The beer was warm but wonderful. And the first small kick of alcohol I'd tasted in twenty-three years suddenly brought on a moment of epiphany, a small one this time.

The revelation being . . . I could scarcely keep my eyes open.

'I'll go out and get some more,' Sheldon promised.

'Something to eat might be a good idea too.'

'Any other requests?'

I thought about this.

'Bread. Straight from the oven, so you can smell it. Roast beef. Apples. Some salad. Fresh. Fragrant. Those are your shopping watchwords for this evening, Sheldon. Here . . .'

I threw over fifty from my remaining wad. I was feeling generous towards him. It must have been good beer.

Then, without even thinking, I asked, 'Does the name "Sister Dragon" mean anything to you?'

He didn't blink. He was thinking. I was willing

to give this some time, because saying the actual words prodded some subterranean mental rock inside my head that had been liberated by the presence of alcohol. Beneath it lay the conviction that I only remembered Sister Dragon because someone, perhaps in interrogation, had thrown around the phrase repeatedly, and drawn a total blank from me then too. Even so, there was something about the context – *my* context, the situation in which the question got asked – that made me feel scared and more than a little shaky, just as I had when Alice had uttered that same phrase. If it was an interrogation, it surely wasn't an ordinary one.

'You mean you never went?' Sheldon asked.

'Went where?'

'It was a place on Humboldt Street. Got closed down twenty years ago, all of a sudden. Overnight, as if something bad happened. Wasn't open for long but . . . wow. Started off as some smart cock-tail bar, all straight and nice and above board. Went sleazy really quick. The way of the world. Dancing. The strip part turned a little . . . partici-patory if you get my meaning.'

It didn't ring any bell I recognized.

'Miriam took me there!' Sheldon continued. 'I remember now. We had margaritas. They were good.'

'Miriam? Margaritas?'

I never remembered her drinking anything but wine, and that in delicate, studied moderation.

'Yeah. She knew the people who ran it or something. I don't recall. This was a long, long time ago. She must have taken you, Bierce. It looked like she was at home in the place.'

'Maybe,' I agreed, knowing I had never, in a million years, stepped through the door of some bar-cum-strip joint called Sister Dragon.

'What kind of a name is that anyway?' I wondered.

'It was something to do with the woman who ran it, I think. Who the hell knows? This was twenty years ago. More. What does it matter?'

'Not much, I guess. Buy me some flowers too. White roses.'

My head hurt. Too much information.

'Flowers?'

'I just want to smell them. Wake me when you get back. And thanks.'

I crawled off towards the steps to the loft, trying not to think about what dank, bachelor pit lay up there.

He wasn't such a bad guy. Nor was his tiny pad, with its mattress on the floor, boxes full of half-folded clothes, and stacks of magazines laid up against the roof walls, as squalid as I expected.

There were probably worse brothers-in-law in the world, I thought, and went to sleep on the wrinkled sheets of the mattress on the floor, to dream about the Pocapo river, and not from the old days either, but as it was now, with the syringes and the condoms, the silver-head trout and Alice

Loong there smiling, unworried, pleased because I was standing in front of her, nervous like a kid, holding a bunch of white, white roses.

She looked as if no one had ever given her flowers in her life, which seemed a shame, and maybe a little unbelievable. Also she appeared to be holding a small and very real-looking handgun, one that hung its short snout very loosely in my direction. And when I looked into her face I realized why she was smiling. She was pleased to see me again, and that was not good news, not at all.

The last part notwithstanding, I was happy in that dream until something shook me out of it. Muzzy-headed and with the beer smog still hanging around my mouth, I opened my eyes.

There was a silver-haired man seated on a chair in front of me. He wore an expensive-looking suit, silk maybe, a white shirt and a red necktie pulled up tight, the way business people liked. On the chair next to him was some huge black guy with the build and muscles of a wrestler who'd been squeezed into a uniform that was similar, though slightly inferior, to that of the individual by his side. This gentleman had my service pistol in his hands and was staring at it as if the thing was an antique. Behind the pair, standing, fiddling with a dark leather bag, was a serious-looking doctor type whose myopic eyes twitched nervously inside thick, rimless glasses.

Sheldon was there to one side of them and he

looked even more nervous than the one with spectacles.

'You s-s-s-said you wanted to meet Mr McKendrick,' my lying, treacherous brother-in-law stuttered nervously. 'I was hoping we could talk this through nice and polite.'

'Oh, Sheldon . . .'

To my surprise, I genuinely did feel more disappointment than anger at that moment. Except about his persistent abuse of grammar.

'And who the hell killed the adverb during my incarceration? Is there a death notice I can read somewhere?'

He hung his head and mumbled a word I seem to have associated with him for most of his sad little life.

'Sorry.' He gulped. 'Those parts weren't. You reminded me.'

'Weren't what?'

'Sale or return.'

Me and my mouth.

The doctor figure was holding a hypodermic syringe in his hand and, just like my new-old friend Martin, was poking it inside a little glass bottle, when he wasn't casting scrutinizing glances in my direction.

I was, I began to realize, starting to lose my childhood fear of needles.

'Is there something I can do to help you gentlemen?' I asked.

'For your sake,' McKendrick said, in a low, coarse

voice that didn't match the silver-haired appearance and the suit, 'I hope so.'

'So, Kyle,' I answered amicably. 'It's been more than twenty years since I busted you for chasing street whores in St Kilda. What kind of stuff are you into these days?'

McKendrick reached inside his grey jacket and took out a small, shiny handgun.

Then he turned round to Sheldon and casually shot him twice in the chest.

My brother-in-law flew backwards five or six feet, a look on his face that was half fury, half shock. A couple of dark shiny patches started to show through his overalls. They were the colour of the old oil that lived there most of the time anyway.

'That kind of stuff, when I feel like it,' McKendrick said, and watched Sheldon close his eyes and go still, propped against a large pile of *Playboy* magazines of some vintage, stacked tidily against the leaning loft wall.

I'm a reasonable man, particularly when there are guns and needles around, and people who've tied me tight to a chair with some nylon rope they appear to have brought for the occasion.

So I looked, first at Sheldon, who didn't appear to be moving a muscle, then at Kyle McKendrick and said, 'You know, you could always ask.'

McKendrick stared at me as if I were some kind of idiot.

'Ask? *Ask*? What the hell do you think we've been doing all this time?'

I shook my head. This was beyond me.

'I'm sorry. I don't understand.'

'Sir.'

Dr Rimless spoke hesitantly, as if worried he might say the wrong thing without knowing it.

'What?'

'He wouldn't remember,' the doctor type said. 'Not necessarily.'

'Remember what?' I asked. 'You people keep talking in riddles. How am I supposed to help if I don't know what it is you want?'

McKendrick sat and looked at me. Then he put a finger up to his cheek, the way TV people used to do when they wanted to look thoughtful.

'Who else have you talked to since they sprung you?' he asked.

'They? You mean like the judge.'

'None of my judges let you out of that jail.'

This sounded strange.

'You mean I escaped?'

'Somehow.'

'Sleepwalking. That's all it can be. See, I was under the impression someone from the law office or whatever came along, let me loose, gave me some money and a drive home. And then . . .'

What the hell had Stape been up to, I wondered? He had those papers, but he kept them. There was the money, but that was plain bills. The truth was I didn't have a scrap of proof that I'd got out of jail legally at all.

'Then what?' McKendrick asked.

'Then somebody nailed some dirtbag called Tony Molloy to a telegraph pole outside my front door, which seemed to have got the real police, and several other parties, chasing me like I'm a fugitive or something.'

He didn't speak.

'OK,' I said. 'So I understand. I *am* a fugitive. Also the person who nailed Tony Molloy up there was you.'

'Me,' the black guy interjected, pointing a finger at his own chest.

'I stand corrected.'

'Frankie Solera never confessed to killing my wife and kid then?'

'Of course the moron confessed!' McKendrick snarled. 'Who'd have thought a jerk like that would get religion?'

'Strange things happen on a man's deathbed.'

'You're in a good position to judge, Bierce.'

'I take your word on that. Just so's I know . . . you're saying those two *did* kill Miriam and my boy?'

Kyle McKendrick sighed.

'You're still playing the innocent, Bierce? This is so tedious. I could stiff you just for that. What the hell did she see in you?'

There were three of them. I am not a man given to fantasies. All the same, a part of me was wishing I could shrug off those ropes, step right up and rip off their heads in one easy movement.

'You and Miriam . . . ?' I asked, not really wanting to know the answer.

'Where did she hide it?' he demanded.

'Hide what?'

Dr Rimless found the courage to intervene again.

'He really doesn't remember,' he said. 'We've tried too many times for him to be hiding that.'

'Maybe he never knew in the first place,' the black guy grumbled. 'In which case, why are we wasting our time?'

McKendrick closed his eyes, the way people did when they were dealing with children.

'Because we don't know for sure. Or whether he's spoken to anyone else.' Then to me. 'Have you spoken to anyone else?'

'I went home. I got up. People started chasing me. Then I came here and talked to my brother-in-law about family stuff until you shot him. What else can I tell you?'

The black guy glowered at me.

'Man says there was someone on the back of that bike you used.'

'Man needs to get his eyesight checked. I haven't been outside a jail cell in twenty-three years. How many friends do you think I have here?'

'None,' McKendrick muttered. 'None coming either. All the same . . .'

He scowled. He was stuck for a course of action and this seemed to be a situation that was new to him.

'Maybe,' the hood suggested, 'they're still looking for him too. We could just pop him here and have done with the damn thing.'

McKendrick put his head in his hands and swore, freely, profusely, worse than a street hood did a quarter of a century ago. I never moved much in billionaire circles, but I didn't expect them to use words like that.

'Jesus,' the boss man moaned. 'I am surrounded by idiots. He *knows*, moron. I was banging his wife for a little while. Maybe that's why he doesn't feel co-operative.'

I wriggled in my ropes, mind blank, not scared, not angry. Just stuck there, wondering.

'If you tell me what I'm supposed to know . . .' I said.

'Miriam took something that was important to me,' McKendrick said flatly. 'I want it back.'

'Something like . . . ?'

The man in the silk suit sighed.

'Stick him now,' he said to Dr Rimless. 'I can't hang around here dealing with this shit. I got a school to open. Then I got to see the ad agency about some corporate branding session at four-thirty. That gives me a diary window in one hour forty-five. Make sure he has something to fill it.'

The grass is short, newly mown, with the lovely fresh green smell I always found ample reward for the tedious task of cutting it. Ricky's running around the garden, kicking a ball. Something sits in the branches of the apple tree. A large animal. Maybe a cat. Maybe something bigger.

I look more closely. It's some kind of bird, grey

and shapeless, with a long sharp beak and wearing rimless spectacles behind which lie two cold black eyes watching me, gleaming. In its claws there's a syringe, from which a line leads straight across the flower bed, through neat rows of lilies and white roses, up the table leg, into my arm.

The creature's listening. I know what it can hear.

My blood boiling in my veins. My mind racing a million miles an hour, searching for something, matching what I think I know against what I'm trying to dig up from my damaged memory.

'Ignore him,' Miriam suggests.

She's in the loose red dress, which is odd, since this is day. Her arms look more tanned than normal. Her face seems tired and a little lined.

'That's easy for you to say. You're dead. Or imaginary. Or both.'

She smiles, a sad smile, one I haven't seen much.

'Did I ever really know you?' I ask.

'How can you say that? We were married for seven years.'

'And for the last few months you were banging some city councillor I'd picked up once in St Kilda, hunting for a whore.'

She folds her arms and gives me a cold, disappointed look.

'You should ask more questions. Those two facts are mere coincidence. Surely you recognize that? Besides, it's always about you.'

Her arms are skinnier than I remember. There

are marks on them. Scratch marks. They look old and some are a little scabby.

'What do you mean?' I say, offended. 'I *am* asking questions. I'm asking about *us*. About the fact we were married.'

I glance at Ricky, who isn't really Ricky at all. His features are blurred and unrecognizable. He's just a shadow with a little colour, chasing over the short grass, like a cartoon character running in a loop in the background.

'And the rest,' I add.

She uncrosses her arms. One hand reaches out and touches me. Or so my eyes tell me. I can't feel a thing.

'No, Bierce. I didn't mean it that way. This *is* all about you. Surely you understand that?'

'Kind of.'

A part of me appreciates what she is saying very precisely. I'm not in the garden in Owl Creek, back in 1985. I'm in Sheldon Sedgwick's loft, with him, dead probably, a couple of yards away, and some bird-impersonating creep in rimless glasses feeding dope into my arm in the hope he can force me to remember something that disappeared the night she and Ricky died, in the beating I took too, from Frankie Solera and Tony Molloy, who were working, probably, at Kyle McKendrick's behest, though it's hard to be sure.

Maybe Miriam is really the creature in rimless glasses, though I doubt that. More likely she's part of me, asking questions of myself, throwing them at some black, empty part of my memory that died over the years, trying to find some answers before Dr Rimless prises them out with his needles and dope.

'I thought I would have known,' I say.

'Known what?'

'That you were having an affair.'

'Cops,' she answers, with a shrug. 'You spend so much time peering into the lives of other people you never really notice what's going on in your own. You weren't there a lot of the time, Bierce. You never realized, I know. And it wasn't deliberate neglect. But you were gone. Days and nights. For a long time on occasions.'

I try to squeeze her hand, wondering if there's any warmth in the flesh.

'So you went to Sister Dragon?'

'Among other places,' she agrees.

'Where was Ricky?'

She looks at the boy. He is my son at that moment. *Our* son. I can see this in her imaginary face.

'Dreaming of seeing penguins,' she says quietly. 'Dreaming . . .'

'They can fly,' Ricky, suddenly sharply in focus, says, except it isn't his voice, it's mine, and hearing it emerge from his young, unspoiled mouth makes me feel more miserable than at any other moment in my too-long life, makes me feel as if I've stolen the breath from my child's lungs and placed my own there in its stead. 'They can fly. I know it.'

'Penguins,' Miriam says, with the careful intonation of the schoolteacher she once was, 'cannot fly. We have been here a million times.'

'Just because you haven't seen them . . .' Ricky or I, it's unclear which, objects.

'Their wings are too short and stubby,' Miriam goes on. 'There are physical laws that mean you don't have to see them not flying to know they *can't* fly. In the promised land, maybe. Here, no. This is the way the world works. This . . .'

She looks into my face and the pupils of her eyes are black, bottomless pools.

'This is the gravity that holds us all down. Cops do not prosper. Penguins do not fly. Children believe daydreams until one day they know better. And then they turn into us.'

She waves Ricky away.

'Also there are these people called "baby-sitters". I believe I explained the concept to you one time.'

'And while Ricky was with a baby-sitter, you were out screwing a thing called Kyle McKendrick. I don't understand.'

'No,' she-says, without emotion. 'You don't. I realize that.'

'Did I? Once?'

Miriam closes her eyes, and this is her, in a way, even if she happens to be nothing but stitched-together memories fired up by Dr Rimless and his assistant. Mistress Dope.

'No. You never understood. Not really.'

'But I knew, right? That night when . . . it all happened. You told me then.'

'I believe so.'

There's nothing there, nothing in my memory to support the question I ask next.

'And we fought? You against me, not the other way round? Which is why they found my skin under your nails?'

I need to know this, desperately. She recognizes that. She says nothing.

'Why?'

It isn't me talking. It's the creature in the tree. Its voice has an inhuman metallic ring to it. If I could move – the line that leads from his syringe into my arm keeps me rooted to the spot for some reason – I would get up and wring his fat feathery neck, long sharp beak notwithstanding.

'Why what?' she asks, of me, not it.

'Why did we fight?' I interrupt, because this is my dream, not his. 'Over McKendrick?'

'What do you think, Bierce? How would you react if you thought I was sleeping with another man? That perhaps I even *loved* another man?'

She makes the distinction very clear. That puzzles me. Either way I'd be heartbroken. I'd sit where we are, at the battered wooden table, staring out at the garden, wondering how we might put our lives back together again, struggling for the means, determined they would, at any cost, be found.

There were women before Miriam, but none

came close. She was . . . is the one. I thought she felt the same way about me. I'm wrong but, even now, when I know, it doesn't make any difference. If you can choose love, it isn't love at all. What more is there to say?

'Where did you hide it?' the creature demands.

'Hide what?' she replies.

'You know.'

She looks at me and we say the words together.

'Do I?'

Something happens in my arm. A cold rush of chemical comes running through the hole there. Some unknown instrument, a bell maybe, or a drone, begins singing at the back of my head, one note, not a word, not even a sound I can recognize.

'You know,' the grey spectacled bird in the tree repeats.

'Tell me,' I ask her.

There are tears in her eyes. Not grief. Fury, with herself I guess.

'I don't believe in ghosts, Bierce, and nor do you. Think about it. Either you have the understanding. Or you don't. Some things you can only do on your own.'

'Then help me.'

She shrugs.

'How?'

She takes my fingers more tightly in hers, winding them round and round, the way she used to.

Miriam, dead Miriam, Miriam out of a dream,

can't take her eyes off me, and for a moment I envy whatever place it is she occupies.

'All you have is what you have. You're the only person who can find it. Not through some chemical fix or a blow to the head or anything artificial like that. You find it by being yourself. There's no other way.'

Then she adds, never breaking her hard, fixed gaze, 'If you really want to, that is. Some things are best left buried.'

'Bierce,' says the other voice, 'it's . . .'

She starts howling. She puts her hands to her ears and the crazy thing is, when she does that *I* am the one who can't hear a sound.

The Rimless Thing falls out of the tree, on to the hard bare ground beneath its branches. It drops the syringe. It's yelling something, over and over again, but my lip-reading talents, such as they are, have deserted me. All I can hear is Miriam, yelling and yelling and yelling, hands tight to her – my? – head, so the sound of her voice stays inside me, fills up everything there, every corner, every dark, fleshy passageway.

I say something and don't detect the sound of my own voice.

I look in the direction of the tree again. The Rimless Thing is gone completely.

Something is changing with Miriam too, and even though I know this is just a dope dream, it makes me want to weep. The image of her isn't so definite. It's fading slowly, her sad eyes, the real eyes now, glassy with tears, slipping back where they came from, down into the lost depths of my consciousness.

My head's starting to roll sideways, towards some abyss that's opening up beneath the garden table.

I feel rotten. I can't keep upright at the table. When I next try to look at her there's nothing on the other side but bright, filmy dust, floating in an unreal breeze.

From out of the line of my vision comes the sound of a man, Rimless I guess, yelling something I can hear but not comprehend. The thought of getting my shaking hands tight around his neck refuses to go away.

'Bierce?' says a distant female voice, and I don't even have the strength to twitch my head around, trying to find where it's coming from.

'I don't know what you're talking about,' I mumble. 'If I did know some time, it's gone. And it's not coming back, not ever. So just kill me now. Who the hell cares anyway?'

'Bierce!'

'Quit shouting, start shooting. *I don't give a shit.*'

I try to find the bird but he isn't anywhere. There is no tree. There's a grubby room with grubby furniture, a body I kind of recognize, heaped against some magazines. It's Dr Rimless, who is back to being a man. He's slumped on Sheldon's floor mattress, looking shocked and hurt. His spectacles lie on his chest, shattered. A large red wound has sprung up from somewhere on his wide forehead.

'Listen, dinosaur,' the hidden woman says. 'We're getting out of here now. Before anyone comes back. Can you hear me? Can you even move?

'Bierce!'

Her shape stops swimming. A long, slender hand the colour of a fading golden rose comes out from the fuzzy part of my universe and starts slapping me hard around the cheek.

'We are going. Now. And who's this?'

The hand is pointing at Sheldon. His eyes are open. He appears to be conscious and breathing. I envy him on both counts.

'Brother-in-law. Treacherous stinking asshole.'

'Then he's coming too,' she says, and jerks me to my feet, an act that leads to my head wobbling wildly on my shoulders, looking for a spare place on the floor, between the beer cans and porn mags, where it can roll off and lie still for a while.

Alice Loong looks me straight in the eye.

'You *will* help me pick up the shot guy,' she orders. 'There are four vehicles downstairs and a million sets of keys. Something's got to work around here. We *need* him.'

Dr Rimless moans and says something colourful.

My slender half-Chinese friend walks over and wallops him hard on the head with the largest mechanic's wrench I have ever seen in my life. He doesn't move or say anything after that.

I struggle to pull together a smile for her.

'I tried to buy you flowers,' I say with a sorry slur, hating Sheldon all the more because I know he never got them.

'You're the most generous man in the world,' she replies. 'Now take his legs. We're gone.'

The thing about pharmaceuticals is that, unlike booze, they usually wear off quickly. Or so I kept trying to tell myself.

We drove out of the Pocapo flats industrial zone in the ancient brown Volvo estate wagon I saw on the way in, now newly vacated by rodents, selected by Alice from Sheldon's small fleet of vehicles deemed too far gone to be collected by their true owners. I sat bolt upright in the passenger seat, suddenly feeling pretty high and talkative. The miracle of chemicals. Sheldon was sprawled out in the back, moaning. Alice Loong was behind the wheel, angerometer touching ten on the Richter scale.

'Where are we going?' I asked.

'I'm dumping your friend off at the hospital. Then I'm taking you somewhere quiet.'

'When will we be there?'

'Shut up, Bierce. I am thoroughly pissed off with you.'

I gave up struggling to put my seat belt on and stared at her.

'For why?'

'You abandoned me, for God's sake! While I was taking a leak. What kind of man does that?'

'Maybe a man who thinks you're better off that way. Besides, I left you money, didn't I?'

A silver Mercedes came speeding the other way, with a now-familiar black figure behind the wheel.

'Uh-oh,' I muttered, and quickly ducked down behind the dashboard.

When I got back up, the Mercedes was still sailing on in the direction of the Shangri-La.

'Evil bastard McKendrick fooling with my wife,' I grumbled under my breath.

'What?' Alice barked.

'You heard.'

'You're full of that stuff they gave you. Why don't you shut up and go to sleep or something?'

'Can't. Thinking. Besides, maybe he was fooling with your mom too.'

She slammed on the brakes. We came to a halt by a couple of newspaper stands that had been vandalized by someone learning how to spell.

'That's it. Get out. Now.'

'I'm serious! Tell her about Sister Dragon, Sheldon.'

He was groaning like crazy on the back seat. But he wasn't bleeding so much. Even doped up as I was, I felt pretty sure Sheldon Sedgwick would live to cheat and lie another day.

'I've been shot!'he whined.

'You got two tiny bullets from a ladies' gun. They clearly hit nothing of any importance, otherwise you wouldn't be squawking like you are now.'

'I've been shot!' he squealed again.

'Don't worry. You're made of lead-absorbent lard. We'll drop you off at the hospital, they'll give you someone else's blood, then you'll pass for an ordinary decent human being for an hour or two before your own stuff starts to kick in again.'

Alice swore, put the car in gear and swerved back into the road.

'How the hell could you sell me like that, Sheldon?' I asked, and sounded a little pathetic too, I could tell. 'Me. Your own brother-in-law, who comes to you for help, *and* passed over a fifty for beer and flowers.'

'Flowers?' Alice asked, bewildered.

'Yeah. Flowers. Never got them either. How could you do it, Sheldon?'

He was well enough to drag his bleeding frame up off his seat, lean over the back of mine and stab an accusing finger at me.

'I didn't know they were gonna pull stuff like that, did I? Otherwise I wouldn't have said nothing.'

'Use one more double negative and I'll shoot you myself, O brother. Why?'

'The landlord guy called this morning. Said they were just interested in knowing if you showed up. One whole month's rent in it for me.'

I brushed off his arm. He fell back on to the seat.

'Oh, wonderful,' I moaned, and looked at Alice in the driver's seat. 'I am cash-flow positive. That excuses everything. And you?'

She glared back at me.

'Me?'

'Yeah. Who *are* you?'

'What do you mean "who am I"? I'm the person who just saved your life.'

'But why?'

She reached down into her bag, pulled out the wad I'd left there and threw it at me.

Sheldon sighed in the back. The presence of so much cash within smelling distance seemed to me the greatest threat his health was likely to encounter all day.

I still couldn't work out whether I felt super-smart or super-stupid.

'I don't like being abandoned,' Alice added. 'And I don't like being patronized. What the hell did you mean by that?'

My head really wasn't running on the right lines. I shook it to see if that would help.

'What?'

'About my mom? And McKendrick.'

'Oh.' It took a second or two. '*Tell* her, Sheldon. About Sister Dragon.'

He didn't say anything. He was hiccuping. Or throwing up. Or both. He did have two bullets in him. He did need medical help.

'Fine,' I announced. 'Leave this to me too.'

I tried to pull myself together and looked at her. She glanced back at me, a little nervous. This wasn't going to be nice, for either of us, and somehow Alice Loong understood that already.

'Sister Dragon was some sleazy cocktail bar

pick-up joint on Humboldt,' I said, speaking very precisely. 'It got closed down years ago. Unbeknown to me, my wife used to go there before she climbed into the back of Kyle McKendrick's Taurus for a quick hump or something.'

'For Christ's sake, Bierce. How can you possibly know that?'

'I *know*. Just trust me. McKendrick virtually rubbed it in my face for one thing. It's not the kind of stuff you'd lie about.'

She winced.

'I'm sorry.'

I waved an arm around loosely.

'No. It's OK really. A part of me knew already. It just doesn't want to vomit up all the rest of the crap it's got hiding down there.'

'Wait . . .' she said.

We'd passed some kind of medical station by the side of the road. There were a couple of ambulances there and an office with – I could just make this out – some people in white nylon coats inside.

'Sheldon,' Alice said, 'it is time for you to discover the joys of private medicine.'

I turned round. His eyes were looking bleary. There was blood all over the back seat.

'Huh?' he moaned. 'I don't have insurance. Don't leave me here. They'll cut me up for parts.'

'No,' I found myself saying. 'They'd only do that if you were the same species as the rest of us.'

Then she helped him out and got him to sit on a trash can by the front door. The white coats

170

inside didn't notice a thing. They all seemed to have their faces stuck to computer screens, one per head, or so it looked like.

Alice went round the corner, where I couldn't see her. It took a minute or so before she came back, but at least we didn't have Sheldon any more.

'Let's go,' she said.

She'd made a phone call. I saw her putting her tiny little pink plastic handset into her bag when she came back. Had I possessed more of my wits, I would have mentioned this. But I didn't, and that, I guess, was why she thought she could get away with it.

'Such efficient, detached care,' I observed instead. 'You could get a job in medicine yourself.'

Alice drove off slowly. She looked as if she wasn't sure where to go. She looked uncertain of herself, if I'm being honest. Somehow I found this reassuring.

'So,' she asked, 'your wife used to go to a cocktail bar and screw McKendrick? And you knew nothing about this?'

'No,' I corrected her. 'My present self did not know knowingly. That is not to say my previous self did not, at some stage, know, not that he's telling. If you follow me.'

'I'm trying. How are you, Bierce? Is there anything I can get you?'

I thought about this.

'I have a serious thirst for a Long Island Iced

Tea, a bucket of buttered popcorn and a plate of steak tartare. Which probably means I'm not good at all. If you could find me some real food and water that would be nice. Before . . .'

She had very nice eyes, the colour of the green you used to get in signet rings. I noticed something else too, when she opened her mouth and half smiled at me. The tongue stud was gone. This was one more invention of the twenty-first century. You could stick lumps of metal in your mouth and make it look as if they'd been nailed there. Then take them out the following day and no one would ever have guessed.

'Before what?'

'Before we visit Sister Dragon or whatever it's called these days. I just want to see. Find out if it sparks any pictures in my head or something.'

She shook her head.

'I don't know Humboldt. Isn't that a really long street? If you don't have a number we'll need to ask.'

I said nothing and hunched up in the passenger seat. A small store – with the iron grille and warning notices about alarms that I was now getting used to – hove up on the right. We weren't a mile from Humboldt in any case.

'Pull over, will you?' I said. 'I need to get some sugar or something inside me.'

She did, without a moment's hesitation.

I dragged a note out of my pocket and walked through the door. I liked this place immediately, with that warm, tears in the eye affection only the truly doped up or drunk can have. It looked as if it hadn't changed much in twenty-five years or more. Just the prices, and the security cameras that seemed to be poking at everyone who entered.

Lurching up to the counter, I started counting through the candy bars, picking ones I recognized, throwing in some potato chips and sundry assorted junk snacks.

There was a time for fine food. There was a time to fill the face.

I picked up several specimens, then let them loose in front of the man behind the counter, a small, elderly individual of wiry build and Mediterranean appearance. Behind him was a large wire cage with a green parrot inside. It kept talking in what sounded like Greek. Dirty Greek.

'Party time,' the counter man said, and laughed.

'Yeah . . .'

I hadn't even noticed the newcomer who'd slid in behind me and walked straight up to pay. I looked at him now. He was about my height, in the familiar uniform of a patrol car monkey, with shorn golden hair and sunglasses tucked back on to his head, like a bad TV cop.

He eyed me up and down carefully, then grinned.

'Don't you go crazy with all that,' he advised, in a slow, stupid drawl.

To this day I have absolutely no idea whether he was serious or not.

Still, if the cops were looking for me hard even

this bozo should surely have known. So whoever the other party on my case was – Kyle McKendrick's rivals, that much was clear – they didn't appear to be wearing a badge. Which made me think it would be very interesting to have a talk with my old friend Stape some time soon.

'You have any flowers?' I asked. 'White roses.'

The shop guy's eyes rolled back into his head, thinking.

'Out back maybe,' he said, then looked at me, as if trying to work out whether I was the type to purloin his entire stock of confectionery and potato snacks once his back was turned. 'Ah, there's a cop here. What's to worry about?'

He went through a little door behind him. The patrolman and I exchanged vapid glances.

I pointed to the security cameras sprouting everywhere, and the signs about alarms and time locks and all kinds of stuff I didn't begin to understand.

'What's the world coming to?' I asked. 'Where are the values?'

He nodded.

'I believe, for economy shopping, sir, you may be better served by a larger establishment such as a supermarket chain. You don't come visit Mr Thanatos for bargains, now do you?'

I closed my eyes and thought about weeping.

'Just a little retail advice,' he added.

When the store keeper came back I saw the roses were getting a little grubby at the edges. I paid

what he wanted, though, which seemed an extraordinary amount, then asked, 'Either of you two
heard of a place called Sister Dragon on Humboldt?
It closed down years ago. A cocktail bar or something. A friend of mine was in town once. Said it
was quite something.'

The uniform looked blank. The store man stared
at me, not pleasantly either.

'That was a whore joint,' he said eventually.
'What kind of friend was he?'

'It was a she, actually. You wouldn't happen to
know the address? She's a nun now. I thought it
might be funny to send her a photo or something.'

'Corner of Vine, south side,' he said.

'And now?'

He said something that made no sense to me at
all, then added, with some finality, 'Good night.'

Back in the car she stared at the roses, then picked
out a couple of chocolate bars and took a big bite
of one.

'What the hell did those people do to you,
Bierce? These are the worst flowers I've ever seen.'

'Limited choice. Sorry.'

'And why?'

'Why'd I go in there? Because I was hungry. And
because I wanted to know if anyone around here
had heard of this Dragon Sister place?'

Her face was taut with interest. I wasn't so doped
up I didn't notice.

'And?'

'I got an address. Humboldt on Vine. The south side.'

'Tomorrow maybe.'

'No. Now. I insist.'

She laughed.

'I'm driving this stolen vehicle, Bierce. You're in no position, or condition, to insist on a thing.'

She put the car into gear. I put my hand on the wheel, firmly, to stop her going wherever she thought we ought.

'No, Alice. I am. I want to go see this place. I want to think about it. And then I want to know the truth.'

Alice Loong sighed and stared at me.

'You're tired and doped up and stupid.'

'All true, but only of late. Just a couple of hours ago I was feeling quite bright and breezy, to be frank with you. Here's one thing I thought back then. You said you knew they were asking your mom about Sister Dragon when they killed her. Which maybe was true. And maybe not. But this I *do* know. I worked Chinatown for a couple of years. I had friends there. I went to parties and festivals. And this I remember.'

She'd put down the chocolate bar and was looking young and worried again.

'The Chinese for dragon is "*loong*". You've got to know that. You said yourself you got brought up by your grandmother who's all Chinese. So why's it so puzzling that someone would be asking your mother about Sister Dragon?'

'Tell me, smartass,' she murmured.

'Because it isn't. I'm putting two and two together here and maybe getting five and a half. But the way I see it is this. Your mom didn't know Miriam and Ricky because she worked in that factory in Owl Creek. She knew them through the bar. Maybe she and Miriam were friends. Maybe she was some secret baby-sitter while I was out at work. Or maybe the place was called Sister Dragon after the person who ran it, which seems to me to make the most sense, since everyone was just beginning to embark upon the cult of self-worship you people all know and love so well today.'

She didn't hit me. She didn't say no.

'So . . . my bet is that Sister Dragon was called that because the person who ran it *was* your mother. And if that's true, then what follows next is obvious. It was called *Sister* Dragon because the guy who owned it was her brother. Your uncle.'

I stared at her.

'Is he dead too?'

She didn't say a thing, just looked a little crestfallen.

I picked up the flowers, which had tumbled to the floor by her side.

'I can get out of the car if you like. I can leave you that money. Whichever, I don't care.'

'No . . .' she said, shaking her head.

I thought of what the man in the store had said.

'It's something called Starbucks now. Do you know what that is?'

'Oh, my God, Bierce . . . You're not fit to be on the streets. It's a coffee place. There are millions of them.'

That sounded a pleasant bell in my head.

'Coffee?' I said. 'That would be nice.'

That, I thought, and the truth.

I have no idea what a double skinny latte mocha with a tangerine shot or something is. But coffee it is not. I sat in this smoke-free, squeaky clean, sanitized dump on Humboldt, squeezed between a launderette and what looked like an appealing book store, feeling I'd wandered into some adolescent's dream of what grown-up life ought to be like.

There were cushions of many colours, meaningless paintings on the wall, soft unmemorable music, and cups of drink the size of Bavarian *Bierkeller* mugs. Most people seemed to be sipping on gallons of warm sweet milk while chewing tiny fancy biscuits that cost the price of a meal the last time I had walked down Humboldt. In between sucks, they played around with little computers on their laps, spoke on their tiny phones and even, in a couple of rare, misfit cases, read something that had once been a tree. I believe I saw one young man and woman indulging in a conversation too, though that may well have been a hallucination. Every last one of them looked fit and well and deeply grateful to have escaped the ravages of the world beyond the door. This was a communal womb with caffeine – or at least a pretence of it – on tap, and I wondered if some of them ever went home at all.

I smiled at the young girl behind the counter as she tried to interest me in some incomprehensible extras.

'Sorry,' I apologized. 'English is my only language. I gather this place used to be a strip dive called Sister Dragon. I don't imagine there would be an adult around here who could confirm such a theory.'

I thought she was about to burst into tears for a moment. Then she just turned her back on me and upped the volume on the Muzak. In my day it came without fuzz guitar, which at least seemed somewhat more honest.

Alice led me to the one free sofa. I sat in it and sank three feet deep into soft, plushy foam.

I tried the liquid in the cup and felt a little nauseous. It was impossible to believe a coffee bean had expired in its making. Also, I wondered how it would get along with whatever else was still floating in my veins. With hindsight, I suspected Martin the Medic's little procedure the day before hadn't entirely slipped my bloodstream before Dr Rimless came along and added his intravenous cocktail to the mix. Pouring a double skinny latte or something on top was, perhaps, unwise. On the other hand, it did just seem to be mainly warm milk.

'I think maybe I should get a doctor to look at you,' Alice suggested.

'A good night's sleep is all I need. If I'm still weird in the morning, nag me then.'

She sighed. Alice Loong was a quick young woman. She knew by now there was no point in arguing.

Instead she looked around the cafe.

'It's hard to believe, isn't it?' she said.

It was just about possible to imagine it as a cocktail bar. The windows must have been expanded somewhat for its present purpose. When I imagined them replaced by the little square panes of glass that were *de rigueur* for drink joints back in my own time, a picture started to form. Bars always had some kind of magic about them that meant the more people came through the door, the bigger the space inside seemed. Empty, the place would have looked tiny. Crammed with fifty or so thirsty customers, it would, I imagine, have sought to attain the status of being intimate. There were also, I suspected, other rooms out back, now used to store millions of cardboard coffee cups and cinnamon aerosol sprays.

I'd never be able to confirm this last part, not without breaking in. The moment Alice parked the old Volvo outside – something she did without even having to check the street intersection – I became ever more sure of one thing. Miriam had never taken me inside Sister Dragon, doubtless for some very good reasons.

'Everything's hard to believe until you start

working on it,' I said. 'So let's begin. Your uncle first. Did he have a name?'

'Everyone called him Jonny. That wasn't his real name, naturally. But not many people speak Cantonese.'

I nodded.

'Jonny Loong. Jonny Loong.'

'Say it, Bierce.'

'I told you. I worked Chinatown for a while. It was standard training when you were new to the department.'

'And?'

She knew what I was going to come out with anyway.

'I heard the name Jonny Loong once or twice. He was a crook. Not a big crook, not in Chinatown terms. Just street lowlife, the kind of man you'd put in front of something to hide who really owned it.'

My memory was very good about some things.

'He owned, or claimed to, a restaurant in Eden. Some of the cops used to eat there cheap, lunch and dinner.'

'Cheap being free. Were you among them?' she asked.

I shook my head, with some insistence.

'No. I pay the same price as everyone else. Either that or I don't eat at all.'

'That must have cut down the availability of dining partners.'

'A little. So what? Did I get Jonny wrong?'

Her green eyes lit up with a touch of fury.

'I was three years old when he disappeared. When my mom died. How the hell am I supposed to know?'

Unbeknown to her, I'd smuggled in a crappy rose in my pocket. I took it out and placed it on her lap.

'Alice,' I said, 'if we're to do anything together, we have to learn to be honest with each other. If we can't do that, nothing works. Not when it comes to finding out what happened to your mom or my family. Nothing else either.'

Her face creased with puzzlement.

'What "else"? Don't mistake what happened in your house for something real, Bierce. I was just trying to get you on my side.'

'No, no, no.' I cursed myself for being so stupid. 'That wasn't what I meant at all. What I'm trying to say is . . . we have to have some trust between us. So we can talk frankly. There's no alternative.'

She did the smart thing. She turned the trust question back on me.

'So you won't stuff a wad of cash in my bag and run off again?' Alice asked sweetly.

'No,' I said, and crossed my heart. 'That's a promise. Now it's your turn. Tell me about your family, please.'

It was, I imagine, a pretty standard immigrant story, with one significant twist. The Loongs had come out of Hong Kong in the sixties, penniless, like most people in their circumstances, but willing to work every minute of the day to make a go of things. They wound up in the city, in Chinatown, slaving everywhere, from the restaurants to the little factories that made tourist junk, and sending what they could back home to help.

The one unusual thing was this: old man Loong never came with them. For some reason Alice didn't know, he stayed in Hong Kong and died there, of lung cancer she said, when her mother was still young.

'So your grandma was on her own with two kids, in a strange city, with no work except what she could pick up on the streets?'

'Correct. Lao Lao had no relatives either. I just heard stories from time to time. She never wanted to talk about it much. It must have been awful. The thing is, people of that generation don't think about the past. She's fine now. Got her own little apartment. Enough money to get by. It doesn't bother her any more. I'm not sure how much that part of things ever did.'

'Losing your two kids would, though. Were they her only children?'

'Yes,' she said warily. 'The rest is difficult, Bierce. I've never had this conversation with her direct. I daren't do that with Lao Lao. We don't have that kind of relationship.'

'So this is just what you've picked up over the years?'

'Correct.'

There was quite a lot there, though. Jonny Loong was a typical teenage jerk, the kind you got when there was no father around to exercise a little discipline. May Loong, Alice's mother, was less inclined to mix with criminal types. Instead, she hung around with the leftovers from the hippie fad that had once taken over the east side of St Kilda. This flirtation with the beautiful people left her briefly in hospital for heroin addiction, busted for softer drugs on a couple of occasions, and, from a passing relationship with someone Alice never knew, owner of a daughter.

Motherhood, it seems, had put May on the straight and narrow – mostly – in the way it sometimes can. She went back to live with Lao Lao, started studying for some kind of college qualification that would one day get her a job as a nurse and looked set to become what, in some quarters, is known as 'a good citizen'.

Alice went quiet.

'And then?' I prompted her.

'She still needed to work to pay for the classes. Jonny came back and said he had a business idea. A bar. Here. He wanted my mom to run it. He wanted lots of pretty women. It was going to be that kind of bar.'

'Meaning?'

'Meaning a bar with pretty women! My mom wasn't a hooker. I *know* that, Bierce.'

'I knew my wife was my wife, and never even

thought of looking at another man. I was wrong. Maybe . . .'

'No!' she yelled, so loud that the youth at the next table gasped in horror and stuffed a pair of white plugs – the kind I'd seen on the idiot walking across the road earlier that day – into his ears.

It takes a while to accept ideas like that. For me it had proved easy, in the end. I'd seen Kyle McKendrick now and knew that, while he was an ugly, lying, murderous lump of crime-slime, on that subject he was telling the truth. There'd been no reason not to.

'What happened?' I asked.

She closed her eyes. I thought there was the ghost of tears there.

'There's a bar four doors down. A real bar. I can't do this without a drink. Are you OK with that?'

I didn't touch my beer for fear of what it might do to me. Alice downed half her Bloody Mary, then let the glass rest on the counter. We were the only customers in there. I wasn't surprised. The place smelled of stale smoke, spilled beer and fryer fat. The solitary bartender lurked out back most of the time, switching seventies rock tracks on the hi-fi system: the Doobie Brothers, ZZ Top and some things I only half remembered. It felt like home.

'As far as I can tell,' she began, 'they only ran Sister Dragon for a few months. I went down and

185

looked at the liquor control records. There's not a lot there. The licence was taken out on 13 May 1985. It was revoked on the grounds that the business had gone bankrupt on 29 July.'

'Four days after your mom and my family got killed? They didn't wait long, did they?'

'I asked about that. The licensing people say they revoke licences the moment someone points out a business has gone under.'

I was about to ask a question.

'No. There's no record of who reported that,' she said, anticipating me.

'Who was the licensee? Jonny?'

'My mom.'

Alice caught something in my expression.

'Is that significant?'

'Was Jonny ever convicted of anything?'

'Not that I'm aware of.'

'So he could have been the licensee but preferred not to be. That means the money wasn't his, and he didn't want anyone to see where it really came from. If he made your mom the licensee, it would be one more obstacle to clear if people started to get nosy.'

I think she'd worked this out already.

'My mom had two drug convictions.'

'Then Jonny had important friends. I don't know what the rules are now – maybe a criminal record is a primary requirement to run a bar these days. But back then any conviction that could attract imprisonment ruled you out as a licensee.'

'Fine,' she snapped. 'My mom and my uncle were crooks. I have the message.'

'It's not exactly big time, Alice,' I pointed out. 'There are millions of people out there doing a little cheating on the side.'

'It doesn't matter anyway. What matters is what happened on 25 July. Your family died. My mom died. And my uncle disappeared for good. Dead, I imagine. It's hard to think of anything else.'

I would be lying if I said I wasn't expecting the last part.

'It's taken me five years to piece this much together,' Alice continued. 'Lao Lao never went near the place. I get the impression she hated the idea from the outset, which, if you knew her, meant it basically didn't exist. I couldn't find anything in the papers either.'

'Any stories about a fire? A fight or something?'

'No, Bierce! *I couldn't find anything in the papers about my mom and my uncle*. I know she got killed. I was there, hiding, when it happened. Lao Lao saw her body too. But then these people who called themselves detectives came round. They took my mom away. They cleaned the place up. And after that . . .'

She finished the rest of her Bloody Mary. I waved away the bartender when he came hovering in the hope she'd have another.

'After that?'

'Nothing. Not in the newspapers. Not from the

police. Not a word. There was no funeral. No mourning.'

This seemed incredible.

'What about the detectives who came round?'

'We never saw them again. When Lao Lao finally went to the police, they denied it had ever happened. They just said my mom and Jonny were logged under "missing persons". I imagine they still are.'

'I worked in the police department then. No one could have hidden something like that.'

'Dammit, Bierce, they did! In case you haven't got the message yet, my mom and Jonny were born in Hong Kong. They were illegals. A little less than human. It goes without saying, Lao Lao still *is* illegal, at least in her own head. Amnesties and stuff like that don't count with people of her generation. They always think someone might come along in the middle of the night and kick them out. That's why they daren't ask questions.'

She pointed a finger in my direction, as if I was the enemy.

'But not me,' she added. 'I was born here. There's not a thing they can do.'

I was starting to appreciate the enormity of what she was saying.

'They – whoever "they" happen to be – can kill you. I think we both know that much by now.'

'Maybe. But they have some weak points, don't they? When it comes to killing a nice white family, where the man just happens to be a cop, they couldn't cover that up.'

188

'No,' I agreed. 'They just unloaded it on me.'

'I wasn't taking a pop at you.'

'Thanks. Do you know what time of day they came round to kill your mom?'

She took a deep breath. It occurred to me that Alice Loong had never had this conversation with another human being in her life, which I found deeply interesting.

'I'm pretty sure it was about one-thirty in the afternoon. I used to go to some free kindergarten for immigrant kids so she could work. I was able to check that. It ran from ten in the morning through till eight in the evening weekdays for those who needed it. On Saturdays it closed at noon, so my mom would collect me and we'd be home for the afternoon. I remember being there a lot, so I guess my mom did need it. Lao Lao worked in a Chinese herbal store till five every day. She still does from time to time. So it must have been in the afternoon.'

She glanced at me, a little nervous.

'The court report said police came round to your house after someone – anonymously – reported screaming around seven p.m.'

'That would be correct,' I agreed. 'I was on duty till four. I had paperwork to do. I wouldn't have got home till six or so.'

'What do you remember?'

I took a look at the beer going flat in front of me. A little sip seemed in order.

'The last thing I'm sure of is leaving work. I think

189

I recall parking in the garage. I *think* – though this may just be imagination – I had logged the fact there was a strange car in Owl Creek. Something modern and shiny. Since we were the only house, that would have appeared a little strange. The industrial places nearby had their own lots. But I'm not sure about any of this. The trouble is, when you try so hard to remember things, events appear in your head anyway, and you're not sure what's real and what's not. The next certain thing I have is waking up in hospital surrounded by people I once thought were my friends looking at me as if I were some kind of monster.'

She reached over and put her hand on mine.

'You said that very easily,' Alice observed. 'It's good to talk about it, I guess.'

'It would be if I had more to talk about. You, on the other hand . . .'

I gritted my teeth. We both knew it had to be said.

'The likelihood,' I went on, 'is they came for your mom first, beat something about Miriam out of her, killed her, then came for us. I imagine you worked that out a long time ago.'

'They took three hours killing my mom, Bierce. She didn't give it up easily.'

'I wasn't blaming her. I'm of a disposition where you could beat something out of me with a feather. If I knew what McKendrick and these others were looking for I'd tell them right now, then catch the first flight out of town.'

Alice laughed.

'I'm sure you would.'

'No. Really. It's just that it's not an option. They wanted something out of your mom and beat her until she gave it them. After that they wanted something out of Miriam. And they didn't get it.'

'Your little boy . . .' Her green eyes watched me carefully. 'No mother would keep something inside her and lose her own child.'

I shook my head.

'She didn't have the choice. I went over the autopsy reports time and time again, trying to understand what had happened. It wasn't like your mom. They killed Miriam really quickly. Too quickly, I imagine. I think she was dead before the bastards even got around to offering the option. After that, Ricky was a witness. And I was an easy scapegoat.'

Something flashed in my memory. Something unpleasant I didn't want to think about, let alone face or discuss with Alice Loong.

'It wasn't hard to make it look as if she'd hit me in self-defence. In a crude way, at least. Some of the forensic stank to high heaven, but by the time I realized that I was past caring. What was there left to fight for?'

She was ordering up another drink anyway. This sudden rush of income brought half a smile out on the face of the bartender. I felt a deep, deep thirst coming on me, slaked down the small glass of beer and ordered a big one to follow.

* * *

191

When he'd gone, I turned to her and said, 'You need to think really hard, Alice. About what you heard when they came for your mom. I know it hurts, but that's the only contemporary evidence we have.'

She stared at my beer, picked up the glass, then leaned over the counter and poured three-quarters down the sink. The bartender watched in horror, but said nothing, nor did a thing to help a thirsty man.

'I've tried. Really I have. I just remember them going on and on about Sister Dragon.'

'They spoke Chinese?'

'No. Not a word. I thought . . .'

She shook her head. Alice's long hair moved gently around her shoulders. I think she was exhausted too.

'It just sounded to me as if they were asking, "Where is it? Where is it?" I thought they meant where was the place. It couldn't have been that, of course. If they'd come to see my mom, they *knew* where the bar was. So she had something of theirs. Or they thought she had. And I guess she must have told them it was round your house.'

She was still keeping something back.

'How do you know she knew Miriam? You said your grandma told you. Then you said she didn't talk about the bar at all. I don't get it.'

Alice frowned and looked guilty.

'I lied. It happens. Lao Lao's never really told me a thing. But I've lived with her from time to time, when I couldn't afford a room of my own. When she's out I've looked around. Even traditional old Chinese grannies keep photographs. I found some of my mom and Miriam and your boy, at least I assume it's Ricky. A bright sunny day outside a place that's got a fresh-painted sign. The two of them look as if they own it.'

One more link back to the past. Alice seemed to be a positive well of them.

'Do you still have the photos?'

'They're at Lao Lao's in the little room she keeps for me. She doesn't know I have them. Otherwise she'd go crazy.'

'I would like . . .' I began.

'I know. They're as much yours as they are mine. Maybe more. Bierce, we can't stay drinking in a bar all night long. We have to find somewhere to stay. There are cheap motels. What are we going to do?'

I wondered how far I could push it.

'You're absolutely sure that, whoever these people are, they've no way of tracing you.'

'You bet. Whoever that fake cop is, he thinks my name is Jenny Wong and I live out in a trailer park on the Peyton peninsula. Stupid I am not.'

'I never doubted that for a moment.' I paused, hoping. 'Lao Lao. Will she put us up for the night? I'll sleep on the floor. Wherever. I'd like to see those photos. Maybe if I talk to her . . .'

She was creased with laughter. I'd never seen her like this. Some small, stupid, doubtless doped-up part of me wished I had some decent flowers in my possession.

'You can't call her Lao Lao,' she said when she got her breath back. 'It means "maternal grand-mother". I can say that. You can't.'

'So what do I call her?'

'I don't know. I never took a man back there who stayed long enough for me to find out. How about "Grandma"? If you see knives come flying in your direction, you know it isn't working.'

One last thought struck me in the car, as we drove through deserted streets, past empty clanking trams, down into the tacky scented neon jungle in Eden that was Chinatown.

'I have a question,' I said as we crawled lazily past an empty tram headed for the terminus. 'How did you find me?'

'That beer was a bad idea, Bierce. I told you this already. One of my bargirl friends heard they were looking for someone.'

'No. I meant, how did you find me today? At Sheldon's.'

I must have been looking over-suspicious.

'Oh, that.'

She reached into her bag and took out some-thing using one hand. To me it looked like one of those odd little boxes people of this century stuck into the white cable plugs they liked to stuff in their ears. I was becoming familiar with them now. One day I'd need to find out what they were.

'It's easy. You can buy these tracker gizmos in drug stores. They're invisible unless you know. I stuck one on you when we were down the river, when I realized I didn't like the sneaky look on your face. After that I can track you anywhere. Today. Tomorrow. For the rest of time. You can never escape me now, Bierce. Never.'

I found myself brushing the grubby suit furiously, cursing this creepy modern world in all manner of flowery ways. I couldn't find the damn thing anywhere. I was about to get *very* mad indeed.

Then I noticed she'd started laughing again.

'Great joke,' I barked.

'You had it coming,' she answered with a shrug. 'Besides, I was making a point.'

'Thank you. So how?'

We were in a back street of Chinatown now. One of the places visiting white people wouldn't go too often, not because it was dangerous, but because the local restaurants hereabouts served things – chicken's feet, thousand-year-old eggs – nice white people stayed away from.

'Listen and learn,' she said, parking the car. 'I knew you had to be going to those industrial places because there was nothing else downriver, and scary people up. So I just walked round banging on a few doors, asking if anyone had seen a man who looked like an extra escaped from an episode of *The Rockford Files*. It didn't take long.'

'Oh. Why didn't I think of that?'

'You would have,' she said. 'In the end.'

It was hard to tell how old Alice Loong's Lao Lao truly was. She was a small, rotund woman, with tiny gleaming eyes that shone out of a face the shape of a shrunken melon. Her black hair looked as if it had been copied from Davy Jones of the Monkees. Home was the top of a three-storey apartment block that had a drunken lean on it and some kind of all-night traditional drug emporium, all stinking dried snakes and pots of rhino horn, on the ground floor.

When we arrived she was wearing a dark, old floral dress and, for no good reason I could see, since the place was frankly a little grubby, a bright pink polyester cleaner's apron.

'Very kind of you, Grandma,' I said, extending a hand in which I had one remaining faded rose bloom. 'I – *we* – appreciate it greatly.'

She looked me up and down and said, in a highly accented voice that sounded as if it was being filtered through several packs of hard-core tobacco, 'I not your freakin' grandma, jerk.'

Then, to Alice . . .

'How come all your men are jerks? You can't find no real men out there or wha'?'

One more brutally appraising look flew in my direction.

'This one *old* jerk too. Jeessuss . . .'

I decided the kiss on the cheek and the general

chit-chat about the lousy state of the world could maybe come later. I was so tired I could barely keep my eyes open, so I made a few noncommittal noises, then asked to be shown somewhere to sleep.

The room was a shoebox littered with old junk and cases of Chinese books and tiny paintings. There was a rickety double bed and a threadbare rug by the side of it.

Alice followed me in and closed the door.

'Can I see the photos?' I asked, remembering.

'You don't like waiting for anything, do you?'

'I've been waiting twenty-three years.'

She swore mildly, then fetched an envelope from one of the plastic storage boxes.

'In fact,' I said, 'at heart I am a very patient man.'

She kept quiet. That was nice of her.

There were six pictures in all. Miriam and May Loong were in each, standing outside Sister Dragon, with a fresh-painted sign in the background. Alice's mother had no make-up on and stood there, smiling at the camera, looking beautiful, a plain, easy, elegant beauty that didn't need any artificial help on its way out into the light of day. Miriam was beautiful too, but then I knew that all along. The two of them were wearing the same kind of clothes. Bright, shiny silk cheongsams with colourful flowing serpents embroidered all over them. May Loong's was purple. Miriam's was pure white. The dresses were slashed way up the

197

leg. In a couple of the photos, the two women were making a point of showing off some thigh. Ricky was in one of these, looking a little baffled. I didn't blame him. I'd never seen a piece of clothing like this anywhere in the house. Miriam never bought anything Chinese, not that I knew of. Nor, or so I thought, was she the type to flaunt herself like this, even for some unknown cameraman, who had to be Jonny Loong, I guessed, and that made me feel distinctly uncomfortable.

I sat cross-legged on the rug and stared at the photos for so long I lost track of time. Alice came back in some kind of nightgown and brought me some long, navy-blue cotton pyjamas, a large fluffy towel, a disposable razor and a tiny throwaway toothpaste set. Then, after some prompting, I put down the pictures and she showed me the bathroom, where I did what I was supposed to, before coming back to look at the photos again.

Lao Lao was downstairs listening to Cantonese TV at full volume.

'I'm OK sleeping on the floor,' I said. 'It's good for my back.'

'Bierce,' she said softly from the bed.

'No, Alice. Please. I'm tired and confused and I feel like crap, what with beer and God knows what else running through me. I just want to close my eyes and disappear somewhere.'

Martin the Medic's words came back then, ringing in my ears.

For in that sleep of death what dreams may come?

Kyle McKendrick surely never employed anyone with a passing knowledge of Shakespeare. A part of me understood that already, implicitly. I'd been improvising when I told Alice there were two parties involved in this particular game, but the more I thought about it, the more convinced I became. There was Kyle's side and there was the side where Stape, good old generous Stape, now lived.

Also, there was a third. The cops. Who surely, even in this new world, must have taken an interest in a convicted killer who appeared to have slipped jail illicitly.

I looked up from the floor at Alice, young, damaged Alice, whose position on most things seemed to be set in sands that shifted beneath her constantly, in ways she couldn't comprehend.

I wondered which of the three, if any, she worked for.

'For pity's sake,' she said to me crossly. 'This is not last night. I know I don't need to go there again. But we need a good night's sleep. Who the hell knows what we have to deal with tomorrow?'

'Bierce?' she whispered again after a while.

'Oh, lord,' I moaned. 'What was that you said about sleeping?'

'I just want someone to hold me, that's all. I don't see anyone else around.'

'That's flattering.'

I put one arm around her and left it at that. She

moved her head closer to me. That was all. We lay there chastely, because it really wasn't about anything else. I can say that in all honesty. Alice Loong, twenty-six, tough, but not as tough as she thought, wanted some simple physical comfort.

Her hair had the wonderful fresh smell a woman's hair has, something I'd completely forgotten. After a while I could sense something else that had submerged in my memory too: the dampness leaking from her eyes on to my neck.

She wriggled into my chest more closely. I shut my eyes tight and tried to think of what the night was like in Gwinett; the howls down the corridor, the rattle of plates on bars, the sound of men getting beaten up.

'Bierce,' she whispered again, so close into me I found it very difficult to stop my arms curling round her slender, tense shoulders, hugging her tightly.

Somehow – I swear I have no idea how this occurred – the ancient springs of the bed creaked.

In an instant, Lao Lao was hammering on the door with her tight little fist, yelling, 'No making out in there. *No making out, you hear?*'

We lay there, unable to speak, giggling like two schoolkids caught necking on the veranda.

Then, unable to stop myself, I kissed Alice Loong on the forehead, just once, for no more than one and three-eighths of a second, or possibly less.

She was as surprised as me, I think. Not that she protested.

Her skin tasted sweet and soft against my lips.

The one small act, and the way she didn't flinch from it, made me feel as if someone had dragged me out of the grave and breathed new life back into my old, tired lungs. Which maybe wasn't far from the truth.

My head swelled with a mix of competing emotions: guilt and pride, certainty and confusion, hope and, behind it, always, the distant siren wail of the onset of despair.

It couldn't stay like this. I knew it. Nothing could be this simple.

THURSDAY

When I woke the sunlight was streaming in through the windows, a little too yellow and faded for my liking, the kind of sun you got at the dying of the day, not its birth. Turtle doves were cooing noisily on the roof. Outside, the racket of the traffic had an afternoon cadence to it, the kind of slow-burn anger people got on the way home.

I looked at the clock by the side of the bed. It was four p.m. and I was alone. Drenched in dope, and just a touch of alcohol, I must have slept for the best part of seventeen hours.

I was still in my fresh cotton pyjamas, for which I was grateful. From downstairs came the loud bark of the TV, an English channel, one which, to my dismay, appeared to be mentioning my name.

Oh, I thought, and walked down the rickety stairs.

The two of them sat in front of the little TV, which was perched on some silver box I failed to recognize. Alice looked horrified. Lao Lao clucked like an old, incomprehensible hen.

The newscast was coming to an end.

'Did I hear that right?' I asked.

Lao Lao threw me a dirty look, picked up a remote control and, to my astonishment, wound back a live TV programme just as if it was on tape.

'How the hell did you do that?' I asked, amazed.

She shook her head in disgust.

In a couple of seconds she'd reached the start of the bulletin. It was the local station. Their lead story was about the execution that morning of a former city police officer who'd been on death row for nearly twenty-three years.

My lawyer ever since, the lovely Susanna Aurelio, was there on camera, live from outside some place I had never heard of, 'the McKendrick County Correctional Facility', tears in her eyes, shaking her head, saying something about how cruel and unnecessary capital punishment truly was.

'But Officer Bierce killed his wife and five-year-old son,' the interviewer objected. 'Doesn't a man like that *deserve* to die?'

Susanna dabbed at her face with a tissue. She looked as if she'd come straight from the opera: all silk and pearls and oncue sobbing.

'Many may believe so, Bruce. But I watched that man go to his death today. I listened to the confession he finally made, and the true and heartfelt remorse he showed at the very end. Had you witnessed those final moments . . .'

'Sure,' the interviewer interrupted with a sneer.

'And there we must leave it. Now, on A1A this morning . . .'

Lao Lao picked up another remote – she seemed to be collecting them – and hit the off button.

'This some kind of record,' she said, looking at me and shaking her head. 'Not only new guy a jerk who's an old jerk. Now he's *dead* old jerk too.'

Being beyond the realm of the living isn't all bad news. For one thing I knew the cops – the *real* cops, like the Tic Twins and my blond-haired friend from the grocery store – definitely wouldn't be scouring the streets, trying to hunt me down. The only people I had to worry about now were the ones I thought of as McKendrick's people and Stape's. The former were, it seemed pretty clear to me, murderous. The latter had, unless I was much mistaken, freed me from jail illegally in the hope either of jogging my memory about the events of twenty-three years ago or pinning some new crime to my chest.

It didn't seem entirely impossible that I could, with no support except that of Alice – for what it might turn out to be worth – no information or intelligence, real weapons or other firepower, defeat the two of them. I could blow the twenty thousand in my possession on an Uzi or some such toy and try to do a kind of real-life Clint Eastwood impersonation. But it didn't seem right. It wasn't me. What's more, I was beginning to think I was getting a feel for this new century.

People weren't that different really. They were just a little more miserable and fearful. And they relied on inanimate objects and nebulous procedures to tell them how to act. When I was a cop and heard someone had done some bad thing, it was easy. All I did was ride round to their home, knock on the door, stare them in the face and ask, straight out loud . . . *Well?*

I'd talked this through with Alice already. What she said confirmed my initial impressions. In this world the first thing anyone did before tackling *anything* was turn on the computer, hunt around for the right instructions, then try to follow them to the letter. Don't think, just do as you're supposed to. As your peers expect. That, to me, seemed to be motto of the century, and if I was in luck, then perhaps it left a little space into which a caveman could throw the odd spanner. Predictable people have predictable weaknesses, if you can find them.

There was one other excellent piece of news, too. When Alice told me she thought no one had any idea who she was, it seemed clear she'd been right. Had Stape or McKendrick possessed the merest hint of Lao Lao's address, they'd have been round while I was sleeping, all guns and noise, with badness to follow. Even the postman hadn't come to call, as Lao Lao mentioned several times in her long litany of moans to her granddaughter, spelled out so loud I could hear them from every room of the apartment.

The truth was this. In Grandma Loong's cramped third-floor apartment, breathing in the smell of dead lizard and God knows what else from the pharmaceutical store below, we were, for the time being, safe.

Or, perhaps, where Alice, and anyone behind her, wanted us to be. I had racked my brain trying to work out whether I trusted her or not. The plain answer was: not. Every piece of her story had leaked out so slowly, requiring such careful extraction, I just knew there had to be more. But was this simple reticence on her part, with some good reason I couldn't guess? Or was there a bigger secret in Alice's life? I couldn't get away from the fact that she was in my house in Owl Creek that night, looking at home, and ready for anything, just a few hours after they let me out of Gwinett. Or more accurately, the McKendrick County Correctional Facility, whatever and wherever that was.

My old dad always said it wasn't worth worrying about problems you couldn't solve. He was right. I should have listened to him more. Over the past three days I'd been shot at, mock-executed and now declared officially dead on public TV. A man becomes sanguine about such things after a while. Alice had saved me from the needle of Dr Rimless. She'd done her best to get me away from the men I assumed to be McKendrick's in Owl Creek too. Whatever other secrets lay inside her smart young head, I didn't want to leave her and miserable old Lao Lao exposed when the smoke cleared.

And that would still require some work.

They watched me slink off to the bedroom, ostensibly to think, after I watched the newscast one more time through Lao Lao's magic silver box. While I was sleeping Alice had gone out and bought me some clothes: cotton pants, a couple of shirts, all the other practical stuff a woman would think about, knowing it would pass me by completely. I dressed, looked at myself in the mirror, and was surprised by what I saw: a middle-aged man, not fat, not thin, not remarkable in any way, dressed in the kind of clothes that seemed to go down well in the twenty-first century. I was anonymous, which was, as Alice, smart, lovely Alice, had quickly realized, definitely look of the month for me.

After a while I went downstairs and joined her. It was now gone six in the evening. A wonderful smell of Chinese food was coming from the minuscule kitchen squeezed next to the bathroom. Lao Lao was working away in there with a wok. Eventually she came over with two plates of noodles and meat and vegetables, dumped them in front of us and said, 'Even dead people gotta eat. I work downstairs for a while now. Old Fred need me.'

I tried the food and, for a moment, couldn't say a word. It contained all the flavours and colours that had been methodically removed from everything that ever went on a plate in jail. I wanted to put it in a box and carry it around, ready to sniff when I started to feel sorry for myself again. For a moment, I thought this new century couldn't be all bad.

When I got my voice back, I said, 'People. She called me "people". Not jerk. I'm coming up in the world.'

Alice shook her head. She'd gone out and got her hair cut that afternoon, the way women did at such idle, uneventful points in their lives.

Or – and I hated myself for this suspicious, conniving thought – when you'd fixed some secretive meeting with the boss.

'She's not so bad. She kept me alive when no one else was interested.'

'How the hell could that have happened? You're smart. You're beautiful.'

'Bierce . . .'

'No. I mean it.'

This had to be asked. She was in a fresh white cotton shirt and pale fawn slacks. Almost business gear. Looking at her, she could have been a tour guide or an office receptionist. Talking to her, you might have upped that to some kind of postgrad student still working her way through college. Her hair was so clean and shiny, and her face, long and intriguing, in an imperfect, half-Chinese way, was definitely the most interesting I'd seen in a long time. Something had happened to Alice Loong and I needed to know what it was.

'Where did your dad come from?' I asked.

'A boat.'

The hard stare told me that wasn't going any further.

I pointed to the small scar above her left eye.

'And that?'

'That what?'

'The scar.'

'Oh. The scar. Fight. A man, naturally. I wouldn't lower myself to fighting other women.'

I waited for more. When she saw I wasn't leaving the subject she went upstairs to the bedroom and came back down with another photograph. This one was more recent. I turned it over and it even had the date printed on the back: five years ago, almost to the day. It was just a kid by the beach, near the larger Greenpoint marina, I think. The ocean was a lovely shade of blue. The same colour as her hair, though I wouldn't have said that was lovely. This was Alice Loong too, I realized. A different Alice, though perhaps one who still lived inside the same skin somewhere.

She was as thin as a rake, bones sticking out from inside a ragged T-shirt and torn jeans. There was hardware everywhere: in her eyebrows, her ears, her nose. Worst of all, she was staring at the camera wearing an expression of intense hatred. For herself, naturally. It couldn't have been anything else.

I put the photo face down on the table.

'The past is done with. I'm surprised you didn't come out of that period with more tattoos.'

'Hated needles,' she said. 'I just got the one.'

'I know,' I pointed out.

'Oh.'

I guess she'd forgotten how she'd briefly stood naked in the old bedroom in Owl Creek that first night. It seemed a long time to me too.

'So what changed?'

'I got older. Got sick of waking up feeling ill and cold and poor. The poor part hasn't changed much. But at least I can function, even if it's only working behind a bar in a miniskirt.'

'You've done a little more than that of late.'

She grinned and scooped up some noodles with her chopsticks, in that expert way some people have. Lao Lao had thoughtfully provided me with a fork and spoon.

'Yes, Bierce, I have. It was my grandma too. She got to me in the end. I think she knew she always would. It didn't matter how bad things were. How lousy the company. How stupid, selfish and offensive the behaviour. She always came along to pick me up from the hospital, bail me out, whatever.'

'She's your family now. And you're hers. She doesn't have a choice.'

'But she does! That's the point. She could have abandoned me.'

There was a flicker of anger in those green eyes. 'You did.'

'No,' I said carefully. 'I left you behind. I thought it was in your best interests.'

'Do you think that now?'

'I don't know,' I answered honestly. 'I'm not sure there's a choice. You need to understand what happened to your mom. Just as I need to find out what the hell went wrong between Miriam and me.'

'Thank you.'

'You're welcome. Besides, if this doesn't work out, I know I'll be walking down some street in Chinatown five years hence and you'll be standing across the road, slumped up against the wall, with blue hair and ironwork in your face again. That I could not stand.'

She nodded.

'I'll try my best. What do we do now?'

The big question.

'I would,' I confessed, 'really love to spend some quality time with my old friend Stapleton. The guy who roped you into all this. I don't imagine he left a phone number or address or something.'

She shook her head.

'How were you going to get paid the rest of your money?'

'He said he'd drop it round the bar where my friends worked. It was all cash. I was supposed to trust him.'

All these answers came so glibly. I wish she could have hesitated, just a little.

'And you talked to him at the bar? Nowhere else?'

'That's right. He didn't feel like a cop. I think my antennae are pretty good on that front. It comes from growing up around here. He didn't feel like a cop at all.'

We'd stopped working as partners some eighteen months before Miriam, and Ricky were killed. He'd disappeared from the police department after that. I assumed this was because he'd moved to another precinct, or perhaps joined one of the fast-car and Ray-Ban squadrons people kept putting together trying to tackle organized crime. A certain type of cop couldn't watch enough *Miami Vice* episodes around then.

'OK. I'll have to find him some other way. But we do need to speak to someone. This isn't going to unravel from us sitting around talking or punching computer keyboards.'

'Who?' she asked, shrugging.

There was, I knew, only one answer.

'I think,' I said, 'it's time I saw my lawyer.'

The last time I saw Pelican Bay it was a small, protected cove that sat between the southern end of the Greenpoint rich persons' neighbourhood and the ragged, unspoilt coastline that ran down to the De Soto bridge. We used to take Ricky there to play and watch the birds and seals. I believe it may be where his penguin obsession started. There was one parking lot, restricted to no more than a hundred and fifty vehicles, a warden's lodge where you could pick up free brochures that described the wildlife, and a single coffee and ice-cream stall, open summer weekends only.

Susanna Aurelio lived here with husband number five, in something called Ocean Vista Gardens. It was getting dark by the time Alice drove the Volvo down the hill, on a brand-new private highway, towards the shoreline. I could see from the twinkling zigzags below that things had changed somewhat. There were hundreds of them: street lights and home illumination, all in that irregular pattern that spoke of money. When they build for the poor and the lower-income classes streets run in straight lines, homes look much like one another. The affluent need to convince themselves they're different from the rest. Even their equally rich neighbours. So I'd no idea where to begin, or where the address we'd found for Susanna, from some law directory Alice had picked up through her computer, was located.

'Swing by the beach first, will you?' I asked. 'I haven't walked on sand in a while.'

'How romantic. Unfortunately that won't be possible. This is private now. I told you.'

She pointed up ahead. We were approaching a large, half-circle iron gatehouse with what looked like a prison warden's cabin by the side of it. There were camera lenses poking in every direction, naturally, and a man in a dark uniform already eyeing us, beginning to get out of his booth. Beyond the rungs I could see wisps of moonlight running across the dark ocean waves and the sheen of the long, flat, perfect sand we used to sit on, breathing in the salt sea smell.

'What the hell is this?' I demanded, feeling more than a little angry.

'It's called a gated community. This is how rich people live today. Actually, it's how anyone with any money lives, if they can afford it.'

'Behind bars, you mean?'

'That pretty much sums it up.'

'The beach. I want to walk on the beach.'

'Well, you can't. That's part of the community. They own it.'

No one can own a beach, I thought. That was just obscene.

I'd imagined I would just walk down Susanna's street, check the house names – hers was called Bellagio – ring the bell and wait for the maid to answer. Some hope. The guy in the uniform was out walking towards us already. He had a truncheon. And a handgun. If I squinted hard I could have mistaken him for a cop, which was, I guess, the point.

'This is private security, right?'

She nodded.

'They get to walk around with weapons wherever they feel like?'

'They get whatever they want. It's just ordinary people who don't get guns. The rich want protection.'

'Don't we all?' I asked idly. 'No. That was rhetorical. No need to answer. I'll handle this. It's best no one saw you. Go drive around. Take in a movie or something. I'll call when I'm done.'

She smiled at me in that slightly condescending way I was beginning to recognize.

'How exactly?'

'Er . . .'

Alice reached into her bag and pulled out a little plastic gadget which I took to be some kind of phone. A ladies' model, since it was that same horrendous shade of pink as the one I saw her use earlier, only somewhat bigger.

'Put that in your pocket,' she ordered. 'If I don't hear in two hours, I'll call. If you need me, just hold down the 1 button till it rings out. It'll call me.'

I said thanks or something and got out quickly. The fake cop was getting near and I really didn't want him to see Alice for a moment. She was gone, not too quickly, not too slowly either.

I stood there, smiled at him and said, 'I'm hoping to see Susanna Aurelio, sir. Would you happen to know if she's at home?'

He was a surly-looking sort in his mid-twenties, clearly pleased to get both uniform and a gun all in the same job. He had the same build as McKendrick's heavy: fat running to muscle.

'She expecting you?'

'Absolutely not. This is a surprise visit. I'm a cousin from out east. We were at school together. Haven't seen each other in five years. My flight got overbooked while I was passing through. So I thought . . .'

I smiled, which was a waste of effort.

218

'Is her husband at home too?' I asked.

He turned back to the gatehouse, expecting me to follow him I guess.

'You can call her on the video phone,' he said, not answering my question. 'If she says you're in, you're in. If she doesn't know you from Adam, you and me are going to have an interesting conversation.'

Susanna came into view, looking as preciously gorgeous as ever. The light came on and lit up my face.

I yelled, 'Surprise!'

She started screaming.

The security guy gave me a cold, hard stare.

'I told you this would be a hoot,' I said, smiling.

It took a couple of minutes. I had to say a few things to convince her I wasn't a ghost. Though quite why a ghost would want to use a video phone . . .

Finally, the gate buzzed. He pushed it open for me. I walked into Ocean Vista Gardens and followed his directions for Bellagio.

It was nice in there. Leafy and smelling of oleander and pool ozone drifting up from the shining blue rectangular mirrors I could see floating around in the back gardens of the vast low villas, each with yet another iron gate in front, that someone had built on my one-time pelican-viewing station.

Mr Security was phoning someone from inside the booth. I couldn't miss that fact.

★   ★   ★

She greeted me at the door, looking as if she'd dressed for the occasion: long silk blue evening dress, low-cut, tight around her still-perfect figure, and a double pearl necklace around her swan-like, unwrinkled throat. I first knew Susanna Aurelio when she was a twenty-one-year-old law student hanging around the city courts, looking for some attorney, any attorney, to 'take her under their wing'.

She was beautiful then, with gentle, innocent, 'who, me?' movie-star looks, short, glossy red hair that bordered on chestnut, perfect white skin, bright, seemingly sensitive eyes that always made you feel you were the only person that mattered in the world. She also possessed a mind so sharp you could open evidence packets with it. Which happened, from time to time, since the wings the lovely Susanna got taken under were many and varied. The police department gossip was that she had the scalps of judges, fellow attorneys, city and state politicians, plus a couple of movie stars and well-known rock guitarists hanging from her bed head by the time she was twenty-five.

Not mine, I hasten to add, though she had tried. This occasion did give me an insight into the Aurelio love technique. I got lured back to her little bachelor-girl apartment on a work pretence. It had all, or mostly, been about me giving her an illicit look at some evidence due to be introduced into court about a young teenage kid she was representing on a dope charge. I let her see it anyway. The kid was innocent and, I suspected, getting fitted up by someone in narcotics because they didn't like his face and background, neither of which came with the word 'white' stamped upon them. She didn't need me in her bed to get that and I told her so, and couldn't work out whether she was happy or deeply offended that she'd finally found a man who turned her down.

Not that I cared. That was Susanna all over. Lots of the cases she took on were good, principled *pro bono* stuff, often on behalf of poor, underprivileged people who may well have been innocent. That didn't stop her pulling every last underhand trick she could imagine in order to get her way. The perfect case for Susanna – the young Susanna anyway – involved social injustice and a pile of suspect evidence that could miraculously be made to go away by some smart wheeler-dealing in the judge's rooms and the simple and judicious application of copious quantities of sex, exploits that were, on occasion, capable of being performed simultaneously.

On pillars such as these are legal careers made.

'Oh, Bierce,' she whispered, covering my face and neck with kisses. 'What the hell's happened here? Come in, come in . . .'

The house could have been described as a 'mansion', but only if it had been made a little smaller. There were two circular staircases winding up on each side of a massive entrance hall, and rooms going off in all directions, doors open so you could see into each.

The floor was shining Mediterranean terracotta or something. Paintings and masks and bits of porcelain hung on the walls. Lots of little tables, all in very dark, almost black wood, stood around, bearing vases full of vast bouquets of roses and lilies. At the end was a long internal window that let visitors see across the grown-up amusement park outside – pool, tennis court, statuary and the rest – straight down to the beach. *My* beach, once upon a time.

I did not feel at home.

'Where's your husband, Susanna?' I asked.

'Out on some Caribbean cruise banging his junior partner,' she said. Her hair had lost none of its fire, maybe through a little cheating. It still hung around her head loose to her slender neck. In truth, as I stared at that oh-so-innocent face I was amazed to realize she'd hardly changed in all the time I knew her, apart, that is, from the ever more expensive wardrobe. 'It's just fine by me. I sent the servants out for the night too when I saw it was you. Seemed best.'

'Dead people don't need servants.'

She was gazing into my eyes with so much love and affection I felt a little queasy.

'Oh, baby,' she moaned, soft hands back on my cheeks again. 'I dreamed of getting you out of that horrible, stinking place all those years. And I never did. And now you're here. What the hell happened, Bierce? Here . . .'

She took my arm and led me through to some kind of living room. There was a tiger print sofa that could have slept a family of six and a flat, thin TV the size of a private cinema screen.

'A drink,' she said.

'I'm fine.'

'Who's talking about you?'

'Maybe a beer.'

She went in the kitchen and came back with two glasses. Mine contained something fancy and foreign. Hers smelled of vodka which had made the passing acquaintance of a thimble of tonic along the way.

I toasted her. She pulled me to the sofa and sat down in the next cushion, very close.

'*Salute*,' she murmured. 'I never said that to a ghost before.'

'You still haven't. It's me, Susanna. Really.'

'I have *eyes*,' she said in the low yet very distinct voice she had.

'And yet . . . I have to ask.' This was a difficult and unusual question to phrase.

'Ask away.'

'I caught up with the TV this afternoon. You seeing me dead and all.'

Susanna Aurelio took a large sip, put her drink on the table and looked at me.

This was more than a little unnerving, because

I felt it was the same look I'd had all those years ago, in her tiny Eden apartment, when she was starting out, hunting for sneak peeks of evidence the easiest way she knew.

'Oh,' she said, almost forgetfully. '*That*.'

'First things first,' I began. 'When I saw you on TV you were standing outside something called the McKendrick County Correctional Facility. Where the hell is that and what does it have to do with me?'

'Are you kidding? McKendrick is where you've been these last eighteen months.'

A little bubble burst in my mind. It was utterly empty.

'I think I would have known that, Susanna.'

'They moved you there from Gwinett. They heard someone was going to kill you. They didn't like cops in jail, I guess.'

No, no, no, screamed some small voice inside my head.

'I went into solitary in Gwinett years ago,' I insisted. 'I stayed there, all the way into the execution wing. No one was going to kill me. They'd have been robbing the state of that privilege, and the state wouldn't have liked that.'

She shrugged.

'I'm a lawyer. Not a penal expert. That's what they said. You didn't object.'

'I didn't know! For God's sake . . .'

The words wouldn't come quite right. She waited for me to calm down.

'They had you sedated in Gwinett. It was for your own good. I went along with that, Bierce. You were terribly distraught, for years. People feared for your sanity.'

'I was an innocent man in jail for murdering my own wife and kid, and about to die for it. What do you expect of a morning? A rousing chorus from *Oklahoma?*'

Her eyes went watery. She stared at her drink. In spite of everything, I felt like a jerk.

'I'm sorry,' I said. It was hard to believe Susanna was pushing fifty. She had the appearance of someone fifteen years younger. But it was more than that. She had the mannerisms and the easy charm to match too. 'It's been a hard couple of days.'

She sighed and placed her hands in my lap. A cloud of something expensive filled the air.

'What do you think it's been like for me? I know you didn't kill them. I couldn't convince anyone. You didn't help. Not with your high and mighty, "If I can't remember, I *can't* remember" act. All the same, I always thought I'd get you out of there in the end.'

There were so many avenues available for further exploration in that conversation. I just leaned forward, took another mouthful of foreign beer and said, 'I know you did. And I appreciate everything. Now tell me why you think you saw me die this morning, please. Because for the life of me – if you'll excuse the expression – I swear I missed it.'

★   ★   ★

The story was this. At eleven the previous night she'd been called at home by the correction facility's legal representative, who'd told her that every last avenue of appeal had been exhausted and I was, without a shadow of doubt, going under the death needle at eight the following morning. This was, of course, some twenty-odd hours after I'd actually been driven out of the place, not that I was going to complicate matters for my faithful, gorgeous attorney at this stage.

Susanna had, naturally, spent most of the night phoning around every last judge and contact she knew – something that had happened a dozen times before, and ended in stays of execution for an ever-diminishing and more inexplicable array of legal niceties. This time round no one was playing. Dead meant dead, and there wasn't a single string she could pull, not one last remaining past lover she could twist around her slender fingers.

So at seven in the morning she'd driven out to Kyle McKendrick's private penitentiary-cum-murder farm, hoping there might be some last stunt she could try on the spot, such as a plea of insanity or – this seemed so bizarre I could only believe her – by claiming I was suffering from some physical ailment that made it improper for me to be executed until I got better. She was always a resourceful woman. The way she told it, I began to believe she felt some genuine remorse at my impending end, though how much was grief and how much fury at losing a case was hard to tell.

She stopped. Her drink was empty. She went to the kitchen and came back with fresh ones for both of us. I accepted, on the grounds it was mine by right; it's not every day a man hears a description of his own death.

'And then?' I prodded her.

'I blew a tyre on the freeway. Would you believe it? That thing cost more than a quarter of a million. Supposedly the best six-litre sports coupé to come out of Italy. Then that.'

'You were late for my execution, Susanna? How could you?'

'I tried and I tried. Hell, Bierce, they shouldn't have gone ahead with the execution without me there.'

'Maybe they thought you were trying to stall them.'

She patted my knees and gave me a brisk, businesslike peck on the cheek.

'You bright, bright baby. That's exactly what that bastard Johansson said to me when I finally got there. Smug as hell with that "You're too late for this one, bitch" look on his ugly face.'

'Johansson?'

'He was the governor. You met him. I promise you met him. He was there when I came to see you. Eleven months ago, I think it was.'

'In this McKendrick place?'

'Yes! We had to talk. About the money. A couple

of decades of representation now. It doesn't come cheap.'

I shook my head.

'I don't remember any of this.'

'It happened,' she insisted. 'You signed the papers. They were witnessed.'

'What papers? No. *No*. Later. I saw you on the TV, Susanna. You stood there telling them how I went out all brave and that.'

She nodded.

'I did.'

'You went in front of the camera and made all that up?' I asked, and tried not to let my voice squeak too much.

'What the hell did you expect me to say?' she snapped. 'I missed my own client's execution because I got a flat on the way? Be realistic, Bierce. As far as I knew you were dead. I have a career.'

This was, I now recalled, the real Susanna.

'But you didn't ask to see a body?'

She looked at me as if I were stupid.

'Why the hell would I want to see a dead body? I'm a lawyer. I represent people who are still breathing. You think I'm some ambulance-chasing ghoul trying to squeeze money out of a corpse or something?'

She looked around the room.

'Does this look like what ghoul work gets you?'

She had her standards, you see. They just weren't those of normal, civilized human beings.

'You said,' I pointed out, 'that I felt remorse.'

She put down her drink at that, took my hands in hers and stared deep into my eyes.

'Bierce,' she murmured, working on the huskiness so that I got sexy on top of sincerity. 'I know you didn't murder Miriam and your boy. But the world out there made up its mind on that subject years ago, and you didn't win. I agonized over what I was supposed to tell those TV people. That you went screaming your innocence all the way into the killing room? No. I wouldn't have been doing you any justice that way. What I said, I said out of respect for you. If people thought you showed remorse at the end, then some of them would think, well, maybe he wasn't all bad. If I said you just kept screaming "not guilty", they'd put you down for an asshole. Which would you prefer?'

'The truth,' I said straight away.

She laughed, then went back to the drink again.

'The truth being what?' my beautiful lawyer asked, dispatching a whiff of raw, expensive vodka in my direction.

She had a point. I wanted to punch holes in her story. It deserved that kind of treatment. But for the life of me I couldn't work out how.

'Your turn,' she said.

I told her, as much as I wanted, and watched her eyes widen all the while.

The funny thing was that, when I was done, she didn't ask a single question. That was left to me.

'The man I saw on the way out of Gwinett . . . I

mean McKendrick, or wherever it was. His name was Stapleton. Do you know him?'

'Stapleton, Stapleton, Stapleton . . . Do you want a sandwich or something? Damn, I shouldn't have sent those servants away.'

'Stapleton. Also known as Stape. He was a detective alongside me for a while. Then he went somewhere else. The secret people, maybe.'

She shook her head.

'It may ring a bell. I don't know. You say he put some money into your bank account?'

'Just a little. Four hundred and sixty thousand. It ought to be there now.'

'I can check if you want,' she said, as if this was the easiest thing in the world.

'How the hell can you check my bank account?'

She actually looked sorry for me at that moment.

'Oh, my. They really did pump you full of stuff in there, didn't they? I've had power of attorney over all your accounts, all your assets, for a long, long time. I can look up your account online. To all intents and purposes, I own Owl Creek. It's held in escrow against your legal bills. Why else do you think the mortgage people didn't foreclose? They'd have been coming up against me if they did.'

'My house?'

'We discussed this. That last time I saw you in McKendrick. You signed the papers.'

'I signed away my house?'

'Don't worry, Bierce. I'm not taking anything

away from you. I couldn't be that cruel. You're alive. That's what counts.'

'My *house* . . .' I said again.

'Let's find out about this money first,' she interrupted. 'Then I can look up some private places you might find this Stapleton individual. Would you like that?'

I answered, truthfully, that I'd like that very much indeed.

'In that case, you've got to come upstairs. I work in my bedroom. It's the one place I can guarantee my asshole husband will never disturb me.'

I could have fitted most of the ground floor of Owl Creek into Susanna Aurelio's bedroom and left space for a Jacuzzi or three. The place had a huge bed, with its slate sheets, opened up, ready for use. A couple of sofas. A grand fireplace with what looked like a fake Adam but real marble surround, and above it the statutory painting of the owner, looking gorgeous and, naturally, naked. Then a small kitchen off, and a door that led to a bathroom that appeared to be stocked with porcelain and shiny marble fittings that could have been stolen from an Arab prince's palace.

I got a good view of the veranda too. I walked up and opened the doors. There was a terrace with several tables, more chairs, a large telescope on a pedestal, then a gentle line of steps down to the garden, the pool, lit by underwater lights, and,

231

at the end, the silver ribbon of beach and the sea, moving with a solitary grace under the moonlight.

'This is what I call the mistress bedroom,' Susanna announced with no small measure of pride.

'You mean the master's is smaller?'

'Just. And pretty soon I'm going to own that too. When Frank gets back from the islands I serve papers. After which . . .'

She came and stood by me, slipping the palm of her hand into the small of my back for one brief moment.

'. . . I am available.'

'Quite,' I said, and moved away. 'Now about this guy Stapleton.'

Susanna's face fell and, just for a second or two, she looked her age. A woman like her wasn't used to getting knocked back and I'd done it twice. She walked over to the long, gleaming desk just a little way from the bed and flicked a switch on the stretched-aluminium box there, pulling up the lid to reveal a screen.

She pushed a button on the keyboard and the panel became alive. It was covered in photos, mostly of Susanna. At the podium, speaking. On TV. Handing out prizes of some kind. It was all a long way from that little apartment where she'd tried to seduce me for a packet of papers from the prosecution files.

'First name?' she asked.

'Radley,' I said. 'Or maybe it was Ridley. It was a long time ago.'

'Never mind. Neither's common. Which is good.'

She typed something, very quickly.

'I have a Radley Stapleton who's a wireless op in the navy. Oh. No good. He's serving abroad.'

'You what?' I asked.

'Bear with me, Bierce. I'm not done yet.'

She typed again.

'Correction. I am. I can't find a single Ridley Stapleton in Google. Which means he doesn't exist.'

'Google? This is this special place you mentioned?'

'No. But generally speaking the special place just has a little more of what Google has. I can try.'

I watched her, feeling like a Neanderthal who'd just walked in on Einstein.

'Nothing,' she said after tapping a few more keys.

'So where does that leave me?' I sighed.

'You said he promised you money?'

It was instructive, I thought, that Susanna's mind, in these circumstances, turned not to the fact that a convicted killer, apparently out of jail illegally, was now standing in her bedroom, but instead to hard lucre.

'He gave me twenty thousand cash. He said there'd be another four hundred and sixty thousand in my bank account this morning.'

'Let's see . . .'

'But . . . ?'

I wanted to scream. This was my bank account. Well, *our* bank account, since Miriam and I did everything jointly, had done ever since we got married.

Susanna Aurelio sat there, let her fingers fly across the keyboard, and shot up the whole thing on to the screen of the machine in her grandiose bedroom in just a second or two.

'No,' she said, pointing at the paltry figure there. 'You have less than three hundred in the account. It's been like that for twenty-three years. If there'd been anything more I could have got you into something interest-bearing . . .'

'W-w-wait a minute! We had more than eighty thousand saved when I went into jail. I put some by every month. For Ricky's college fund. For the future. It was hard. Miriam used to give me a tough time for putting all that aside.'

She wheeled round the leather chair in which she sat and eyed me seriously.

'Do we really want to talk about this?'

'Yes! Where the hell's my money?'

'OK,' she answered, shrugging her bare shoulders.

She tugged on the pearl necklace for a moment, then started hammering the keys again.

'They don't have statements from the eighties online. But I'm your attorney. I digitized everything to do with your case. To do with you. Standard practice with everyone. Here . . .'

Something else popped up. It looked like a paper bank statement, the kind I recognized from when the world was real.

Except this one could not be true.

It showed a cash withdrawal of eighty thousand, dated Wednesday, 24 July 1985. Just about every

234

last cent we owned had been withdrawn from our joint bank account the day before Miriam and Ricky got killed.

'This is not possible,' I said, shaking my head. 'That kind of thing can't happen without my knowing. Why didn't anyone tell me? Why the hell didn't you say something?'

'Because I was trying to keep you alive, Bierce!' she snarled. 'That's what attorneys are for.'

I was quiet. Susanna didn't lose her temper without reason.

More buttons got slapped around on the keyboard. Another piece of paper appeared on the screen.

I stared at it and, not for the first time, wondered if this was all really just one long dream, a bunch of illusions filtering through my mind in the brief moment between Martin the Medic putting in that last needle and the long, dark, empty place rising up to claim what it was owed.

There was no way of knowing. Right then, I wouldn't have minded either way.

What was on screen were two cheques. The first moved eighty thousand in cash from our joint account into the private one I'd held from my single days. It was signed by both of us, as it would have to be, since sums of this nature required mutual agreement. The second appeared to move this selfsame money, our life savings, on to some account I'd never even heard of.

'This is a fake,' I said. 'I never signed either of

these. Also, that doesn't look like Miriam's signature. Not if I recall right.'

Susanna nodded.

'I have handwriting analysis on it. They said there's a 90 per cent possibility your signature is genuine. Just 10 per cent on hers.'

'This is ridiculous. What the hell would I do with all that money?'

'I can tell you that too. You tried to transfer it abroad. The second cheque only needed your signature of course.'

She pulled up a letter from a bank in Liechtenstein, one that had some sort of mythical bird with spiky wings and a dragon's head at the top.

'It never got there. They froze your money transactions the Monday after the murders. Then they seized it for costs.'

'Where the hell is Liechtenstein? *What* is Liechtenstein?'

'It's a small principality in Europe. Between Switzerland and Austria. Back in the eighties, some people used it for laundering cash they didn't want anyone else to see.'

I put my finger right on the screen. She looked at it until I took it away again. This was apparently bad manners.

'I did not take money out of our joint account. I did not try to move it to some country I've never even heard of. This is someone else trying to forge my signature, Susanna. You know that.'

She nodded.

'I would have tried to argue that if I'd needed it. Handwriting analysis isn't foolproof.'

'So why the hell didn't you?'

'Christ, Bierce! Stop making me repeat myself. I was trying to keep you alive, and God knows, with what they had against you, that was hard enough. Did you really expect me to introduce into court something that suggested you'd raided the family bank account and moved all that cash abroad one day before they died? Think about it.'

I did, and she was absolutely right.

'I was trying to paint you as a good and responsible husband and father,' she went on. 'Putting stuff like this in front of a jury just places more doubts into their heads, and there were plenty there already. Besides, even if they believed me, that these signatures were fakes, what did it do for you? This was a real bank account. Someone opened it. Unless I'm mistaken . . .'

She flailed the keys. Something popped up on screen. It had the same fancy bird logo on it and a line of figures.

'It's still sitting there.'

Even a financial idiot like me could read what was on the screen. On 2 July 1985, three weeks before my family died, it appeared I'd opened the account with a deposit of a couple of hundred. Bank charges over the years had reduced this to a mere thirteen and fifty cents. I guess the Liechtensteinians, or whatever they called themselves, were still hoping.

'What this shows is someone was messing around with us.'

'Who?' she demanded.

'I don't know! That was the job of the cops.'

The words got out of my throat before I could throttle them.

'You were a cop,' she pointed out. 'If anyone should have been able to prevent this kind of thing, it was you. Right or wrong – and I think it was right – I felt this would have done us a lot more harm than good.'

Her incisive and apparently guileless eyes bore down on me.

'And by the way, you really don't want to know what I had to do *personally* to keep all this out of court. It was above and beyond the call of duty. Even for me.'

I felt miserable. I felt stupid. I walked over to the bed, sat on the edge, rested my elbows on my legs and struggled to understand just one iota of what she'd told me. Susanna had seen the truth all along, and kept it from me for my own good. Someone had ripped the heart out of my family, in more ways than I knew, and done it with a methodical, deliberate, calculating audacity, right under my unsuspecting nose.

She came over, sat next to me.

'Don't give up, sugar,' she insisted. 'That was then. This is now. Things are different.'

'I noticed,' I observed drily. 'So I'm broke. I'm an illegal fugitive who's skipped jail. Except I also appear to be dead from getting executed this morning.'

She nodded.

'That about sums it up. I can work with this. If we play it right, it could turn out fine.'

I shook my head.

'What happened this morning, Susanna? Why would they announce I was dead?'

'Maybe because they want to cover up the fact you're free. What other reason could there be?'

'No . . . Stapleton said that Solera had confessed. It was there. A judge had seen it.'

She took my face in her hands and shook my head gently.

'Stop thinking so hard, Bierce. You'll explode. No one's been talking to me about your case since I saw you last year. It can't have gone in front of a judge. Whatever they've been telling you was a bunch of lies for some reason. I mean . . . four hundred and sixty thousand dollars. If you'd done twenty-three years in jail on a wrongful conviction we'd have been coming at them for *much* more than that.'

She corrected herself.

'We *will* come at them for much more than that. I mean it.'

'And now?'

She smiled at me. Susanna could look so innocent sometimes, so full of sympathy and understanding too, that it was impossible to believe she was thinking about anyone else in the world, herself least of all.

'Now I keep you safe and sane. Tomorrow, we drive south to a house I own. It's just over the state line, so if anyone starts throwing writs around I can drown them in paper from a safe distance. Even if they found you I'd have a year, maybe two, before they could put a thing in court here. You're not going back inside, Bierce. That I promise. I take on people for life. Rain or shine.'

I nodded. A part of me wanted to sit back and do whatever she wanted.

'Now,' she said. 'I'll be back in a moment with some food and drink. In the meantime, you go raid Frank's wardrobe for some decent clothes. The Gap-reject look doesn't suit you.'

While she was gone I wandered along the corridor to another, slightly smaller bedroom, where I went through everything husband Frank owned, thinking. I picked out a pair of impeccably pressed blue linen slacks and a white polo shirt. Then I went and showered before putting them on.

Water made my head start to work again, or at least believe it was doing so.

I walked back into Susanna's bedroom, framing a few questions.

Susanna was there with an empty glass and a look that said: enough booze for now.

She patted the cushion beside her on the sofa and said, 'You know, you're the only man who's ever – *ever* – turned me down.'

She pondered this statement for a second or two.

'Apart from my Uncle Joe and he doesn't count.'

'I'm flattered by these intimate confidences. What about Kyle McKendrick?'

Her faultless features wrinkled up with disgust.

'Please! A lady doesn't tell. But in the case of that creep, no. I do have standards. Maybe they weren't high enough for you back then . . .'

'I was married,' I reminded her.

'That stopped a lot of men.'

'Happily married.'

Or so I thought.

'Well, you're not married now. You've not been near a woman for twenty-three years. How does that feel?'

She dented the soft sofa again. I shook my head and stayed where I was.

'I haven't given it much thought.'

'You will.'

Something made a noise, and vibrated too, in my pocket.

I took out the pink phone Alice had given me. There wasn't a button to push anywhere. I hadn't a clue where to begin. Finally, with Susanna looking on, awestruck by my inability to cope with such a simple device, I managed to lever the bottom edge free. The phone opened up like two seashells on a hinge. I could even hear a voice coming out of the earpiece.

'Yes?' I said.

'I don't want to worry you.' Alice sounded anxious. 'But I've done something stupid. Some people came looking for Lao Lao's apartment. She's safe round the corner for now. We need to pick her up. Also . . .'

She didn't seem keen to say this.

'I could be wrong but I thought I saw that black cop guy of yours go past me in a car, headed your way. Just a minute or two ago. I found a parking space by the public road at the end of the beach. Just walk to the shore, turn right and I'll be there.'

'Fine,' I said, unsurprised, and put the phone back in my pocket.

'So you do have friends,' Susanna murmured.

'Only in ways you wouldn't understand.'

I walked over, bent down, kissed her softly on the cheek, reached round the back of her warm, slender neck and gently unhooked the string of pearls from her throat. She made small, soft squealing noises in my ear.

Then, while her eyes were still screwed shut with anticipation, I took both her hands in mine. I'd removed the cord from the silk dressing gown I found in husband Frank's bedroom. I looped her left hand through the noose I'd made there, then the right, and finally pulled her up and round so she had her back to me, managing to gently tie her together at the wrists, just like I once did with suspects and plastic cuffs a quarter of a century ago, before she could begin to say much at all.

I turned my lovely lawyer round and sat her back on the sofa, as comfortably as I could manage. I genuinely believe Susanna thought this might all have been some kind of foreplay for a moment. But the silence didn't last long.

'Bierce! *Bierce*!' she began to yell, flailing her legs around, up and down in fury, trying to struggle free.

'I'm sorry . . .' I began to say.

'No man says no to me twice,' she yelled. '*No* man.'

That was Susanna. The refusal hurt most of all.

A fake electronic bell chimed. Then a small video screen lit up by the side of the bed. Stapleton – *Ridley* Stapleton, I recalled – was there, looking both puzzled and mad.

I walked up to the screen and gazed into the little lens above it.

'Stape,' I said. 'I am in dire need of male company, friend. There are so many women in this world of yours. Meet me tomorrow morning, Pier Twenty-seven, the one for the Stonetown ferry. Eight-thirty. Come alone or the deal's off.'

'What deal?' he bawled, wide-eyed and furious.

'I got my memory back. *That* deal.'

He didn't say a thing.

'And by the way,' I added, 'the price is now a million. Cash. Paid into an account in Liechtenstein. Maybe you know the number.'

Susanna's fury was building up nicely. Until something happened that defeated even her.

It was a deep, growing, roaring sound, like two gigantic jet engines strung on wires, getting dangled low over the roof of her mansion in Pelican Bay, so close, and so powerful, they shook the room. I could feel my skin vibrating over my bones. I watched as a couple of paintings worked themselves off their hooks and tumbled to the floor.

She looked a little scared at that moment. I'd already guessed she'd called Stape when she went downstairs. The wide-eyed ignorance she'd shown at his name, and that little game with the computer, never really came across as convincing. I don't imagine she expected, for one minute, that some vast, dark helicopter would materialize in the night sky as a result.

'You know,' I yelled above the racket, pointing upwards at the beast in the sky, '*that* has really ruined the mood.'

I walked over to the desk, unhooked the computer and the power cord and stuffed them under my arm. Then I hopped through the French windows and down towards the beach.

I'd love to say I eluded Stapleton and his flying machine through a combination of low athletic cunning and intellectual guile. But I'd be lying. By the time I made it to Susanna's pool, breathless, panting and finally realizing I was either out of condition or old or both, Stapleton's helicopter appeared to be hovering just a couple of inches above my head. Beams of bright silver light were beginning to swoop across the perfect clipped lawn and a voice was coming out of a loudspeaker, barking commands I couldn't decipher.

Then, as I leapt over the iron gate at the beach end of the garden, the sensible part of my mind asking, somewhat drily, why the hell I was headed for the only place nearby where a helicopter could land, something happened. The painful hot down-draught of the rotor blades stopped. The chemical stink of avgas disappeared, a little anyway. For some reason the helicopter decided it had better things to do than chase an out-of-condition escaped convict struggling through the back lot of a private paradise in Pelican Bay.

I stood on the soft sand, beneath the fringe of a palm tree, coughing and wheezing, fighting to get my breath back, listening in amazement as the machine flew off south, away from the lights of the city, to some private landing strip hidden from view in the dead flat lands along A1A, I guessed.

They were gone, and there could be just one explanation. Stape called them off. Something I'd said over the video phone gave him pause for thought. It could only be the one thing, of course: *I knew*. And the fact this made him send his scary buzzing thing home could, naturally, mean just one thing too: it wasn't there as luxury transportation to take me to some desert island where we might discuss the state of the world over cocktails and canapés. It was there to scoop up my awkward ass once and for all, until the moment I let on that I now recalled what it was both my former colleague and the charming Mr McKendrick wanted so much to hear.

The latter was a lie, naturally, though I had fast come to the conclusion of late that lying – and stealing Susanna's valuables – seemed small sins next to everything else happening around me. It felt bad enough being dead, without having people wanting to kill me. What are a little untruth and theft next to that?

Also, my head hurt, in a way I was coming to recognize. Not so much pain as muzzy confusion, a state of mind that hovered between the real world, if I could call this strange place that, and some dark corner of my imagination trying to poke its way through to take a look around. I'd felt like this ever since waking up after Martin the Medic's needle. If that's what I did. The needle from McKendrick's Dr Rimless hadn't helped. Nor had the beer Susanna had come up with either.

'I need a break,' I murmured to myself, then looked up, towards the gentle incoming tide, with the rippled reflection of a full moon on the small, regular wavelets, and felt my heart sink straight through my boots and bury itself deep in the sand, whimpering all the while.

When I say I saw Miriam standing in the water I don't actually mean she was *there*. This wasn't my sanity taking flight. It was the lost part of my mind trying to crawl back into place and find some perspective by running through a few games it thought might help me comprehend. Miriam had been dead for twenty-three years. The only place any fraction of her survived was in the memories of those who loved her. Recent discoveries taken into consideration, I still counted myself among that club. She cheated on me somehow. But then someone cheated on both of us, big time, in a way I'd yet to comprehend. They gave Jonny Loong money to start Sister Dragon. They roped in Alice's mom as smiling front of house, and somehow Miriam signed up too, putting on her sexy cheongsam with the slit up the side before getting down to business.

And while doing that, my wife and Alice's mom and uncle found out something that got them all killed; Ricky too, as what the military men like to call 'collateral damage'. I am not a naive man. When Susanna showed me those cheques and the bank account in some far-off country I still couldn't picture, I saw one possible explanation instantly. Miriam had faked my signature on cheques before. Several times. It was necessary, she'd said, when she needed to pay for something big that went over the single-signature limit on the joint account and I was out working somewhere. Occasionally she had good reason.

It was entirely possible she had written both signatures on the joint account – making mine good and hers bad in case things went wrong. And then forged my name again to move the money from my personal account – which normally had just a couple of hundred in, a hangover from my single days – before transferring it offshore.

247

But why? And where was she getting all the help from? She was a smart woman, but setting up bank accounts in foreign countries required the kind of knowledge that was surely beyond her. Was she planning on running off with someone she'd met through Sister Dragon, leaving me to deal with the awkward questions? Or was it possible a figure from outside had done all of this, without her direct knowledge, and killed her and Ricky and the Loongs when the truth trickled out?

'Well?' I asked of the figure standing in the waves, holding her scarlet skirt up out of the water that lapped around her knees.

She didn't look dead. She looked beautiful. But that was only to be expected. This wasn't Miriam. It was my memory of her, ripped from my mind by the various chemicals floating round my blood-stream, then turned into some kind of simulacrum of my long-dead wife because she was the person I wanted to see more than anyone else at that moment.

This Miriam made by my memories looked at me, smiled and said, 'Not now, Bierce. You don't have the time.'

'Prevarication is an ugly thing after all these years.'

'My, you learned a lot of long words in jail. Here's a short one. *Run.*'

'Yeah, right, Miriam,' I snapped. 'Here I am, trying to work out whether I'm alive or what. Whether you loved me or hated me or . . . I don't know. And all you can say is . . .'

There was another sound too. Several of them. Voices. Shouting. Some way off, but loud too.

'Run.'

It wasn't her voice at all, that last time most definitely. When I looked up from my sudden fury there was no Miriam there. Just a ghostly white kid's paddle boat bobbing up and down on the rippling black waves, with a transistor radio on the seat, still playing, its tinny voice singing a song I remembered from back when. A lone pelican sat on the back, beak on chest, eyeing me miserably.

Music's odd. It defies time. It sits in your synapses, apparently forgotten, then jumps back out of nowhere when you hear two notes on a guitar or a lone male voice singing a single word from a refrain that should have been lost over the years.

This time it was Fleetwood Mac and 'Go Your Own Way' and the sound of it dragged me out of whatever stupid, selfish hole I'd fallen into, straight back into the dark, threatening night of the now I so wanted to avoid.

Something in my pants pocket started vibrating just at the moment a high-pitched voice began singing.

She'd adored that album, had played it over and over again, until the needle scratched the surface – we were still a pre-CD family – and I had to go out and buy a new copy.

I pulled out the pink phone.

'Run, Bierce,' Alice screamed. 'Run!'

*   *   *

To my right, close to where I said I'd meet her, a vehicle was flashing its lights. To my left I could hear another engine gunning over the beach. I looked. It was some huge thing, like a Jeep on junk food, churning through the sand with flood-lights attached to its two front corners, searching, lost, I was glad to see, for where to begin.

I loped steadily towards her, thinking about what I'd seen, what I'd heard these last few hours.

'Let me drive,' I said, when I got to the car. 'I know the lanes around here.'

'Bierce . . .'

'Please.'

She watched me throw the computer into the back seat and then went ominously quiet. The gigantic lights on the beach had seen us and were roaring our way.

This time round there was no argument. Alice shuffled along the bench seat and let me drive. I put the old Volvo into gear, was relieved to discover my head was working well enough for it not to worry too much about driving again, and turned off the concrete parking slab by the shore, heading inland and uphill, wondering how long the lead we had on them, a quarter of a mile at best, might last.

Away from the carbuncle of Ocean Vista Gardens, this area hadn't changed much at all. Tiny single-track roads criss-crossed the hills that led back to the city, a remnant of the time this was poor farmer land for settlers trying to stake a claim

to a couple of acres and dig a living for their families out of the ground. My mind began to work
overtime, recalling all the occasions we'd got lost
here, looking for picnic places, even before Ricky
came along. I had half an idea of where we were
going, and the right direction to follow. In a warren
of tracks like this, that was worth a head start or
several.

At times we could hear the Jeep thing bellowing
angrily below. But these were still little more than
lanes made for the horse and cart era. It didn't
belong, and pretty soon we heard its ugly voice
no more.

After fifteen minutes of slow, patient driving, we
were clear of Pelican Bay altogether and Alice still
hadn't said a word. This couldn't go on. I drove
into a deserted lay-by in one of the public park
stops near the summit of the hill, close to the
highway, turned off the engine and the lights, then
looked at her.

'So what happened?' I asked.

'I did something stupid. I called the ambulance
service to see how Sheldon was.'

'You what?'

'He'd been shot. We took him in. I needed to
know.'

'Sheldon is a lying, cheating, venomous scumbag
who tried to sell me to Kyle McKendrick.'

She looked miserable and grumpy. But she also
looked as if she was telling the truth. I was starting
to get an inkling for these things. It was all to do

with the eyes, whether they peered straight at me or not. A simple thing, I know, but I hadn't stared into many faces for quite a while.

'He regretted what he did, don't you think?' she said. 'He's doing OK in hospital, in case you're interested.'

'I knew he'd be OK! How many shot people do you think I got to see when I was on the streets?'

All the same, it shouldn't have exposed us.

'How did they know?' I asked.

She frowned.

'I think I heard it in their voices when I called the ambulance people to check out where they'd taken him. I told you it was a privatized service. They'd been ordered to listen out for someone calling about Sheldon, I guess.'

'Privatized? You mean McKendrick?' I asked.

'Who else? I guess they tracked back the phone number. Lao Lao phoned me soon after I dropped you off. She's pretty smart, you know. The people in the medicine store called up from downstairs to say someone was asking. She went out by the fire escape and walked round to some bar a friend of hers runs. We need somewhere to stay, Bierce.'

'I'm thinking,' I lied.

'Well, that's good.'

For the life of me I couldn't work out why she seemed so angry with me.

'What did you do after you left?' I asked.

'You mean after getting the call from my grandma saying some people with guns were out looking for us? I drove around a little. Then I found that way down to the beach.'

She hesitated.

'After that I walked along the beach. They don't seem to patrol it so much at night.'

'No.'

That had struck me. But that part of the bay was pretty difficult to reach by any major public road. I guess they felt secure behind whatever sea of electronic devices they'd installed in their fake palaces.

'Your lawyer isn't much of a one for closing the curtains, is she?' Alice stated. 'Also you smell somewhat . . . fragrant. If you don't mind my saying.'

'Ah.'

If you'd been someone peering in through an open window it must have looked pretty damning.

'Did you used to kiss her in jail too?'

So that was why she was mad with me.

'No. I was trying to work out how to get what I wanted out of her, and then get free before the goons answered her call. That's all. Susanna knows things about me I don't know myself, though I ought to.'

I told her about Gwinett and the supposed move to McKendrick, Susanna's account of my 'execution', a little of the missing-money tale, and not a word about the meeting I hoped I'd set up with Stapleton the following morning.

She thawed a little.

'What did your lawyer tell you to do?'

'Go south with her, over the state line, and engage in long-range fisticuffs with the legal system. What do you expect? But then, while she was out getting a beer, she called Stapleton. The rest . . .'

I opened my arms wide.

'Alice,' I said, 'I'm sorry. I am not the kind of man you think. Part of me's still locked to what happened twenty-three years ago, and I can't stop that part talking in my head, much as I'd like to. I don't have whatever it is men of this century are supposed to possess in terms of manners or morals or charm. For instance . . .'

I reached into my pocket and pulled out the double string of pearls.

'I stole these along with Susanna's computer. I wanted to give them to you. I thought they'd be a present. I now realize what a dumb, thoughtless idea that was.'

She looked at the two rows of luminous spheres shining in the dark.

'Are they real?'

'You saw the house. Do you think she'd own fakes?'

Alice ran her fingers along them, then took her hand away.

'They're not me, Bierce.'

'No,' I agreed, and a part of me was glad, because it was thinking, if you give her a present and she takes it smiling, you'd *have* to trust her, wouldn't you? We were both, men and women, made that way.

'I got a little of what I wanted out of Susanna, then left. And here I am talking to you, still feeling like some slow-witted fool who's got the big picture waiting inside his head and just can't see it.'

I pulled the creaking Volvo back out into the road. There was only so much time and energy I could expend on banging my head against that particular wall. I needed to think about somewhere to stay, somewhere Ridley Stapleton and Kyle McKendrick would never find us. Lao Lao was waiting for us in a Hawaiian bar in Eden, three blocks from home. She had a plastic bag with some belongings in it, a drink that looked more fruit and paper umbrella than liquid, and an expression that suggested an evening of pleasant banter around an open fire, with the odd glass of good cognac, was probably not scribbled on her to-do list.

'Thanks, jerk,' she muttered as I helped her into the car.

I didn't hear another word from her, even when we pulled into the Seaview Motel. Lao Lao shuffled off to her room without another word. Alice hung around as I raided the vending machine for soft drinks and snacks and a way into the awkward conversation which now had to ensue.

We'd passed the Seaview on the way back from Pelican Bay. Some part of my childhood said there was a rule about 'hiding in plain sight' or something. They wouldn't be looking for us just three miles from Susanna Aurelio's mansion, I thought. In fact, I doubted Stapleton would be looking for me at all. I'd made the appointment for the following morning. Being a man of substantial resources – as the helicopter showed – Stape doubtless thought he could keep this meeting, hear me out, then, if need be, grab me there to shake out any facts which remained undisclosed. Which was perhaps true, though I planned to do my best to avoid that particular eventuality.

The Seaview was a place teenagers of my generation took their girlfriends for a few hours of shared privacy. You could rent rooms by the afternoon or the evening. If you were feeling exceptionally generous you could stay overnight, though this was not a common event. It was more than thirty years since I'd set foot in the place, for professional reasons – that missing teenager I later found dead under the De Soto bridge. Nothing much had changed in that time. It still was furnished in garish red velvet with plastic furniture and cheap prints of places – Paris, Rome – that hadn't seemed so exotic even back in my youth.

I asked for three separate rooms, which surprised the gawky youth behind the desk. It didn't take more than a moment to prise out of him the fact that we were the only guests that night. In fact, I rather suspected the Seaview hadn't enjoyed an overnight paying customer in some time, judging by the way he made us wait in the lobby while he went to check the rooms were actually fit for human habitation.

They weren't, of course, but I wasn't going to argue. The place was a classic of its type, little more than a line of low single-storey cabins running either side of the reception, each with a door opening out on to the wooden deck in front. It would do.

'Was the Bates Motel full?' Alice asked, as we walked outside towards the accommodation. The three rooms were in the left row, with Lao Lao at the end, and me willing to go wherever was empty and quiet enough to sleep.

'A cultural reference to the twentieth century,' I noted. 'I am impressed. When this is over and done with I will take you to the Overlook. Or its equivalent.'

'I don't know that one, Bierce. Don't push your luck.'

I reached the first cabin. 'I wouldn't dream of it. Can I borrow you for a moment?'

I held up Susanna's computer.

'Instinct tells me there might be something in here that's useful for us. And that perhaps I could communicate with the outside world if necessary.'

She frowned. The skinny receptionist was out of his cubby-hole watching us, looking suspicious.

Alice walked over and asked, 'You got wi-fi?'

He looked at us with an expression that I believe was meant to appear tough.

'It's twenty a day. Cash.'

I handed over a note and got some grubby voucher in return.

He shuffled around on his cheap sneakers.

'No web cams in the room. That's one of the rules. We don't want no one pushing out live porn from here. Someone down A1A got busted for that last month. I don't want trouble.'

I put my hand on his arm. He jumped, just a little.

'I promise you. No web cam.'

'Unless,' he added, looking her up and down and licking his lips, 'you need an extra or something. I got some acting experience, if you know what I mean.'

She looked ready to hit him, which was all we needed.

'I wish you well with your career,' I replied, and opened the door of the first cabin, ushering her in front.

'The places you take me, Bierce,' she grumbled. 'Will I ever forget them?'

'In time,' I said, holding out the computer. 'You now have twenty minutes to teach a stupid old man everything he needs to know about how to survive in the twenty-first century. After that you go next door and we both get a decent night's sleep. Agreed?'

It was easy really. You just clicked things and pushed things and typed here and there. Then Susanna's computer coughed up its secrets all in a rush. And, if it couldn't find any answers there, it went hunting and pulled them out of thin air from this distant, amorphous place even I'd heard of in jail. Somewhere known as the internet, which I asked Alice to explain to me, then waved her into silence after thirty seconds.

We started off with my financial affairs. How she did it I'll never know – or, I hope, need to – but Alice somehow managed to find everything that Susanna had shown me, and a little more. It lived, she said, inside this silver thing, along with countless other letters and case files and messages and faxes . . . It seemed most of Susanna's entire professional life of the past twenty-three years was in there somewhere.

Alice hammered away at the thing, typing furiously, running her finger across some strange little pad, watching the screen like a hawk every second of the way.

After a while I could only ask, in astonishment, 'How the hell do you learn this stuff? Do they teach it at school?'

'Only to old people. How did you learn to use the phone?'

'I picked it up and started talking.'

'Snap. You know, I can't believe she's got all this just sitting there. No password. No security. Nothing.'

That made sense to me anyway.

'Susanna's obscenely rich and lives behind big iron gates. This thing never sets foot outside the bedroom.'

'I'll take your word on that,' she said slyly.

'It's psychology, a much-neglected art in your century if you ask me. Rich citizens of Susanna's persuasion believe security is something they pay other people to do. She *knows* no one can break into her beautiful mansion and start tapping away at the keys of this thing. So why worry?'

'It's a generational thing,' she said, shaking her head. 'She's about your age, isn't she?'

'A little younger.'

'Really beautiful too. From what I saw on the TV. She does a lot of TV. I remember seeing her before.'

'Yes,' I agreed. 'She's very beautiful.'

Alice waited, her fingers still for the first time in several minutes.

'Fine,' I sighed. 'I will say this just the once and never return to the subject again. A very beautiful woman is not necessarily a sure-fire signal that a man should turn off, even temporarily, all sentient thought for the well-being and security of himself and those he admires in return for nothing more or less than thirty minutes of predictable, albeit usually pleasurable, physical activity. You may find it hard to believe, but many of my sex also think this way.'

'You haven't met many of your sex in a while,' she muttered, shaking her head.

'That is the end of the Susanna Aurelio discussion, Alice. I appear to be damned if I want the woman and damned if I don't. The truth is I don't.

Never have and never will. You just work out which of those two possibilities you'd prefer to believe, then take it as read I agree, absolutely, that was the way it was.'

I took her hands off the keyboard. They'd started fidgeting, not typing.

'Well?' I looked her in the eye.

'I know you didn't do anything. It's just . . . twenty-three years. People have needs.'

'Agreed. I need you to tell me everything that's in that machine. Now, will you look at my case records? Please.'

She swore, then got back to typing. I watched the screen. It filled with line after line of impenetrable jargon.

'How the hell am I supposed to read this stuff?' I grumbled.

'You can't. These are just file names. Lists of all the documents that have been lodged as part of your case. They're all there. Look.'

She pointed to the names scrolling down the screen.

'Witness statements. Forensic reports. Officer reports.'

'I was awake when all that stuff came in. I heard it in court. It's no use to me.'

'Then . . . what can I do?'

One thing that puzzled me still. Why were they convinced so absolutely I was the one who killed Miriam and Ricky? The bank account had never made it into the trial. All I got thrown at me was the fact they didn't like my line about not remembering anything to do with the attack. Plus they had traces of my skin underneath Miriam's fingernails, and some bloody prints of mine on the floor and the stairs. This was flimsy material on which to hang a murder prosecution. The skin could have got there a variety of ways. Through making love even. The prints might have been the result of me crawling upstairs after being attacked myself.

'Can you narrow this down to reports from the DA's office? Before they went ahead with the case?'

She did something magical. Three documents appeared on the screen.

'There's got to be more than this,' I pointed out. 'I've worked murder inquiries. We used to drown in paper when we were trying to persuade these people to go ahead with a prosecution.'

'In that case, they're missing,' Alice said. 'It's a computer, Bierce. They can't fall behind a filing cabinet. These are the only documents from the DA's office which mention your name.'

It wasn't hard to guess what I'd find there either. They were all about the money movements, out of our joint account, into this thing in Liechtenstein. The first two reports were wailing on in excited terms about how this was cast-iron proof that I'd been planning to murder Miriam all along, spirit away our money, then, I assume, enjoy a life of untold abandon in Austria, wearing short leather pants presumably and gorging on sausage. There were caveats even then. As a motive, this was all a little neat and tidy. Some anonymous individual had pointed out we had the reputation for being a loving, devoted couple. If they wanted to pursue this line, they really needed something that burst that particular illusion. They didn't have it, which was a shame, because right then I would have very much liked to have known myself.

In any case, it all became irrelevant. By the time of the third report the money evidence had been shelved, through a bunch of legal technicalities only someone with several degrees in gibberish would have understood. Susanna's wiles – whatever they had been – had worked. There was one interesting thing there, though.

Someone had scribbled in the margin, close to the end: *And we can't use the call either. Great work, surveillance!*

'The call?' Alice asked.

'I have no idea. None whatsoever. The law directory that listed Susanna's address did that because she works from home. It only listed an office number. Can you find her private phone number on this thing? She's got to be ex-directory. Also, can you see if she's been in touch with McKendrick recently?'

'Yes . . .' she replied cautiously. 'But you're being uncharacteristically slow here, Bierce. If you call her on the mobile I gave you, or worse, on the hotel phone, you can be traced.'

'I know that. I know Susanna too. Trust me. Please.'

She gave me a long, somewhat worried look. Then, shaking her head, to herself I think, not me, she began typing again.

It took her three seconds to find the number. After a minute I could see that there were indeed contacts between her and McKendrick, but they appeared to be the kind of social things rich people liked. Invitations to public occasions and charitable events. I knew Susanna well enough to recognize her tone. With McKendrick it was distanced, even chilly.

I used the little pink phone, interrupting her on the first syllable of 'Hello', and said, 'I don't want to know why you called Stapleton. I just need to know this. Did you phone McKendrick too? Was that his giant Jeep thing chasing me up and down the sand?'

The line went quiet. Alice was glowering at me.

'I did not . . . I *would not* phone that man.'

'Well, that's a relief. You only called in one person to kill me. Please don't do that right now, will you? I'm hiding in a convent full of saintly nuns and it would be a real shame if they got wasted by that big black helicopter of his.'

There was an ominous silence on the phone. Alice was giving me the 'nice try, smartass' look.

'Bierce,' Susanna said eventually, 'what the hell have you got yourself into? What am I supposed to do in these circumstances?'

'Listen to your client, I would have thought.'

'I have more than one client. Sometimes their needs conflict.'

Ah. Something clicked.

'I had no idea he'd call in the air force or whatever,' she went on, oozing her special kind of sincerity. 'I thought he was coming to get you out of trouble. The Jeep was nothing to do with him. I swear that's the truth. Please believe me.'

'I'll try. Here's one more question. When you kept out the evidence about the cheques, there was something else. Someone's scribbled on the file. Something about "the call". What was the call, Susanna?'

It would have been so easy to have objected . . . *Search me. You want perfect recall of a scrawl on a piece of paper from twenty-three years ago?*

Instead she said, 'They never told me, Bierce. And believe me I asked. There was a lot they never told me about you. And you know something? There was a lot you never told me, although you wanted me to believe that was because you really couldn't remember. Was that true too?'

'I believe so, but after all this time I really don't know. And that's the honest truth.'

'Can I still help?' she asked quietly. 'Or did I screw everything this evening?'

'Probably,' I said, and cut the call.

I didn't master the twenty-first century in twenty minutes. But, thanks to Alice Loong's patient and skilful tuition, I did learn how to find things, fetch things and even send the President of the United States an email, from something called a Hotmail address which Alice kindly set up for me.

After which we went through everything we'd found among my attorney's private files, cursed the fact that blackmail wasn't our calling and decided that, the scribble on the third DA's memo apart, there really wasn't much of interest at all.

'It's just a machine, Bierce,' she said, and yawned.

I couldn't help but notice she looked at the bed at that moment. She noticed I'd noticed and both of us pretended we hadn't.

I pulled the pearls out of my pocket and held them out in my hand.

She stared at them, close up this time, seeing them for what they were, not a part of the image of me and Susanna she'd had in her head when we were in the Volvo.

'They're beautiful,' she said, not really able to look away.

I reached up and fastened them round her neck. They nestled against Alice's smooth olive skin, seemingly at home.

'They look a million times better on you than they ever did on their owner,' I said truthfully. 'Go see. Keep them if you like.'

We got up and stared into what reflection remained among the cracks and stains of the motel mirror. Alice looked lovely just then. Composed and intelligent and completely in control of herself. I seemed old and out of place next to her, and that was both a shock and a disappointment.

'I'll think about it,' she said, fingering the two lines of shining oyster spit balls. 'Tomorrow . . .'

Tomorrow I had an appointment.

'Let's talk about that over breakfast,' I said. 'Just now, Alice, I need some sleep.'

There was suspicion in her eyes again. She wanted me to see it.

'You'll be here, won't you?'

'Where else would I be?'

'I don't know. You're sneaky sometimes.'

'Not at all. I'm a very old-fashioned man,' I insisted. 'I thought you might have noticed.'

I hesitated. This needed to be said.

'You've got a gun,' I said. 'I saw it in your bag this evening. In the Volvo. It wasn't there before.'

She blinked, took her cheap little plastic bag off her shoulder, opened it and pulled out an old automatic.

'Lao Lao gave it to me,' she explained. 'She thought I might need it.'

'For me? Or someone else?'

Alice Loong sighed.

'How many times do I have to save you before you give up on this fantasy? If I wanted to shoot you, I could have done it that first night.'

She put the gun back into her bag. For some reason, that made me feel scared. Alice looked vulnerable at that moment. I had the horrible feeling she was going to tell me something, and I didn't want to hear it. No confession. No sudden truth or revelation. The shifting semblance of some plan was starting to hatch at the back of my damaged brain, and it had taken so long to get there I couldn't countenance anything – particularly not something personal – getting in the way.

'You're not what I expected,' she began to say. 'You're not . . .'

Before she could utter another word I kissed her, very quickly, on the cheek, then, for just a microsecond, on her full, pink lips, in a way, I hoped, that could have denoted either attraction or affection. Or maybe, in truth, a mixture of both.

'G'night . . .' I whispered, and, to my relief, she said nothing, leaving without another word.

I waited until I heard the door to the adjoining cabin slam before opening up the computer, trying to remember everything she'd told me. Finally I tracked down Kyle McKendrick's email address and began hunting and pecking across the keys.

Kyle! You rogue, you. Shooting my miserable SOB brother-in-law like that (he's still alive, friend, you should take gun tuition, soon please).

And making out with my wife all those years ago! How'd you do that? Did the cheongsam help or hinder? No. This is your secret. Keep it. I never had a clue. Not the slightest. Talk about dumb cops. Here's one more thing. I don't care. If Miriam wanted

268

to cheat on me that was her right, just as it's mine to say: to hell with the bitch, she had it coming.

All this is in the past. I am a forgiving man. And I forgive you everything. Well, almost everything. You go eat the food in that correctional facility of yours and see how you like it.

Most of all, though, I am alive and I would like to keep things that way. To this end I can offer you a bargain, the best you'll ever get.

You post a million dollars in cash into my account in Liechtenstein, the details of which I'll put at the end of this message. You do this first thing in the morning. Then around noon I'll give you the little secret you want, because – here's the rub – Dr Rimless and his magic needle worked. If you'd just turned up before my rescue party I'd have poured out everything, heart and soul, right there in the loft of Shangri-La Motor Repair, where you could have listened, taken notes, then popped me just like you popped Sheldon, except with more care.

Such is fate. But here's the thing. Now I have experienced once more what it's like being alive, I quite like it. So as well as the money I want your assurance that, once we both have what we want, no one's going to come looking for me – or anyone else among the few people I happen to know in this shiny new world of yours – with a gun or a syringe or anything. I have researched your present status on this marvellous toy you call the internet. You are, I see, a man of great renown. A charitable human being, with many generous endowments and political connections that must make for a lot of tedious dinners. I wish you well in all your many ventures. But should you break this part of my munificent bargain, there is a cost. Just the usual. Some incriminating documents and the rambling story of my life, in every last damning detail, deposited this night with a lawyer, to be dispatched to every mainstream media outlet in the country should I expire of anything other than the most natural of causes at any period over the next ten years.

Being rich, I'm sure you'd stay out of jail, of course. But here's the bad news. You'd be a pariah. Look it up if you don't know already. No more society receptions and free champagne. No nights at the opera. When you open the post in the morning all you'll see is bills not invitations. Hell, you'd be just like the rest of us. Nasty, huh?

I'll book a table at Loomis and Jake's for twelve-thirty (just to take away the taste of that prison food of yours). If you're amenable, this is over. Expect my call.

Yrs, Bierce

PS The lobster's on you

I hit send and wondered how long it took for these things to arrive. Were there morning and afternoon deliveries? Did Kyle pick up these things for himself or have a secretary read them out loud from the computer?

However quickly they turned up, I didn't expect him to be sitting, waiting for them, at thirty minutes past midnight. I had time, to think, to plan and, most of all, to prepare.

Kyle McKendrick would not, unless I was very much mistaken, put one million dollars into that bank account in Liechtenstein. Though he no longer knew it, he was a crook first and a businessman second. Had it been the other way round, things might have been different.

Still, I would settle for some guarantee that I – and Alice and Lao Lao – got out of this safely, maybe by leaving the city altogether, though even at this stage I found that idea unappealing. I'd never lived anywhere else. Where would I go? Also I deserved that meal at Loomis and Jake's. The place had memories for me and an ad in the restaurant guide I'd found in that grubby room revived them. They hadn't even changed the artwork: badly drawn lobsters and crabs and a promise of the best food in town from a kitchen

271

that had been run by the same family for nearly eight decades. The father of Mickey Carluccio, my one childhood friend, owned the place along with the city fish market, where he employed me when I was a school kid chasing pocket money. He had other connections I didn't know about till later too. Miriam and I used to go to eat there before we were married, when money hadn't seemed so tight. Ricky came along once or twice when he was old enough, and got his face covered in tomato sauce when we bought him his favourite, the *cioppino*. It was a landmark that had sat down by the Piers for half a century or more, with a view of the boats and the ferries, the sea lions and the gulls. It was impossible to think of the city without thinking about Loomis and Jake's, at least for me. And when this mess was over, I would, I swear, buy Alice Loong one good, expensive meal there, before working out what happened next.

There was just one obstacle along the way.

I had no idea, not the slightest clue, what it was that Stape and McKendrick lusted after so badly they seemed willing to kill anyone to get it.

Bringing McKendrick into the loop came from the stated wisdom of my old man on the subject of mad dogs. Never fight them yourself or try to run away. Just find another mad dog and let the two of them sort it out between themselves.

It was the kind of advice I would have handed out to Ricky when he was old enough, since fathers are supposed to come up with that kind of plain, sensible fare, even though I doubt anyone spouting such nonsense has ever tried it out in real life.

Weren't these creatures mad to begin with? In which case how could you apply any logic whatsoever to their actions? And what if they decided they liked each other and turned on you instead?

The Fleetwood Mac song I'd heard on the beach came back to taunt me.

Go Your Own Way.

That was what I was trying to achieve really. Something, anything that was the opposite of Stape's and McKendrick's expectations. These two men had money and organizations and access to gadgets and stuff a caveman from the eighties couldn't begin to imagine. There was no way I could play them at their own game; I needed them to play me at mine.

And here's the truth. I was a lousy cop at most things. I couldn't shoot straight. I was never much good in a fight.

My one talent was this: I could talk to people, high and low, big and small, crooked and straight. This was no small gift for one very good reason. When I became a cop there was one thing I noticed very quickly. People don't shoot you while they're speaking. Guns only come into their own when the talking stops.

To this end I tried to develop a little sly charm and persuasiveness. Now it was time to gauge how much had survived the years in jail.

When I went outside my heart was up in my

mouth. I walked along to her room, knocked twice, gently, so as not to wake the person next door, and waited.

Lao Lao opened the door in a lurid violet floor-length nightdress. She was smoking a cigar and had a glass of amber spirit in her hand.

'What took you?' she muttered, and ushered me into the room.

'Do you believe in ghosts?' I asked.

'What kind of question's that?'

'The simple kind,' I said, shrugging. 'Like, "Can I call you Lao Lao?" Alice does. It makes things easier for me.'

'Sure you can. I just wanted you to ask.'

'Your English is good.'

'When I want it to be. It's useful being some dumb Chinese grandma occasionally. You got a first name?'

'Bierce works either way. Let's not complicate things.'

She sat down on the bed, pulled out her bag from beneath the mattress, brought out a bottle of cheap whiskey and poured some into a plastic tooth mug she'd kept by the chair.

I politely turned it down.

'I need a clear head for the morning. Big day.'

'Every day's a big day.'

'Some are bigger than others. You didn't answer my question.'

She gulped at the whiskey and winced.

'Lots of Chinese believe in ghosts. Me, I dunno. Someone once said, if you believe in them, they exist. If you don't, they never pester you. Why'd you ask?'

There was no point in hiding it.

'I keep seeing my wife.'

Lao Lao looked interested.

'Does she say anything?'

'Nothing useful. Not so far.'

She stubbed out her stinking cigar in the sink by the bed.

'Alice says your memory's not so good. Maybe this is one way it's trying to make itself better.'

'That had occurred to me.'

'Best listen, then. Best get it talking.'

'How?'

She held up the bottle.

'I've had more stuff pumped into me than you can begin to imagine, Lao Lao. It didn't work. And I don't want any more.'

She hunched her shoulders and stared at her knees.

'What would really help,' I went on, 'would be some information.'

'I'm just an old woman. Why do you tell me this?'

'Because whatever happened, it began with that club that Jonny and May started. Sister Dragon.'

She waved a compact, wrinkled fist at me.

'Just Jonny. You leave May out of it.'

'She was there. She ran it. The licence was in her name.'

'No! She was just doing her stupid brother a favour. She had a good heart. Like her daughter.'

'It killed her. It killed them both. And my wife. And my son.'

Lao Lao was starting to look as if she regretted allowing me into the room.

'What do you want from me, Bierce?'

'Something that can help me understand what these people need so much.'

'They think you know that!'

Clearly Alice talked to her grandma rather more than she let on. Either that or . . . I didn't want to think too much about the alternative just then.

'They're wrong. And tomorrow I've got to tell them something. I don't know what. This has got to come to an end. We'll run out of places to hide. We'll run out of patience with each other.'

'You're a smart man in some ways,' she said, which was, I believe, quite a compliment.

'I've spent a lot of time in jail for something I didn't do. How smart is that?'

'You should have seen some of the jerks she brought home. So what's wrong with my granddaughter? You too good for her?'

'There's nothing wrong with her. I've other things on my mind right now. I need some help.'

She shuffled her round body on the bed, steeling herself to say something awkward.

'You got to remember, Bierce. I came here illegal, forty-four years ago, when May was two and her brother just a couple of years older. I thought my husband would follow in a few months. Instead the stupid man died. I was on my own. I didn't get protection from no one. Not the police. Not my own people. That's good education. You learn to stay out of the way. To talk stupid when you're around people you don't know. You learn to make yourself invisible.'

'I can understand that,' I agreed.

'Yeah, but try telling it to your kids. Jonny and May didn't think they were Chinese at all, not really. This was their home. They could do what they wanted. Except . . . they were still illegal. They just didn't know it. So they walked around pretending they were something they weren't, and when it all went wrong they had nothing. Except me, yelling at them. What else could I do?'

She put down the drink. Lao Lao was an interesting woman. That didn't surprise me.

'Listen, Bierce. I'm saying this once and once only. I tried to put them straight. Then I gave up. When your kids go bad, you can talk till you've got no voice left. If that don't work, all you can do is wait and hope. I couldn't fix Jonny. He was a loser, always was. Never did a thing for anyone. But May was the sweetest kid I ever knew. She was always getting him out of trouble and never a word of thanks, nothing. That was how she was. Everyone loved her. She would have come good once she'd got all the nonsense out of her system. She *was* coming good when Alice came along, and Alice is her daughter through and through. A few years ago you wouldn't have recognized *her*. She was just a bum, living with bums, a real mess. Then she changed.'

I'd a good idea what had done that too.

'When she decided she needed to find out more about her mom?' I asked.

'Like I said, you're a smart man.'

'And if she doesn't work this out?'

She picked up the whiskey glass again and just looked at me.

'Alice doesn't tell me everything. She's her mother's daughter in that way.'

That had occurred to me already.

'Is she in trouble?' I asked.

'We're all in trouble, aren't we?'

That wasn't good enough.

'You know what I mean, Lao Lao. Alice came to me. It wasn't the other way round.'

She knocked back some more of the drink.

'I already told you, Bierce. If a child doesn't want to tell you, there's no making them. Not a way that works.'

That particular avenue was clearly closed, though it was apparent Lao Lao knew full well what I was talking about. I tried something different.

'Who gave Jonny the money to open the club?' I asked.

'I don't know.'

'If you lie to me I can't help anyone. Alice. Me. You. It's too late for that. Don't you see?'

'We've got money. We can move somewhere else.'

'Then Alice won't know, will she? And maybe these people she's been working with will get even madder than they must be at the moment.'

'Don't try this emotional stuff on me, Bierce.'

'Emotions matter. You love Alice. She loves you. That matters more than anything else in the world.'

'Really?' she snapped. 'What do *you* love? Huh? Not even yourself from what I see. Where do you think that's going to get you? Fix yourself before you think you're good enough to fix the rest of us.'

'I'm just like Alice. I want to know what happened,' I said weakly. 'After that . . .' I honestly hadn't given it a thought, but I wasn't going to let her bludgeon me out of the room before I'd pushed a little further.

'Jonny mixed in bad company. Alice told me. Did he get the money for the club from some local crooks? Kyle McKendrick, say?'

She laughed.

'Kyle McKendrick. Some stuffed-up white guy in a fancy suit. I'm Chinese, Bierce. We got crooks, real crooks. People who could pick up Kyle McKendrick by his ankles right now and throw him in the ocean. All these white guys . . . they want it both ways. Want to be crooks and big citizens, in the paper, everywhere. Chinese crooks know who they are. They don't need dinner dates with politicians to pump up their egos.'

In some roundabout way Lao Lao was, I believe, trying to tell me something.

I'd worked that part of the city. I knew the four

rival triad groups who fought to control it. I could still remember their names. They weren't the kind of thing you'd forget: Wo Shing Wo, San Yee On, 14K-Hau and 14K-Ngai.

'So if it wasn't crooked white money, maybe it was crooked Chinese money?'

'This was Chinatown! Half the restaurants and bars there were opened on crooked money. You think I'd be worried about *that*?'

What few working gears remained in my mind crashed at that moment.

'I give up. What's left? The National Rifle Association? Opus Dei? The Boy Scouts?'

She was staring at her old, gnarled hands, looking deeply miserable. I wasn't proud of myself for not letting this go, but there wasn't an option.

'Tell me, Lao Lao,' I said. 'Tell me now or I walk out of this room, out of this place, for good. I had a wife who lied to me once. I never knew it at the time but it screwed us all up. Cost her and my son their lives. Maybe it killed May too. I don't know, but I know this: I am not dealing with that kind of deceit again. I can't.'

I sat down on the bed next to her, took her old hands and peered into her face.

'I won't,' I said. 'I mean that.'

She dragged her fingers from out of my grip and hugged herself.

Then she looked at me, half resentment, half relief perhaps, because I don't think this was a secret Lao Lao liked much either.

'It was the gov'ment,' she murmured, then poured herself some more of the whiskey.

She looked scared. Truly scared, and it even came through in her speech, which wandered back into the crude, half-English I imagine she used among most white people.

I wanted to stand up and find some way of kicking myself. Lao Lao had been trying to tell me this all along. She was an illegal immigrant, in her own head, still. She'd die that way. A woman like her would spit in the shadow of made-up hoods like Kyle McKendrick. She probably took tea with the wives and mothers of the four triads and listened to them moaning about how hard it was to get out the bloodstains from their men's best suits.

When every other possibility has been laid to rest, look at the most improbable.

'Tell me,' I said.

'Nothing much *to* tell! I scream and scream at Jonny not to get involved in this shit. He so stupid. By the end it like he not my son at all. He just live in some dream world where he was this big shot who could have anything he wanted. Then one time, when I'm yelling at him again, he turns round on me, like I'm an idiot or something, and says, "What do you know, you old witch? It's the gov'ment that's giving me the money. It's all some big, secret thing the gov'ment's doing, and when it's all over, you just look at me. I'm a big man.

So big I won't even have to talk to some miserable immigrant bitch like you."'

The glass bobbed up and down, got emptied, got filled again.

'Three weeks later Jonny's gone for good. And I'm coming home and my little girl's dead on the floor, just some bloody mess there I don't really recognize, and that half-white kid of hers is going crazy in a cupboard.'

There was a shine in her round black eyes and I felt deeply, sickeningly guilty for putting it there.

'That's all I know,' she added. 'All he ever told me. It was enough. I can't explain to Alice. She wouldn't understand, would she?'

'Probably not,' I agreed.

'Besides . . .' she added, and didn't need to say more. There was a secret Alice didn't want to share either, and it concerned me.

She'd given me a clue herself. She wasn't an immigrant. She wouldn't lie back and take the kind of humiliation a woman of Lao Lao's birth and generation would swallow, then try to forget. She'd make noise. She'd do what it took.

'Tell me, Lao Lao. Are the Wo Shing Wo still the big people in Chinatown? Or did one of the other three steal their thunder while I was in jail?'

She stared at me, then laughed.

'What the hell kind of man are you? How do you know people like that?'

'I'm the sociable kind. I talk to everyone. High

and low. Good and wicked. It's the one small skill I own.'

'Small?' She had a hold on her emotions again. The question interested her. 'Wo Shing Wo are the men. No one messes with them. Also, they never harm anyone outside the societies. Not if they can help it. It's a matter of principle. If you got to have criminals, best you have people like them.'

I nodded. In my time Wo Shing Wo were also the biggest importers of hard drugs through the Yonge docks. If they were still in charge, that couldn't have changed. But I wasn't in a position to be picky.

'You still know a few people there?'

'Not for a long time, Bierce. Not since Jonny got killed.'

'You can call someone, though?'

She shook her head.

'You can never beat the gov'ment, Bierce. Never.'

One way or another I seemed to be kissing a lot of women since I left jail. So it seemed only natural that I leaned over and placed a gentle, filial one on her wrinkled, walnut cheek.

'We don't need to beat them,' I said. 'We just need to know their game.'

I walked outside, past Alice's door, back to my own room. Then I waited an hour, thinking, before quietly sneaking outside.

The weather forecast Alice had found for me was turning out to be dead right. When I walked to the edge of the parking lot I could see a long finger of fog rolling in across the bay from the north. It would reach the city by sunrise. Tomorrow the sun would be gone for most of the day, trying to burn off this grey shroud that would trap every district, rich and poor, in a cold, damp sea mist of the kind anyone who'd grown up here had come to know from an early age.

I wished I could have left them the gun; the weapon Lao Lao had given Alice was so old-looking it maybe didn't work well, and was doubtless the only one she had. But I did count out ten thousand from my stash, then placed the rest in an envelope that I pushed beneath Alice's door on the way out.

I left a note by the computer. It said, 'Believe me when I say this. I am not abandoning you. Whatever it is you want, I will try to find it for you. Wait for my call.'

They could have the car too. I noticed on the way in that the spotty receptionist appeared to keep a pushbike at the back of the property. We were so out of the way here – and the thing was so decrepit – that he didn't even bother to lock it.

So I hopped on the hard, worn saddle, felt my muscles seize as they tried to accustom them-selves to a form of physical exercise they hadn't encountered since we'd been teenagers together, and pushed myself out of the drive of the Seaview Motel, grateful for the bright silver light of a full moon that shone in fat beams through the conifer forest that ran all the way to the city outskirts.

It was a good thing it was downhill. I didn't feel too short of sleep, but I was stiff and out of condition. I freewheeled as much of the way as I could, first through the deserted business streets of Westmont, then on through Eden, where the Chinese restaurants and gambling parlours were still operating, even in the morning hours, and the odd tram clanked its way noisily along the road.

Susanna Aurelio and Lao Lao had given me a few answers, ones that begged more questions, naturally. But there was a limit to the number of places I could pose them. Everything, I was coming to believe, hinged on one place. The house where Miriam died, where they found me afterwards. The house where something crucial in our lives had gone deeply, irrevocably wrong, and I'd never noticed, not for a moment.

I couldn't imagine Stapleton or McKendrick had the interest or the resources to keep Owl Creek under surveillance day in and day out. They didn't need it now either. They had an appointment with me, and, being the big, important men they were, they understood that was all they needed. They could come along with their guns and their might and everything would roll over straight into their laps.

For all I knew, they might be right.

I didn't mind. Something told me I needed to go back to Owl Creek that night. When I wheeled the pushbike into the cul-de-sac, there was nothing there. Not a vehicle. Not a sign that anyone was watching, or much interested in my presence.

I let myself in. Then, using a flashlight I'd picked up at an all-night store along the way, I finally plucked up the courage to go back up to our old bedroom and lie down, exhausted, on the mattress.

A few of Alice's things – cheap clothes and underwear – still lay on the floor. A tang of her perfume, something exotic, continental, and un-sophisticated, continued to hang around the room.

A part of me missed her already. A part of me wished I could sit down with her and beg her for the truth, not that I thought it would come easily. There was some internal struggle going on inside her too.

You're not what I expected.

Someone had given her a few ideas beforehand.

I tried to force these thoughts from my mind. I came back to Owl Creek because this was the place to find answers. The place to stare the ghost that lived inside me straight in the eye and ask: *why?*

So I lay down and fell asleep almost instantly, expectant, waiting for Miriam to appear.

What was it that Lao Lao had said? If you believe in them, they'll come. If you don't, they won't.

Miriam never entered my mind at all that night, though I seemed to spend a lifetime searching for her, in the kind of landscapes a Dalí on dope might have painted in his strangest dreams.

Then the phone was ringing, the little pink one Alice gave me, sitting by the bed, buzzing like an angry wasp.

I dragged myself off the sheets, still dressed. It wasn't yet dawn.

'Yes?' I said, not quite awake.

Someone was screaming. A female voice, yelling something wordless, over and over again.

This went on for a good minute or more. They wanted to make sure I got the message.

I felt cold. I felt small and stupid and powerless.

Eventually the shrieks stopped and I knew why. Someone had dragged her away from the phone.

'McKendrick here,' said an amused, cold voice.

'Morning, Kyle.'

'I have your girlfriend. Make me happy today, Bierce. I hate it when I have to put down something beautiful.'

FRIDAY

They gave her the phone when I asked. Kyle McKendrick was, you see, a professional. At least in his own eyes. He only resorted to kidnapping, torture and murder when there was no commercial alternative. I believe that, in his own head, he was simply a highly successful entrepreneur who'd managed to circumvent the conventional venture capital route to power and affluence.

I listened for a minute or more, then asked for McKendrick.

'Kill her, Kyle,' I said. 'If that's what turns you on. We're supposed to be doing business with one another. I feel deeply disappointed you should attempt to complicate matters in this way. This isn't personal, is it? Please . . .'

He spluttered for a moment. With people like this, it's always best to say and do the opposite of what they expect. And let's face it, what else did I have?

'You talk to her again,' McKendrick yelled when he'd got his voice back. 'I'm through listening.'

The screaming started once more and I wasn't

sure whether he meant he was through listening to me or her. I'd half recognized what was going on the first time round, once the initial shock had subsided. The clue was this: it was fury, not fear that was causing all that volume. And now it was flying in my direction.

When the swearing had stopped, she yelled, 'What the hell do you think you're playing at, Bierce?'

'Me? *Me?* You're my lawyer, Susanna. Not my girlfriend. Why don't you explain *that* to him. It might put a different complexion on things. Also what are you doing there?'

'I am trying to clear this mess up, you moron! That's what I do.'

A part of me felt sorry for her. A very small part. Susanna Aurelio was out of her depth, very possibly for the first time in her life. No amount of cooing and cajoling was going to help. I doubt Kyle McKendrick cared whether she was clothed or not. All this must have hurt.

'Did you call him? Or did he come for you?'

'Number two,' she answered, with a little less heat.

I thought of the big Jeep wheeling around on the beach. And the guard on the gatehouse, too nosy for his own good. Just one more minion on the McKendrick payroll, I guess. It was obvious he'd be watching Susanna. I should have seen that.

'What kind of mess are you *in*?' she asked. 'I had no idea . . .'

For Susanna, I realized, life basically boiled

down to reading torts in between sex. There was no real connection between what was happening out there and the insular existence she enjoyed in her pampered mansion or three. It hadn't always been like this.

'My kind of mess.'

'Well, that's informative. So what do you want?'

'Kyle knows that. I want him to buy me lunch. No. Correction. Now I want him to buy *us* lunch. It's the least he can do. I mean . . . does he want to piss off the Bar Association or whatever? How's that going to play the next time there's a vacancy on the Opera House board?'

Susanna went off the phone. I could still hear a little of what was going on. It sounded pretty bad-tempered. I'll say this for the woman. She had guts.

'He says no,' she said when she came back. 'Either you come up with whatever it is he wants. Or . . .'

'Or what? Put him on.'

After a second or two McKendrick's voice began to blare out of the earpiece. I waited till he had to pause for breath, then broke in.

'Quiet. *Quiet.* Please. Listen. Threatening to kill well-known telegenic lawyers is beneath you. If you don't know that, you need to change your PR people. The situation is simple. I have something you want. I have stated my price. This is just a case of supply and demand. Either we come to some agreement, or we don't. In which case I look for another buyer. Did your guys in the Jeep see the helicopter last night? Jesus, what is that Stapleton guy spending your hard-earned taxes on now? If he can afford that, he can afford to buy a little something from me, don't you think?'

It went quiet for a while. Then . . .

'Don't *dare* threaten me, Bierce.'

'Kyle, Kyle,' I said, in a hurt voice. 'You are one amazing individual. I've been in jail for the best part of my life. I've lost my wife and my kid. I've been stabbed with needles and filled with dope. And now, as far as I can work out, I am officially *dead* thanks to you. And what happens? I come up with a nice, simple solution to all of our problems, and you just turn nasty. This is not the behaviour of a gentleman.'

'Bierce!'

'Listen to me. There is no rule in the world which says that, in order for you to win, I have to lose. Or vice versa. I am offering you a way out of this mess, one that doesn't pose any legal risks for either of us, and will make all our present problems go away. You get what you want. I start all over again. A little late, being fifty-two, but it's better than my prospects were a few weeks ago. What's wrong with all that?'

He didn't come back straight away. This was good.

'So?' I asked after a while, cautiously but with a degree of firmness that told him, I hoped, I wasn't budging. 'Are we doing lunch?'

'There's no window at twelve-thirty! You think

I don't have better things to do than deal with all this crap?'

'Window? *Window*? What the hell are you talking about? Whoever it is you're supposed to meet, are they really more important than me? Well? Are they?'

'Yes,' he answered. 'They are.'

'But at that particular moment in time . . . ? Think about it. Ask yourself this too. How long is it since you ate at an ordinary place like Loomis and Jake's? Checked tablecloths with yesterday's stains on them. Waiters who spill your beer and dare you to complain. Fresh cooked lobster and clams. Nothing fancy. The world like it used to be. One relaxing hour, some nice food, a little pleasant conversation and then we're done. Both happy, both safe. You give me what I want. After which I point you to where you can find your heart's desire.'

Silence.

'So . . . Where's the harm in that?'

'I'll get a table for two. You don't get a penny in that stupid bank account of yours until I have it.'

'I can agree to that. Make that a table for three, though. Buy Susanna something nice and I think we can both guarantee not a word of this will go on the cocktail circuit. We can make it for twelve-fifteen, if you like,' I added graciously. 'Outside. Don't you love the sea air?'

'Don't push me, Bierce. I have my limits.'

As have we all, I thought, and cut him off.

★   ★   ★

He could probably trace me back to Owl Creek just from that. But somehow I didn't think Kyle McKendrick would bother now. He was in the same position as his opposite number, Ridley Stapleton. Both men knew they were going to meet me. Both felt sure they'd get what they wanted. Their older, baser parts were probably already imagining what they'd do to me once all that was over.

Crooks had changed while I was in jail. The ones like Kyle McKendrick had put on airs and graces. Some of them anyway.

I picked up my watch and stared at the phone. It was four-fifteen. Business people worked weird hours these days. Perhaps everyone did.

Unable to help myself, I called.

'Where are you?' she asked softly.

'What happened to "Who are you?"'

'Let me add caller ID to the "must teach him" list. Where *are* you?'

'Owl Creek. I had to. I can't explain it. There's a note by the computer. You should talk to Lao Lao too.'

'Too late. I've done both. You made a hell of a racket when you left this morning.'

'The only thing I do well is talk. And I'm not so sure about that any more.'

'Have no doubts.'

'Thanks. McKendrick's got Susanna Aurelio.'

'Oh, my God!'

'I thought it was you.'

I really would have been lost if that had been the case. What would Kyle McKendrick have cared about a struggling cocktail bar waitress whose one prize possession in life, a 1993 Kawasaki 500, was now dead and bent and rusting in the Pocapo river, all thanks to me? What would he have done to squeeze out of her the secret that I didn't even dare ask for?

'We have to get her out of there, Bierce.'

'I know. I know.'

'How?'

'Working on it. Talk to Lao Lao. Make those calls she'll tell you about. Let me know when you're done.'

She didn't drop the line.

'Did you see any ghosts?' she asked.

'Not a one,' I answered. 'But I'm looking.'

And look I did. Everywhere. In the garden. In the shed. In the garage and the cellar where I'd been planning to build Ricky a model train network on the old dining table when he was old enough to appreciate it. Or when I found the time. I worked my way through every bedroom cupboard, through sheets and dirty clothes that had gone musty and damp over more than two decades, through boxes of toys that made me weep remembering them, and all the assorted junk seven years of married life had accumulated in the timbered loft.

Forty-five minutes later, when it was supposed to be daybreak, I was covered in dust and scratches, cursing everything I could point my tongue at. I'd looked everywhere, in every stupid hidden corner, all the fancy, pointless places that attracted Miriam to Owl Creek to begin with.

It didn't help that I had no idea what I was searching for in the first place. It didn't help that Miriam's shade refused to crawl out of my ear, materialize in front of me and say, with a sweet, self-deprecating smile, 'Oh, *that?* You mean the thing that got us killed? Third cupboard on the right.'

I needed a coffee. I needed to think.

I went into the kitchen. On a good summer day the sun would be filtering down at this moment, sending golden shafts between the ugly, thick branches of the lumbering apple tree. If it had been like this while Ricky was around I'd have been ordered to take a saw to the branches.

I walked out into the garden and picked a couple of apples, came back in, still eating one. There was a jar of instant coffee by the sink. Alice had come prepared, as best she could. So I made myself a cup, black, strong, sat down to finish my apple, and began to accept there was going to be no sudden flash of revelation, no moment of epiphany in which everything fell into place.

The finger of fog I'd first seen in the distance from the Seaview Motel was now working its way into the city. I could feel its chill, damp presence already. Soon it would drift everywhere. I'd grown up with this kind of weather. It interested me.

When I was on duty it meant I could set my motorcycle on its stand anywhere in the city and sit there, unseen, even in uniform, listening to the invisible gulls cawing from the rooftops and the trams working their way through the tight, narrow streets of Eden, bells ringing, wheels squealing, the old-fashioned sound of metal upon metal.

The fog was good. An acquaintance, if not a friend. I'd been living with it in my head for so long it didn't bother me any more. But for people like Kyle McKendrick and Ridley Stapleton it must have seemed foreign and threatening. They thought they were better than the rest of us, different, immune. But when the fog came we were all equal, just walking animals with a few clothes on our backs, stepping through its chilly, opaque embrace, trying to work out what was happening up ahead.

I bit into the apple and sipped the coffee. Instant, like I used to make for myself when Miriam wasn't home, but out somewhere, with Ricky – was that true? – shopping or visiting or doing one of the many things she cited as 'getting out of the house'.

Such as putting on a cheongsam and taking Kyle McKendrick into a back room at Sister Dragon for a little quiet time together.

It was twenty minutes, twenty-five, no more, down to the Piers on my stolen pushbike. In this weather no one would see me. No cop would complain about the lack of lights. No street hood would get interested in what I was carrying: a wad of ten thousand, an old police handgun and a little remaining ammunition.

I was free. Kind of.

The coffee tasted better than it should have done. In fact, it tasted just like the coffee used to back then.

The fog was closing in, and it was thick and curling, a fat sinuous cloud of grey that seemed to want to make its way everywhere.

The kitchen door was still open. The shroud of mist began to work its way into the house.

'Nice timing, Miriam,' I said, and cursed the coffee.

'The coffee?'

'Yeah,' he says. 'Where'd you get it? I don't own any that tastes this good. Mind you . . .' Ridley Stapleton casts me a look that says, *lucky man.* 'I'm just a bachelor living on my own. If I had some beautiful wife to find me these things—'

'Colombian,' I interrupt. 'We pick it up with the coke and smack we get from the Yonge gangs. They deliver now, Stape. I thought you might have known that. What with you being in this all-new secret-squirrel thing the government's setting up.'

'Secret squirrel?' he asks. 'I never heard it called that before.'

He's wearing a dark suit cut very tight and has that moustache I always thought he'd copied from some bad black cop movie. He thinks it makes him look good.

'So what should we call you?' Miriam asks.

'I am a public servant,' he replies coyly, and picks at a morsel of pizza. 'You don't want to know. Trust me.'

It's the end of April. That last year. We've invited people round, colleagues, friends, a few neighbours from our old days when we lived in Miriam's studio apartment. The spring is so warm we take them into the garden, about twenty adults or so, and Ricky with a couple of friends riding their bikes around the apple tree.

'Secret squirrel?' she asks. 'Is that why you're drinking coffee when we went to the expense – the unusual expense – of buying in wine?'

'Strictly speaking, I'm on duty,' Stape says. 'You know, I can't believe they never gave the police department a decent raise this year. How do you people live on that kind of money?'

I lift my glass of white Pinot Grigio, trying to forget how much it cost, and say, 'Mostly I take bribes. Though I continue to hope the male prostitution market will pick up again soon.'

'But why secret squirrel?'

Miriam's feeling persistent.

'Because,' I go on, 'they all have nice clean coats and bushy tails. And they scurry around from tree to tree, so you know they're there but you can't quite see them. Listening. Looking. That right?'

'*You* have never seen my tail,' Stape says, grinning, and a part of me thinks he has actually thrown a wink in Miriam's direction. 'Oh. Excuse me.'

He pulls something out of his black jacket pocket. It's the size of a brick but black too. With white buttons, numbers on them.

He walks away from us and starts to talk into the thing.

I am getting mad.

'What's wrong?' she asks.

'Manners.'

'It's a phone, Bierce. They say we'll all have them some day.'

'Not me.'

'What's the big deal?'

There's an exasperated inflection to her voice, not far off anger.

'Everyone needs somewhere they can be on their own,' I point out. 'Privacy. Somewhere they can think.'

'Everyone needs money. How much do you think a secret squirrel gets?'

'I have no idea. We have a house, don't we?'

She glances back at the white timber garden frontage, then kisses me, just.

'My own pet caveman. When do you start dragging me around by the hair?'

'He doesn't do that already?' Stape asks, now he's finished the call.

He's still holding the big, brick phone, just so we can see it.

'Only in private,' Miriam says. 'How do you like it normally?'

He grins and it's ugly.

'Sometimes it's good slow,' he says. 'Sometimes fast. Today . . .'

'Ridley!' she says, laughing. 'I meant the coffee.'

I can't quite grasp what I'm hearing. She knows his first name. He's learned this little refrain of hers.

'Gimme that . . .' I say, and try to grab the phone from his hands.

'Bierce . . .' Miriam whines.

'Gimme that!'

I snatch the big, ugly hunk of plastic from him and dash it to the ground. It bounces on the soft grass. Ricky is watching, with his friends, still on their little bikes, eyes shining with shock and disbelief.

I kick it to one side, hard, and I'm screaming mad now. The rest of them, all these strangers, are going quiet. They're looking at me as if they half expect this. It's not just the noise either. There's something in my hands.

A sledgehammer.

I didn't know we owned that. I've no idea where it comes from. Still . . .

I swing it once. It bites the paving stone in the slender winding path where the brick phone now lies. Dust and dirt rise up from the ground, make a small storm cloud in the unnaturally warm spring air.

'You'd think,' Stape's voice says behind me, 'a man would know his station.'

I look at the phone. This time the hammer

doesn't miss. The thing breaks into a million flying pieces, cheap plastic and wire, circuit boards and buttons bursting everywhere.

The funny, not-funny part is this: there's blood spurting up from this shattered piece of junk. Gouts of it, small rivers. I can feel the spots hot and sticky hitting my face, smell them too.

I stop. I'm tired. I'm sweating and I'm cold.

'Miriam?' I murmur, closing my eyes.

When I open them they've disappeared. Every last dead one of them. All that remains is the cold breath of her voice deep within my ear.

'And you thought it was all about me?' she asks, teasingly.

I sit in the kitchen, the real kitchen, cold coffee in front of me, not daring to touch it or finish the apple.

I'm shaking and shivering, miserable and afraid.

The little pink phone rings. I stare at it, wishing I had a hammer right now.

Then I pick it up.

'Bierce? Are you OK?'

'Never better,' I say after a long moment. 'How's things?'

'Good,' Alice replies. 'I think we're ready. How about you?'

In the shadow of the apple tree I can see something moving.

I hold my breath. A large grey cat leaps into the lower branches and seizes a sparrow picking at the heart of a half-rotten apple dangling there. The dying bird struggles in its sharp claws, a cloud of soft, insubstantial feathers now stained with blood.

'Ready.'

I cycled through the fog, navigating on memory and the sound of the trams, listening to their iron wheels clanking, old bells chiming, through the invisible streets of Eden, past Fair Meadow and Leather Yard, God's Acre and Silent Street, on into Westmont, where gigantic black limousines were starting to vomit up their breakfasts of suited executives looking to rule the coming day.

These streets used to be my life. The red-brick squares of late Victoriana, the long, narrow lanes of timbered stores and homes. Beyond the grey shroud it was, I knew, changed. In Westmont, huge shapes loomed above me, dark monoliths, with dim yellow lights burning in offices that probably never slept. On the low, two-lane carriageway of Broad Street, once a grassy plain for cows and linking Eden with the port, video stores and fast-food outlets shone like neon spectres risen from what was once parking lots and storage areas, a place the sensible never went.

Everywhere vehicles glided past me, oblivious to my presence. Only the middle classes cycled these days, I guessed. They started work late. And few would be found at the Piers.

That change had begun in my childhood. As the

Yonge docks grew steadily grubbier and more dangerous, the city stepped in to preserve a little of its 'heritage'. The unions were losing their power. More and more ships arrived, from Japan and Europe, bringing their wares in containers, not open holds. That meant fewer men and less pier space. Eventually the full extent of the commercial waterfront – thirty-seven piers – was too much. So they hived off everything except the first nineteen, demolished twenty and twenty-one to build a new concert hall, as a landmark between the good part of the city and the bad, and dubbed the rest 'the Piers'.

Some were commuter ferry stops, bringing in workers from the islands and suburbs along the coast. The rest were tourist attractions: restaurants and bars, fairground arcades and rides, stores selling everything from kids' toys to Chinese furniture and Russian furs.

Only Pier Twenty-six stayed the same in all of this. It was here, for three-quarters of a century, that the city's fishing fleet had brought its catch. In the great glass hall of the fish market locals and visitors crowded to buy salmon and scrod, mussels and oysters, and, as its fame grew, fancier stuff from further afield, Alaskan spider crab and Maine lobster, South American tilapia and red snapper from Jamaica.

I knew this place well from when I was a schoolkid. During the holidays I used to come down and earn a little cash, scrubbing mussels and scraping out the meat from fresh boiled crab. Then, when the morning's work was done, I'd wait around for the real reward, which was a seafood stew, made with tomatoes and garlic and wine, just the things your mom would never use at home, thrown together by the stall bosses themselves, and handed out for nothing to anyone who'd put in a good morning's work.

They fed me every time, on two accounts. I always earned my money. More importantly, my best friend, the one who got me into this tight little community, which was almost exclusively Italian, was Mickey Carluccio, son of the man who owned this part of town.

The Carluccios were a sprawling second-generation family from Salento in Puglia and proud of the fact. Their fiefdom covered Pier Twenty-six and the tourist candy and drink stands that roamed the entire area, from one end to the other, selling identical junk food to identical dumb tourists gasping for a sugar refill.

If you wanted to trade in Pier Twenty-six you saw Mickey's old man, Arturo, a large, smiling individual who had a habit of patting my head every time he saw me.

If you wanted to hawk your goods to the dullards meandering the piers and the waterfront, you hired your cart from the Carluccios too. Breaking either of these rules was a sure-fire way to get yourself roughed up a little, then dumped back in town with a reminder to be more polite next time round. They also owned Loomis and Jake's, after Loomis, who'd long ago bought out his partner, defaulted on some gambling debts. This was before my time, but everyone said the food, which was wonderful before, just got better and better after the Carluccios arrived.

The month we discovered Miriam was pregnant, a porter looking to get paid found Arturo at his desk in Pier Twenty-six. His face had been shot off. Before that happened someone had removed his fingers with the large, curved knife he often used to gut big fish like tuna and halibut. Arturo liked to mix with the real men in the market hall, doing what they did, all his life.

We never got a soul in court, naturally. The gossip was that one of the bigger crime firms, a *real* crime firm, had walked in and asked Arturo to front some kind of a dope-smuggling operation through the boats he used to bring in imported species from South America. Arturo had a family the size of a small country. Like Liechtenstein in all probability. From what little I recalled of him, drugs would be something he wouldn't touch, not from a mile.

So they took off his fingers, then shot away his face. Remembering this reminded me it wasn't all sunshine and lemonade in my time after all.

I'd lost touch with my schoolfriend Mickey long before that. When I chose my particular calling the relationship had cooled on both sides. But I'd phoned him a few days after, asking whether he minded if I came to the funeral. I always loved being around his old man, particularly after my own father was gone. He was funny. Alive and real in a way most of the Italians on Pier Twenty-six seemed to be. They didn't have much money, in truth, and what they did have they spent on food and drink and family.

Mickey said he thought it best I stay away. I got the message. He kept the business the way it was. As far as we knew in the police, no one ever came to him asking the Carluccios to front a dope operation. Unless Mickey had changed greatly over the years, he would have told them where to go, especially after what happened to his old man.

Never threaten the *Salentini*, Arturo told me once, when he'd had a few glasses of wine. It was just counter-productive.

He was fifty-four when they killed him. A different generation, I thought, as I cycled down to the waterfront.

Or, my head reminded me, someone just two years older than I was at that moment.

Time has a habit of catching you unawares on occasion.

I leaned my stolen pushbike against the corrugated ironwork of the market and peeked inside. It was seven-thirty in the morning. The only living things around at this time would be the professionals: fish merchants and restaurateurs looking to steal the best prizes before Joe Public arrived and got sold the rest, and flocks of white cawing gulls screaming for the scraps of flesh that found their way out of the building and into the water below.

The smell of raw fish and the sea hit me in the face and flung me back forty years in an instant. If I'd had an ounce of Italian blood in me I could probably have got a job here myself, under Mickey's wing. And then what would have happened?

Maybe something worse.

I walked through the doors. The place was bustling with people haggling over white trays of fish and clams and scallops. The layout looked much the same. In the corner where they made the stew, someone was frying down tomatoes and onions already. The vast iron crockpot, black and burnt on the base, looked like the same one Arturo used to tip fish scraps into, singing some song in Italian, with a bottle of cheap wine hanging from his left hand all the while. The sight and the smell made my stomach start to rumble.

The Carluccios' office was in the same place too: on the first floor, overlooking their territory through long wooden-framed windows. I wondered what Mickey would say when someone he hadn't seen in almost three decades walked through the door, a dead man at that.

I was still thinking that when an arm grabbed me, rough and hard, dragged me under the first-floor overhang of the office above, so quickly I couldn't even protest.

By the time I'd got round to wondering what was happening I found myself pinned up against one of the ribbed metal pillars the Italians used to strike their matches on in the old days, before smoking and food got divorced.

A man I didn't recognize had me by the throat. He looked old: almost completely bald, with a florid, pockmarked face and watery eyes. He was strong, though, and big. I couldn't move an inch.

'Bierce?' he asked, not letting go of me for a moment.

'Mickey?'

'Who the hell else?'

'Apologies. It's been . . . what?'

'A long time.'

'Right. You know what puzzles me?' I asked.

He shook his head.

'Why everyone gets older. And I just stay the same.'

'Maybe,' he said, 'that's because you're dead.'

He relaxed his grip. I held out my hand.

'Aren't you?' he added.

'Very. Does that mean we can finally talk?'

Five minutes later I was sitting in Mickey Carluccio's office with a big cup of steaming cappuccino and a warm sausage ciabatta in front of me. He had a picture of his old man on the wall. Apart from that, the office didn't look different at all. Good coffee, good food and a small, comfortable room that had scarcely changed since I was a child. I could have stayed here for the rest of my life.

I told Mickey as much as I thought wise. He listened carefully, nodding his head, thinking. It *was* him, too. The same gestures, the same thoughtful, considered habit of letting someone get through a story without interruption. He'd just got older, that was all, in a way that was much more marked than anything that had happened to me. I'd kept my hair, my teeth, my physique. Probably thanks to the regime in jail and the regular check-ups they kept giving me there. Very regular, now I thought about it. I guess if they were pumping me full of dope to a schedule, it was important to understand how I was holding up under the strain.

Mickey had been out here in the real world all along. Which for him meant two marriages, both now over, six kids, all of them still beloved, and a young girlfriend who worked as the front of house manager for Loomis and Jake's. I didn't ask which came first, the job or her.

When I finished, he gulped down the last of his coffee, shook his head and said, 'Why you, Bierce? That's what I don't get. Of all the people I ever knew, you seemed the straightest. The one who'd end up retiring at fifty-five, living off a comfortable state pension, watching the grandchildren. You seemed so *stable*.'

Miriam and I had gone out for dinner with him

and his first wife, just a couple of times. It hadn't been easy.

'I don't know,' I answered honestly. 'One day it all seemed to be there. The next . . .'

He stopped shaking his head and walked over to the long window overlooking the office.

'I never liked her,' he said, his back still turned to me.

'What?'

'Your wife.'

He came back and sat down, so that he could look me in the face.

'It was always as if she was waiting for something to come along. As if what she was doing with you was the warm-up. I don't know. It's a stupid thing to say. Ignorant too.'

'No, no. I'm interested.'

I'd told him how screwed my memory was when it came to certain periods.

'Did the two of us argue much?' I asked.

He shook his head, vigorously.

'No. Nothing like that. I'm talking crap, Bierce. Tell me to shut up.'

'I don't want you to shut up. Did I ever look as if I could have been violent to her?'

'You? Give me a break. I don't remember you getting heavy with anyone. It just wasn't the way you were. Always. I remember when we were ten, eleven. There were jerks around at that school. I was little then. None of this fat. You stuck up for me. You didn't need to punch anyone to do it. You just told them what a bad idea it would be if they didn't go along with what you wanted. That was enough.'

I racked my brain.

'I don't remember that.'

'I do. It was the reason I stuck with you to begin with. That and the way you could gut sand dab twice as fast as anyone I knew. I *never* did like that job. Still don't.'

I laughed. It was easy.

'And when you heard Miriam and Ricky were dead?'

He squirmed in his captain's chair, spinning it from side to side, playing with a pen. The very image of his father, though I doubt he knew it.

'I don't believe for one minute you could have killed a child, Bierce. Not anyone's.'

'And Miriam?'

This had to be dragged out of him.

'Like I said, I didn't much care for her. I could imagine how she could drive a man a little crazy. Perhaps even you. She had that beautiful smile some women use the moment before they take everything you have. You want to know what I wondered?'

I did.

'I wondered whether she had done anything to that boy of yours. And that what happened then was . . .' He sighed. '. . . some kind of consequence. Is that possible?'

'I don't think so. No. I don't believe it's possible.'

'Then . . . I'm sorry. What do you need? Money? A way out? What the hell is your status anyway? Are you on the run or what?'

I shrugged.

'I'm dead, I guess. On paper. So if a couple of people come along and make that for real, who's going to know?'

'That's all I need. I'm getting you out of here.'

'Not yet,' I said quietly.

'Bierce!'

'There are people who know what happened, Mickey. I think one of them's responsible too. I can't just leave it at that.'

He groaned.

'These people being?'

'Half of them are hoods, though I imagine they'd tell you they were businessmen now, at heart.'

Mickey Carluccio swore. He seemed familiar with that concept, which I found interesting.

'And the other half?'

'Some kind of government team. Federal, I guess. Fill in the spaces. The kind of people you never hear about, not even when . . . or if . . . something comes to court. They exist. They're necessary. They're just not the sort who like you getting in the way.'

He went quiet.

'Mickey?' I asked.

He stayed quiet.

'OK,' I said. 'I understand. It was stupid of me to think I could come and pester you like this. Stupid and rude.'

I got up. His hand was on my shoulder. He was a strong man. I wasn't leaving, not yet.

'Don't rush me,' Mickey Carluccio grumbled. 'There's something we need to get out of the way.'

He didn't look happy having to say this.

'I know you thought my family were involved in all that mob stuff. It wasn't that simple. My pop was no hood, for God's sake. He was just on the edges of it all, a little guy who made good food for people the rest of town preferred to think didn't exist. He was their clown, for God's sake. He never did a serious thing for any of them. All he did was fool around and talk too much from time to time, when the wine got flowing.'

He glanced at the photo on the wall.

'So a couple of them listened to him in his cups, came round asking for something he'd never deliver and this got him killed. I have six kids, two wives and a girlfriend to feed. I am not going the same way.'

'I appreciate that,' I said, feeling a little anxious. 'I don't want your money. I just wanted a little assistance. I'm going to be having a conversation with someone important very soon.'

I looked at my watch.

'In thirty-five minutes to be precise.'

'Oh! *Oh!* I appreciate the advance notice.'

'I'm a dead man trying to walk here, Mickey. I want to have this conversation undisturbed. Your guys can make sure of that. Especially in weather like this.'

'No shooting,' he said. 'Nobody dead.'

'That I guarantee. If it all goes well, the person concerned won't even be on your territory after eight-thirty.'

'And if it doesn't?'

'Then who's to know? I'll be gone anyway. And the Chinese won't talk to anyone.'

His watery eyes lit up with alarm.

'The Chinese! What the hell do they have to do with this?'

'Nothing that matters to you. Are they so bad?'

'How the hell do I know? It's hard enough keeping a bunch of Italians happy without messing around with the Chinese. Get 'em in and out quick.'

He stared at me. I liked what Mickey Carluccio had become. He had authority and style. He looked like the boss around here.

'And the rest?' he demanded.

I opened my hands.

'What do you mean?'

'That sounds much too small a thing to have you come sneaking into my fish market at this time in the morning, looking guilty and scared as hell.'

'Just the one thing. I have a lunch appointment at twelve-thirty. Loomis and Jake's. Table for three.'

'You have good taste. I will make sure the food's superb. You can have some wine from my private cellar. Italian wine you won't see in the shops. The lunch is on me.'

'I'm dining with a man and a woman. The woman you can forget about. The man is, I think, something big in the mob, not that he likes to let on about that these days.'

'You didn't have to tell me that, Bierce. You already got a free meal and the best wine we have.'

'I intend to deal with the mob guy's protection, kidnap the man himself, then bring him and the other one together so that, between us, we can sort things out.'

Mickey was fidgeting on his chair, rubbing his brow with one big fist.

'I'll need you to do more than look the other way for that,' I added.

He kept on staring at me.

'*What?* After all I've said . . .'

He looked ready to throw his old schoolfriend out of the place that very instant.

'After all this you want me to help you snatch some kind of *capo* or whatever they call them? Have you listened to a single word I've said?'

'I don't have a choice, Mickey.'

He sighed.

'I am truly sorry to hear that. The answer's still no. Ask me for something I can give. It's yours.'

He looked around the room, the hall outside.

'This has been ours for seventy-eight years. The two sons I have who are of an age to run it don't want to know. Law and medicine, would you believe? How does that stack up to gutting a sand dab?'

'Mickey . . .'

'No.'

I glanced at the photo of his pop on the wall.

'The guy concerned was just some rising politico back then. I'm sure the people who knew him understood what he really was. Ambitious mostly. The kind of ambition that wasn't good for anyone who stood in his way. Do you know who killed your old man?'

'I know,' Mickey snapped. 'This conversation is coming to a rapid end now. Get out of here! Or I'll call one of the big guys.'

He had his hand on the phone. Throwing out bums was beneath this Mickey Carluccio.

'The man I'm having lunch with,' I added, 'is called Kyle McKendrick. One way or another, he's going to be in jail or dead by the end of this day. Him or me.'

He stared at me the way someone stared at a madman. But he put down the phone.

'McKendrick?'

'I think maybe it was him who had Miriam and Ricky killed. He was building some big empire back then. Don't ask me why he did it. I can't tell you. I was wondering. Did he . . . ?'

'Don't ask!' Mickey yelled. 'Don't *dare* ask. Christ, Bierce. I've spent half my life trying to swallow down what happened to my pop. Do you think that's easy?'

'I had a wife and a kid. I know it's not.'

'Oh, yeah! Oh, great! Lay that on me too. Jesus,

what did I do to deserve this? You walking in looking like you've been stuck in a freezer for a couple of decades. I'm an old guy, Bierce! I got responsibilities. People looking up to me.'

'I'm sorry. If there was an alternative.'

'Find one!' he bellowed at me.

'I can't. Besides . . .'

'Besides what?'

'When someone kills a person you love you have to find some way of balancing it out. I don't think you ever did that. Did you?'

He kept quiet. He was staring at the photo on the wall, tears starting to run down his cheeks, shaking his head, grinding his teeth, swearing and gulping for breath.

I felt inordinately ashamed of myself at that moment.

'You know why they cut off his fingers?' Mickey asked after a while.

'I've no idea.'

'They said it was a question of taste. He had this party trick. He used to play the piano. Really badly. *It was a joke!*'

My old friend Mickey Carluccio thumped his big fist on the desk and sent the contents, bills and pens, a mobile phone and some loose change, scattering all over.

'It was a joke,' he said again softly. 'McKendrick watched while that evil old bastard Guerini butchered my pop. A few years later Guerini's dead in a car somewhere out on the peninsula and everything's McKendrick's. He owns the whole damn city.'

'That was after I'd gone to jail.'

'I guess. Guerini was a buffoon. If people wrote histories of these scum they'd say McKendrick was the main man all along. They'd say it was all changing anyway, and men like my pop were just part of the dead generation who never understood that. This isn't the world we were kids in, Bierce.'

'I noticed.'

'I wish it was. That's a place you can't go back to. Not me. Not you. Not anyone.'

'I don't want to go back there,' I said emphatically. 'I just want things set straight. And I want my memory back. Nothing more.'

Mickey shrugged. He was in control again.

'Those were the things I heard,' he added. 'I think they're true. I can't guarantee it. What I *can* tell you is that McKendrick's a big man. Bigger than ever today.'

I nodded.

'He's a hood in a silk suit, fooling himself he's something else,' I said. 'Your pop would have said that was a sure sign of weakness. That a man should be what he is, not what he thinks he should be.'

Mickey grimaced, then reached into his desk and pulled out two cigars. I turned down the offer and watched him light up.

'We used to get up to some stuff, didn't we?' Mickey said with a shadow of a grin.

'I believe so.'

He laughed, a wreath of smoke curling round his bald head.

'Why the hell does it have to be me, Bierce? Do you really have no other friend in the world?'

'Not a one,' I lied.

He got to his feet, looked out of the window and stared down at the market floor.

'Keep talking,' he said.

Alice was outside, next to the chowder stall by the gate, shivering in a blue Chinese jacket. The fog was turning into a bad one. Somewhere over the curved roof of the market hall I could just make out the hazy silver disc of the sun struggling to fight its way through the thick grey haze. It wasn't making much impact. The city got cold in weather like this. It always fooled the tourists, who came out, spent thirty minutes shivering on the streets and the trams, then fled back to the hotels and cafes of Eden to try to stay warm, wondering how they'd fill the rest of the day.

This suited me wonderfully. Also, there was a steady rush of long-faced commuters dribbling off the ferry piers and starting on the long walk to their cubicles in Westmont, a small river of humanity flowing in one direction, unwilling, for a moment, to stop for anything in its way. Stape might have lots of hardware and knowledge. He wouldn't come alone either, though, because he understood I was no fool. But his helicopter wouldn't be flying. I had opportunity and more than a couple of surprises up my sleeve.

And I had Alice and her gang. Six surly, slovenly Chinese youths who stood by her, sniffing at the chowder getting made, snarling at the girl preparing it because there wasn't a bowl yet ready to eat.

They didn't look the smartest, nicest people on the planet, but right then I wasn't in much of a position to get picky.

One, the tallest, about twenty, with a long, arrogant face and the aggressive demeanour of a street punk, came up to me and said, 'Money. Mr Ho say you got money.'

I smiled.

'Who the hell is Mr Ho?'

He glanced at Alice. She gave him a vicious look in return.

'Boss,' he said simply.

'Mr Ho is a well-informed man.'

'You pay now. Cash in advance.'

'Do I get a receipt? Is this tax-deductible?'

He stared at me, unable to work this out.

I took his arm.

'Here's the deal, er . . . I didn't catch your name.'

'No name.'

'OK. Here's the deal, No Name. You do the work.'

I took out my wad and waved it under his nose.

'You get paid. You do it exceptionally well and I hand over a little more, not that I'm telling Mr Ho that. Agreed?'

He looked me up and down, smiled, nodded, then walked back to talk to the rest of them. They didn't return. I took this as a sign they were in agreement.

'Where the hell did you find these people?' Alice hissed at me when they were still mumbling among each other, out of earshot.

'I didn't. I thought you did.'

'You and Lao Lao put this together, Bierce. Don't blame me.'

This would have been interesting had I possessed the time.

'I can't imagine Lao Lao knows little punks like this,' Alice continued.

'She called someone for me. Maybe that person called someone else. Who cares?'

Alice waved a finger in my face.

'I don't know who these kids are, Bierce. Bear that in mind. I don't know . . .'

There. It happened again. One more moment where I could have stepped in and torn down the walls between us.

Instead I said, 'All this plan needs is a little muscle.'

She brightened up a little at that. We were both relieved, I guess. Then she slapped her gloved hands together.

'There's a *plan?* Well, that's a relief. I thought we were just making this up as we went along.'

I refused to rise to that particular bait.

'Am I to be allowed to share in this information?' she asked.

'Sure. Today, I – *we*, if you like – kidnap two people. One being the government agent I suspect talked Jonny and May and Miriam into the whole Sister Dragon idea in the first place. The second is Kyle McKendrick.'

'Because . . . he was having an affair with your wife?'

'No. Because one of these two people ordered a couple of lowlife crooks-to-rent called Frankie Solera and Tony Molloy to kill your mom and my family in order to keep them quiet about what had been going on.'

She nodded.

'Which one?'

'I don't know. Plus, there's a personal matter too. One of them somehow talked Miriam into thinking he was going to run away with her. Or maybe set her up in some new life in Europe, with all the money they were stealing from our joint account, and whatever else they could take from the Sister Dragon scam.'

Alice considered these possibilities.

'And when you – *we* – find out? Then what?'

'I don't know that either,' I answered honestly. 'Do you have any suggestions?'

'Not legal ones.'

'Me neither,' I agreed. 'Can we trust these Chinese kids?'

She smiled and shrugged.

'I'm just a cocktail waitress with a background. How would I know?'

'Can you understand them?'

'It's Cantonese. I can get it up to a point. They speak really quickly. These are gang members.' A shadow crossed her face. 'I guess they're what my Uncle Jonny was once.'

'Talk to No Name. Get him on our side.'

'All that takes is money.'

'Then that's what he gets. As much as it takes.' She hesitated.

'Do you really want to do all this at Owl Creek? Won't that be the first place they'll look?'

I'd thought about that already. I was beginning to have a feeling for this time I was living in. It felt it was smart. In some ways, perhaps. In others . . .

'These people aren't like that. They'll stare at their computers, call a meeting or three. Try to think it all through. We used to just blunder in and hope everything worked out OK in the end. I think that's considered a little . . .'

'Neanderthal?' she asked.

'Your word not mine.'

'Neanderthal,' she said again, and stared at the ocean, which was fast disappearing behind a wall of grey mist.

The eight-twenty-five ferry from Stonetown was for people who planned to start work late. Maybe they were lucky or hung-over or just plain idle. But there were plenty of them. I had to fight against a struggling tide of besuited, shivering, unhappy humanity as I tried to make my way up Pier Twenty-seven for my appointment with Ridley Stapleton, glancing around me to see what kind of interested company I might be picking up.

None that was obvious. The secret squirrels were good at their job. The problem they had was one they shared with all the covert people I'd briefly encountered during my time as a uniform cop. They lived inside their own little world, so much they thought it was real, and the rest of us were just marionettes going through the motions.

The squirrel mentality demanded, too, that there could be no easy way to do anything. You had to check out everything first.

I didn't have time for that. Neither did Stape. The difference was I'knew it. I also knew why I was there. Not to deal with Stape, or kill him, which was probably what he believed. But to snatch him from right under the noses of his colleagues. Here was my strong point. They were focusing on me when, in truth, they should have been focusing on him.

I'd borrowed a fisherman's jacket from the market and a woollen hat I pulled down low over my face. There were scores of men dressed this way in the fog. I didn't look out of place for a second.

Once I'd pushed through the throng of commuters I made my way slowly towards the head of the pier, stopping by the rusty gangplank where the passengers came off. I took a good look around. Stape was no fool. There were men – and women – hanging about. The next ferry back to Stonetown left at twenty to nine, another, to the larger suburban town of Rainport, five minutes later. Some of the bodies nearby would be people waiting to travel home against the normal flow of traffic this time of day. Some would be his.

Naturally, I made myself late. Stape was desperate to meet me. If I didn't turn up he would have to face the possibility I'd bumped into Kyle McKendrick along the way. If I was late, he would start to get uncomfortable, and the first rule in dealing with anyone you're trying to do bad things to is . . . make them feel as awkward and ill at ease as possible.

After five minutes of hanging around the gangplank, though, I was starting to get a bit restless myself. Mr Ho's little gang was there, crowded together by the billboards on the jetty, ostensibly checking out the latest movie posters. The ferry was making moves to go. This being the 'wrong' direction, and Stonetown barely more than a village, the return trip at this time of the morning would often be almost empty apart from the crew. On a day like this you could sit outside, up front, wreathed in mist, listening to the foghorn all the way on the steady ten-minute trip across the water to Stonetown. It should have been perfect.

Then I saw a dark crook-backed figure wending its way through the huddle of coated bodies on the jetty.

About time, I muttered to myself, and carefully

slipped my old police handgun out of the pocket of my jacket, into my tight fingers.

He was looking. The ferry was getting ready to go. Any second now the gangplank would go up and the grubby little tug-like ferry would be on its way.

I nodded to Mr Ho's gang. They saw their man. I waited until the ferry crew started walking towards their ropes.

Then I let off two shots into the grey foggy air and yelled, 'Stape, Stape, you murdering bastard, you . . .'

Fill in the obscenities as you see fit. Most of the ordinary men and women didn't hear them, not clearly anyway. Because, you see, I was screaming them out loud while racing as fast as I could along the jetty *back* to dry land.

By my count there were a good five squirrels following in my tracks. One of them had bright white hair and a limp. I guess Martin the Medic didn't walk away from the wreck of his Hyundai completely unscathed.

The sight of him, the memory of his sharp, pricking needles, inspired me to let loose a couple more shots up into the fog when I got back to the chowder stand, where Alice was screaming blue murder. Sheldon's old Volvo was up on the sidewalk, revving, ready to go.

'Get in,' she screeched.

★ ★ ★

When we turned south, driving very slowly and carefully, towards the Stonetown jetty, fifteen minutes or so away at this time of the morning, just a little slower than the ferry, I allowed myself a look back.

Mickey had been as good as his word. It looked as if the entire population of the fish market, a couple of hundred people by that time of day, had emptied out on to the wharf and were now milling around, looking lost and angry, blocking the narrow exit of the pier, spreading out on to the cobblestones of the pierside road.

However many little silicon toys they had tucked away in their furry pockets, the secret squirrels would be struggling against that unforeseen eventuality for an hour or more. From what insight I'd gained into their management methods, it seemed quite probable to me that, before they settled upon their next course of action, it might well be necessary to convene a meeting, with someone to take notes, and run through a re-evaluation of their goals and targets, their *modus operandi* and trade-craft.

At some stage – though not soon, in all this murky fog and human confusion – they might work out that Ridley Stapleton was missing. At some stage they might even come to realize that a small party of Chinese youths hopped on to the departing Stonetown ferry very, very quickly, with such a rapid, deliberate motion they just might have swept up an unsuspecting middle-aged man in their midst, and sat on him, lightly, but not too much I hoped, outside on the front deck for the short journey across the water to Stonetown.

Not that any of this mattered, I thought, as Alice drove carefully to the pier stop, where, dimly, we could now see the ferry moored, silent for the morning, with a handful of crew seated outside the terminal, cigarettes beaming like small orange beacons through the fog.

There was a rusty red van with some Chinese writing on it parked a little way along from the exit. I left Alice, then opened the van doors and got in. Stape was there, his hands in front of him, bound with rope.

He had a black eye and a bloodied mouth.

'Hey,' I said to No Name, 'I told you not to damage the goods.'

'Stupid old guy got punchy,' he muttered, and hit Stape lightly on the shoulder.

The vehicle began to move, with the awkward bumping motions old vans have.

'That is *so* out of character,' I said, shaking my head. 'His stuff?'

No Name passed over a handgun, a mobile phone, some kind of radio, a set of headphones with a curly wire coming out of the back and what looked like a mike dangling down beneath. Plus something that looked like a shrunken video cassette made out of aluminium. It was just big enough to fit into a pocket. The thing had a large screen blinking colourful patterns and a few silver buttons on the front.

'What the hell is this?' I asked him, and got no reply.

'Palmtop,' No Name answered.

'A what?'

'Palmtop.'

He pressed a button. The screen filled with a street map. A red star was flashing on it, moving gently along the selfsame road we ought to be using.

'What the hell are they giving you squirrels these days, Stape?' I asked.

'Nothin' special,' No Name interjected. 'My uncle got electronics shop. He sell this shit. Cheap too. Palmtop. GSM. GPRS. GPS. You can play videos and MP3s on it too.'

He tapped Stape on the shoulder, gently this time.

'Next time your boss want some more, come to Chinatown. We do a good deal.'

'You don't want to get involved in government purchasing schemes,' I said. 'It's not your field.'

They all stiffened at the g-word. I reminded myself not to use it again.

After which I took out my gun and placed it on Stape's temple. The Chinese boys stiffened even more at that. Someone turned up the radio. It was playing old Western pop.

'The suspicious part of me keeps saying there must be something in this magical device that tells people where you are. For your sake I hope this isn't true. Because if we get disturbed, Stape, I will, I swear, put a bullet through your temple before I even so much as consider what to do next. So?'

He pointed a finger at the side of the thing. I held it closer to him. He pushed at a little slot. A black plastic card the size of a thumbnail popped out.

'Oh . . .' No Name grinned, grabbing it. 'SIM card! Free gov'ment phone calls!'

They laughed.

'Where are we going?' Stape asked after a while.

'Please,' I answered, and gave him a playful pat on his shoulder. 'You're kidding me. You mean you really don't know?'

'What do you want, Bierce?' he murmured.

'I want . . .'

The radio was damn loud. A familiar tune. One that was starting to get to me.

The van stank of old perfume and Chinese herbs. I closed my eyes. She was there.

Sing to me, Bierce.

I can't sing.

Then pretend.

'I want to bury Miriam, Stape. Don't you?'

I was never a den man. No time and, if I'm being honest, no interest. Work and family were what mattered to me. The basement of Owl Creek belonged to Miriam. It was her territory and I

333

knew to keep out unless invited. She had a desk down there, for what she called her 'house routine'. She put in an old TV and a VCR. I never got the attraction myself. The room was the length of the house, undivided, but dusty and always damp. There was scant light coming in from the narrow ground-level windows that sat above the dampcourse collecting algae and mud. It always felt to me like a grave with electric lighting. Ricky didn't want to go in there either. It scared him. Ghosts or demons or bogeymen lurked behind the cobwebbed corners.

Perhaps that was why she liked it.

We passed Alice's Volvo, parked in the street, then Mr Ho's young acolytes drove their red van into my drive. I hopped out, opened up the garage. They reversed in and, thanks to the wonders of house design in the 1890s, we were able to take our captive straight to the basement through a side door that led down from inside the garage.

No one saw or knew a thing as far as I was aware. It couldn't have gone more smoothly.

Every last light bulb worked. They should have done. I'd checked them that morning, changing two for the replacements Alice had brought that first night, when she was trying to make the place live-able in. I told No Name to tie Stape to one of the six old kitchen chairs tucked beneath the ancient wooden table we found here when we moved in.

I walked round the room and ran a finger through the thick dust on the table.

'Sorry,' Alice said, with a smile. 'I never even knew this place existed.'

'And you?' I asked of my guest.

Stape didn't seem much interested in a conversation. He sat there, No Name's rope around his chest, under his arms, his hands tied in front of him. He was hovering between being awkward and being scared, with the former winning at that particular moment.

'You are *so* out of your depth here, Bierce. Trust me. The best thing you can do is let me go now and pray I'm feeling generous once I get outside this dump.'

No Name had sent the others back to the van. He was wandering around with a big, stupid smile on his face, looking at all the junk, the washing machine, the central heating furnace, the typewriter sitting in the middle of the kitchen table, touching stuff, pressing keys and buttons, laughing to himself. Judging by the amused look on his face, he thought he'd stepped into a time machine. He wasn't even in the womb the last time I'd been in this place. So maybe he was right. It was from another world.

'Best you go see what your boys are doing,' I suggested.

He was, I now tended to believe, a distinctly creepy individual.

'No. We done a good half of the job. We get good half of the money.'

'When the . . .' I started to say.

Then I stopped. No Name had walked up to

the old TV, a junk thing even in our day, with a mechanical rotary dial and a picture that shook from time to time. He'd punched some buttons on the front. A picture came up, bright and good. Black and white, but who'd complain? They built things well back then.

It was a newscast. It seemed the biggest story of the day was the fog. That was good to hear.

'Turn it off,' I ordered. '*Turn it off!*'

No Name was hunting round the kitchen table. It struck me after a second or two. He was looking for a remote.

I walked over to the TV and pressed the power button. Miriam had put a VCR next to it not long before the sky fell down on us. It was still there, still dusty.

It rang a bell, one I couldn't place.

I pulled out something like a thousand in notes, showed No Name there was lots more where that came from and said, 'I am, by nature, a generous individual. But only for good boys who do as they're told.'

He took the cash, grinning.

'I want watch you, Bierce. You interesting guy. This better than chasing rent down Chinatown. I learn from you.'

'Yeah. You can learn how to end up in jail. Alice?'

She stared at me, a little mad because she knew what was coming.

'Take him upstairs. I'll be along in a little while. Then we go back down the Piers.'

'This involves me,' she insisted.

'We need a few moments of private time.'

I patted Stape on his grey rodent's head.

'That's right, now. Isn't it?'

He muttered something obscene.

They went. I took out my gun, held it loosely in my fingers, angling it in his direction.

'The first time you lie to me, Stape,' I said, 'I will shoot you in the knee. The next time in that busy little groin of yours. The last time in the head. Do those three statements leave *any* room for misunderstanding between us? Because if they do, best we clear it up now.'

I should have remembered something. Ridley Stapleton had, by this time, been a government employee, a fully fledged secret squirrel no less, for a quarter of a century. He was institutionalized by that experience just as much as I was by the time I'd spent in Gwinett and Kyle McKendrick's private convict quarters, sweating and staring at the walls.

What guile and imagination he'd once possessed had been surgically squeezed out of him by some endless round of focus groups, managerial assessments and bonding sessions. He thought like a robot. A scared, sneaky robot with the moral backbone of a jellyfish, but a robot all the same.

All I had to do was press the right buttons and off he went. For one very good reason. Stape, my old patrol-bike buddy, the man I thought I'd saved from a life of corrupt policing, genuinely believed me guilty. He just wasn't quite sure of what any more.

We began with Sister Dragon, since that was something I was beginning to get a feel for anyway. There were only a limited number of reasons the squirrels would set up a sleazy nightclub in St Kilda and governmental privatization was not among them. It was a sting operation. They'd got their sights on someone they wanted very badly indeed. Someone smart enough to stay out of legal harm in the natural way of things.

So they did what smart squirrels did in the eighties – and ever since, for all I knew. They invented a situation in which crime could flourish and be seen to flourish, then they sat around, collecting all the evidence, waiting for the day they could jump out from the wings and say, *Surprise!*

It didn't come, of course. What did arrive was 25 July, killing day for the Bierce and Loong families. Stape didn't look too happy about that outcome either when we went over it. I'll give him that.

Ridley Stapleton looked at me and asked, 'Why are we going through all this, Bierce? Am I really expected to believe it's all news to you?'

'Yes . . . Because it *is*. What do I have to do to convince you?'

'Find a time machine,' he said instantly. 'She had your skin under her nails. You don't get that through a handshake.'

'Married people do not shake hands. Did you find my skin under May Loong's fingernails too?'

He lost his temper and yelled, 'It wasn't just Miriam and May!'

I blinked, wondering whether this really was news to me. My old partner was staring at me as if I were the devil incarnate or something.

'We lost seven other people that day. Some bastard tipped off McKendrick's people. You want to see? Pull that gadget out of my pocket. Give it here.'

I took out the thing that had the street map on it and put it in his right hand. He had just enough movement to hit the buttons and press at the screen.

'Here. This is Sister Dragon. The way we found it.'

I let him flick through the photos on the little screen while I looked. It was the kind of scene you used to see on the news in Beirut and places. Bodies and blood everywhere. Arms and legs sprawled out in that awkward, crooked way dead people fall.

'This is supposed to mean something to me?' I asked. 'I didn't know any of these people.'

'Is that so? The only two of our operatives who didn't get killed were May and Miriam,' Stape went on. 'They weren't there at the time. Not that it did them much good.'

'Were you screwing Miriam too?' I asked, not really wanting to know.

He closed his eyes.

'It was a business relationship. Nothing more.'

Something in his face made me rest the gun on his knee and play with the trigger.

He squeezed his eyes tight, then screeched, 'OK! *OK!* It was just the twice. In that damn club.'

'Why?' was all I could manage.

'Because she was beautiful! Because she wanted it. Because . . .'

The sweat was starting to bead on Stape's face. He went quiet, scared.

'Because . . . ?' I prompted.

'Because it was in that place. Don't ask me for an explanation. Or an apology. You don't get either. We set up that club to be somewhere people could check in their identities at the door, then become someone else. We – and I give most of the credit to Miriam – did that very well. You left it behind when you walked out.'

I wanted to laugh.

'You don't honestly believe that, do you?' I asked. 'Still?'

'I slept with your wife twice, in some squalid little sex club in Humboldt Street. She seemed pretty pleased with how it went at the time. That's all there is to say on the subject. Besides . . .'

He wasn't scared any longer. He was just full of hate.

'You got her into all this, Bierce. Or is that a part of your memory that got burned out too?'

The gun was starting to feel a little damp in my

fingers. I put it down, wiped my hand on my pants and took it up again. A part of me wanted a drink.

'You're saying I came to you and *asked* you to whore my wife for whatever faceless grey-suited bureaucrats pushed your buttons?'

He nodded.

'Pretty much.'

'I did this in person? Was I buying the beer or was it you?'

He wriggled. This was something he had to remember.

'No. Miriam came to me. She said it was your idea.'

The weapon twitched in my hand.

'Oh, right . . .'

'She said you told her there was some civilian undercover work going. She didn't specify what interested her. Neither did I. When we spoke it was kind of obvious . . .'

'*What* was kind of obvious?'

'She was bored. Bored stupid. She said you knew that. You'd talked about it. You both thought a little . . . experience might help your marriage.'

'So you never heard it directly from me?' I asked.

'This was Miriam! Why the hell would she make up something like that? Why the . . . Jesus, Bierce. *Jesus!*'

I let loose two rounds close to his right leg. The shells bounced off the hard stone floor and winged their way around the basement, whistling in different directions. Then they buried themselves in the woodwork somewhere. I wasn't looking. It didn't seem important.

'That wasn't a lie!' Stape screamed.

'Correction,' I said calmly. 'It was not *your* lie. It was Miriam's. That's why I missed.'

'What is it you want?' I asked. 'A memory? A cassette? A photograph? What?'

Stape sighed and shook his head. I lifted the gun again.

'You are seriously starting to get to me,' I warned. 'There's something missing here. You think I know about it. I swear I don't.'

'OK,' he snapped. 'I'll play this game. I should be used to it by now. We had some fancy state-of-the-art surveillance system in there. No one had ever used it before. There were these little cameras, big cameras, all kinds. The mob people weren't stupid. They had stuff they could sweep a place with too.'

He frowned. The memory was painful.

'The big local man at the time was Guerini. McKendrick was just his puppet on the council. But he had ambitions.'

Stape stared at me.

'Guerini was in some deal to get into bed with people from the east. We had one room, very private, all wired up through a video chamber behind in a way they couldn't detect. Miriam and May worked that with their clients, then dealt with the tapes after. When they weren't using it, the mob people would go in and talk. Sometimes it got a little mixed up. A bit of both. That was when it turned really valuable.'

'And?'

'Don't look so freakin' bored, Bierce. We weren't talking about a bunch of mid-rank punks running local rackets. They were all going to hook up, become something *huge*. Maybe legitimate mostly.'

I shook my head.

'What place is there in this world for the little man?'

'We could have taken them all. Guerini. McKendrick. Those bastards from the east. We had agents from all over waiting and watching for the day. Then, when our backs are turned, someone walked in and slaughtered every last one of them.'

He was glaring at me now.

'We got it all down on two tapes Miriam had cut for us in the video room. When we'd washed up the blood we found they were gone. All our work. All our evidence.'

I got the accusing look again.

'Which means,' Stape went on, 'they knew where to look.'

'That must have been a blow. You shouldn't have turned your backs.'

'Screw you,' he grumbled. 'We lost everything. The mobs merged. Guerini got blown away by his underling one day after playing golf. McKendrick became the local don and the city benefactor too.

Result? This is the Wild West now and no one knows it. The trains and the buses run on time. If you walk down the street you'd think the crime rate wasn't too bad at all. It doesn't need to be. *They own it all anyway.*'

Which was, in a very fuzzy way, very much what I'd begun to think for myself.

'So,' I asked carefully, 'if I did all these favours for them, how come I wound up in jail, sitting on death row, getting needles up me all the time?'

'You tell me.'

'I do not know.'

'How many answers can there be, Bierce?'

'Just the one, I guess. I was trying to screw them. Or someone was.'

'Correct.'

'With these tapes?'

He didn't need to say a thing.

'And if you had them now?' I asked.

'There'd be people falling down all the way from here to the Atlantic, McKendrick being one of the smaller ones. Why do you think he kept you alive in jail all those years? He needs the things, still.'

I must have been getting smarter at that moment. Because the next question worked so well it made me think I could have been a decent detective – sorry, *dee*-tective – once upon a time.

'And when Frankie Solera got religion and coughed this all up to his priest or someone?' I asked.

Stape's mouth creased with the ghost of a smile.

'Then bingo. McKendrick knew you'd be coming out soon. Which to us meant that one way or another you'd be dead before long. He'd had you for more than two decades, pumping you for what he wanted. If he couldn't get it and you had a ticket to freedom, then . . .'

He frowned. I think he couldn't work out whether to say what was on his mind or not.

'We'd prior warning Solera was going to get talking before he croaked. We lifted you out of the correctional facility six weeks ago and put you in some fake jail rooms we made out some place we have in the forest,' he continued, and for some reason that news depressed me deeply. I really had been out of things not to notice such an event. 'All that crap on the TV about the execution was just McKendrick trying to cover his tracks. We tried our best to . . . get through to you too. It didn't work. Still, you're alive. For the moment.'

Inside No Name's ropes my old partner shrugged, the way a doctor might if some cough medicine hadn't worked correctly.

'We thought we'd try a few last tricks. No luck. Then we thought we'd let you come home. See what happens.'

His two rheumy eyes never left me.

'You always were a smug bastard, Bierce. It was your name on that bank account. And the rest.'

I thought about the document on Susanna

345

Aurelio's computer. And that scribble in the margin.

'I saw something on the court documents. About a call I supposedly made. Which you couldn't use. Why was that?'

'Illegal phone tap. I thought maybe it was admissible because Miriam knew about it. She put the bug on your line.'

'*Our* line.'

'Your line,' he said, gripping his little toy. 'Do you want to hear?'

'Sure,' I said, and I knew from the quick and easy grin on his sick face that this was probably the last thing I'd want, ever.

His fingers started working the screen.

'We picked this up four hours after the shootings at Sister Dragon. Straight after May Loong was murdered. We don't know where the call was made from. Back in those days we couldn't work that out so easily. This was you calling Miriam, after you'd worked out she wasn't going to play your game.'

Coming out of the tinny speaker of his little gadget it sounded scratchy, the way old recordings do. But it was me all right. And I sounded mad. Very mad.

'Miriam. *Miriam!*'

There was a silence on the line. Then, 'Bierce? Where are you? What's wrong? Please come home. We can work this out. I love you, sweetheart. I love you.'

The terror in her voice sounded so real.

'*Damn your love!*' this old me on Stape's gadget roared.

'Ricky's going to bed soon, darling. Don't wake him. He hates it when we argue. Please . . .'

'*Damn your lies!*' I bellowed.

The call ended suddenly. Someone, me supposedly, had slammed down the phone somewhere.

Stape stayed quiet, looking smug.

The basement felt alive with her presence, strong and pervasive, like the sweet damp wood smell of the old timbers rising with the dust.

The TV's on. She has the VCR hooked up to it and something new. A large, shiny video camera.

'Miriam! *Miriam!* Where'd this come from? We can't afford things like that.'

It sits on a tripod, staring back into the room, big and ugly, connected to the VCR by cables. I've no idea why it's there. Ricky's at school. I've come home a little early. She isn't around when I arrive. When she turns up she looks flustered, excited. Perhaps a little embarrassed.

She rushes me down to see the camera when I ask her where she's been.

'It's not bought, silly. You know Caitlin Sanderson?'

'No.'

'You do. You just don't recall. Her husband works for Sony or someone. He has these things coming out of his ears. They hand them out. To get consumer feedback or something.'

'You mean it's free?'

'It's free.' She sighs. 'What's the problem? Look . . .'

She messes with the buttons on the VCR. It seems to me as if it was recording already and she stopped it. I know nothing about these toys, though it occurs to me that Miriam loves playing with them more than anything. Then a picture comes on the TV, Ricky fiddling with his face, looking bored. Finally he sings a song, something from *Sesame Street*. He seems embarrassed.

'How cute can something be?' she asks. 'Think of the memories.'

I tap the side of my head.

'This works just fine for me.'

'You're prehistoric, Bierce. Look . . .'

She puts a tape in the hi-fi, something I only half recognize, then stands in front of the microphone doing her best impersonation of a rock chick, wildly throwing her hair around, screeching the lyrics.

After a minute she stops and looks at me.

'Your turn,' she says, pointing at the camera.

'No, no, no.'

I'm not in uniform. I'm in plain clothes, and have been for a couple of weeks, staking out a dead and empty warehouse on the edge of Yonge. It had got so boring I even told Miriam a little of what I was doing. I *complained*. This was not like me.

'Do this for me,' she says. 'I like this new stuff.

Cameras and things. There's so much you can do. It's like Hollywood.'

'Hollywood's a bunch of dreams. Or nightmares.'

'It's cool.'

'I find it hard enough dealing with what we have already.'

'Don't worry. I'll deal with it for you. Stand there.'

I get pushed in front of the camera, stare into its dead glass eye. She fast-forwards the tape. I listen to it squealing. Then the monotonous thump of a bass drum, some scratchy banjo, harmony singing, male and female in unison, so high and perfect I couldn't imagine how people would even think of something like that, let alone perform it.

The bass falls in. The anguished voices roll.

'Sing it, Bierce,' she orders over the music.

'I don't know the words. I can't sing . . .'

'Listen. *Sing!*'

She turns down the volume of the hi-fi. It's almost like a backing track now. Inviting me.

'Come on. Just for me. *Please*. Then we can go upstairs and I'll do *anything* you want. Even . . . I don't know. You name it.'

This isn't like her at all.

'Miriam . . .'

She lifts up her scarlet dress, starts swirling it around her long, tanned legs, lifting it to the insistent rhythm of the music. I blink. She's got nothing on underneath.

'Here's an idea,' she snaps. 'If you don't want to sing it, just *say* it. Imagine I'm a movie director or something. *Act*, Bierce. Pretend for once in your life. Do this for me. *Please.*'

I hate disappointing her, even when I feel like a fool. But we're in our dusty old basement where no one can see. And afterwards she'll hide it, in the drawer behind the TV, which sits on a table facing the wrong way towards the wall, because the front legs are so weak and rickety that's the only position in which it can stay upright.

I mumble the refrain and they're words full of anguish and hatred.

'*Act*, Bierce,' She yells at me. 'Get mad. Get human.'

'Don't want to,' I complain like a child.

'Give me feeling! Give me fury, goddammit!'

She walks up and slaps me hard in the face.

I stare into the camera and yell, loud and hurt and angry now, hearing the refrain of the song, trying to match my pained grunting in time to the music, the way she wants it.

And I sing, because these are the words coming out of the hi-fi over and over again, '*Damn your love, damn your lies.*'

She hits the off button, for the VCR and the hi-fi, before the end of the song. The room falls into a sudden, stark silence.

'That was good,' Miriam says. 'Now we can go upstairs and . . . Oh.'

She's looking at her watch.

'I'm sorry. It's late. I have to go fetch Ricky.'
She kisses me quickly on the cheek.
'You don't mind, do you?'
'No,' I say, and mean it.
She points at the camera.
'Play with the thing some more if you like.'
'No,' I say firmly. 'It's beyond me.'
'Poor Bierce,' she says, and walks up the steps to the garage. Soon after I hear the sound of her car, gunning hard and loud, as the vehicle lurches noisily out into the road.

Stape regarded me carefully for a few moments, then said, 'Forty minutes or so after you made that call they were dead. It wasn't us. I don't think it was McKendrick. It was you and Solera and Tony Molloy, doing what you did at the club, and at May Loong's, trying to screw us all.'

This was interesting. Not what he was saying but the uninterrupted way he said it. I thought I'd been out for a good five minutes or so. To him it had all happened in an instant. The miracle of jail dope flashbacks. Or something.

'I was on duty that day,' I replied quietly.

'Kind of. We checked. You were on plain-clothes surveillance. You had been for weeks. On your own. No supervision. You could do what the hell you liked.'

When I closed my eyes I could see Miriam bending over the VCR, punching the buttons, hooking wires up to the hi-fi, doing clever things, copying and editing, words and pictures and sounds, managing to change things, meld things in ways I could never begin to understand.

I like this new stuff, she said.

I walked over to the table, leaned around the back, found the drawer that didn't really look as if it existed at all. There were only so many places you could hide something in Owl Creek, and the squirrels clearly didn't have the imagination to find any of them. The tape was still there, inside its cardboard case. I turned on the VCR, wondering how reliable these things were after two decades, and pushed the plastic slug through the dusty slot. It took a minute of button punching to get something on the screen. The picture was crackly and coarse, from all the dust I guess. But I'd found the right one.

Ricky, dead Ricky, just a few ghostly shapes now, trapped on a piece of tape, was singing his song from *Sesame Street*.

The poor kid didn't look cheerful. With the benefit of twenty-three years' hindsight I thought there was, perhaps, something in his face I'd never noticed at the time, and should have. Some unhappiness. Some awkward, inner fear.

My captive squirrel was struggling against his ropes, excited all of a sudden.

I found I was crying. I wiped the tears from my eyes with the sleeve of Susanna's errant husband's shirt.

'Sorry,' I said. 'Wrong tape.'

Then I hit the stop button and went upstairs.

★   ★   ★

'Are you OK?' Alice asked.

I didn't answer straight away, so No Name jumped in for me. He was driving. The two of us were upfront. His underlings bounced around in the back of the van with all the restaurant smells.

'He's fine,' No Name insisted. 'I watch this man. He handle himself good.'

We were heading through the business district, downtown Westmont, all tall office buildings and anonymous grey people on anonymous grey sidewalks.

I looked at her and said, 'I keep remembering. It's the house, I guess.'

Her fingers wound their way into my hand. I looked her straight in the face and wondered how long it was going to be before I knew exactly what it was she was lying about.

'Did he tell you anything?'

'Not really.' That's the thing about lies. They're infectious.

A few minutes later No Name stopped the van by the goods entrance. Mickey Carluccio was there already, as he promised. Loomis and Jake's sat round the corner, on its own small pier overlooking the sea lions and the gulls, just far enough away from the fish market to escape the smell.

I checked my watch. We had twenty minutes to spare.

'How are you feeling now?' Alice asked, and I think she was worried.

I thought about it, wondering how I might

inform her politely that this question was starting to bother me.

'Hungry,' I replied.

Mickey gave us an outside table. It stood at the end of the miniature wharf, with three gigantic lampposts pumping out heat and light from gas canisters in their feet. It was cold, but only when you strayed away from the table. The fog had cleared just enough for me to be able to see the black, slug-like shapes of the sea lions basking on the rocks below and the gentle wash of an incoming tide over the long hanks of green seaweed around them.

I was enjoying a glass of tomato juice laced with some comforting Tabasco when a large, white individual, twice as wide at the shoulders as he was at the feet, walked over towards me very purposefully.

He kept his hands stuffed deep in the pockets of his grey suit. I had a momentary flash of fear as they came out when he reached the table.

'Mr Bierce?' he asked in a slow, patient voice.

'No one else.'

I stuck out a hand.

'May I be of assistance?'

'I am Paul,' he announced. 'Mr McKendrick will be here momentarily.'

He had just the one earpiece with a curly cable coming out of it, then running down to the collar of his jacket. His face had a bland babyish appearance that was almost fetching. Paul didn't look threatening at all. He was front-of-house security, not the muscle guy I'd met the day before.

'What work do you do, Paul?'

'I am Mr McKendrick's engagements officer, sir,' he replied.

I pointed at the earpiece and the curly cord.

'Can you get sports scores on that?'

'No, sir,' he replied very seriously. 'I regret that is not a possibility.'

'Seems a shame. I was thinking of hiring an engagements officer myself. How much does a man like you expect to earn these days?'

He wriggled inside his suit, uncomfortable.

'I guess the . . . going rate is thirty thousand up.'

'*Thirty thou?* All that responsibility. You having to carry a gun and all?'

He swallowed. For such a large man he had a remarkably small Adam's apple.

'You *do* have a gun, don't you? Kyle and I have made a few enemies over the years. I'd hoped you were here to protect me as well.'

He nodded.

'I do own a gun, sir,' he said quietly. 'Legally.'

Poor Paul. He really was just front-of-house security. He'd no idea why he was there at all.

'Now will you excuse me for a moment?' he added.

He went back to the fire escape that led down to the lower level of the pier. A couple of feet along was the end of the kitchen block. The double wooden door still stood there as I remembered it. Waiters would bounce through at regular intervals with plates of steaming soup and seafood stew. It was a little early for that now, though. And from the brief conversation I'd enjoyed with Mickey Carluccio on the way in, I gathered that Kyle McKendrick's special of the day was likely to be more special than most.

I was just finishing the tomato juice when they arrived. Susanna appeared tired, perhaps a little worried even. McKendrick just looked angry. He sat down, shouted for a vodka, then got round to moaning about the fact we were outside, in the fog, listening to the horns of the nearby ferries and the gulls squawking on the railings from the piers beyond.

'I thought you'd want privacy, Kyle,' I said when the rant ended. 'We can go inside if you like.'

'No,' he snapped. 'This isn't going to take long.'

The waiter had turned up. It was Mickey himself, servile inside a striped shirt and blue apron.

'Gimme a plate of something hot and a glass of New Zealand Sauvignon,' McKendrick ordered. 'Plus some peanuts.'

'You know they make this wonderful seafood stew here,' I said. 'It's what the bosses used to prepare for the market men once the work was over. Fish, shrimp, mussels, clams, tomatoes, wine, garlic . . .'

'Yeah, yeah, yeah. Three of them.'

'Thank you,' Susanna said coldly, then put down her menu.

I smiled at her. It was a one-way thing. From the expression on her exquisite face you'd have thought I was the one who'd organized that morning's kidnap.

'First things first, Kyle,' I said the moment Mickey had gone off with the orders. 'I don't want anyone involved with this except us. It's nothing to do with Susanna. Or any other people you might get to hear I've encountered during my brief sojourn in this outside world of yours. Is that agreed?'

He pulled a sour face. A weird noise came out of his jacket pocket, like a tinny, fake symphony. McKendrick pulled out a silver phone, spoke on it as if we weren't even sharing the same planet, then came back to us just as Mickey returned with the drinks. Our genteel host downed a shot of vodka, then a mouthful of Sauvignon, and threw in a handful of peanuts along the way.

'Listen to me, Bierce. This is beneath me. *You* are beneath me. Give me what I want. Then nothing will drag your miserable sorry ass into my consciousness ever again.'

Susanna took a sip of wine, leaned over and said, 'I would venture the opinion that sounds like a yes.'

'How clear do you want it?' he asked. 'Please me and you live. Piss me off and I'll feed you to those damned birds out there. Her too if she jumps into the conversation one more time without getting invited.'

'No,' Susanna interrupted. 'I am not listening to this. I will *not* negotiate under this duress.'

'Shut up,' McKendrick ordered.

'Shut up,' I echoed.

She did, but not without the filthiest of glances in my direction.

'The money?' I asked.

He laughed.

'The money. *The money!* Here you are, eating my food, nothing in your hands, no proof or anything, and you're talking about money.'

'You wouldn't expect me to bring you the tape straight out or something. All those people getting shot in a little sex club you and your friends used for screwing and talking business. Come on, Kyle. Let's not be foolish here.'

He stared across the table, brows furrowed, eyes close to being crossed with fury. It occurred to me there were several things you weren't supposed to do around people of his stature, one being to call them fools.

Mickey arrived with three deep bowls of steaming stew. Just the smell made me want to take one to a corner somewhere with a whole bottle of semi-frozen wine, then eat and drink myself into oblivion.

After the plates were on the table and we were alone again, McKendrick asked, 'So when did you remember that?'

I laughed.

'You're a smart guy. I always knew that. Miriam did too. She never underestimated you, Kyle.'

'When did you remember?' he asked again. 'At that bum's garage?'

I shook my head.

'Keep trying.'

'This is not some stupid game!' he yelled, leaning across the table, spitting red tomato and fish pieces everywhere.

'See,' I said quietly. '*That* is why we're eating outside.'

An interesting thing: Paul, the engagements officer, didn't move a muscle during this outburst. He surely knew his place.

'When did you know?' he asked one more time.

'Always,' I said. 'Right from go. But what's a man supposed to do?'

He was spitting food again.

'We pumped you full of so much dope! I even got you moved to that correctional facility so's they could do things we couldn't get away with in Gwinett.'

Susanna was staring at me wide-eyed and with a flattering degree of sympathy. I have to say that dressed, with no make-up, and a glass of wine in her hand she did look wonderful. Back in my bachelor days I would have dreamed of dining at Loomis and Jake's with a woman like her sitting across the table, particularly if someone else was paying.

'Sorry,' I said. 'See it my way, Kyle. If I gave you everything in jail I was dead.'

He was slurping down his stew. He seemed to like it.

'Well?' I went on. 'Wasn't I?'

'Of course you were dead,' he snarled.

'So I kept it to myself.'

'Those doctors pumped you full of such shit . . .'

'The medical profession. Can you believe a word they say? This isn't a proposition from Wittgenstein. I just wanted to live.'

I raised my glass.

'Now I'm out again I just want to live a lot more. Also, I have had the opportunity to check the tapes were where I left them. And in good condition. No one likes selling shoddy goods. A satisfied customer is a happy customer. I want you to be happy, Kyle. Is that so wrong?'

He grunted. Susanna was still eyeing me with a mixture of shock and alarm.

'The money,' I said again.

'I put a thousand in that bank account you gave me,' he said. 'Just to see if it was active.'

Then, without warning, he belched. A loud one.

'Excused,' I said. 'And is it?'

'Yeah, yeah, yeah. You don't get a million, Bierce. You get . . .' He belched again, and this one sounded even worse than the last. 'Twenty thou and your life,' McKendrick finished weakly.

'I need more than that.'

'OK you get fifty thou and I leave the life out. And . . .'

The belching came back.

Susanna reached over and patted his arm.

'Kyle, dear. Are you OK? Would you like to go to the bathroom or something?'

'Stinking fish,' he snarled. 'Stupid Italians can't even cook right.'

Mickey was hovering at his elbow.

'Is everything well with your food, sir?' he asked, laying on the toadying a little heavily for my taste.

But Kyle McKendrick was dashing for the double doors to the kitchen, clutching his guts, letting loose an Uzi-like burst of gas along the way.

Mickey followed. I took a good look at Paul. He was shuffling on his tiny feet, seeming lost. I could see his hand hovering over some hidden button in his jacket. This was not good.

'Bierce!' Susanna snapped at me. 'What the hell is going on here?'

I took her hand.

'Just walk away quietly now,' I said. 'Take a cab home. Stay inside. Don't let in any strangers. Not till I call.'

'I haven't finished my food!' she yelled.

'Did you not see what it did to our good friend Kyle?'

'Yeah, but that's because you and your Italian friend put some stuff in it or something. Kyle may be stupid and blind but I'm not. I will not . . .'

There was a commotion beyond the doors. Loud and violent.

'I'm gone,' she said, and by the time I'd reached Paul she was nowhere to be seen.

He had his hand on his little hidden button. I had mine on my gun.

'Please,' I said, and ripped the thing out of his ear, then reached inside his jacket and retrieved the piece nestling in the holster there.

It was as clean and shiny as a cop's badge the first day they give it to you.

Paul stared at my weapon, gulped, sending that tiny Adam's apple on a long journey up and down his very large throat, and asked, 'Are you going to shoot me, sir? Because if you are I should tell you I have a girlfriend. And we were hoping to start a family real soon.'

'Of course I'm not going to shoot you, Paul,' I snapped back at him. 'What kind of man do you think I am?'

'I dunno. Sometimes Mr McKendrick meets people . . . I don't know at all.'

'Did you call anyone? With that magic earpiece of yours?'

'No,' he replied instantly, with a sad, earnest openness. 'If I'd been a little quicker like I should have been I would've, though. That's why Mr McKendrick pays me.'

The noises in the kitchen next door were getting

a little less loud. Pretty soon they ought to have McKendrick down in No Name's van. I just hoped that whatever stuff Mickey had put in his food had stopped making him throw up by that stage. It smelled bad enough already.

Mickey walked out of the kitchen, wiping his hands.

He stared at Paul.

'What are you going to do with him?'

'Can't he stay here?'

'No! We got a full house. What do you think this is? Some holding tank for hoods?'

'He's not a hood,' I objected, before Paul was able to make that point for himself.

'Well, he's not a waiter and he's not a cook. So he can get the hell out of here.'

'For God's sake,' I muttered. 'Paul, hold out your hands.'

Mickey went and got some rope from one of the lobster-pot decorations to tie him.

'What's going to happen to me?' Paul asked, with his gigantic hands stuck out in front of him.

'We're going for a ride,' I said automatically.

His big featureless face turned a deathly shade of white.

'No, Paul. I didn't mean it that way. We're just . . . going somewhere.'

I barked at him to get down the back stairs, then go round to the trade entrance, where we found No Name's van.

Kyle McKendrick hadn't heaved in it, thankfully. But he didn't smell very good at all.

Thirty minutes later we were back in the basement, Stape and McKendrick and Paul, bound on chairs, Paul to one side because to be honest I really hadn't planned on having him there.

Alice was watching me. So was No Name, who'd now had his second stab at my remaining money and still looked as if he was waiting on a tip.

Whatever it was Mickey put in McKendrick's stew seemed to have worn off, judging by the way his mouth had rediscovered its purpose in life. He was yelling and cursing and shouting the kind of language that came most naturally to him.

I looked at Paul and shrugged. Even he was a little embarrassed. Come tomorrow he'd be looking for a new job, that was for sure. If he got out of this alive, a qualification that had to be running round the heads of everyone in this room, except perhaps for No Name.

It was bothering me more than most. Because now I had them here – Stape and McKendrick, one of whom *must* have sent Frankie Solera and Tony Molloy round to kill Miriam and Ricky, and me along the way – now they were seated in our old basement, tied to chairs, there was something wrong.

It was this. *They didn't look guilty.*

Mad. Puzzled. Expectant. But neither of them

was acting the way I'd expected, the way that could have got me out of this mess.

Alice said it. Once a cop, always a cop. I know what guilty men look like. I can spot that shifty look in their eye, the way they wriggle and squirm when you talk to them.

Guilty men act the way they do for one reason and one reason alone. All along they're thinking . . . *does he really know?*

And I wasn't getting that kind of self-conscious doubt from Stape or the jumped-up hood pretending to be some big-time businessman.

There's only one person I was getting it from. Me.

McKendrick finished his latest bile-laden tirade and yelled, 'Do you even *have* this God-damn tape, Bierce?'

I didn't answer.

Stape was glowering at me too.

'You know,' he added, 'I was sort of wondering that too. Sooner or later my people will find their way here. You're already looking at kidnap and conspiracy charges, along with all the rest. If I had the tape maybe I'd have something to bargain with. If not . . .'

'What is it with you people?' I asked.

I nodded towards Alice.

'One of you got her mother killed. My wife, my kid, at least one of whom was innocent. Both probably, if I'd been a better husband.'

'I didn't order them dead,' McKendrick insisted. 'Maybe when the smoke had cleared and I'd worked out what kind of stunt you bastards had been playing in that club I would have done. But not then.'

I pulled up a chair in front of him and looked Kyle McKendrick in the face.

'But you did send Solera and Molloy round to the club to . . . clean up, right?'

He winced.

'What if someone did? This is supposed to be a free country. No one wants the government setting up places to spy on its own citizens.'

Stape laughed.

'Yeah, right. "Citizens". Let me tell you something, Kyle. Citizens are people who pay taxes, go to work every morning and generally get through their lives trying to stick to the law.'

'I know,' McKendrick snapped. 'I employ plenty.'

'Well, then . . .'

'Hey, hey,' I interrupted. 'This is not the time or place. The point I am endeavouring to establish is this. Did you send those two murderous bastards round to Sister Dragon, Kyle?'

He pulled a sour face and said, 'OK. Listen to this. You get an anonymous call saying people have been making movies of you screwing and talking private to your buddies. What would you do?'

'I'd try to buy them back,' I said.

'Not first off you wouldn't. You'd try to *get them*. That's all the answer you're gonna get.'

366

'And after the club you went for May Loong?' I persisted. 'Then here?'

'Are you serious? After we'd trashed the damn place we realized the tapes that mattered weren't there anyway. We were way too busy making preparations to get out of town to start chasing a couple of women. No one went after them.'

'Someone did!' I yelled.

'Seems to me,' McKendrick said with a smug look on his face, 'that's a question you should be asking a little closer to home.'

They were only looking in one direction at that moment, even Alice. My direction.

'Oh, no, no, no,' I shouted. 'I did not go to extraordinary lengths to put you two in my basement in order to hear this. Alice! Join me, please.'

She watched me storming towards the stairs.

'Where are we going?'

'To give the men what they want,' I barked back at her, then pushed the gang of Chinese teenagers out of the way and stormed into the garden.

I couldn't help but notice she gave No Name a look at that moment and said something short and low in Chinese, something that sounded very like an order.

It was cold and foggy and the only noise I could hear through the mist was the distant shrieks of hungry gulls. I couldn't even make out the silhouette of the apple tree or the line of the surrounding walls.

'Is this the right thing to do?' she asked, and came close to me.

'I don't know any more,' I answered. 'I thought I'd just get those creeps here and it would be . . . maybe not simple, but apparent. Something I could touch and feel.'

I stared around the garden, then back at the outline of the timbered house behind me.

'Maybe the answers are here. But if they are they're not what I expected.'

Or, I realized, wanted either.

Alice was shivering. If I thought she'd do as I suggested I would have given her every last piece of money I owned and told her to get out of the city for good. But it wasn't going to work and I knew it. We'd come too far.

She put her hand on my arm.

'Do you really know where these things they want are?'

'I think so.'

'Will they help?'

'I have no idea. But there's nothing else left. Not that I can think of.'

When I got out of Stape's fake jail I'd been in a haze. It had never really lifted. Owl Creek had swallowed me up, tried to hug me tight to what I dreamed were my memories of the place. Were they lies? No, not really. They were just parts of a bigger truth, one that was more ugly and more complicated than I wanted to remember.

Some details still grated, though. And one of

them was of picking up my old gun from the place I'd left it, the place Miriam and I had both agreed upon.

My memory was always good until I got hit that black night all those years ago, and then spent a couple of decades having dope shot into me. I had a feel for things. People. Places. Objects.

Even after twenty-three years, something had felt wrong when I went to retrieve my old police handgun watched by an Alice Loong I no longer recognized. It just took a while for the realization to sink in.

'Here,' I said, giving her Paul's shiny pocket piece, showing her how to take off the safety catch and then handing over a small oyster knife I'd taken from the kitchen in Loomis and Jake's. 'I took a gun off Stapleton too. You'll find it underneath an upturned fruit bowl on the sideboard next to where I parked Paul, McKendrick's bodyguard. Take that when you get back too.'

She stared at the lump of metal I'd placed in her hand.

'I already have a gun.'

'That thing Lao Lao gave you belongs in a museum. Use these.'

'I'm not sure I *want* to, Bierce.'

Here we were again. Dancing around the same old unasked question: what was it she was chasing really?

'That's very sensible but you have to think ahead. If it turns awkward in there for some reason we may not be able to cope. I want you to get Paul's ropes off and give him a weapon. The shiny one. Since it's his he'll be more familiar with it. I don't think he's a bad guy. We may need him.'

'Why?'

That made me angry.

'Will you stop throwing questions at me?'

She stood there and let the gun droop in her fingers. Her eyes were glassy.

'Bierce . . .' she said softly.

It was coming. All at the wrong time. And I didn't want to hear it.

I took hold of Alice Loong, I put my arms around her and held her tight. She was frightened. I think there was something in her face that told me she was a little ashamed too.

'There's something I have to tell you.'

'No,' I said, and put a finger to her warm, smooth lips. 'I don't want to hear it.'

'You do. I can't . . .'

'*Please*. What's done is done. I don't care about it. All I care about is . . .'

I ran out of words. I kept thinking . . . all I care about is you, which is exactly the way I felt about Miriam, who betrayed me somehow, set me up for all this black nonsense and paid for it with her life.

Alice Loong looked at me steadily, with that calm, self-assured wisdom I was fast beginning to appreciate.

'What if it *was* you?' she asked. 'Neither of those two look worried.'

'You noticed?'

'So why don't we just walk away? Take the money. Buy a bike. If you don't remember, would you still be the same man?'

'I think so,' I answered straight away.

She put her arms round my neck and looked into my face, hopeful, uncertain.

'We could leave them to the Chinese. Drive somewhere. Right now.'

'How far would we have to go?' I asked.

She thought about it and answered, in a quiet, pained voice, 'Forever.'

The tapes were there. They had to be there. I remembered the way things felt. It was Miriam who was the forgetful one.

'That's too far,' I said.

We walked down the path to the lean-to by the south wall, close to the shattered door we'd left behind when we made our swift exit with Alice's now-deceased Kawasaki two days before. I didn't need the shovel this time. The cement lid was on neat and square. I picked it up by the rusty hook and threw it to one side, then peered down, as far as I could.

There was something there, beneath where the box, with my old spare gun inside, had lain. It was a good place to hide things. Only two people knew about it. One of them was dead.

I got down on the ground and strained with my right arm, deeper and deeper. Finally I got my fingers round a soft, familiar object covered in dirt and mouldy leaves. I pulled it out.

Ricky's old school bag, the blue one with plastic red piping, fell on the lawn. The school was on vacation when he died. I guess it hadn't been needed.

She watched me as I brushed away the cobwebs and the dirt. Then I undid the buckles and prised it open.

Miriam had bundled everything up in three plastic trash bags, bound in duct tape, tight so no water would get in. It took me a minute to rip them open. Inside were three video cassettes in plastic covers.

'You knew?' she asked, and I didn't feel comfortable about the tone in her voice.

'I guessed. At least, I think . . .'

You knew.

How many times had I been asked that question for more than two decades, almost a quarter of a century now? Did I know? And if I didn't, was that what Alice was coming round to thinking?

'How could you guess something like that?' she insisted.

'Because when you live with someone you start to understand a little of how their head works.'

Even someone who turns into another person, in a flimsy cheongsam, when you're gone.

Alice didn't look convinced. To be honest I didn't blame her. All the same she said, 'You don't have to . . .'

'No. I do. *We* do.'

I carried what I'd found down into the basement. Alice followed. Stape and McKendrick sat quiet, watching me as I held up what I'd found.

No Name was still there and for some reason this seemed wrong. This was a private matter. Paul, quiet, baffled Paul, I could live with. No Name . . .

I threw some more money at him.

'There's the tip,' I said. 'Go outside. Listen to the radio. Tell your buddies there's a little more to come after we've done some private business.'

'What private business?' No Name asked.

I held up the tapes.

'Private, private business. OK?'

'OK.' He shrugged and walked off.

Two of the tapes had dates. One didn't. Not knowing quite why, I picked the one without a label, removed the tape that was already in the VCR, slotted the new one in its place, then pressed the play button.

Alice stood by me all the while. I watched the screen flicker. I think she squeezed my hand but I'm not sure. After a moment or two she'd walked away in any case, to stand on the far side of the room, beyond McKendrick and Stape, close by the scared, confused Paul.

All things considered, I was grateful for that.

It's the club, can't be anywhere else. There's a date stamp running along the bottom like some small tattoo: 25 July 1985, 12.52. No wonder Ricky never made it to Pee-wee Herman. I still don't know where he really went.

Miriam, my wife, I now know about. I see her, naked on some kind of single bed, face up to the camera, hair splayed back against the pillow. A man is over her. They are . . . making love is the polite term but it's not the right one. They're screwing. Hard and physical like animals, and the noises that are coming out of Miriam's mouth aren't the sounds I know. Soft and loving, excited and intimate. They're grunts, not pleasure, not pain but some strange place in between where all the notions that are supposed to go along with this act – passion, affection, some shared pleasure in a small common miracle – are entirely absent.

I can't work out who the man is. All I can see is the back of his head. Dark hair, pale skin. The video's black and white. That doesn't help. But a part of me's convinced I'm not meant to see him either. This is about Miriam, about seeing some part of her I've never witnessed before.

I start to shake. I walk over to the VCR and try to stab at the buttons. Nothing works.

They're driving at it hard now. The sounds increase. She's using words that don't fit right in her mouth. She's screaming and yelling and rolling her eyes.

My fingers flail at the machine. I start to think I could shoot it maybe.

Then the images stop anyway. There are white crackly lines like static and a hissing noise.

'That was worth a million dollars?' Kyle McKendrick says, and before I know it I have the gun in his face and I'm fighting to stop myself blasting his ugly head off.

But something's coming back on the screen. It's Miriam again. The time stamp says 16.11. Not long before I got home, if what they said in court was right. She and Ricky have maybe an hour left to live.

'You see, you see, you see . . .' she whispers.

Her face is in the camera. This is somewhere else. She's frightened, terrified. Her hair sticks to her skull. She can't stop brushing it back with her shaking fingers, frantically, more often than it needs.

'Listen', she says. 'I don't know who you are or whether anyone will ever get to look at this. I just want it *down*. OK? I don't know . . .'

She goes out of view of the camera. We see the basement. It's cleaner. A little. There are things on the table: clothes and stuff. And in the corner a case and some travel bags, though I'm the only one who'd really notice. To everyone else they might as well be junk.

'He'll be back some time. If I'm lucky me and Ricky will be gone. I know I shouldn't . . .'

She pauses, does the neurotic shuffle with her hair again.

'I want someone to *know*. It was him. It was Bierce who told me to do this. I didn't want to . . .'

Miriam stops. There are real tears in her eyes. She looks as if she can't control herself.

'He *forced* me to do these . . . things. With all those other men. Crooks. Their friends.'

Her mouth makes a pained, crazy O-shape.

'I didn't want to, Bierce. For God's sake, why'd you make me do that? We didn't need the money that bad. I feel so . . .'

She wrings her hands and shakes them as if they're wet and the water won't come off, not that it's doing anything at all.

'Filthy.'

She looks straight into the lens. A serious expression. Miriam is saying: *I have a hold on myself again.*

'He sent me down to see those government men. He said to do what they say. Everything.'

A pause. The hair.

'*Everything.* And wait and wait. Because some time at the end of it there's a kind of prize so valuable someone will pay big money for it. More money than a uniform cop could earn in ten lifetimes. Money he could use to do anything. Go abroad. Be someone else. Take Ricky and me anywhere in the world so we can live in a big house by a beach or something. He says . . .'

She gulps, as if this is difficult.

'. . . we just sell this thing to whoever comes up with the most. The crooks. The government. Anyone. And . . .'

Miriam sighs, tired, frightened.

'I don't believe him any more. I never should have. Bierce is crazy.'

She leans into the lens.

'Listen to me. *Bierce is crazy*. He doesn't look that way. Everyone sees him and thinks he's more normal than normal. But it's not like that. You don't see what I see. Here. In the house. He's mad and bad and violent and . . . I don't think he means this at all. I don't think he wants me and Ricky along. I don't wanna go anyway. *This is wrong*. I did . . .'

More tears. The O-shaped mouth again for a few seconds.

'I did these things. In that place . . . And now I'm just scared I'll disappear. He could do that. He could do anything he wants and no one would know.'

She stops. From somewhere there's a noise, though a part of me, the small, still-sane part, says maybe it's just her kicking hard with her foot on the floor.

'Oh, my God. I think he's here. He said he'd get these people killed. We'd hold out for some money. But he *scares me*. And now he's here. Jesus . . . *Jesus*. I've got to hide us somewhere. Hide . . .'

The TV goes black. White noise comes out of the tinny old speaker again. Crackly lines run across the dark, empty screen.

They look at me, each in their different way.

Stape, saying: *I knew it was you all along.*

McKendrick, thinking: *this is certainly screwing up my schedule.*

And Alice. Poor, lost Alice.

Alice stares across the room, eyes glazed with tears and rage, mouth trembling, trying to say something . . .

'No, no, no, no, no . . .'

The word just trickle out of her mouth in a conjoined mumble.

I don't hear. I don't want to hear.

Then she yells, 'It's not true, Bierce. Tell me it's not true and I'll believe you.'

The old question, the one that always catches me out.

I lift the gun. I put the nose against my temple.

I stutter what I always stuttered, the words that come out so easily now it's as if they're programmed into my head.

'I don't remember. I don't recall.'

And all it takes is something simple. A little light pressure on that warm stub of metal nestling against my index finger, a flash of momentary agony.

Then there is no such thing as memory. No pain. No chance of it again.

Something falls hard against the back of my skull. The old hurt, the familiar one.

I open my eyes. I'm falling. There's the sound of people, a babble of voices.

And a man standing over me, a weapon in his hand, with blood on the butt.

I look at his Chinese face and think, 'Ah . . .'

★   ★   ★

Lying on the floor of the basement, slugged by some hood's pistol, I finally realize. This face has a name. Two in fact. And I am stupid, the stupidest man on earth.

I roll upright. My weapon's gone, scattered across the floor. No Name and the rest of the Chinese kids are there, nervous and a little scared, because this whole thing has surely taken on a dimension they never envisaged, not in all their teenage fantasies. This is out of their league. Someone is going to die, and that is both frightening and fascinating at the same time.

The individual who stands above me is staring straight at Alice Loong, who's walked across the room to stick a gun down at my face, hesitantly because the barrel's wavering, between me and the empty, grubby floor, to an unnerving degree. His own weapon is down by his side. He holds it there, confident.

'Be nice to your Uncle Jonny,' I find myself saying, quietly, and hear the catch in her voice, see the terrified look in her eyes. 'Or Mr Ho. Take your pick. Which was he to you?'

'You knew,' she says, and it's not a question. 'I think . . .'

Her face is troubled, perhaps even undecided.

'. . . think you're good at hiding those things, Bierce. From yourself sometimes too.'

Is that true? I've no idea. All I know at that moment is I can't take my eyes off the figure next to her, the Chinese man with the lean, damaged face, skinny body tight in a dark hood suit. A man who is wearing a grin that could frighten children from half a mile away, not that Alice sees this, because that's what family does to you.

Jonny takes a little bow.

'Course he knew,' he says. 'One smart guy. Like I told you, girl. He worked this out himself, all those years ago. When he killed your mom and those other people.'

Jonny walks over and kicks me hard in the gut. It doesn't hurt as much as it ought to.

'Bierce knew I ran away, now didn't you? He just didn't expect me to come back.'

There's now a fresh stabbing ache in my stomach. It's not the worst thing happening at that moment.

'No,' I sigh. 'I don't know him. I never did any of that . . .'

I look Alice straight in the eye.

'I *am* sure. The amnesia only works for that afternoon, Alice. Nothing longer. This man's a stranger to me, not you, and I should have realized that. It took getting hit on the right part of my head. Sorry . . .'

Her gun is pointed more at me at this moment and it isn't wavering.

'Not that you or anyone here's going to believe it,' I add. 'I can't blame you.'

I shake my head, trying to clear it, then take a good look at him.

'So you went away? And then you came back?'

'Right first time.'

He strokes his face.

'Got this done in Singapore. You like it?'

Jonny has a short, snout-nosed automatic by his side and can't decide who to laugh at more. Me or his niece, who, for once, is uncharacteristically blind to what's going on. Alice has tears in her eyes and a part of me thinks she likes that because it blurs the fury of acceptance in her face as she stares at me.

'Nothing to compare it with,' I say. 'You mind if I stand up?'

'Sure,' he answers, grinning. 'You finally got round to handing out the tapes?'

'Finally,' I say, and point to the two remaining ones sitting on top of the VCR.

Stape is trying to barge his way into the conversation. He has his serious, let's-do-business face on. I feel like weeping with mirth.

'I still represent a federal agency in all this,' my treacherous one-time partner says, with a marked quiver in his cracked oldman's voice.

He tries to look dignified inside the ropes.

'I promise you we can cut you a deal. Money. Witness-protection programme. You name it.'

'Witness protection?' Jonny laughs, and kicks me again.

Alice keeps her gun pointed in my direction. Jonny has a genial-seeming, carefree nature. I can imagine he'd be a lot more fun, in the short term anyway, than me.

'Why the hell would I wanna mess with crap like that?' he wants to know.

'Security, sir,' Stape answers very seriously.

Jonny didn't say anything. Getting lectures on security from a man strapped to a chair in someone's basement, with a room full of armed Chinese teenagers waiting to do what they like . . . I can understand that.

'Tell them, though, will you?' I ask. 'Please. Do this for me. No. Do it for Alice.'

'Tell 'em what, Bierce?' Jonny replies, not quite understanding.

'What happened,' I say, and just the words make me feel cold and scared and angry.

The big grin gets bigger, like that on the Cheshire Cat I once imagined lived in the apple tree outside, pouncing on birds it thought too fat and lazy to live.

'Oh. What *happened*?'

He makes a little bow to her. It all looks very nice.

'See, Alice,' Jonny Loong says kindly. 'You're a grown-up girl. A good-girl. Who helps her family. So you can hear grown-up things. The truth is, we were all friends together. Your mom and me and Miriam and Bierce. Good friends. Sometimes I'd bang Miriam. Sometimes Bierce'd bang your mom.'

'No, no, no, no, no,' I start, but then his gun comes up and I fall silent. Not so much for the gun, but out of respect for the pain visible on her beautiful face.

'We had this little deal together. We work for the man here. We take his money. We get something precious of his. Then we sell it. Except . . .'

He shrugs.

'Stupid white jerk gets greedy. Wants it all for himself. Gets these hoods in. Kills your mom. Kills Miriam.'

'Ricky too,' I interject. 'Don't leave him out.'

'Yeah. Would've killed me if I hadn't run.'

She glances at me. Some small part of her still doesn't know what to make of this. She'd like that part to go away.

'You see?' Jonny asks her. 'I told you. Right from the start. Bierce is a bad man. Would kill us all if he could.' He puts a hand on her shoulder, an uncle interested in his niece's welfare.

'And now?' I ask.

He shrugs.

'Now Alice knows.'

He looks at the VCR.

'Now I got something to sell.'

He looks at me.

'Now you get dead.'

'Shoot this jerk after,' McKendrick interrupts. 'Look, Loong. Get me out of here. I'll arrange double anything this fed moron offers. And you don't get to pay tax on it either.'

'Lot of money for a couple of tapes,' Jonny observes.

'It is indeed,' McKendrick agrees.

'Thing is,' my new Chinese friend goes on, 'I talked to some people out east this morning. They say they could be very embarrassed if those tapes start getting round.'

McKendrick nods, listening carefully, looking very corporate.

'Damned right. That's why I'm prepared to be very, very generous.'

'They say, only some kind of real jerk could lose that kind of thing in the first place. Then screw up getting it back. They pay better than anyone too.'

'Hey!' McKendrick yells, straining at his ropes, the old part of him coming to the surface now. 'Cut the crap, Chinaboy. Get me out of here so we can talk business.'

'Here's business,' Jonny says, then empties four bullets into Kyle McKendrick's silk-clad torso.

The room's quiet after that, except for a gentle little sobbing coming by way of Paul in the corner.

'What happened . . .' Jonny repeats quietly, looking at Alice, not me. '*What happened?* You screwed us, Bierce. We had a deal and you broke it. I gonna kill you. I wait years for this.'

The short black barrel of Jonny's piece rises up to greet me. Two bullets left, I guess. Not that he needs more than one at this distance.

'No.' He checks himself. 'Alice?'

She's just a couple of feet away, glaring in my

direction in a way that makes me feel worse than anything else I've experienced in the last few days.

'He murdered your mom. You got the right. You kill him. That way it all gets even. Yin, yang. All that shit. We take our money, we do what we like with it after. You're a good clever girl. I been watching you a long time. I know. We can do things.'

Alice Loong can't take her eyes off me. I pull an old dusty chair out from beneath the table, sit on it and open my hands.

'Say something,' she murmurs.

'Like what? I'm out of answers, except the obvious ones. How about this? It was Jonny and Miriam. They put it all together in bed or some-where. Maybe they were both planning on cheating each other too. Maybe Miriam was going to dump him the way she planned to dump me. When he found out . . .'

'You . . .' Alice began to say.

'Me? *Me?* I just walked in on the whole horrid party, an idiot at the feast. What else can I tell you?'

'Listen to family, Alice,' Jonny says. 'You think I'd murder your mom? My own sister? What kind of man could do that?'

'Yeah, listen to family,' I suggest. 'Ask Lao Lao. Ask his own mother. Does she know who Mr Ho is? That he's been talking to you all along? Did she know it was his bunch of charm merchants she was calling into this party today? Or was that down to you?'

Alice says nothing and thereby gives me her answer.

'Is she even aware this lying, murdering, blood-thirsty offspring of hers is still alive?' I add, just for good measure.

Jonny walks over and slaps me hard around the face. I wipe away blood from the edge of my mouth. Broken lip. I don't even feel it.

'Just tell me you didn't do it,' she says.

'I didn't do it! Any of it!'

'The tape, Bierce. We *saw* the tape.'

'I can't explain that. I know myself, who I am.'

Two words, a vicious caveat, form in my head: *I think*.

The big question, the biggest, one so many people have thrown at me over the years, is forming at the back of her mind. I just know it. I understand, too, what I'll say.

'Do you *know* you didn't do any of these things?' she asks, and the room goes quiet, because they understand, even dead Kyle McKendrick wher-ever he may be, what my answer will be, *must* be. The one it's always been.

'Oh, my God, Alice,' I whisper, hearing my voice break with exasperation. 'How many times do I have to go through this? With people I hate. With people I love. I don't remember. Not much. I don't . . .'

I close my eyes. What does it matter?

'Kill me for being so stupid I never saw this coming, then or now. But not for that. Unless you don't believe me, in which case do what the hell you like. The truth . . .'

There's an important point to be made here, though I'm not entirely sure what it is. Last words often come this way, I guess.

'The truth . . .'

I begin to say, the smells of dry old wood and Kyle McKendrick's blood feeling their way into my nostrils, so strong I start to shake, while, from the peripheral edge of my vision, a black cloud begins to work its way ever inwards.

'The truth,' I repeat, and no one hears, least of all me, because there's a sound rushing towards me, fast and hot and angry, a roaring, devastating blast that can be one thing and one alone.

The truth is this, nothing but, world without end, amen, and now, in these closing moments, it comes racing into my mind, so vicious and vivid nothing can squeeze it back into the closed compartment in my head where it's stayed hidden, festering all these years.

It's that afternoon. I park in the drive and walk through the garage to the garden. I can hear voices there, angry voices. Miriam and Ricky, arguing.

It's hot. I'm tired. I feel stupid from all those long hours staring at an empty building, pointless work, work I don't understand.

When I get there he's punching her, little fists hammering on her knees. He's screaming and, as I look at them, I feel my head getting heavy because this is something new, a side to them I've never seen before.

They are my family and family spells love. These things do not happen.

'Ricky,' I say, and he stops hitting her, clings to my legs, crying, furious.

I look at Miriam and there's something in her face I don't recognize. Plain, bitter fury. With the boy. With me for interrupting them maybe.

'You're early,' she says accusingly.

She's covered in dust and cobwebs. It looks as if she's been scrabbling around in the cellar for some reason. She's been doing that a lot of late.

'I couldn't keep my eyes open any longer. What's wrong?'

'Bad mommy, bad mommy, *bad mommy*,' he screams, and tries to go back to thumping her with his small tight fists, though I stop him, pulling him back, bending down to look into his eyes.

My son's more full of grief and rage than I've ever known. This is all so foreign.

'She said we'd go to a movie!' he spits at me.

'Well, Ricky. Sometimes grown-ups say things they can't always deliver. Life gets busy.'

'She said to tell you we did.'

'You know I . . .'

My mind goes blank. There's nothing to say. I can't imagine what's happening here.

She's got Ricky by the hair now.

'Go to your room, you little bastard,' Miriam screeches at him. 'Go to your room. *Go now!*'

And I blink at what I see. She hits him. Not hard, but hard enough, a slap across his pale, flawless face. There are more tears, on his part, more screaming, then he runs, over the too-long grass, past the scattered toys, the second-hand bike with stabilizers I got down the charity shop because we didn't have the money to buy new, the cheap balls and tin trucks, into the house, screaming, screaming, all the way through the kitchen and up the stairs.

I look above me. The curtains of his room are drawn in a sudden sweep. Angry, bitter words fly down at her, not me. Then a kind of silence.

There are birds on the roof. Three black crows, watching me, watching us all.

This is like a bad dream. Or coming back to a place that looks like home, smells like home, has people in it that seem like family, but it's all wrong, foreign. Nothing's real or as it should be.

She's tense and tired-looking too. Her face is gaunt. She's wearing a white shirt and long dark slacks, grubby from the basement, and a part of me thinks: *she dresses like this when we go places.*

Not that it happens very much, and I'm ashamed by that thought.

Her hair's a mess. I don't see that often either.

'You're early,' she says again. 'Is it too much to call?'

'I live here,' I say gently, not as some kind of admonition.

'Me too. It's just . . .'

389

She's struggling to work out what to say.

'I thought you and Ricky were going to the movies?'

'Pee-wee Herman,' she snaps. 'I decided I'd save that joyous occasion for you. Though I guess that particular masterpiece may be long gone by the time the opportunity comes around.'

'Miriam . . .'

'This isn't convenient. I've got to go.'

'Go where?'

'Somewhere else.'

'When? For how long? Why?'

'Forever!' she yells.

I don't know what to say or do.

'I get bored easily, Bierce. You mean you never noticed?'

I shake my head. I feel stupid.

'I don't understand.'

'This is over,' she says, waving her hand horizontally across the tall grass and the scattered toys, a look of intense fury in her eyes I simply do not recognize. 'Everything. Me, you, Ricky. Owl Creek. All gone for good, never to return. And you know the best news?'

I stare at her, not a single word forming in my mind.

'They'll put it all down to you. I'll be somewhere else, with a different name. And all they'll think of is putting you in jail while I have the time of my life. *My* life.'

She turns. I put a hand on her shoulder. She

flies round, hands tearing through the hair at my face. I feel her nails scratch deep into my skin.

'Don't touch me! Don't *ever* touch me!'

I try to hold her and then she's gone, in through the open kitchen door, looking for something, racing round the room, frantic. I stand there, mind frozen, immobile with shock.

Finally I follow in her footsteps, bleating, 'Miriam. *Miriam*?'

She's not there. But someone is. Not one visitor either. Two. Possibly more.

Then I hear it. Ricky screaming again, loud and frightened this time, not the anger of before.

Ricky is screaming, and somewhere upstairs so is Miriam. It's her voice, even more than his, that makes my blood run cold, for the way it's veered from hatred to terror in just a few short breaths.

There are men in the house and they're murderous.

And before I can do a thing, raise a fist or a voice even, something falls upon me, so heavy I tumble, groaning, to the floor.

I roll over and stare upwards. It's a new face, one I have never seen before in my life, though some insidious cerebral connection takes me from that moment to now and says: *Jonny Loong*.

'She was expecting you,' I say, tasting the blood in my mouth.

'Stupid white bitch,' he mutters. 'Thinks she can screw with me.'

In his hand there's a sledgehammer. There's blood on it. Lots.

'Get the hell . . .' I start to say, then my vision goes black, my head feels as if it's about to fly off my shoulders.

It sounds as if the biggest church bell in the world has rung between my ears. I roll, I tumble, try to scream and know my voice means nothing in this place.

When a little of my vision returns I see him reach down and straighten my face so he can look into my eyes.

'Where are they?' he asks.

'Miriam,' I mumble.

'She dead. Can't tell me.'

My breathing's not working right. My whole body's pulling in on itself to try to disguise the pain.

'Dead like you,' he says, and pulls back his two arms, the hammer rising behind his head.

No, I think. Not say, because the words have gone from my throat now, scattered like gulls fleeing the city waterfront when the foghorns start to bellow through the mist.

Struggling, rolling around on the floor, waiting to die, I can see his face, try to freeze it in memory. And I think . . .

I remember it all.

Four simple words, an entire universe inside them. These thoughts and recollections and fragments of a life as it was lived: . . . they embrace everything. They give my dead parents a semblance of life. They let me think of my little lost child and wonder what he might have become.

They make me wonder about Miriam too, and how I failed her. In what small, invisible ways I allowed our marriage to fall apart and never noticed a thing.

I open my eyes, desperate to speak, to say those few short words I never thought I'd be able to utter.

'I didn't kill anyone,' I mutter. 'I *know* I didn't kill anyone.'

Except something's happening already.

Jonny Loong is looking at his long-lost niece, holding on to his chest with two hands, staring at the pumping red wound there in disbelief, staring at her too.

Alice extends the gun towards him.

'You lying bastard,' she says, and fires one more time, straight into his torso, and I try to think, hard, because there's No Name in the room, and six green but troublesome Chinese youths, who are surely more than a match even for Alice Loong and the weapon in her oh-so-steady hand.

'Paul,' she yells.

On the far side of the cellar I see the big figure in his grey suit. My baby-faced, wedge-shaped captive is out of his seat already, shiny firearm tight in hand, roaring at No Name, who's screaming and shouting on the floor, clutching his leg, backing into his little band of fake warriors, face contorted with pain and fury.

'I am in control,' Paul bellows at them. 'I *am* in control.'

I just know there must be an instructor in some training school somewhere who would look at this young man and see a job well done, because there are six young thugs crawling in the dust, doing every last thing he asks, throwing knives and guns across the stone tiles, pleading for mercy.

Alice walks over and lands a fast, hard kick into Uncle Jonny's torso.

I get up, brush myself down and take a look at him.

'Doctor . . .' Jonny begs, beginning to cough up thick red blood. 'Family.'

She's got the gun up again. I take it quickly. She doesn't object. Not much anyway.

'Not my family,' she spits at him. 'Not mine.'

He isn't listening.

'Mr Bierce?' someone asks from across the room.

I blink. I haven't heard the 'Mr' part in a very long time.

'Paul?'

He waves his weapon towards No Name and his terrified companions.

'What do I do with them?'

I stare at the gangly youth. His bravado has departed, for a while anyway.

'No Name. Go. Do not cross our path again.

Tell no one a word of what you saw here. Otherwise . . .'

He's shaking, nodding his head, terrified.

Paul watches them struggle up the stairs in silence. He's doubtless deeply aggrieved Kyle McKendrick isn't going to make his next appointment, and the anger that has put on his cherubic features gives me pause.

I am, I realize, a terrible judge of character.

I look into Alice's cool green eyes.

'You didn't wait for me to say it?'

'Say what?'

'That I didn't do it.'

She sighs.

'For pity's sake, Bierce. Do I have to explain everything?'

She's shaking her head, unable to believe I finally got round to pressing this matter, the delicate shifting bond of trust between us.

Alice looks at Jonny, who's groaning in a lot of blood on the floor, and says, 'I had to shoot someone. It felt better shooting him than it would have done you. Is that good enough?'

'I guess,' I say, feeling stupid.

'I never really thought you killed them,' she adds. 'Not from the moment you wouldn't sleep with me. It's just . . .'

She glowers at her stricken uncle on the floor and for a moment I think she might be about to kick his wounded gut again.

'Sometimes it's easier to believe a lie than accept the truth,' she says carefully. 'Because the truth causes more pain, I think.'

This is a conversation for another time. I turn to my old colleague. He must have been out of the front line for a while. He's sweating and scared and looking as if he might throw up at any moment.

With this last in mind I see the little oyster knife from Mickey Carluccio's kitchen sitting on the table, where Alice must have dropped it when she freed Paul. I cut him free. He wriggles his arms, struggling to get back some feeling.

'Bierce . . .' he begins to say.

'Shut up and listen.'

I point to the VCR and the tapes.

'The deal is this. You get these and Jonny Loong, who's yours to deal with as you see fit. You clean up this mess. You get everything off my record. You never come looking for any of us, me or Alice or Paul. We saved your life here and if you *ever* show a lack of gratitude for that I will be very pissed off indeed. Are we agreed on this?'

He's looking at the gun in my hand, the one I took from Alice. He's suspicious.

'How much?' he asks.

Alice rolls her eyes.

'C'mon,' Stape goes on. 'I need to know. This is government. We got to raise paperwork and stuff. If it's a real lot of money – and I'm not saying that's impossible – you may have to get it in instalments. Offshore, natch.'

I look at her and say, 'Tell him.'

To my delight, Alice picks up the spare video cassette and drops it daintily in his lap.

'Mister,' she says, 'we'd pay *you* to take this crap away. If we had any money, that is.'

He's speechless, then he's nodding. A little voice at the back of my head is screaming at me for being an idiot, but I soon silence it. There is still one thing left.

Jonny Loong is on his back, gasping, in pain, but nothing necessarily fatal. This can be altered.

I place the barrel of my large police weapon square in his face, between his scared eyes, and say, 'How did you know, Jonny?'

'Wha'?' he squawks. 'Get me a doctor, for God's sake.'

'You won't need a doctor if you don't talk to me right now. Miriam thought she had this all pat. She left all this evidence. My blood under her nails. The bank account. Everything. It fell apart because you found out.'

He wriggles, not wanting to look at the gun.

'How did you know?' I ask again.

'Stupid women,' he spits. 'She called May at the club and told her to go home, play sick or something, 'cos something bad might happen. Next thing McKendrick's people coming round shooting everyone, screaming the tapes aren't there. I got out of the back, went home, saw May. Solera and Molloy wanted more money than

McKendrick threw their way. So we got it all out of her in the end. She was a stubborn bitch. Tapes gone. Miriam gone. Always was one greedy, crazy bitch. Not hard to work out, huh?'

'And for that,' I say, feeling the trigger get hot and sticky under my finger, 'you beat your own sister to death? My wife, my kid too?'

'I was mad at them!' he bawls. 'OK? We were supposed to be partners, selling it all together! Didn't I screw her scrawny white hide enough or something?'

I mutter something bad and out of character, then pull the trigger. Jonny Loong screams and puts his bloodstained hands over his eyes. The hammer falls on nothing. It's my gun. I haven't fed it any more bullets since loosing off the four shots in the fog when we took Stape that morning. The two slugs Alice put in her Uncle Jonny were the last ones. I never was good with numbers.

'Please,' Alice says quietly, and takes the weapon from me. I am still wondering if it's worth beating Jonny Loong to death when she places her strong, purposeful hand on my arm and turns me.

'Please,' she says again.

There's a noise from the TV behind. I turn.

The crackly lines have disappeared. There's a picture again.

There's more.

'Bierce?'

She's back on screen and she's laughing. After

all these event-filled minutes when nothing but interference and white noise came on the screen, Miriam's there on the TV again.

'Note to self,' she says in a dead, robotic voice that's foreign to me. 'Must erase end of tape.'

My dead wife shakes her head.

'So much to do, so little time.'

She closes her eyes tight shut, concentrating. Then she goes . . .

'Listen. I don't know who you might be or whether you ever get to see this. I just want it *down*. OK? I don't know . . . Oh.'

There's a line of vivid cursing. She did an amateur theatre production once. The rehearsals never came easy.

Miriam looks into the camera and her eyes have a genuine, deep sadness that cuts into my heart.

'How many takes do I have, Bierce? You'll be home soon.'

She folds her arms, the way she did when we had a conversation and the point she had to make was serious. To her anyway.

'What will you say when I tell you? Shout? Scream? Cry? Try to stop me?'

She shakes her head.

'You know something? I could do anything to you. I could beat you half to death and you still wouldn't put a finger in front of your face to stop me. I could ball half the men down the Yonge docks, one after the other, right in front of your eyes, and you'd just watch, puzzled, waiting for an explanation you could live with. You're like a little dog. Always coming back for more.'

She makes tight, harsh claws of her hands, as if to mark me with her nails.

'I'll scratch you and you'll never notice. They can convict a man for homicide, even without a body. I looked it up. I can screw you. I can screw Jonny. All of them. There's people out there who want these things so badly . . .'

There's a tape in her hand.

'I took them. Me. The little homemaker. The mother of your child. The woman who fills your refrigerator and irons your stupid khaki shirts. I took them, then I phoned Kyle, who's been in every last part of me and still doesn't know my voice. I said a friend needed for him to hear something. Bye-bye, Jonny. Not that you'll ever know. Exciting, huh?'

She laughs. Then she's serious. All this happens in a split second.

'More exciting than a lifetime of living off a cop's wages. Dreaming of the time we can take a vacation in some dump all the other drones go. Me driving the kid to school, then driving him back. Did you never wonder why there wasn't another one?'

She's scrabbling in her bag. Something comes out. She waves it furiously in front of the lens.

'It's called the pill, Bierce. I've been taking it for four years, all the while we've "been trying". And you never noticed. You're not the kind of man who'd look in a woman's bag or think to ask a personal question.'

I think, as I look at this dead woman on the screen, that you only remember the good elements of a person, the parts that have a place in your heart. It is Miriam and it isn't. At that moment it's principally a stranger, full of hate.

Her face comes closer.

'You know what *I* want. No. You never asked. I want to go to Paris when I feel like it. I want to pick up a man, screw him and wake up to find him gone. I want everything, now, instantly, and then I want something else in its place when I'm bored.'

Everything drains from her at this moment. All life. All feeling. All humanity.

'I *hate* you, Bierce. I hate what you and Ricky and *this fucking life* have done to me.'

She stops. Something inside is choking her. I recognize this woman again. I knew her.

Her eyes close. When they open again she's back to being herself, what I lazily, stupidly think of as her 'real' self.

Then, almost as an aside, 'Look after Ricky. He's a sweet kid if a kid's what you want, and it always was. A kid. Not me.'

There's a sound from somewhere out of view.

'Note to self,' she says, a little anxiously. 'Must erase end of tape.'

LATER

The fog never lasts. It didn't come back again that summer at all. The day we ate lunch at Loomis and Jake's – real lunch, by which I mean Susanna Aurelio was paying, so we managed our way through three courses – I wouldn't have wanted to be anywhere else in the world. The temperature was moderate enough to walk around without feeling uncomfortable. You could see miles in every direction. There were crowds of boats bobbing on the water, white sails, big and small, fluttering in the gentle ocean breeze. And the company was . . . interesting.

Partway through the first course Susanna watched Alice walk off to take a call, pushed aside her plate of Mickey Carluccio's finest lobster and said, 'She's too young for you, Bierce. It won't work.'

I shook my head.

'Oh, no. I'm not going there.'

'Come on. Are you seriously telling me you two aren't doing it?'

I nearly choked on my halibut.

'Doing it? *Doing it*? Not that it's any of your damn business but no . . . we're not "doing it".'

405

She winked at me.

'You're figuring it won't take long, though.'

'No! Enough! You make too many assumptions. You add up everything correctly, then push on an extra one just for good measure. Which makes you wrong, in case you hadn't noticed.'

'Is that a denial? That would be rich. A real denial. Not the "don't know but think so" I've been getting for a quarter of a century or so.'

'It's a "what the hell does it have to do with you?", OK?'

'It's got everything to do with me! I'm your lawyer, remember? Your closest friend. Your only true ally. None better. Also you're into me for a quarter of a million dollars in unpaid fees. So I have a personal interest too.'

There had to be a reason for the lunch, naturally.

'Send the bill to Stape. Tell him if he doesn't pay I'll throw the mother of all lawsuits at him.'

Susanna smiled. She was wearing a two-piece red business suit and something gold and heavy around her neck. She was looking very pleased with herself. The divorce papers had been filed two days before. According to a story in the newspaper that morning, one she'd doubtless leaked, the prenuptial agreement – one more modern concept I was still trying to grasp – had been primarily written by her firm on her husband's behalf. So it was going to be an expensive summer for Frank.

'I *love* lawsuits. I'm so good at them. Give me

a chance. No win, no fee. Just 20 percent on the nose when I come through, all expenses included.'

It ought to have been tempting. I'd managed to claw back the freehold of Owl Creek from her, on the grounds that I was clearly not compos mentis when I signed it over. In return she'd seized the thousand Kyle McKendrick had deposited in the Liechtenstein bank account. So all Alice and I had between us was what remained of Stape's original twenty thousand, which was disappearing at a speed I still found hard to believe.

Susanna did what she always did. Persisted.

'What do you have to lose?'

'How about my chance to get back into the world? It's not *my* world. Not really. But it's the only one there is. Either that or slip into being a hermit. Or . . .'

Or what? I really didn't know. A uniform and a badge worked for me then, but they wouldn't now. I was fifty-two. I felt pretty fit and well now my head had cleared. Not quite seventeen again. Or at least in one way only, in that I was staring at this big empty thing called the future stretching out in front of me, wondering.

Mickey Carluccio came over with a couple of plates of extras: sautéed razor shells and clams. I picked at them. It must be nice to live like this every day.

He gave Susanna a knowing glance.

When he was gone I said, 'You know, I think the owner's got his eyes on you. I'm not sure the present girlfriend will last.'

She slapped down her napkin.

'I don't do retail.'

I nodded down at the fish market.

'Mickey's wholesale too. Also, he cooks. That stew you just ate? He learned it from his father. Have you ever dated a man who could cook?'

She was peering at me as if I'd transferred down from Mars.

'One word, Bierce. *Restaurants.*'

I wasn't listening.

Alice was coming back, beaming. She'd spent some of our diminishing money on clothes that morning, specially for lunch. She had a cream shirt, silk, but from somewhere in Chinatown where it cost a fraction of the price of the stores. Plus some sleek blue slacks that looked as if they were tailor-made.

She seemed as happy as anyone could be. We both had plenty of reasons for that, I guess. Stape was as good as his word when it came to the law. Neither of us had a black line against our names. I got a fresh start. Alice now knew she'd never be going back to blue hair and chains. And Jonny Loong, the man responsible for the deaths that had haunted us for so long, had disappeared from the face of the planet, into the arms of Stape's men, presumably to work up a prosecution some time. Not that I expected to see that happen. I was at one with this world now. I had come to appreciate how it worked.

She sat down and said, 'It's outside.'

'What's outside?' Susanna demanded.

'A 1993 Kawasaki 500 twin,' I answered.

My lawyer shook her head.

'This is a lawnmower or something?'

'A bike,' Alice replied. 'Not the colour I'd prefer. But it'll do.'

'Wow,' Susanna gasped. 'You bought her an antique used motorcycle. You surely know how to treat a woman, Bierce. Back to business . . .'

She took a folder out of her bag.

'The thing is . . . I have a certain amount of discovery work I need doing on a couple of cases. I could put this out to the usual agencies. But you need a break. And I've got to give you this: you're resourceful.'

She glanced at Alice.

'Both of you. Hire her as a secretary or something. What you do with the money is up to you.'

'Susanna . . .' I tried to say.

'All legal and above board. Also, as long as you're working for me, I'll happily put *my* claim against your assets to one side.'

The Aurelio smile shone across the table.

'That *is* a good idea. Believe me.'

Alice looked businesslike and efficient.

'Are you seriously asking us to do some sort of investigation work for you?'

'Why not?' Susanna demanded. 'Listen, kid. There are a million agencies out there with long names and fancy offices and all they do for my money is stare at a computer. I can Google myself if I want. You two are a neat combination, professionally anyway. You can do the modern stuff. Bierce here can go out and talk to people face to face, and frankly that's becoming a lost art.'

Alice gave me a knowing look and got back to eating.

'Maybe later,' I said.

Susanna stared at me in disbelief.

'When you work for me, Bierce, you soon come to appreciate the word "later" is not in the approved vocabulary.'

I leaned forward, picked up a razor shell, slipped it on to my plate and repeated, very firmly, 'Later.'

Alice looked up from her plate and the two of them caught each other's eye for a moment. I'm not sure I liked what I saw there. It resembled two predators agreeing on which part of the herd they were each going to eat.

'An office, a salary, a guarantee of six months' work plus free legal indemnity insurance,' Susanna said.

Alice sighed and shook her head.

'Not even close. An investment of two hundred thousand, for which you get a minority stake in the firm,' she said. 'Plus the work guarantee, the legal indemnity insurance, and something else I haven't dreamed up yet.'

Susanna thought for a moment then nodded. 'OK.'

Then the two of them were staring at me, a little cross, because I'd got up from the table and was starting to leave.

In unison, both pairs of eyes firmly set in my direction, they said slowly, carefully, 'Bierce?'

I turned back, smiling, waved the keys and kept on walking.

'Where the hell are you going?' Susannah yelled across the crowded terrace.

Having no idea what penguins say or do, I replied simply, 'Oink, oink,' and flapped my arms.

It was beautiful outside. I sat on the saddle of the old green Kawasaki, thinking about the open road, waiting.